Adultery for Beginners

Sarah Duncan has tried various careers beginning with 'A' – Archaeologist, Art historian and Actress. She was famous for five minutes playing Rodney's girlfriend in *Only Fools and Horses* but after the first minute decided she didn't like it so became an author instead. She has written several non-fiction books and a screenplay but *Adultery for Beginners* is her first novel. She is married with two children and lives in Bath.

SARAH DUNCAN

Adultery for Beginners

CORONET BOOKS
Hodder & Stoughton

Copyright © 2004 by Sarah Duncan

First published in Great Britain in 2004 by Hodder and Stoughton
A division of Hodder Headline

The right of Sarah Duncan to be identified as the Author
of the Work has been asserted by her in accordance with the
Copyright, Designs and Patents Act 1988.

A Coronet paperback

1 3 5 7 9 10 8 6 4 2

All rights reserved. No part of this publication may be reproduced,
stored in a retrieval system, or transmitted, in any form or by any
means without the prior written permission of the publisher,
nor be otherwise circulated in any form of binding or
cover other than that in which it is published and without a
similar condition being imposed on the
subsequent purchaser.

All characters in this publication are fictitious and
any resemblance to real persons, living or
dead, is purely coincidental.

A CIP catalogue record for this title is
available from the British Library

ISBN 0 340 82930 3

Typeset in Plantin Light by Palimpsest Book Production Limited,
Polmont, Stirlingshire
Printed and bound by Mackays of Chatham, Kent

Hodder and Stoughton
A division of Hodder Headline
338 Euston Road
London NW1 3BH

For my own Isabel.
With love and apologies for not getting
round to changing the name.

MORAY COUNCIL LIBRARIES & INFO.SERVICES	
2O 12 27 65	
Askews	
F	

ACKNOWLEDGEMENTS

This book wouldn't have been written without the wonderful support of my writing friends: Rachel Bentham, Sue Swingler, Linnet van Tinteren, Lesley Sylvester, Linda Ewles, Kate Page, Jane Riekemann, Nancy Kinnison, Sarah Stone, Sue LeBlond, Beverley Grey, Geraldine Lindley and Maria Thomas. Jane Riekemann and my sister, Annie Love, provided the information on ex-pat life – I still hope to use the riveting details of the Dutch tumble dryer method of wife swapping at some point. Thanks also to my agent, Lavinia Trevor, and my editor, Mari Evans, for taking me on and to the Romantic Novelists' Association for their help and encouragement. Finally, thanks to Jannina Henderson and Jago for putting up with me being extremely boring for four miles every morning.

I

Damn, Isabel thought, feeling a cooling trickle of stickiness on her inner thighs. Neil lay heavily on top of her, as if the effort had given him heart failure. The huffing and puffing seemed to have expelled all the air from him. Perhaps he wasn't breathing. His body, hairy, sweaty, still rumpled with sleep, swamped hers. She felt her arms and legs sticking out from under his body, flat as a gingerbread woman. The tissues were out of reach, supposing there were any left in the box. Damn, damn, damn, she thought. I only changed the sheets yesterday. He stirred slightly and nuzzled her neck. Not dead then. She gave him a little push.

'You're heavy.'

'Sorry.' Neil rolled off her, their skin peeling apart. He heaved himself out of bed and shambled off to the shower room, yawning and scratching his chest unselfconsciously. Isabel lay flat under the duvet, listening to the water cascading next door and Neil singing and apparently slapping himself. What could he be doing? And why did he make so much noise? She had learnt quickly that the walls in their new house were thin, but Neil hadn't modified his behaviour at all.

The sheets were clammy under her. Too late to do anything about it now. According to the Sunday papers, she thought, this is my sexual prime. Men peak at eighteen, women at thirty-six. Thirty-six. It seemed awfully old.

Neil came back in, humming to himself, apparently not bothered by the way his tummy overhung the towel around his hips, and started to get dressed. He was a big man, broad about the shoulders, with a smattering of freckles, already fading now no longer exposed to strong sunlight. She noticed that his skin, usually taut with good health, had a slackness about it. Two months of desk work, two months of pale sunshine. It had been a terrible summer.

The duvet was all fluffed up, giving the disconcerting impression that her body had disappeared. She took her arms out from under it and pressed them to her side so the fabric stretched taut across her chest, defining her shape. All those years abroad she'd slept in a loose cotton T-shirt but returning to a damp English summer required something warmer. Thinking of the winter to come she had been tempted by head-to-toe winceyette but settled for a long nightdress. Pretty, but not exactly sexy. Neil didn't seem to care.

'Perhaps there'll be a brilliant job for me in the paper today,' Isabel said brightly. 'People coming back from their holidays, deciding to change jobs or get a promotion.'

'Mmm?' Neil was rummaging through his chest of drawers.

'The trouble is, they'll want experience or qualifications. Neither of which I have.' She saw Neil wasn't listening, preoccupied with testing socks for holes. They looked like glove puppets on his hands.

'I want a job,' she said in a squeaky voice, moving her fingers as if they were in the socks and talking. Neil looked at her, his face blank. She let her hands flop back onto the bed. 'Don't put them back in the drawer if they've got holes. Chuck them onto the bed.'

Neil gave her a look that said, 'Might as well tip the whole bloody lot out.'

'I'll get you some more today.' At some point her life had turned from shopping and fucking to socks and sex. The same actions, she supposed, just a different mental attitude. Neil found a satisfactory pair and sat on the edge of the bed to put them on.

'You don't have to work, you know. We can manage.'

'Only because we let out my father's house. It's not just the money.' She squinted at the ceiling. 'I want something more, I suppose.'

'More.' He rolled his eyes. 'Like what? What could you do?'

He doesn't mean it to sound like that, she thought, pleating the duvet cover with her fingers. What could she do? She'd been rejected for the only jobs she'd applied for, hadn't even made the interview. 'Something in an office. Filing?'

'Darling, it's easy to see it's years since you've been in an office. No one does filing any more; it's all on computer. Never mind.' He patted her feet. 'If you want to do filing, you can always help me. God knows, I could use a hand with the paperwork.'

'It's not that I want to do filing, it's just, I want . . .' Nebulous sentences buzzed in her head. I want to do something, I want to be different, I want to be . . . I want . . . I want . . . Instead she said, 'But doing a job wouldn't stop me from helping you. I could take over all the household stuff. Pay the bills, keep track of the statements, that sort of thing.'

'If we relied on you the phone would keep on being

cut off.' He paused with his trousers half on and laughed. 'Do you remember when you lived in that flat and the electricity got stopped, and you had to chat up the man to come round and reconnect it because people were coming to supper?' His voice was amused, indulgent. Isabel felt mortified.

'But that was years ago. And it only happened once.'

He shrugged and turned away. 'We went abroad after that.'

Isabel twisted a dark strand of hair. 'You said you wanted help.' Even to her, her voice sounded childish, sulky against Neil's briskness.

'No, it's sweet of you to offer, but better not.'

Isabel traced the pattern of the duvet cover with her index finger. She really should stop biting her nails. People said you grew out of it, but it hadn't happened yet. Her nightdress was rucked up at the back. She shifted in the bed. Neil was choosing a shirt, one she'd erratically ironed the day before while listening to Woman's Hour, daydreaming of being interviewed by Jenni Murray as a woman with something worth saying.

Neil hummed as he did up the buttons. His moustache hid his upper lip, making a secret of his mouth. He held up two ties against his shirt and looked at her, eyebrows raised in a question. He did this every morning. Isabel felt exhausted, limbs turned to lead.

'The one on the left,' she said, without looking. 'Why don't you shave your moustache off?'

He looked surprised. 'Why?' he said, concentrating on doing up his tie.

'I don't know. For a change? Something different?'

'Kissing a man without a moustache is like eating a boiled egg without salt.'

She wrinkled her nose, trying to remember when she'd last kissed a man without a moustache. Too long ago to remember. 'And how would you know?'

He shrugged. 'It's what my granny used to say.'

'That's not an answer.'

He kissed her forehead. 'I'd better be off. D'you want me to bring you up a cup of tea?' He checked his watch. What would he do if I said yes, she wondered. But that wouldn't be playing the game.

'No thanks. I'll get up in a minute. You don't want to miss the train.'

'See you later.'

'Usual time?'

'The usual.'

Isabel lay in the bed, quite still. How odd to have established a 'usual time' so quickly. A move of two thousand miles, a new country, and yet within a few months they had acquired patterns to hitch their lives to. But England wasn't a new country. It was *their* country – their home. So why did she feel out of place? Stranded in some no-man's-land between the cloistered and cosseted ex-pat life and the demands of the strange new England. A home that had become harsh and modern in her eighteen-year absence.

She turned to look at her bedside clock. Five minutes till she had to get up. Sometimes she lay in bed until she heard the front door slam behind Neil but today she felt restless and swung her legs over the edge of the bed. Five minutes extra. What was it that magazine articles were always saying? Get up five minutes earlier every day and exercise, write a poem or practise deep breathing to release stress. Breathing seemed the easiest option. She inhaled deeply, breathing in through her nose, feeling her ribcage expand, holding it – two, three, four – and then releasing it through her mouth in a gentle whoosh. There. One thing she could do.

Then she remembered. There was a coffee morning for new parents at the school that morning. A chance to meet other mums, the notice had said. Isabel bit her lip. She was used to coffee mornings to meet new ex-pats; new people were always coming onto the compounds. She shouldn't be nervous, but knew she would be. Smarmy on the outside, squirmy on the inside. They can't eat me, she told herself, standing up and stretching. With her remaining extra two minutes and thirty-seven seconds she'd wash her hair in honour of all those new mums she was going to meet.

Isabel slammed her foot down onto the brake to avoid the car in front, forgot she wasn't driving her old automatic, and stalled. She was part of a line of cars on the road to the school, all swerving into spaces or pulling out without looking. It was as if every parent in Milbridge had decided that 8.46 a.m. was the ideal time to drop the children off for the first day of school. Out they clambered, straining with the weight of schoolbags on backs, while sportsbags were dragged along the ground trailing football boots tied by the laces. Isabel thought they looked like refugees as they made their way to the school gates.

'Eyes peeled for a parking space,' she told the children, who made no response. Michael was reading his fishing encyclopaedia, and Katie was tracing faces on the side window. Isabel shook her hair out in front of the heater, regretting her impulse decision to wash it. It had made them late and it would never dry in time, even though the heater was set on max and the air whooshed out at blast furnace temperature. The wretched coffee morning for new parents was straight after the school drop. Her armpits prickled with anticipation. If she kept the heater on at this level she would be sweating like a pig by the time she got there. She felt nervous enough as it was. 'Horses sweat, gentlemen perspire and ladies gently glow' her mother used to say. No mention of pigs. To be on the safe side, she turned down the heater.

She managed to find a parking space as another parent moved out – obviously the opportunity to meet new parents over a cup of coffee was not universally attractive – and hurried the children out of the car and into the playground. A large sign pointing the way to 'New Parents Coffee Morning' made her stomach contract. She wished she hadn't eaten breakfast.

St Joseph's was a small private school on the edge of Milbridge that liked to call itself a preparatory school, as if pupils were automatically wafted off to the major public schools on leaving. The headmistress had pointed out facilities and pupils equally – 'Now, that child's father is a major local landowner, and here we have the junior dining room.' The headmistress's snobbery almost decided Isabel against the school. Neil had said she was oversensitive. Isabel knew it was going to be hard for Michael and Katie to adjust and hoped the smaller classes would lessen the culture shock. At least the teachers seemed reassuringly normal, sensible women in cuddly cardigans, Katie's future teacher being particularly cosy and understanding. And she liked the country feel to the place, the open spaces, the old-fashionedness. Nothing was modern; even the few computers were out of date, with tiny screens in enormous monitors and chunky keyboards.

The school was in a Victorian house, with a cedar tree on the lawns that swept up to the playing fields. When she had visited, it had been calm but with a distant hum as if each classroom contained a hive of diligent bees. The sun had shone into the entrance hall, striking dust motes and photographs of past glories – the Under IX netball team holding a large cup, the headmistress presenting a Save the Children cheque to a minor royal.

Now the entrance hall was full of women talking at the tops of their voices, greeting each other, waving, talking about holidays. One woman was lifting her skirt to show a group of others a spectacular set of bruises on her thigh. Isabel could hear them roaring with laughter as the woman described how her horse had kicked her. Holding the children firmly by the hand she wove her way through to the classrooms. She dropped Michael off first; he was the elder and seemed more confident about the new school. She lingered for longer than was necessary in Katie's classroom, anxious about leaving her, anxious about going outside, only leaving when she realised that she was the last mother in the class. She had hoped to have a chance to nip into a loo and check how her hair looked, but felt inhibited about using the children's cloakroom.

Isabel followed the coffee morning signs and found herself in what had once been a stable block and was now a gym with climbing ropes and ladders on the wall. Confident voices echoed around the room, bouncing off the high ceiling and mingling with the clatter of spoons and cups.

She hesitated at the door, not daring to go in and face the other parents. There wasn't a man in sight, she noticed, only mothers, and they all seemed to know each other. Some were dressed casually, others in suits as if for work. Isabel felt dressed too brightly, the colours bold and garish in the soft September light. Without thinking

Isabel touched her earrings, bought on one of their Dubai jaunts, bright Bedouin beads strung on gold wires that chinkled softly as she moved. She made a mental note to wear something beige next time.

Isabel looked around to find someone to speak to and noticed another woman on her own, standing stiffly and holding a coffee cup as if she might drop it unless vigilant. Isabel was impressed to see she was wearing full make-up and had blow-dried her hair. She had an angular face, as if she had been designed by someone with only a ruler and set square, and an impressive set of teeth, including one gold one, which gave the impression she could actually eat Isabel. But her expression looked how Isabel felt, so she took a deep breath, then went up to her, hoping that her hair didn't look too peculiar.

'Hello,' she said. 'Are you new here too?'

The woman nodded and smiled slightly. 'Year Two. Millicent.'

'Katie,' Isabel said. 'Year One. And Michael, he's in Year Four.'

'My son, Rufus, is in Year Four. Not here though. At another school.'

Isabel waited to see if she was going to say any more, but the woman just stared at her, as if playing a game of Follow My Leader where Isabel had inexplicably been selected as the leader. Isabel ran her hand over her hair, hoping to smother any excessive vitality. 'We've only just moved here,' she tried.

'From London? We've just moved down too. Is your husband commuting?'

'No. I mean, yes. Sorry, I'm not being clear. We didn't move from London, but yes, he is commuting.'

'Where did you come from?'

'All over the place: Syria, Saudi, Thailand. My husband works for a big engineering company, so we've gone wherever we've been posted.'

There was another pause. Isabel realised that the woman, despite the hair and make-up, was even more nervous than she was.

'Where did you live in London?'

'Twickenham.'

'I went to school near there,' Isabel said.

'Not Richmond House?'

'Were you there too?'

'I was. Gosh, what a coincidence.' The woman's cheeks were flushed and she seemed less nervous at having made the connection. Isabel also felt better.

'Wasn't it a dump?'

'Awful. When were you there? I left in seventy-nine.'

'Eighty-two, so I doubt you'd remember me. I was Isabel Cooper originally, Freeman now.'

'Helen Delapole then, Weedon-Smith now.' Helen shrugged her bony shoulders. 'What a small world it is.'

Isabel was about to ask Helen where her family had lived, when a cup of murky brown liquid was thrust into her hand.

'Coffee?' a voice said. She turned and saw an imposing woman wearing a pink sweater decorated with a herd of sheep, of the sort that Isabel remembered people wearing when she'd left England eighteen years before. Perhaps there was a shop in Milbridge selling time-warp clothing.

'Thanks for the coffee,' Isabel said, managing to slop half of it into her saucer.

'I'm Mary Wright, Chairman of the PTA. And you are?'

'Isabel Freeman,' Isabel said, resisting the urge to step back a pace or two. The herd of sheep were neatly arranged in fluffy white lines on the sweatshirt looking off towards Mary's right armpit, drawing attention to Mary's expansive chest. One had an odd expression and was facing the wrong way from the rest of the flock, just how Isabel felt. She dragged her eyes away. 'I'm new here.'

'Of course you are; I'd know you otherwise.' Mary turned to Helen who obediently supplied her name. Isabel took a mouthful of coffee; bitter, instant with a meagre splash of milk.

'And where do you live?'

'In Battleford,' Helen said, stammering slightly. 'We've just moved in.'

'Ah, you must be the new people in the Hurstbourne's old house.' Vigorous nodding. 'An accountant, I believe Vicky said.' Mary asked more questions. Helen racked up lots of points: accountant-in-the-City husband, the Old Manor, double-barrelled surname, pony in a paddock. Isabel thought the headmistress must have loved her.

'My Clemmie's in the same year as your daughter. You must bring her along to the Pony Club,' Mary said graciously, then added, 'I run it.' Surprise, surprise, thought Isabel. Then it was her turn.

She could see that her real life would score *nul points* on Mary's system, so instead she said, 'We live in the Old Palace, my children are called Raphael and Hermione, and my husband is an international troubleshooter, the engineering version of Red Adair.'

'Really?' Helen's eyes were wide.

Isabel laughed. 'No, not really. We live in a brand new house, Neil's just an ordinary engineer and the children are called Michael and Katie. But the international bit is true. We've lived in nine different countries since we married.'

'How interesting,' said Mary, who looked as if she

hadn't appreciated Isabel's pretend life. 'Well. Nice to meet you, and you must come to all the PTA events. Now, I should circulate, but before I go, I must make sure you're labelled,' Mary said. With what? thought Isabel, feeling labelled already with 'Not to be taken seriously'. Mary was scanning the chattering mass of women.

'Ah, there she is. Justine!' she called, waving.

A woman squeezed through the crowd. Her blonde bob looked as perfect as her clothes, which managed to be both smart and casual at the same time. Isabel felt dishevelled and garishly bright, like a moulting parakeet confronted by a peregrine falcon.

'Justine, none of these people have labels,' Mary said.

'Never mind. You carry on and I'll make sure they get labelled.' There was nothing in Justine's attitude or voice to suggest that she was saying anything untoward but Mary gave her a suspicious look.

'I must circulate,' she repeated and went back into the crowd, the women parting like the Red Sea in front of her.

Justine gave a pussycat smile. 'Mary's put four children through this school, which may explain why she acts as if she runs it. The thing to remember is that it's not just you she's patronising, she does it to everyone equally.' She pulled a roll of labels from her bag. 'If you could just put your name and your children's year onto these and stick them on. Then you can find the other mothers in your children's years, and go up and introduce yourselves.' Justine tore off two labels and handed them out. 'Have you both got a pen?'

Helen started writing out her label while Isabel rummaged in the bottom of her bag. 'I think so,' she muttered, feeling car keys, loose coins, lipstick and what felt like thousands of pieces of paper.

'Never mind. I've got one.'

Isabel straightened up. 'Isabel Freeman,' she said as Justine wrote it down in neat blue ballpoint. 'I've got Michael, Year Four, and Katie in Year One.'

'Year One,' repeated Justine. 'I've got a daughter in Year One. Rachel. In Mrs Baker's class.'

'So is Katie.'

'Brilliant; they've been completely swamped with boys. Rachel will be thrilled another girl's joined them. Perhaps you and your daughter would like to come and have tea with us after school one day. If you're not busy.'

'That'd be lovely.'

Justine handed Isabel a business card.

'Here. My number's at the bottom.'

'How smart.' Isabel peered at the card. 'Is this you?'

Justine nodded.

'Wardrobe, Colour and Image Consultant,' Isabel read out. No wonder Justine looked so immaculate. 'It must be odd being on show all the time,' she blurted out, and then blushed at her gaucheness. 'I mean, I expect you feel you always have to be an advertisement for your business.'

Justine cocked her head to one side. 'Yes, but once you know what you should be wearing, then it stops being an issue. Everything looks right.'

'It obviously works for you,' Isabel said, knowing that short of waving a magic wand, she would never look as smart as Justine. Her hair was all wrong for a start. 'We lived abroad until the summer and I can't get used to the weather here. I'm either freezing, or boiling because I've put too much stuff on.'

'It's not just colours. I can organise your wardrobe and help with what you should be buying,' Justine said.

Isabel hesitated. The idea of someone rummaging

through her things appalled her, however much she might need it. It seemed too personal, too exposing.

Justine touched Isabel's arm lightly. 'Don't worry, I'm not going to do a hard sell on you.'

'I've always meant to have it done,' Helen said.

Justine gave her a card. 'Give me a ring if you want to know anything more.'

'I will. I could do with a clear-out. I've still got loads of work clothes from before I had children.'

'Do you still work?' Isabel asked, wanting to change the subject from clothes.

Helen pulled a face. 'Lord no, the children are quite enough for me.'

'What about you?' Justine asked Isabel.

'It's almost impossible for ex-pat wives to work; you move around too much and in a lot of the countries we've been in, women aren't allowed to work. But now we've settled back in the UK I'm looking for a job.'

'What sort?'

'I don't know. I've only done a bit of TEFL before.'

'Teffle?'

'Teaching English as a Foreign Language. I rang round the local language schools but they all wanted the new qualifications – my old TEFL certificate doesn't count. The alternative would be to get experience through casual work, but that would be next summer and I want something now. So I'm not sure what I'm looking for. Anything, I think, just to get started.'

'Can you type?' Isabel nodded and Justine continued, 'I do know someone who's looking for somebody to work in his office, part time. He offered it to me, but to be honest, now I'm single again, I have to work full time.'

'Part time sounds wonderful.'

'I don't think it's very exciting, just basic office stuff.'

'No, that would be fine.' Isabel didn't care what the job was. She felt adrenaline join the caffeine already racing through her veins and had to stop herself jigging up and down.

'If you give me your phone number, I'll find out if the job is still going, and if it is, get him to give you a ring.' She handed Isabel one of the PTA labels.

Isabel started to write down her phone number, then had to check it with her address book. 'It's silly, but I still can't remember it by heart.' She thought that didn't sound very organised, so she added quickly, 'I don't usually have a problem remembering things.'

'Don't worry, he's the world's most disorganised person. Anyone would seem a paragon of efficiency next to him.' Justine gave her a long look, as if considering. 'In fact, I'm probably not doing you a favour,' she said. Isabel wanted to ask her what she meant but was distracted by Mary's voice calling from the far side of the hall, effortlessly overcoming the noise of the other women.

'Justine! Labels needed here, please.'

Justine wrinkled her nose. 'I must go and avert disaster. Mustn't have anyone unlabelled, you know.' She touched Isabel's arm again. 'I'll try and remember about the job.'

Isabel watched her squeeze her way through the crowd, then turned to Helen. 'I suppose that's networking,' Isabel said, wanting to sing. 'It probably won't get me anywhere but . . .'

'You never know.' They said it together and Isabel's heart lifted. Perhaps she'd found a friend.

2

Isabel got back from the town centre and slowly unloaded her shopping. Other women managed to do one shopping trip a week, but she found herself having to slink back several times. It wasn't so much that she ran out of food, more that she ran out of things she knew how to cook. And then there was the unaccustomed luxury of having so much choice. She would buy a head of fennel, excited by the bulbous shape, the elusive scent of aniseed, the wholesomeness, but then once home it would sit there, slowly liquefying in the vegetable rack. After all, what did you do with fennel? The children wouldn't eat it, and Neil had pulled a face and pushed it to the side of his plate when she tried braising it. It was like skate wings. A lovely idea that didn't quite work in practice.

Having stored the food, she thought she would eat something as it was lunchtime. It was strange, cooking for one after years of cooking lunch for Neil and the children in the middle of the day. Now, most days she didn't bother with lunch, just picked at bits and pieces. It wasn't worth cooking properly just for herself. Today what she really wanted was a peanut butter sandwich, with squishy white bread, but she got out a low calorie instant soup instead. She scanned through the post while waiting for the kettle to boil. Neil sorted it before going to work and usually took out his letters for reading on the train. Isabel got left with catalogues and junk mail. She poured the hot water on the powdered soup. It looked thin. It tasted thin. Would it make her thin? Wistfully she thought of peanut butter sandwiches. Still, as she'd been so good, just having the soup, she could let herself have one biscuit.

She selected one of Katie's red felt pens, checked that the tip hadn't completely dried out, and sat down with the local paper. Pen in one hand, biscuit in the other, she turned to the recruitment section. Hundreds of jobs, it promised. Packers, salespersons, fork lift truck drivers. Nurses, welders, executive this and that. Trainers, FE lecturers, waste disposal operatives. So many jobs, none of which she could do. She munched another biscuit, scattering chocolate chip cookie crumbs over the ads. None of them seemed to want what she had. They all wanted different things – HGV licence, NVQs, RSA III. Two years' experience minimum in an administrative capacity.

She reached for another biscuit and realised she had eaten half a packet of chocolate chip cookies. Far worse than a peanut butter sandwich. Oh well, at least they had been two packets for the price of one so she hadn't wasted money. She'd start her diet properly tomorrow. The packet of biscuits could be a final fling.

Her weight had crept up over the last two years so she couldn't even put it down to having babies. Thinking about it, she realised that she could remember days spent at home in Syria, isolated and bored, comfort eating. She couldn't even get in a car and drive somewhere; for security reasons staff and their families were forbidden to drive. But that was there, she thought to herself. We're in England now. No restrictions on women working. I'll get a job, and I'll lose the weight by Christmas she decided.

Isabel got out a piece of squared paper and began to draw up a chart, weeks running along the top, weight running down the side. She then drew a line marking a two-pounds-a-week weight loss. I could easily be back to the weight I was two years ago by Christmas, she thought. And if I exercised as well . . . She drew another line for three pounds a week. The line dropped steeply away off the page. Minuscule by Christmas, vanished by March. No more buttons bursting off, no more tight waistbands. She scrunched up the empty biscuit packet and chucked it in the bin. She felt energised, as if she had lost two stone already.

The phone rang and she went to answer it, tripping on a stray chunk of Lego and falling, wrenching her ankle. She struggled to her feet, propped herself up against the mantelpiece and picked up the phone.

'Ow. Hello?'

A man's voice asked, 'Is that Isabel?'

'Yes, speaking.'

'You sound in pain.'

'I fell over.'

'I see.' The deep voice paused. 'My name's Patrick Sherwin. I hear you're looking for a job.'

'Yes.' Isabel stopped rubbing her ankle and grimaced. Fell over indeed. She must sound like a complete disaster area. Think 'good telephone manner'. She took a deep breath. 'Are you Justine's friend?' That sounded wrong, too like something she'd say to a child – are you Justine's little friend, dear? She stood up straight. Get a grip. Just act normal, she told herself.

'Is that what she said? Yes, I suppose I am.' He sounded amused.

'That was quick. I only spoke to her this morning.'

'She moves fast.' Isabel thought his voice was wonderful, as rich as handcream. 'I need someone to come and help out with my business. Nothing too alarming, keeping the paperwork in order and up to date, answering the phone. That sort of thing. Are you interested?'

'Absolutely.'

'Why don't you come round to my office and we could chat. Would tomorrow be possible?'

'I'm not sure . . .' she said, thrown by the thought that it might actually happen.

'I'm flying to Rome late that evening, so . . .'

'No, no, tomorrow's fine,' she said, not bothering to look at the calendar, knowing that it was blank for weeks ahead beyond 'collect Neil's suit from the cleaners' and 'children to dentist'.

'Good. I'm at number forty-five, Downton Street. Do you need directions?'

'I'll look it up on the map.'

'I'll see you there at, say, twelve thirty.'

'That's fine,' she repeated, hoping that her voice sounded as calm as his.

'Until tomorrow, then.'

She put the phone down and hugged herself. A job interview. She'd got a job interview.

Isabel could hardly wait until Neil came through the front door. The minute she heard his key in the lock she rushed up.

'Guess what? I've got a job interview.'

'Well done. What's the job?'

Isabel rubbed her nose. 'Just general office admin stuff, I think.'

Neil let his briefcase drop to the floor and stretched. 'Sounds good. I'm just going to pop upstairs and change, and then you can tell me all about it. Are the children in bed?'

'Sorry. They were so tired after school that I put them to bed early.' Automatically she picked up his briefcase.

'Never mind. I'm late myself.'

'I've got supper waiting for you.'

'Great. I'll be down in a second.' Isabel watched his feet trudging upwards. Not so long ago he would have taken them two at a time. She put the briefcase into what he and the developer grandly called the study, a cupboard of a room by the front door. It niggled slightly that the hallway was spacious, giving a deceptive indication of the room sizes. The space would have been better added onto the kitchen in her opinion, but Neil had liked the hallway.

She went into the kitchen and took the fish pie out of the oven, settling it on a trivet next to the salad bowl. She sat down and waited, picking at the dry and crusty edges of the dish, till Neil came down. The kitchen units were new, blonde wood with stainless steel handles, but cheaply made. Already some of the doors were scratched and there was a grubby look around the edges that wouldn't shift, however hard she scrubbed away at them.

'So, what does the business do?'

Isabel doled some fish pie onto Neil's plate, trying to think.

'Um. I'm not sure. Help yourself to salad.'

'Thanks. What's the business called?'

'Not sure.' She mumbled deliberately, she'd replayed the conversation in her head so many times she knew she didn't know the answers to Neil's questions. But the tactic of incoherence failed as he asked her to repeat herself. Neil looked puzzled.

'What did it say in the ad? Show me.'

'It wasn't from an ad.' Isabel felt her excitement seep away like water in sand. 'Someone said that they knew someone who wanted someone and, well, he rang up and asked me to come for an interview. Networking. You know,' she said with a bright smile, hoping she looked confident.

'So who rang up?'

'His name's Patrick—' Sherman? Sherden? 'Patrick Sherwin, I think. He's a friend of a woman I met at the new parents' coffee morning. She suggested me.'

'And do you know her name?'

'Oh yes. Justine. She's got a daughter in Katie's class.'

'It all sounds a bit dodgy to me. Where are you going for this interview?'

'Forty-five Downton Road.'

'Where's that?'

At least she knew the answer to that one, having looked it up in the A–Z.

'Close to the centre, on the far side of town. It's the bit that has loads of those Georgian artisan's cottages, painted in pastel colours. Terribly pretty.' She could see them quite clearly; they had window boxes, and slate roofs. Neil had dismissed them when they were house hunting as being too small, too expensive and too impractical. He had refused to waste his time by going inside.

Neil grunted. 'Is it an office address?'

'He said it was.'

'Doesn't sound like it.' She had to admit he was right; it didn't sound like an office address. She watched his face as he finished his meal, trying to gauge his mood.

Perhaps she could divert him away from office addresses.

'Guess what, I met someone from my old school at the coffee morning. It's a small world, isn't it? Her name's Helen, and her husband's called George Something-Smith. He commutes to London on the same train as you. They live just outside Milbridge and she asked us all over to Sunday lunch next weekend. She was three years above me at school. She seems very nice.' Her voice trailed off.

Neil pushed his plate back and sucked his moustache. 'I can't say I like it, Bel.'

'The fish pie? Oh dear. Sorry.'

'No, not the fish pie. This job.' He rested his elbows on the table, clasped his hands in front of his face and looked at her over them, rather like a kindly headmaster (firm but fair) about to admonish a small boy sent to him for some minor misdemeanour. 'You don't know what the business is, what it's called, the name of the man who rang, or what you're going to be asked to do.'

'I do. It's typing and answering the phone and things.'

'You think.'

'Neil, don't spoil it. It's the only interview I've got so far. I thought you'd be pleased.'

'Pleased? Darling, England is not the place it was fifteen, ten years ago even. I really don't think it's safe. You don't know anything about these people. This man could be anyone.'

'He sounded all right on the phone.' He'd sounded gorgeous, in fact, but she didn't think Neil would be impressed with that.

'Isabel.' He leant back in his chair and raised his eyes to the ceiling. He looked so pompous and sure of himself, Isabel felt she could hit him. And she'd cooked him treacle tart. She took it out of the oven and started cutting it up, stabbing at the pastry. Unfair, unfair. She flipped a slice onto a plate and plonked it in front of him.

'Are you saying I can't go?'

'I'm only concerned for your safety.' He calmly picked up his spoon, then paused. 'Aren't you eating any?'

'I'm on a diet.'

'Since when?'

'This afternoon.' She folded her arms and watched him eat, tracking each mouthful. Her jaw ached from clenching her teeth. It was unfair. She'd been so excited and now Neil was ruining everything.

'You just don't want me to work, do you?' she blurted out.

'That's nothing to do with it.'

'Isn't it?'

'I'm concerned—' he started, but she cut him off.

'You make it sound so reasonable. It's just so I look in the wrong, but I know I'm not. You don't want me to go out. All you want me to do is look after you and the children. Just washing and cooking and cleaning for ever and ever.'

'Don't be ridiculous.' He sounded almost bored as he stood up.

'And don't go off. This is important, I want to talk about it.'

'Perhaps when you've calmed down.'

'I am calm,' Isabel shouted.

'Thank you for supper.' He pushed his chair in and smiled at a spot just above her head, a tight smile that left his face untouched and his eyes shielded. 'I'm going to watch the News.'

'I'm more important than the News,' she cried, but he

was gone. I *am* more important, she thought. I *am*. She cleared the plates into the dishwasher then, slowly and deliberately, she cut herself a large slice of treacle tart and drowned it in cream.

The next day Isabel couldn't decide what to wear. A job interview meant a suit, which she didn't have, so it would have to be a skirt. Although it hadn't sounded like a formal sort of set-up. She shied away from thinking about Neil's questions. She opened the wardrobe gingerly – one of the wardrobe doors had already started to hang crookedly on its hinges, too flimsy to take the weight – and started to rifle through the tightly packed clothes, ticking them off in her mind. Too tight, too short, too old-fashioned – how could she have worn all those pleats like an Austrian hausfrau? She knew she should throw it out, but she found it hard to discard clothes, and instead moved on. The corporate wife stuff was shrouded in dry cleaning bags, obviously wrong. Her hand paused on her favourite dress, white splashed with pink hibiscus. Too bright. Too girlie. No, the only possibility was a long, straight, dark navy skirt, which she hoped would make her look taller and slimmer. It was all very well to say that men preferred a cosy armful, but when it came to clothes it was definitely better to be a size ten.

She sucked her tummy in as she pulled the zip up and looked in the mirror, arching round to check the rear view. No excessive bulges, although her legs looked ridiculous, protruding from the bottom hem, two inches of solid white flesh then black ankle socks. Her feet looked enormous, and strangely flat. She slipped the socks off. The elasticated tops had left a ring of vertical red lines around her fat calves. It didn't look very attractive.

She stood on tiptoes to see if the skirt might look any better with high-heels, squinting in an effort to imagine opaque tights. It would work but she didn't have the right sort of shoes. Back to jeans then. Perhaps black ones, with a jacket over them, long enough to cover her rear. The problem then shifted to her middle. Unless she sucked her stomach in, it spread over the waistband. Realistically she was going to have to breathe at some point so that meant wearing a cardigan or sweater under the jacket to hide the bulge. She knew even without trying on the combination that it would make the jacket sleeves too tight plus today was the hottest day they'd had since they'd been back.

So what if she was a bit overweight? She was a mother, not a model. She made a face at herself in the mirror for minding about how she looked. She was a respectable married woman who was meeting someone about a job possibility, not heading for a casting couch session. Neil's words flashed through her mind but she pushed them away. Why should it matter what she looked like? Why should she have to starve herself in an effort to look young and sexy? Her abilities were what counted, surely. She looked at her reflection, pushing her hair away from her face and wishing that just once it would lie sleekly like Justine's instead of frizzing out. Why would someone employ me? she thought. What can I do? How do I sell myself?

I've got O levels and A levels and a TEFL certificate. I've taught children in schools where the nearest clean water was two kilometres away. I can whistle and hum at the same time. I can drive a jeep up sand dunes and I'm better than Neil at wadi bashing. I've read the whole of *War and Peace*, even the boring bits, and I find Anthony

Trollope funny. I love nineteenth-century literature and baroque music.

None of which seemed to be relevant attributes for a woman looking for an office job. But I want to be useful, she thought. I want to do something beyond sitting around drinking coffee and playing the occasional game of tennis. She sniffed, then picked up the discarded skirt lying crumpled on the floor and briskly shook it out. She would wear it with flat shoes if need be, she decided, but if she got a move on there might be time to pop into town and hunt for a new outfit. After all, it was about time she treated herself to something other than doughnuts.

3

'Great shoes,' Mr Sherwin said, raising one eyebrow. 'Thanks,' Isabel said, slightly flustered, both that he'd noticed and also commented. She had meant to buy something sensible, with a lowish heel. Useful shoes. Not plum-purple suede with three-inch high-heels and a finger's-width band of snakeskin across the extravagantly pointed toes. For a second in the shop she'd rebelled against being sensible, so the low-heeled shoes remained on the shelf and the plum-purples had been bought. In their honour she'd also bought hardly-there tights in the finest denier and slipped them on in the car, squeezing awkwardly under the steering wheel, trying to remain decent. She could feel her feet arching over the instep, rubbing gently against the shiny golden lining. To balance she had to stand very straight with her hips pushed out, shoulders back and her bottom tucked in.

'Let's find you a place to sit.' He looked around him. Every surface of the room appeared to be covered with papers. He bundled some of them to the side, careless of scrumpled corners, uncovering part of a faded chintz sofa. 'Here.'

Isabel sat down and tensed as the sofa springs threatened to give way. She perched on the edge.

'The office proper is upstairs, but that's even more chaotic. I'm just going to get myself a chair,' he said over his shoulder as he left the room. Isabel could hardly imagine anywhere more chaotic than the room she was in. She'd remembered correctly when talking to Neil: Downton Street was a terrace of Georgian artisan's cottages, neat as doll's-houses. The downstairs hall and room had been knocked through so the front door opened straight onto the paper-strewn living room and the stairs ran up one side.

Patrick came back in with a kitchen chair. 'As you can see, I desperately need someone who can sort out my paperwork. I meant to have a go at the weekend, which is why there's lots of stuff down here but . . .' he shrugged, palms up. 'Paperwork's not my thing,' he added. Isabel could see that. She wasn't sure if paperwork was her thing either.

'What do you do?' she asked. Neil hadn't actually said she wasn't to go, but she knew he didn't approve. The least she could do was ask his questions.

'I set up computer systems for people, supply software, hardware, whatever's needed. You don't happen to speak Italian, do you?'

'No,' Isabel said, thinking she'd blown it. She didn't think failing O level Latin counted.

'No matter,' he said. 'It would have been a bonus. I have clients in Italy as well as here, that's all.'

Isabel wondered if he was Italian himself. He was dark skinned with dark brown hair, but it was his gestures that seemed Italian, the way he shrugged. And the obviously expensive clothes. Most of the computer guys she'd met before who worked for Neil's company were quite different, bearded and slightly earnest and badly dressed, uncomfortable in suits, as if the coat hangers had been left in them. But his accent was impeccably English.

He leant back in his chair. 'Tell me about yourself, what you've done workwise. That sort of thing.'

Isabel clutched the handles of her bag, trying to remember what she'd worked out. It was quite hard to make nothing sound impressive. 'I haven't been working recently, not formally at least. My husband's job has meant that we've had to travel around, often to countries where women aren't allowed to work. We came back to the UK this summer which is why I'm interested in this job. You said you wanted someone part time?'

'You have children?'

Isabel nodded. Somewhere, at the back of her mind, she was sure she could remember that employers weren't allowed to ask prospective employees about children. It was the sort of thing Neil would know.

'I've got two,' she said, pushing Neil out of her mind. 'Katie's six and Michael's eight. They're both at school.'

'Does that mean you can't do a full day?'

'Well, yes, really.' She bit her lip. 'The school does have an After-school Club, so I wouldn't have to go early. But I'd rather not use it, at least, not in their first term.' Her voice trailed away.

'So when would you want to go?'

'Three?'

'I see. And in the morning?'

'After the school run. I could be here really early, before nine if you wanted.'

'Mmm. I'm not famous for being an early riser.' Patrick looked at her as if considering.

Isabel inwardly cringed. She knew that she was doing the interview all wrong, that she should be talking about all the positive benefits she could bring to the business, rather than the times she couldn't work. On the other hand, she wasn't sure what positive benefits she could bring to Patrick's business. Perhaps if she knew more about what he wanted.

'What exactly were you looking for?' she tried.

'Someone who can manage all this,' he said, waving a hand. 'Also, answer the phone and deal with clients if I'm out and generally act as a PA. I want someone who's prepared to be flexible about what they do and not expire in horror if I ask them to take cheques to the bank or pick up my dry cleaning.' His eyes dropped to her feet as if in doubt that anyone who would wear such shoes could do anything as mundane as going to the dry cleaners.

'I wouldn't have a problem with doing that,' Isabel said, tucking her feet under her, trying to make the shoes less obvious. She was starting to get excited. There was nothing that Patrick had said so far that she couldn't do. Picking up dry cleaning, going to the bank and answering the phone were definitely within her capabilities. It was the more conventional secretarial abilities like touch typing and shorthand that she lacked.

'I work mainly on computer—' he paused. 'I take it you can use one.' She nodded and he carried on. 'I use most of the standard office software – Sage, Word, Excel and so on. Are you familiar with them?'

'We've got all of them on the computer at home,' Isabel said truthfully, omitting that it was Neil's computer and that she'd hardly ever used it.

'And the Net?'

'Oh yes,' Isabel said, relieved that she could offer some evidence of her skills. 'I'm an ex-pat. The Net's the easiest way to keep in touch with friends when they're scattered all over the world.'

'Good.' Patrick frowned. 'Did you bring me a CV?'

Isabel shook her head, excitement being sucked away like dust up a vacuum cleaner. Nervousness was making her mouth dry, the lining as wrinkled as a lychee skin.

He scratched his nose. 'So what sort of work have you done before?'

'Before I married I worked at the BBC as a researcher.' No need to tell him that it was two months' unpaid work experience one summer. 'And I've taught English abroad, both privately and in schools.'

'So you're a teacher.' Mr Sherwin checked his watch. He sounded bored.

'No. Well, yes. Sort of. I taught English as a foreign language.'

'I don't think I need that.' He smiled, and Isabel tried to smile back. 'So no office experience to speak of, in fact,' Mr Sherwin said.

Isabel stared at the floor. All those years and nothing to show for it except a fast-fading suntan and a competent backhand. What had she been doing with her life?

'No, but I have spent many years running a household, often in quite difficult circumstances.' Unconsciously she sat up straighter. 'From what you've said, you need someone with organisational abilities rather than specific office skills.' She put what she hoped was a confident, efficient expression on her face but inside she felt close to tears. It seemed desperately important that she was successful, just to show Neil that she could get a job, even though it looked like she'd be spending her days tidying up.

'I wouldn't want more than fifteen hours' work a week. That's five hours on three days,' he said, and she looked at him, startled at the thought that he might be about to offer her the job. 'Mid-week would suit me best.'

'You mean, Tuesday, Wednesday, Thursday? That would suit me too.' She could hardly breathe with excitement.

'Look, why don't you start next week and we'll see how we get on. Call it a trial period, no strings on either side.'

'That sounds fine,' she beamed at him. He could have said anything and she'd have agreed with it. The first job I go for I get, she thought. Not that hopeless after all. She felt wonderful. A job, a real job. A job meant purpose, and validation and wages and . . . Oh! She realised she had been so bound up in the getting of the job that she had completely forgotten about the money. She swallowed.

'Um, can I ask about wages?'

'Ah. I thought three pounds fifty an hour.'

Her ego deflated rapidly. 'That's outrageous. I mean, that's less than cleaning ladies.' She'd been horrified when she'd discovered what the going rate was in Milbridge. But perhaps cleaning ladies were harder to find than would-be office workers.

He shrugged, unperturbed.

'Five pounds,' she said, breathless at negotiating.

'You've no experience, no qualifications. You could say that I'm offering you on-the-job training.'

'That's taking advantage. Supermarkets pay more than that.'

'Then take a job in a supermarket.' He leant back, completely relaxed, totally confident that she didn't want to work in a supermarket. Which she didn't.

'Four pounds.'

'Three pounds seventy-five,' he countered, smiling at her. The smile irritated her.

'Four pounds,' she repeated, determined not to give in. She didn't want him to think she was a pushover. 'It'd make the maths easier.'

He laughed, and stood up. 'Let it not be said that I'm taking advantage of inexperience. Four pounds an hour it is. Deal?' He held out his hand.

Isabel stood up too. She'd forgotten about the plum high-heels, and the factory-smooth soles slid on the rug under her feet. She nearly stumbled, grabbing at his hand to steady herself. His grip was warm and firm.

'Deal,' she said.

I've got a job, I've got a job. The words sang in her head. Paying peanuts, but Neil had said that the money wasn't important, and if Neil said it . . . And she had negotiated the wage herself. She collected the children from school.

'We've got to stop at the supermarket and get some eggs,' she said.

'Can we have some sweets?' Michael asked. Both children were unused to the abundance of sweets in shops, having been brought up mainly in Syria, and Isabel had been trying to keep it that way.

'Sure,' Isabel said, and smiled at his surprise.

She wandered around with a wire basket over her arm, dropping in chocolate cake and wine and a pot of winter cyclamen and anything else that took her fancy – tea lights and ice cream, mango-scented shampoo and estate-bottled olive oil. When the children asked again for sweets, she doled out a pound each, and they scampered off, chattering excitedly. At the till she realised that she'd forgotten the eggs and had to dash up and down the aisles searching for them, unused to the store layout.

Neither the obvious boredom of the shop assistant nor the surprisingly large bill could dampen Isabel's spirits.

I've got a job, I've got a job. She could see herself telling Neil, imagining his delighted surprise. 'Good for you,' he'd say. 'Well done.' She replayed the interview in her head, the dreadful moment when Mr Sherwin asked about her CV, the sagging sofa, the mounds of paper everywhere. She giggled inwardly. She'd never seen anyone so messy, no wonder he needed someone to sort him out. In her mind's eye she pictured the living room without the layer of paper, the office tidy, everything filed away alphabetically with herself at the centre, a Miss Moneypenny figure with striped shirt neatly tucked into a slim waistband, unchewed biro in hand. Her vision expanded and she was running a vast office, an office where pot plants grew in lush profusion on the desks of the happy workers clicking at their computer keyboards. Phones rang with a pleasant chime and were answered courteously with sweet voices saying— Her daydream stopped suddenly as she realised that she'd forgotten to ask Mr Sherwin the name of his company. Neil wouldn't be impressed.

Neil wasn't.

'I don't understand why you didn't ask,' he kept saying. 'What's the big secret?'

'I didn't think to ask,' Isabel said, feeling stupid and wishing she hadn't told him, had kept it quiet. Neil had been in such a bad mood when he'd got back from work that she'd avoided telling him about the interview. On Saturday afternoon they had driven into town to buy a sofa. Sitting in the passenger seat, waiting to get into the central car park, she'd been lulled into thinking it wouldn't matter, that he'd have forgotten his objections. But no such luck. Neil couldn't leave the subject alone. He worried at it, picking away at the edges of Isabel's pride in her success.

'Look, I'll find out on Tuesday. What about this one?' Isabel sat on a sofa at random, ignoring the children who were bouncing on and off leather armchairs further down the aisle. 'It's very comfortable.'

'I think it's hideous,' Neil said, the corners of his moustache drooping down.

'We wouldn't have to have the same cover. Try it for comfort.' She patted the sofa beside her. Neil sat down, and leant back, his eyes closed as if about to go to sleep.

'Aren't you pleased I've got a job?' she tried.

'Of course I am, darling.' Neil sat up with a sigh. 'It just seems very dodgy to me. It's in this man's house, you don't know the name of the company, there's no job description—'

'I know what I'm supposed to be doing. Personal assistant things.'

'Such as?'

'Filing. Sorting. Organising. That sort of thing. Nothing I can't do.'

Neil rubbed the back of his head with his hand and stood up. 'It's not a question of what you can or can't do. It's a question of safety.'

Isabel stood up too. 'You didn't want me to go to the interview because of safety but it was fine. Not everybody is a mad axe murderer or serial rapist you know.'

'But you didn't know, that's the point. He could have been. You went to meet this man at a private address. No one knew where you were or who you were with.'

'But it was fine.' Isabel felt as if she were back at school and being told off for something she hadn't done, the injustice of it burning inside. 'And you knew where it was, I told you, those Georgian cottages you said were too small for us. And that wardrobe woman from the school, Justine, she knows him.'

'Great. Well that's all right then. The wardrobe woman knows him. Whoopee.' He set off down the aisle. Isabel watched him peering at the sales tags and then letting them drop with a sniff. He straightened up and looked around the sales floor as if, of all the sofas lined up, none of them could possibly be worthy of him.

Isabel marched up to him and pulled at his sleeve to get his attention.

'Why are you being so bloody unpleasant?' she hissed, keeping her voice low so no one else would hear.

Neil looked past her left ear. 'I'm sorry. I don't mean to be unpleasant,' he said in the reasonable voice that always drove her mad. 'I'm concerned that you're being—'

'What? Stupid?'

'No, not stupid. Naïve. Inexperienced.'

'Neil, I'm a grown woman. I'm not a child who needs looking after. I've spent all these years trailing after you, going from one country to the next, and that's been fine. I've accepted that there are certain constraints living in a different culture. It was the life we chose.' She bit her lip, concentrating on sounding as reasonable as Neil, not over-emotional and out of control. 'But we're not there now, and I'm not going to live as if I'm in purdah. This is my home.'

'I'm only concerned for you.'

'You don't need to be.'

There was a short silence. Isabel found the combination of flat neon lighting, low ceilings and no windows on the shop floor was giving her a headache. And the 'Buy now for Christmas' signs so prominently displayed in September were depressing reminders of passing time.

'I don't like these square ones,' Neil said, touching the arm of the nearest sofa with his fingertips. 'I'd rather get something with cushions.'

'You mean more traditional.'

He shrugged, then moved along towards the children on the far side of the shop floor. They'd found a garden swing seat and were rocking backwards and forwards, eyes shut, feet dangling in complete relaxation. For once they weren't bickering and squabbling, but swung gently in perfect accord.

Why are we always arguing? Isabel thought. Since we've been back it's been one thing after another. Neil used to be my closest friend, but now we're always fighting. Perhaps we shouldn't have come back.

She trailed after Neil, who had settled on a large sofa with scrolled arms. She sat on the other side, very conscious of the space between them.

'D'you like this one?' she said finally.

'It's not bad,' he said. 'I like this stuff.' He stroked the sofa arm, his fingers lingering on the soft fabric.

'Chenille,' Isabel said. 'I was thinking that loose covers would be more practical.'

'It's a nice colour too.'

It was a dreary in-between brown, not cream, not chocolate, but a nothing colour. 'You can choose whatever colour you like,' Isabel said.

'I like this one.'

'Don't you think it's a bit, well, dull? I mean, we could have something like this.' She pulled out the book of fabric swatches and handed it to him, open at a vibrant terracotta. He took it as if the swatch might surge up and swamp him, like being attacked by a vat of tomato soup.

'I know this is a silly job,' she said. 'I know it's not important, or clever, or anything really. It's not what I want to be doing for the rest of my life, or even for more than six months. But it's a start, and I have to start from the bottom.'

'Why do you have to start at all?' he said, thumbing through the swatches.

'Neil, we've been through this so many times. I want to work, I want to be useful. The children are at school all day, so what else am I supposed to do with my time?'

'It didn't matter in Syria.'

'The children were younger then. And it was different. I had to shop every day, and make everybody's lunch, and there weren't opportunities to do anything else. It's not like that here. And everything's so expensive here, we could do with the money.'

'It's hard to imagine what they'd look like from such a little piece,' he said, frowning at the swatches. 'I think the one it's got on is the best.'

Isabel said nothing as she looked at the sofa. Sludge would be the most apt description. She took the book of swatches from him and flicked wistfully through the squares of jewel-bright colours – sapphire, emerald and ruby. Still, she supposed that sludge would go with almost any other colour. And she had insisted that he come with her to choose; it would be unfair to then ignore his choice.

'So you'd like this one?'

'Yeah, why not?'

'Don't you think we should look at some others?'

'No, this'll do.' He paused. 'Look, I accept you want to work. I don't see why it has to be this job.'

'Because I've not been offered anything else,' Isabel wailed in exasperation. 'I can't pick and choose. I've no experience, no qualifications. I probably couldn't even get a job selling sofas.'

'You can sell me a sofa any day. Come here and give me a kiss.' So that was the end of the discussion. Isabel thought about pushing harder for a different colour, but as he had relented about her working she shuffled along the seat to him. He put his arm round her. 'That's better. Now, how much do they want for this? You're sitting on the label.'

'Sorry.' Isabel shuffled away and pulled the tags out from behind her. 'It's quite a lot.' She tried to work out how many hours of working it represented, but got confused with the maths. Could it really be as much as five months' pay?

'C'mon, let's grab the kids and go and pay.'

Isabel scanned the room at all the sofas they hadn't looked at. 'But we haven't looked at everything.'

'I thought we'd decided.' Neil stood up and waved at the children. 'By the way, how much are you getting for this job?'

'Four pounds an hour.'

He looked at her then. 'You're kidding. That's less than the minimum wage, you know.'

'I didn't,' Isabel said, rubbing the chenille up the wrong way and then smoothing it down with her fingertips. 'I didn't know there was a minimum wage.'

'Oh, Isabel. What shall I do with you?' Neil stared down at her. 'You really are hopeless.'

How was I supposed to know there's a minimum wage? There wasn't one when I last lived here, she thought, as the children charged over and bounced on the sofa Neil had chosen. At least I got the job. Mr Sherwin didn't think I was hopeless. The idea that he might have thought her a mug skittered across her mind. After all, he had originally offered her three pounds fifty an hour. But then, remembering the chaos, she thought it more likely that Mr Sherwin hadn't heard of the minimum wage either. And I don't care anyway, she told herself. It doesn't matter how much I get, it's the experience that counts. After a few months I can look around for something that pays better.

She followed Neil and the children to the sales desk where Neil negotiated a price reduction for the sofa in the showroom. The sales assistant's probably relieved to get rid of such a boring colour, Isabel thought, and then felt disloyal.

'We could deliver on a Wednesday, Thursday or Friday,' the sales assistant said.

'It'll have to be a Friday,' Isabel said, feeling immensely proud. 'I work on Wednesdays and Thursdays.' It was wonderful to be able to say that. Neil snorted into his moustache but said nothing to her as he got out his wallet and paid for the sofa. Perhaps she could think of the colour as being baby donkey. She could team it with speedwell blue.

As they walked back to the car, Isabel tucked her hand into Neil's arm. 'It's only for a trial period,' she said. 'Just to see how things work out. No strings on either side.'

Neil patted her hand. 'If it's what you want,' he said. 'Though it beats me why.'

Isabel squeezed his arm. 'It'll be fine,' she said. 'You'll see.'

4

Isabel stood on the doorstep and examined the door, currently painted a cheery parrot-green but with enough chips to show other layers of colour underneath, like a half-sucked gobstopper. She rang the doorbell. Nothing. She knocked, a sharp series of raps. Still nothing. She looked up and down the street, feeling conspicuous and uncertain what to do next. She wanted to shout out, I'm supposed to be here. She knocked again then tried to peer in through the window, trying to avoid the startling pink froth of the nerines that were sunning themselves at the base of the house wall. It seemed very dark inside. She'd hassled the children to get to school early, turfing them out of bed and into the car, letting Michael get away with unbrushed hair because it would waste five minutes while he argued against it. She felt cheated. She'd come all this way and now there was no one here.

She took two paces back and stared up at the windows. The curtains were drawn and she wondered if Mr Sherwin lived there as well as using the house as an office. Perhaps he was still in bed, despite the fresh morning sunshine. She remembered him saying something about not being an early riser. But she couldn't believe he'd forgotten she was coming. She walked to the gate, reluctant to leave, frequently turning back as if the door might have opened in her absence. The front garden needed weeding, couch grass pushing up through the herring-bone bricks of the path. A few palest pink buds, stained cappuccino-brown around the petal edges, clung onto a straggly rose bush that might, once upon a time, have been a standard.

She hovered at the gate, unwilling to let it clang shut behind her, wondering what to do next. Then she realised that a man was strolling down the street, a newspaper tucked under his arm and a pint of milk dangling from his hand, and in the next second recognised him. Mr Sherwin gave no appearance of hurry as he sauntered along the pavement towards her. Halfway down he stopped, pulled out a mobile phone and started talking into it. He was still talking when he registered Isabel. With his free hand he brushed the palm of his hand against his forehead, universal sign of forgetfulness – or stupid-ity – and grinned at her, still chatting into the phone. He walked past her to the house and unlocked the door, handing her the newspaper and milk so he could dig out his keys from the depths of his trouser pockets, phone clamped between ear and shoulder.

He had to duck his head to get through the doorway, then beckoned her in. Isabel obediently entered, trying not to eavesdrop on his jargon-filled conversation. The room looked even worse than it had done the previous week. Obviously any thoughts he may have had of sort-ing through his papers had vanished over the weekend. She hesitated then carefully stacked some of the papers into a ragged pile and sat down carefully on the sofa. The springs had mainly given up the struggle, leaving her the alternatives of lolling back in abandonment against the soft feather cushions or sitting bolt upright as if tightly corseted. She sat with knees together, back straight and newspaper and milk in her lap, watching him stride around the room talking, as if oblivious to her presence.

After a few minutes she realised she must look like a presidential candidate's wife listening avidly to her husband making a speech. She pretended to look for something in her bag instead, while she tried not to listen to a voice in her head that said, what are you doing here? As Mr Sherwin talked on, the voice of reason got louder. She stood up.

'Look, I must go,' he said. 'Ciao.' He turned the phone off and looked at Isabel, who was inwardly seething. He could obviously have stopped talking any time he wanted.

'Isabel. Is it Tuesday already? I'd quite forgotten about you. Never mind, it's good you're here. I'm up to my eyeballs at the moment.' He gestured vaguely at the room. 'What would be great is, if you could tidy all these into some sort of order, and then make us a couple of coffees – the kitchen's through there – and then I can run through what I want you to do today. I've got a few calls to make, but I'll do them in the garden. You can bring the coffee out there. Got to make the most of the sunshine, right?' And with that he left the room, already dialling on his mobile.

Isabel stood blinking in the empty room. Well, that's put me in my place, she thought. How Neil would laugh at this. But I'm here, and here to work. She put the newspaper and milk on the stairs then started to collect up all the printed matter ready to sort into piles – newspapers, brochures, letters. She wasn't sure how else to sort them, not knowing what they were about. As she went through she registered certain names and made new piles for them. Invoices, bills – an alarming amount of red reminders – glossy advertisements for computers, bits torn from newspapers. Some were written in what she recognised as being Italian. The telephone rang and her hand hovered over it, uncertain if she should answer or not, but it stopped ringing before she could decide. Bank statements, financial reports, cuttings from the *Financial Times*. Official-looking letters from Customs and Excise and Companies House. By the end she had lined up the material into eight rough piles along the top of the old oak dresser and not a paper lay on the floor. And she now knew the business was called Patrick Sherwin Associates.

She followed where he had gone and found herself in the kitchen, a large room almost entirely filled with a huge pine farmhouse table, big enough for a family of twelve. There were dirty plates and mugs in the sink, and foil dishes indicated that Mr Sherwin had been eating a lot of takeaways over the weekend. She filled up the kettle with water and switched it on. While she waited for the water to boil she did the washing-up and chucked the takeaway containers into the bin, hoping that she wasn't setting a precedent. It was bad enough clearing up after two children and a husband without adding an employer as well.

Having finished, she looked around for something else to do. The kitchen now looked functional but impersonal so she went back out to the front garden and picked some of the nerines. The fragile pink flowers were unscented but beautiful as she put them in a jam jar on the kitchen table, long petals arching away from the carmine centres, edges frilled like underwear. She started to explore the cupboards. Mr Sherwin appeared to have only real coffee, not instant, so she made a cafetière-full. She fetched the milk, poured some into a jug, then put the rest back into a fridge that was empty except for two bottles of Pinot Grigio, a wizened piece of cheddar and four plastic canisters containing camera film. She added two mugs to the tray along with the cafetière and milk, and went out to the back garden, screwing her eyes up against the sunshine.

Mr Sherwin was seated at one end of a garden table, legs crossed and feet on top as he rocked the chair backwards, still talking into his phone. As soon as he saw Isabel he put his legs down and finished off his conversation.

'Thanks, that's just what I needed.' He smiled up at her. 'As you can see, it's all go at the moment, but hopefully it'll calm down later. What I'd like you to do today is answer the house phone and take messages, and start sorting the office out. It's the room upstairs, at the back.' His mobile started to ring, and he reached for it. 'Sorry, you're going to have to make it up as you go along today. When you've finished your coffee, can you find out about flights to Milan on Friday? Returning Sunday – from Heathrow, if possible – use the Net to get the best deal. The computer's in the office.' He looked at the phone display. 'Christ, it's that fool Andrew again.' He pressed the answer button and, with a big smile, said, 'Andrew! What can I do for you?'

It was embarrassing sitting there doing nothing, trying not to listen to Mr Sherwin's phone conversation. Isabel sat for a minute then took her coffee inside. She decided to do the flight booking while he was safely outside and yabbering on his mobile so he wouldn't see her first attempt at booking something over the Internet. She rinsed out her mug, then went upstairs to discover the office.

The office was the back room, not the one with the closed curtains. The room had obviously once been used as a bedroom, with a mattress sagging against the wall. More papers were stacked on the floor or spilled off the edges of the bookcase. There were two large cardboard boxes filled with a tangle of electrical leads and crocodile clips, while computer monitors and keyboards were stacked haphazardly in the corner. Propped up on top of them was a pinboard nearly hidden behind multiple pieces of paper skewered at strange angles, business cards stuck into the frame corners, and a couple of photographs of a gleaming sports car, lovingly polished to a high shine.

Other photographs were pinned on the walls, landscapes mostly. Isabel recognised several local landmarks. They weren't snapshots but what Isabel thought of as proper photographs. She remembered the film canisters in the fridge. He was obviously serious about photography.

One photograph traced the contours of a woman's body in silhouette, just discernible in the darkness. A solitary square of golden light illuminated a patch of naked skin. Mr Sherwin's wife? Or someone else? Isabel peered intently at the photograph, trying to make out the woman's features, but they were hidden in soft darkness. A noise downstairs made her jump, and she left the photograph.

In the middle of the room was a desk, and on the desk was a computer. She eyed it nervously. Although she'd told Mr Sherwin that she knew what she was doing, she'd only used the Internet for email before. Neil had given her a computer lesson at the weekend. It had reminded her of him teaching her to drive, endlessly patient with her mistakes. A good teacher. I must remember to say thank you properly she thought, smiling at the memory of his tolerance. She hesitated by the sole chair placed directly in front of the computer. Mr Sherwin had obviously been using it earlier; the machine was on and two empty mugs sat to the right. She touched the monitor. What if she couldn't do it?

The room felt stuffy so she opened the sash window and leant out. She inhaled the clean morning air deeply, letting the freshness fill her with confidence. If she got into difficulties with the computer she knew Neil would help her, would come to her rescue with technical support. Dear, dear Neil. He was good. She looked down and saw Mr Sherwin in the garden below. It seemed an odd thing to do, give a stranger a free hand with sorting through your papers and possessions. But he seemed an odd sort of man, very casual and not businesslike at all. She couldn't imagine him working in Neil's office, for example. She wondered how old he was. There was no sign of his hair thinning, even from this angle, whereas poor Neil already had a bald patch and receding hairline.

A rustle behind her made her realise that the breeze from the window was threatening to disperse the papers even more thoroughly around the room, so she pulled the sash down. Then it seemed a pity to shut out the freshness so she pushed it up again, to leave a crack for the air. Time for work, she thought.

The first priority was the flights. She quickly ran through the different airlines and came up with a selection of times and prices that she wrote down in her neatest writing, as she imagined an efficient secretary would do. Rome the weekend before, Milan this. It seemed very glamorous. Perhaps, she thought, she and Neil could go one weekend. They could ask his parents to look after the children. She'd never been to Italy before, having missed out on being a student and backpacking around Europe.

Flight information sorted, she turned her attention to the room. There was an old filing cabinet in the corner. She opened the drawers in turn and discovered that it was almost empty, just a few manila folders lurking among the suspension files. She wrote labels for the front of the drawers: Clients and Accounts were obviously the first two drawers. The magazines, newspaper articles and advertisements could all become Information in the third drawer. And everything else could go into the bottom drawer marked, for the time being, Stuff. That settled, she began to work through the piles of paper, dividing them into the categories.

Underneath some computer magazines she found a scarlet clipboard, complete with pen. She made a list of what she had to do. Flights. System. Sort out office. Sort out sitting room. The list grew longer as she thought of things to do until she came to the end of the piece of paper. She ticked off the first two.

As she looked at the clipboard with a sense of achievement the phone rang. She found it on the floor underneath the table.

'Good morning, Patrick Sherwin Associates,' she said in the sort of voice she imagined an efficient personal assistant would use. 'Can I help you?' She inwardly prayed they wouldn't ask any awkward questions. Which could have been almost anything. But luckily the caller simply wanted to speak to Mr Sherwin.

Isabel opened the window. 'Mr Sherwin, Mr Sherwin,' she called down into the garden, waving her hand. 'Telephone.' He looked up and round at her. 'Telephone,' she repeated, miming holding a receiver to her ear.

'I'll take it downstairs,' he called back up to her. 'Who is it?'

Isabel grimaced. 'Sorry.'

He shook his head. 'No matter.' Isabel felt dim for not asking. An idiot would have thought to ask who it was. She turned away from the window when he called her back.

He was squinting up at her, eyes closed against the sunlight. 'You don't have to call me Mr Sherwin.'

'Oh.'

'Patrick will do fine.'

He nodded, then went into the house. Isabel turned back to the phone.

'He's just coming,' she said, forgetting to put on her ultra-efficient voice. She then waited until she heard the click as he picked up the downstairs phone. Then she put the phone down, thinking about calling Mr Sherwin Patrick. It seemed almost disrespectful to call an employer by their first name. Or was that old-fashioned, a remnant from living abroad for so long? But then, he doesn't call me Mrs Freeman, she thought. Neil would probably think he ought to. But then Neil thinks I ought to be at home washing his socks or something. Instead, here I am – at work. And it feels good.

'You'd have been very impressed by your old mother,' Isabel said to the children as they ate spaghetti, spattering tomato sauce over the table. 'I even did the bit with the credit card when Mr Sherwin had chosen the flight he wanted.' She'd got used to calling him Patrick over the day, but felt reticent about using his first name to the children.

'Does that mean I can have a Playstation?'

'Nope.' She mopped round Michael's face, despite his protests. 'Mr Sherwin is half-Italian.'

'Why can't I have a Playstation?'

'Because.'

'Won't you have lots of money now you're working?'

'No, and it's a matter of principle, not money, anyway. I don't want you to have a computer in your bedroom.'

'Everybody else has.'

'Tough. Listen, don't you want to hear about Italy? It's where spaghetti comes from.'

'I thought you got it from the supermarket.'

'Very funny. Eat up, Katie.' Katie was sucking up long strands of spaghetti, leaning back as if that would help. With one final suck, mouth like a goldfish, the spaghetti strand disappeared.

'I'm being Lady,' she said, starting on the next strand. Isabel was confused, then remembered the Disney film. 'Oh, *Lady and the Tramp*. Yes, they have spaghetti in an Italian restaurant, don't they?' Katie nodded, eyes popping with the effort of sustained suction.

'Yeuch, kissing.' Michael made a gesture as if putting two fingers down his throat, and added retching noises.

Typical boy, Isabel thought, not without pride. Whatever you did with them, children divided on gender lines, the boys liking guns and battles, the girls liking puppies and princesses.

'Mr Sherwin's very untidy, much worse than me.'

'Do you tell him off?' Michael asked.

'Of course not. He's my employer. C'mon you two, eat up. There's chocolate cake for afters.'

'Mmm.' Katie started to eat properly.

Only bought cake, not home-made, because she didn't

have time to make her own. The first pangs of working mother guilt gave her an illicit thrill. No longer merely someone else's adjunct, but a working woman too busy for trivia, rushing from one meeting to the next. A life filled to the brim with purpose. She cut each of them a tranche of cake, including herself on the grounds that she deserved a little treat. And although it wasn't as nice as home-made, it was still satisfyingly squidgy.

She sang to herself as she cleared up the tea things, and the good mood continued all the way through Neil's return home. He asked a few questions about her day, which she answered as neutrally as possible, not wanting to trigger any unpleasantness. She hoped that if she kept it low key, Neil would accept her working for Patrick. She'd sent a few emails to her friends about the new job, including one long one to Frances, her closest female friend, halfway across the world on a posting to Thailand, but she wanted to talk to someone about it.

She fished out Justine's business card from her handbag, now dog-eared and creased, unlike the immaculate Justine. She used the phone in the hall, away from Neil in the sitting room, safely ensconced in his armchair in front of the television – so like his father.

'I just wanted to say thank you. I've started working for Patrick Sherwin.'

'I heard.' Justine sounded amused.

From him? Isabel wondered what he had said about her. She wasn't sure she liked the idea of Patrick and Justine discussing her. No, she was being silly. Patrick had probably just said something in passing. She paused, uncertain of what to say next.

'I don't want to rush you, but I was just on my way out,' Justine said.

'Somewhere nice?'

'Just the usual crowd.'

The usual crowd. She imagined Justine sipping sapphire gin and tonic in a club, spotlights shining on her hair, perched on a bar stool while a group of admiring men leant against the polished brass rail.

'I wondered if you and Rachel would like to come round for tea after school one day next week?' Isabel blurted out.

'That sounds good.' They fixed a date for the following week.

'Look, I must dash. I'll see you next week. I expect you want me to dish the dirt about Patrick,' Justine added.

'No, no, of course not,' Isabel responded, but couldn't stop herself from asking, 'Is there any dirt?'

Justine laughed. 'Gotta go. You'll just have to wait.'

Later, Isabel undressed for bed as Neil sat in bed reading some company report. She wondered if he would notice if she grew a thick coat of body hair all over or developed a third breast. She pulled her nightdress over her head and hopped into bed. After a minute she snuggled up to him. He carried on reading but put his arm round her. With her head against his chest she could feel his heart beating, strong and regular.

'Neil—' She paused to get his attention. 'I'm really grateful for all the help you gave me with the computer.'

He squeezed her shoulder. 'I'm glad to help. You know that,' he said, turning the page.

She snuggled closer, letting her mind drift back over the day. It had been tiring, and she had a long way to go before Patrick Sherwin's affairs were in order. But she'd enjoyed it, bringing order out of chaos. And he'd been impressed by what she'd managed to do.

'It's funny; I never do the bills or anything like that at home, and here I am doing a complete stranger's. Perhaps I could take it over.'

Neil grunted. 'Only if we wanted to be getting final demands all the time.'

'You just won't forget that will you?' Isabel rolled away from Neil and settled down to sleep, back towards him. 'Anyway, Patrick says that no one in business pays until the last moment. It's called cash flow management.'

'Bloody poor management, if you ask me. Completely irresponsible.'

Isabel could just picture the expression on his face as he said it, unconsciously mimicking him under her breath. Completely irresponsible. You could tell he'd been a prefect. It made sense to her, making the bigger companies wait. They could afford it.

'And since when has this man been called Patrick?'

She froze for a second. 'Oh, since birth I suppose,' she said airily, and turned out her bedside light. 'I'm going to sleep now.'

'You know what I mean.'

And she did. 'Don't be so old-fashioned. I bet you call everybody else in your office by their first names.'

'That's quite different and you know it.'

'Well, I don't think so.' She hunched her shoulder into her duvet. 'I'm tired. Good night.'

She screwed up her eyes against the light from Neil's bedside lamp, willing for sleep to come quickly. In the half-darkness she could hear him turn the pages of his report. Strange how such a little noise could fill the room. After a while he laid down the report with a sigh and turned his light off.

A whisper of breath.

'Isabel?' A hand sneaking towards her, groping its way up past her nightdress.

'I'm tired.' The hand pawed an inert breast. A cold, thick hand with stubby fingers. She closed her eyes, not that Neil could see in the dark.

He pressed against her and asked, as he always did, 'Is this . . . ?'

Pointless to say no. She always said yes, because yes was easier than no. No meant discussion, fumbled attempts to arouse her that she found deeply embarrassing. No nearly always meant giving in later. She got more sleep with yes and, most of the time, sleep mattered more. Tonight it mattered. She swallowed, a small sound in the darkness.

'It's fine. Go on.'

'Sure?'

As if in answer she hooked her leg over his hips to draw him towards her. Needing no further encouragement he plunged in, losing himself to the physical sensation, a dance that both of them knew, smooth and practised over the years. Practised to the point when it had ceased to have any meaning. Once, of course, it had been the most wonderful thing ever, but eighteen years and two children later, sex had dwindled into a routine activity. She didn't think she was unusual, judging from what other women said.

Sex with Neil was like a hobby, like playing golf. Neil was still keen and Isabel, supportive wife that she was, joined him. Sometimes it engaged her, held her interest, drew them together. Other times she merely strolled around the course with him, breathing deeply, applauding Neil's good shots, and vaguely hoping that the exercise at least was doing her good. It was nothing to be either unhappy or happy about – just another facet of married life.

But that evening there was something else, a lurking question: is this it? There should be, ought to be, something more. Acceptance was not the same as contentment. No matter how Neil pumped away, she felt empty. It seemed insignificant, no more important than a putter rattling in a golf bag. An unexpected hot tear slid out from under her tightly closed eyelids and suddenly she wanted nothing more than to be alone.

Knowing it would hurry him up she dug her nails into his arms, breathed more heavily, muttered, 'Go on. Now.' Encouraged by those sparse tokens of passion he reached the eighteenth hole and collapsed down onto her. His body felt heavy, replete and contented. He kissed her, then rolled off and settled himself down for sleep. Curling up into a foetal position, she realised that she couldn't remember when he'd last bothered to ask if it was all right for her.

5

When Helen had invited the whole family over to Sunday lunch, Isabel had been thrilled at the invitation, their first since coming back to the UK. Now, standing outside Helen's large Victorian house in the countryside outside Milbridge, she was not so sure. She hardly knew Helen, and had never met her husband, George. The links between the two women – both new to the area, both having gone to the same school – didn't seem enough to justify the formality of a Sunday lunch. Neil rang the bell, an ornate piece of cast-iron work that pulled out on a chain.

Silence.

'Perhaps I've got the wrong day,' Isabel said, shivering. It was cold out of the sunshine and she wished she'd brought a coat. She wanted to tug Neil's sleeve and whisper, 'Let's not bother, let's just go home.' But that would be childish.

'Sunday lunch, you said. It's Sunday.' Neil rang the bell again.

'Perhaps I've got the wrong week.' But no, there were footsteps inside, and Helen opened the front door, her cheeks flushed. Then it was introductions, children being sent off to the playroom, and drinks for the adults – mean dribbles of gin and vast slurps of tonic. George and Neil recognised each other from the station platform and

Helen exclaimed about yet another coincidence.

'Hardly,' snorted George. His eyes were pale blue and surprisingly large in his red face, like a Hanoverian portrait. 'Everybody takes the seven twenty.' His voice was contemptuous and Helen seemed to shrink down a size.

'What a lovely house,' Isabel said quickly, although she thought the house depressing.

'We were so lucky to find it,' Helen said, brightening. She launched into a long story of estate agents and probate, surveyors and footpaths. 'It took nearly a year.' They talked about houses and house prices, then moved on to soft furnishings. Helen confided that you could get amazingly cheap fabric from the market that really wasn't bad at all. It was the sort of conversation that is excruciatingly boring to anyone not involved but completely absorbing if you are, the equivalent to snuggling down on a Sunday afternoon with a fresh cup of tea and a packet of chocolate digestives in front of a black and white film starring Bette Davis.

Isabel couldn't remember having had such a conversation before; the houses on the compounds just existed, boxes for living in. Now she leaned forward to listen to Helen talk, a feminine conspiracy of sofa throws and beaded tea light holders. She wasn't sure if it was her attention, or the fact that George and Neil were deep in some masculine bonding session of their own that seemed to be based on the best way of travelling from Hull to Bristol, but Helen became positively girlish. Although Helen and she hadn't been exact contemporaries at school Isabel could imagine her discussing the merits of pale blue eyeshadow or whether Rimmel mascara was better than No. 17.

Helen was in the middle of describing some magic

netting (available by mail order) that stopped rugs from creeping on solid floors, her teeth gleaming with enthusiasm, when Rufus and Michael came in, on the scrounge for food. Helen flapped her hands while Rufus helped himself to handfuls of crisps.

'Oh dear. Don't do that. We're eating any minute.' Rufus continued to cram his mouth with crisps. He had the same hair as his mother, the colour of wet sand and growing straight down, dense as a shaving brush. He was nearly a head taller than Michael who had followed him, hands in pockets. Isabel raised her eyebrows at him, wordlessly checking that he was happy, but he frowned at her. She assumed that meant he was happy, but would be embarrassed by any maternal displays.

'Where do you go to school, Rufus?' she asked.

'Benedict's,' Rufus muttered through crisps.

'Weekly boarding,' Helen said. 'So much nicer than full time.'

Isabel loathed the idea of sending Michael away to school, however 'nice' it was. It would be like paying to have your arms ripped off.

'I don't know how you can bear it,' she said.

'Oh, but he loves it, don't you darling? And you'll find at St Joseph's that most of the boys leave for boarding school by the end of Year Four so it must be a bit lonely for the ones left behind. Benedict's is hardly any distance away so I can always go and watch matches and things. Can't I, darling?' She reached out an arm for Rufus.

'Mu-um.' He shrugged her off. 'When's lunch? I'm starving.'

Helen got up, her face suddenly anxious. 'I'd almost forgotten about lunch.'

'Can I help?' Isabel offered, but Helen told her to stay sitting, she could manage, and hurried to the kitchen. In ten minutes they were all sitting round a large polished table in a formal dining room while George hacked chunks off a large joint of overdone beef. The walls were painted green and hung with framed prints of dead pheasants. An elaborate bowl of fruit stood on the highly polished mahogany sideboard, framed by twisting silver candlesticks. It could have doubled as a stage set for a Sunday teatime family drama series. All that was missing were starched pinnies and maids saying 'Lawks!'

George was making a sterling attempt at impersonating a Victorian paterfamilias. Isabel looked across at Neil, wanting to share her amusement, but he was talking to Helen. Helen was nodding, but with an abstracted air as if counting spoons. Isabel could imagine the litany in her head – pepper, salt, mustard, gravy, horseradish sauce – and realised with a stab of sympathy that Helen was not going to relax until all the food had been eaten and the children were running about in the garden or watching a video. It was as if she felt that her whole value as a woman was measured by her ability to produce a traditional Sunday roast.

'This is wonderful, Helen,' Isabel said. 'Such a treat. We haven't had a meal like this for ages, have we Neil?'

'No, more's the pity,' Neil said, tucking in with gusto. Isabel felt guilty. She'd forgotten how much Neil had always enjoyed his mother's cooking when they'd come back to the UK on holidays. But they weren't on holiday now; they were home for good. She ought to be preparing this sort of meal for Neil.

'In hot countries you often don't want to eat big meals, do you?' Helen said with her soft voice, smiling

sympathetically across the table at Isabel. 'Just salads and
pasta and things.'

Isabel smiled back and opened her mouth to speak,
when George butted in.

'Got to have decent food. Sunday wouldn't be Sunday
otherwise.'

Isabel tried to think of witty things that, while not
actively offensive to her host, would show him up for
being a pompous twit. But the phrase that would allow
her to be both exquisitely polite and downright rude at
the same time escaped her, so she made no reply. She
talked a little to Helen, mainly about the PTA, and helped
Katie cut up her meat despite a few derisory comments
from George about mollycoddling.

As she had predicted, Helen didn't relax until the last
apple crumble plate was ensconced in the dishwasher
and the coffee was on the table. Rufus slid off his chair
with a sidelong look at his father, busy expounding on
the follies of the euro. Michael hesitated, looking across
to Isabel. 'Is it okay for the children to get down?' she
whispered to Helen, who nodded. 'Run along and play,
darlings.' Katie and Millie scampered off hand in hand.
Isabel watched them wistfully. She quite fancied running
along and playing, rather than sitting in the formal and
stuffy room with her waistband threatening to cut her
stomach in half.

George brought out brandy and two glasses, which
irritated her. Not that she wanted a brandy, but she felt
he should have asked. She looked across to where Helen
was sitting, listening to the men talk. George was persuading Neil to join the Golf Club, and for some reason Isabel
thought of Patrick. She stirred her coffee slowly, watching the cream swirl into psychedelic patterns. She'd hardly

thought of him all weekend but now she had, she could imagine him all too clearly – leaning back on his chair, relaxed, his deep voice mocking George's pretensions. She frowned. She should have been pleased that Neil was getting on so well with George, but instead she felt slightly disturbed. Both men were now leaning back, George's red checked shirt straining across his stomach, the squares distorting into op-art patterns like a Bridget Riley painting. He lit a small cigar.

'So,' he said between puffs. 'How did you two meet up?'

'At a party,' Isabel shrugged. 'Same as most people.'

'Come on, darling. Hardly like most people.' Neil was beaming at her, brandy glass in his big hand. She smiled tightly at him, hoping that would be an end to it.

'Aha. There's a story here, I can tell,' George said, cheeks shining like a raddled cherub.

'It was a very hot summer night, a mini-heatwave in fact, and—'

'Neil, they don't want to know. It's too long a story,' she said to Helen, shaking her head.

George thumped the table. 'Come on, spit it out.'

'As I was saying, it was a very hot night—'

George topped up his brandy glass. 'You've said that before,' he crowed.

'So I have,' Neil said, amiably. Isabel realised that he'd had more to drink than she'd thought.

'Neil, I really don't think—' Isabel started, but Neil cut her off.

'It's a good story. Don't be silly.' He waved his hand dismissively at her. 'Anyway, this party. A joint eighteenth and twenty-first, I think. So long ago I can hardly remember.'

'Lin's eighteenth and Peter's twenty-first,' Isabel said,

trying hard to think of a way out of this conversation. 'Lin was at Richmond House too,' she said to Helen. 'Did you come across her – Lin Hetherington? Her mother drove a sports car.'

But whether Helen could remember Lin or not, Neil was determined to carry on. 'Whatever. The parents had really pushed the boat out, marquee, dinner, band, dancing. The works. Really good do. But it was boiling in the marquee. So, some bright spark jumped into the swimming pool – fully dressed, you understand – and soon everybody was going in. Including Isabel.'

'Neil, you didn't save Isabel from drowning, did you?' Helen sounded impressed.

'Better than that,' Neil said with satisfaction. 'Now, I'd spotted Isabel earlier in the evening. Obviously she was the prettiest girl there, but she was also dressed differently from the other girls in this long, floaty thing.'

'It was a second-hand dress I'd bought from Portobello Road market.' She could remember the dress clearly. Fine navy crêpe, splashed with scarlet and white flowers, buttoned down the front with strawberry-shaped buttons, seams piped in scarlet reaching to the ground. It had a sharply defined waistband and was the sort of thing worn by Hollywood actresses in the Forties. A collector's item now; then it was a cheap way of dressing. She thought back, how lacking in confidence she had felt alongside the other girls with their generous clothes allowances and shopping trips to Harrods on Mummy's account card. She couldn't compete with that, but her market dress had sidestepped any question of competition. And the Forties style suited her, emphasising her small waist (those were the days) while skimming over her more generous hips. 'I loved that dress,' she said, more to herself than to the others.

'So, what happened?' prompted Helen.

'Isabel was one of the swimmers, but then she got out and went into the marquee.'

'The water was cold – it was Surrey, not the Tropics after all. I wanted to warm up again.'

'She starts dancing, right? But each time she moves, this dress tears a little.'

'Tears?' Helen looked at Isabel, eyebrows raised.

'I think it must have been the chlorine in the swimming pool. I don't know if the dress was synthetic, but the fabric just couldn't cope.' It was like candy floss, the damp fibres pulling apart. Not tearing or ripping, more melting, dissolving with each gesture, each movement. She could remember so clearly, looking down and seeing—

'This is so embarrassing,' she said to Helen, hopeful of female solidarity.

Helen looked confused. 'Perhaps we should have coffee in the drawing room.'

'Nonsense. Get on with it, Neil,' George said, patting his stomach.

Isabel tried to send telepathic messages to Neil. She hoped her face was smilingly casual, with an underlying hint of steel that Neil would pick up. 'Please Neil, stop there.'

'But this is the good bit. You see,' Neil said, untouched by telepathy, utterly unmoved by her embarrassment, 'she wasn't wearing anything underneath.'

Isabel wanted to curl up and die. They were all looking at her, Helen wide-eyed, perhaps slightly shocked, Neil pleased with the effect his story was having, and as for George, his eyes had been designed for boggling.

'It was a very hot night,' was all she could think to say.

'I should say,' said George. He didn't actually wink and nudge Neil in the ribs and say 'Phwoar', it just felt to Isabel as if he did. She tugged at her cardigan, barricading herself against George's prying eyes that were fixed firmly on her chest. And suddenly she felt eighteen again, exposed, distressed, with people laughing and pointing. She had scanned the faces in the darkness round the dance floor, looking for help, for a friend, and with each turn the dress quietly shred a little more. She crossed her arms over her breasts, feeling the back give way, and walked to the side, moving slowly to minimise the damage and the humiliation, laughter echoing in her brain, and then there was a man holding out a dinner jacket. 'Take this,' he'd said and wrapped it around her shoulders. It was still warm from his body, the satin lining slippery against her damp skin.

'But that's so romantic,' Helen exclaimed, her eyes shining, as she smiled at Isabel. Isabel shrugged, sliding a look across at Neil, one-time saviour, now humiliator. How could you? she asked him wordlessly, but his eyes weren't focused on her.

George's eyes glittered. 'I hope she was properly grateful.'

'I think so,' Neil said smugly. He even winked at George as if to convey all sorts of sexual adventures, whereas Isabel knew that the evening had ended with him driving her back to the flat she shared in Fulham, then a few kisses over the transmission of his Ford Mondeo, gearstick acting as a latter-day chastity belt. She would have asked him up, probably would have slept with him, but being the sort of man he was it didn't occur to him to ask. 'Nice girls don't on the first meeting' was so ingrained in him that he'd not registered the opportunity.

For some reason an image of Patrick came into her head. Would he have rescued her, or would he have been part of the laughing crowd like George? A rescuer, she thought. She could see him, slipping his jacket over her shoulders, but then he would have happily taken advantage of her gratitude and ravished her behind the marquee. She gave herself a little shake. What an extraordinary thing to think, she told herself.

Katie came into the dining room and sidled up to her, thin arms about Isabel's neck.

'What is it?' Isabel said, relieved at the distraction, slipping an arm around Katie's waist.

Katie put her mouth by her ear. 'I want to go to the loo,' she whispered, her breath hot.

'Can't you ask Millie?' Isabel whispered back.

'I want you.' Katie's face was small, eyes screwed up in embarrassment.

Isabel excused herself to Helen, grateful for the reason to escape, and went with Katie into the hall. She realised that the loo door had no lock, which was why Katie was anxious. Isabel stood outside, guarding Katie against unwanted intrusion, not that the boys were anywhere to be seen or heard. This seemed to her what motherhood was about. The little things. Tiny noses gently wiped. Small clothes washed, dried and ironed, woolly socks in pairs. Cool hands placed lovingly on hot foreheads. Eggs boiled and then dunked in cold water so the whites were hard but the yolks were runny, and the toast soldiers buttered with the crusts cut off just so. Bumps that could be cured with kisses. Love bound by a thousand daily intimacies, a thousand daily acts of service.

Katie came out, unself-consciously pulling up her knickers with both hands. Isabel smoothed her dress down.

'Shall we go and find Millie?'

Katie nodded. Isabel took her hand and they went to the playroom where Millie was playing with a doll's-house. Katie left Isabel and crouched down beside Millie. Isabel watched them playing, enjoying the freshness of their skin, the seriousness of their conversation. Millie had very decided ideas about what went where, and which dolls had to do what. Mother dolls were in the kitchen, the babies and children were upstairs in bed, or being naughty in the sitting room. Isabel knelt down beside them. She could remember her own doll's-house, random furniture of different sizes so the house looked as if it belonged to the Three Bears rather than a pallid felt doll with a faded smile and curly wool for hair.

'What about the father doll? What does he do?' she asked.

Millie paused in her arrangements. 'There isn't a father doll,' she said, matter-of-factly, and went back to discussing with Katie where the cat should go in their exclusive little world of mothers and babies. Isabel picked up a tiny teapot, painted with a carrot, carefully holding it in her palm. But although the lid came out there was no hole for the spout. The teapot could never function. There would be no dollies' tea parties. Isabel turned it round between her fingers, feeling as disappointed as Hunca Munca in the Beatrix Potter tale, although she restrained herself from bashing the plaster lobster with the miniature coal scuttle.

The little girls were talking, a continuous murmur. They were not excluding her; rather there was no place for her in their self-absorption. Isabel got up, feeling her knees creak. I'm getting old, she thought, and went back to the world of adults.

They left late in the afternoon, George promising Neil to nominate him for membership of the Golf Club. Isabel was cross with Neil on the way home for what she saw as his betrayal, but he was unrepentant, unwilling to acknowledge that there was any problem.

'I've told that story to loads of people,' he said yawning, despite two coffees.

'And I've never liked it,' she snapped back.

It wasn't strictly true. But a story told to friends under the relaxed blue skies of the Middle East was quite different to hearing one's past revealed under the gaze of George's bulging eyes on a grey English afternoon. Would she have minded Neil telling Patrick? She wondered what Justine would say about Patrick when she came to tea.

'I like this house,' Justine said looking around Isabel's kitchen, the bell of her hair swishing round like a girl in an ad.

'I don't,' Isabel said, then realised how odd that must sound. 'I mean, it's all right, and there are enough bedrooms and the kitchen functions and all that, but it's not what I wanted. Still, that's what comes of looking in a hurry.'

'You must have stunning views over the town from upstairs.'

'Mmm.' Isabel sipped her tea, thinking about houses. 'I would rather have lived in something older. We've been living in modern houses for such a long time, and I suppose I dreamed that when I got my own house it would be more traditional. And I thought we'd live in the country rather than a town.'

'A cottage with roses round the door?' Justine sounded amused, her eyes sparkling with gentle mockery. Isabel couldn't decide if she liked her, but she enjoyed Justine's acerbity after Helen's cosy conformity.

'Something like that. I don't know, I spent all my child-hood traipsing around from one house to another, and I always promised myself that my own children would be settled in one place.'

'Was your father in the army?' Justine asked.

Isabel drank the rest of her tea, hoping that Justine would think she hadn't heard the question, then carried on talking. 'The alternative was going into rented accom-modation and I didn't want to do that. We only had a couple of months' notice you see. This time last year we didn't know we would be here.'

'How come?'

'You never know. That's the way the company works. Oh, you can put in your preference about where you want to be sent but you take what's available. If we'd stayed abroad our next posting would have been either Nigeria or Eindhoven, neither of which appealed. And I wanted to come back to the UK anyway, so Neil applied to go into management at Head Office. We looked at anywhere close to a station that ended up at Waterloo. So here we are.'

'Well, it seems very nice to me. Very spacious.'

Spacious. Isabel winced inwardly when she heard it; it seemed such a non-word, the sort of word used by estate agents. A bland word, like pretty, and tasty, and saying you were fine. Don't be mean, she told herself. Justine's only trying to be positive about it.

'Magnolia everywhere works wonders.' She looked around the kitchen, her own personality asserted over the blandness by the addition of copper pots from Morocco and a string of scarlet chilli peppers like an archaic coral

necklace. 'We're lucky, we had a house in London which
we let out while we were abroad, so it meant it wasn't
such a shock when we came back.'

'Do you still have it? It must be worth a fortune,'
Justine said.

'I don't know about that,' Isabel said, embarrassed. 'But
we've still got it. If we'd had more time we'd probably have
sold up and bought something else down here, but we've
got good tenants and the way prices are rocketing in
London it's probably best to hang on to it.' She frowned.
Neil had wanted them to sell her father's house, complaining about the cost and hassle of maintenance, but she knew
her father would have preferred that his house be saved
for her children rather than financing a more impressive
home. Secretly she hoped that it would provide whatever
fees the children needed to go to university: her father had
always regretted that he didn't have the chance to go.
Thinking of the children brought her back to the present.

'I suppose I ought to start getting the children's tea
ready. Does Rachel like pasta?' Justine nodded. 'I try and
think of different things for them, but they won't try
anything new and I end up eating it, so I tend to stick
to the old reliables,' Isabel said. 'Neil said the other day
that only three things in life were certain: death, taxes
and pasta for lunch.' She fussed in the kitchen area,
putting water on to boil, getting out a saucepan and
cheese grater. 'Do you know Patrick Sherwin well?' she
asked, as nonchalantly as she could.

'Oh, Patrick,' Justine said, leaning back on her chair.
Isabel hoped the chair back was up to it.

'Do I know him well?' Justine said slowly, as if buying
time before her answer. 'I've known him for about . . .
um . . . eight years.'

'Quite a long time.'

'It seems like forever. Goodness, we were both married when we met.'

'So he has been married,' Isabel asked, feeling guilty about talking about Patrick behind his back, but unable to resist. 'But he's divorced now, isn't he?'

Justine let out a snort of laughter. 'Don't you know?'

Isabel prodded the spaghetti down into the saucepan, watching the stiff strands bend and become supple in the hot water. She felt foolish and naïve.

'Perhaps it's not surprising you don't know. Patrick can keep very quiet when it suits him.'

'I wouldn't expect him to talk about something personal like that,' Isabel said, feeling she was sounding prissy, but reluctant to launch into discussing Patrick.

'But you want to know, don't you?'

Isabel shrugged, not wanting to say yes.

Justine stared up at the ceiling. 'I don't think Patrick or Caro were suited from the start. She was very much part of the hunting and shooting set round here. Still is, in fact. After their divorce she married some man with two thousand acres towards Petersfield.' Justine fiddled with a biscuit on her plate. Isabel realised Justine hadn't eaten any of the hand-made cookies she had bought from the WI market especially for the occasion. No wonder she was so slim. Isabel had already eaten four.

'It's funny how the rich always seem to marry the rich, isn't it?' Justine said.

Isabel blinked. 'I don't know. Do they? Perhaps that's how they get to be rich.'

'How they stay rich anyway.' Justine crumbled a bit of biscuit, squashing it flat under her index finger. 'One thing you'll learn is that there are an awful lot of people with money round here. Not so much in the town, but outside in the villages. Stupid money. Some of it's from the City but a lot of it's inherited.' She sniffed.

Isabel didn't know what to say. The conversation seemed to have nosedived rapidly away from Patrick and Caro, and she wasn't sure how she could steer it back again.

'So Caro's rich?' she tried.

'Rolling in it,' Justine said. 'You'd have thought with all that money she could afford to dress decently.' She sounded as if the way Caro dressed was a personal affront. Then Isabel realised that it might be.

'Did you do your wardrobe thing with Caro?'

'Sure, she had the full wardrobe consultancy, colours, clear-out, the works. Not that it did her much good. Or me come to that,' Justine added like an afterthought. Isabel wondered what she meant but Justine looked cross so she didn't like to pry.

'Tell you what, the pasta's nearly ready. Why don't you call the children down?' Justine got up and went out of the kitchen. Isabel quickly laid the table with three places, drained the pasta and made a sauce by adding a knob of butter, some cream and a mixture of quickly grated Gruyère and cheddar. At the end of this activity she was slightly surprised that none of the children had yet appeared and went out to the hall.

'Hello?' she called up the stairs. 'Children. It's tea.' Silence. She called again, and this time she heard sounds of movement. Michael came first, slouching down the stairs in a manner that would befit a teenager, Rachel and Katie next and lastly Justine, who was saying, 'Come on girls,' in a rather hearty manner. Isabel had the distinct feeling that she hadn't been fetching Rachel and

Katie for tea but had been having a quick scout upstairs. Justine smiled as she passed her, shooing the children into the kitchen. Isabel shrugged. There was nothing she could do about it, except hope the bedrooms weren't disastrously untidy.

Justine was very complimentary about Isabel's cooking skills, gushing about how clever she was to knock up something so delicious, so quickly. Isabel was uncertain how to react. It was obvious that the dish was simple, so Justine's praise seemed excessive. She was now standing and looking along the mantelpiece at the clutter of postcards, finger paintings, dusty treasures and 'to do' lists.

'Is that Neil?' she asked. Isabel turned in her seat to look. Justine was pointing to a photograph of a man standing, hands on hips, relaxed, confident, while behind him a massive sky was streaked with the beginnings of sunset, turning a range of jagged mountains gold.

'Mmm. That's the Arabian peninsular, the Empty Quarter.'

'It's not empty, you know,' said Michael, shovelling in pasta. 'That's just what they call it.'

'Don't speak with your mouth full,' Isabel said automatically. 'And don't interrupt.'

'That's all right,' Justine said, making Isabel feel like a harsh and repressive mother. 'What's in it if it's not empty?'

'Lots of things. Birds and animals and people.'

'Sand?' Justine's voice had an attractive lilt to it, almost as if she were flirting.

'Oh yes,' Michael said, oblivious. 'There's lots of that. Can I have some cake?'

'When the girls have finished.' Isabel noticed that Rachel was struggling and said she didn't have to finish. Justine cut in quickly.

'I have a rule that children have to finish what's on their plates.' She smiled tightly at Isabel, who was nonplussed. Rule twenty-three of mothering: never interfere with another mother's discipline. But it seemed unfair to expect the child to eat food she didn't want in a strange house. And unnecessary. Nobody benefited from forcing a child to eat.

'I think I gave Rachel quite a big helping in the first place,' she said carefully. 'I should have asked how much she wanted. It's quite filling so perhaps this once . . .' She smiled across at Justine, who rather grudgingly said Rachel didn't have to finish.

Isabel collected up the plates, then cut the cake. Out of the cardboard packaging it seemed smaller than she'd thought. In her hurry, she cut pieces individually, with no regard to where the centre of the cake was, rather than cutting a cross and then halving each piece.

'I seem to have made rather a mess of this,' Isabel said, licking her fingers, puzzled at how the cake had turned out. 'From the WI market I'm afraid. I used to make my own, but now . . .' One piece was short and fat, the others long and thin, like a trigonometry question in Michael's homework – how many of these are scalene triangles, how many isosceles? Michael and Katie squabbled over who had the largest piece. Isabel felt flustered, especially as Rachel was sitting quietly eating her own misshapen slice. Her manners were impeccable. Perhaps Justine was right to insist on good table manners at all times, regardless of the circumstances. Justine was looking at Neil's photograph again.

'I've always liked that photograph,' Isabel said. 'We'd only just got married, and Neil had given me a camera.'

'He looks young.'

'We've been married forever. Neil was twenty-six and I was just nineteen.'

'Nineteen!' Justine's eyes were alert with speculation. 'Nobody gets married at nineteen nowadays.'

'I know.' Isabel pulled a face. Yet again she'd have to make it clear that she and Neil didn't have to get married because she was pregnant. 'Neil was just about to start a two-year contract in Saudi, and I couldn't go with him unless we were married. And then, under their law, I became his property and so they paid for my airfare, and provided us with suitable accommodation for marrieds. Otherwise Neil would have had to stay in a ghastly sort of hostel place.' She shrugged. 'And there wasn't much to keep me in the UK, so we got married, went off to the desert and lived happily ever after.' Occasionally – usually after a row – she wondered what would have happened if they hadn't had to get married so quickly. Recently the thought had become more insistent, popping up in unlikely places. 'More cake?' she added, handing round the plate of squished triangles.

Katie and Michael, having finished their cake, pushed their chairs back and ran from the kitchen, but Rachel lingered. 'Please may I be excused from the table, Mrs Freeman,' she said, her hands neatly in her lap.

'Call me Isabel, do, Mrs Freeman makes me feel so old. And of course you can get down if you've had enough to eat. Go and find the others. What lovely manners,' she said to Justine, while Rachel ran after Katie.

Justine smiled, gratified, and started to clear up.

'No, no, leave it. I'll do it later. More tea?' Isabel asked, thinking wistfully of the sitting room and a conversation that didn't involve children and domesticity. A conversation about other things. Like Patrick Sherwin. But Justine had taken over, clearing things away. Isabel felt embarrassed at the number of utensils she seemed to have used to make such a simple meal. She really wanted to dump them in the sink and sort it out later. They had just finished clearing up when Neil came into the kitchen.

'You're home early,' Isabel said as he kissed her cheek.

'I caught the four twenty.' He turned to Justine and held out his hand. 'Hello. Neil Freeman.'

She took his hand. 'Justine Torens.'

'Justine's daughter is in the same class as Katie,' Isabel chipped in, hoping that Neil would go upstairs or into his study and shut the door. But he didn't. He stood there drinking tea and chatting to Justine and showing no sign of disappearing. There were things she wanted to talk about, to ask Justine. Instead they were talking about one of Neil's favourite projects, a huge dam which had provided hydro-electricity for hundreds of thousands of houses but in the process had also drowned several villages in a remote valley. Isabel glowered. How could Neil imagine that Justine was interested in all that? Although Justine was doing a good line in nodding and asking questions, Isabel could see that her attention wasn't held.

Finally Justine ended it. 'I really must be going,' she said, picking up her bag. 'I've completely outstayed my welcome.'

'Not at all,' Neil and Isabel said together, Isabel mechanically and Neil with a beaming smile as if he meant it. 'Have a drink,' he added.

'That's so kind but, no, thank you. I must be on my way.' She went into the hall and called up to Rachel then turned back and held her hand out to Neil. 'It was so nice to meet you. Your work sounds fascinating.' Rachel came clattering down the stairs, followed by Katie. 'Thank you so much for having us, we've really enjoyed ourselves, haven't we Rachel?'

Rachel nodded obediently. Isabel found herself opening the front door. Normally it took hours for people to go: children disappeared, one shoe lost, toy left in the garden, that sort of thing, but Justine was leaving rapidly. As she passed through the doorway she paused.

'I was going to tell you all about Patrick, wasn't I?'

Isabel nodded, conscious of Neil hovering in the hall behind her. 'Another time, maybe.'

'There's really not much to tell. I mean, he doesn't keep his skeletons hidden in his cupboard. If anything, Patrick's skeletons are thoroughly out and probably drinking with him down at The Mason's Arms.' She shot a glance past Isabel towards the hall and whispered, 'You know what they say about him, don't you?'

Isabel shook her head. 'What?'

'They say . . .' Justine looked sideways at Isabel as if gauging her reaction, 'he's very good in bed.'

6

Good in bed. Isabel sorted the post into letters, junk mail, bills. Good in bed. The words seemed engraved on her brain, so that some of the letters seemed addressed to 'Patrick Sherwin, Good in Bed', not 'Mr Patrick Sherwin, 45 Downton Road'. Who were the 'they' who said it? And how did Justine know? Had she and Patrick . . . ? Isabel thought about it as she made coffee for Patrick in the cafetière. She knew Justine was divorced, but little else about her.

The phone rang. 'Patrick Sherwin Associates,' she answered. Good in bed, she thought. 'I'll just see if he's in.' She held the phone to her chest while she hollered for Patrick upstairs. 'He's just coming,' she told the caller, then waited for Patrick. He came clattering down the stairs and took the phone from her. 'Yup?' he said. Isabel tried not to listen to his conversation. It was boring anyway, something about a computer not working. Patrick was trying to work out what the problem was, long-distance. He wasn't very successful at keeping the irritation from his voice, she thought, as she handed him his coffee. He smiled as he took it from her and she felt herself blush. Good in bed. The phrase nagged like a football chant in her head. She could imagine cheer-leaders, ra-ra skirts twirling: 'Good in bed!' – clap, clap, clap – 'Good in bed!' – clap, clap, clap.

She went back into the kitchen and made tea for herself, dreamily lifting the tea bag from the mug and dropping it into the sink tidy. What was it that made a man good in bed? She'd always thought that, for women, it was their own mental attitude that made the difference. Certainly for herself she thought it was true, although her own experience outside Neil was limited and seemed a long time ago. Perhaps it was experience that made the difference. But the man might just be repeating the same moves, over and over. Or he'd learn what suited one woman, and then have to learn new tricks for the next. So he'd have to be sensitive. Considerate. Receptive. Not qualities traditionally associated with men. At least, not with the few she'd known. Perhaps all women liked the same things. But that was like saying everybody liked potatoes. Most people did, but some liked chips, and others went beyond baked, roast and mashed for more exotic variations such as duchesse and dauphinois.

She frowned. It couldn't be size – well, not just on its own. And as for inventiveness, there seemed something offputtingly mechanistic about ticking off the various positions. Up a bit, left a bit, bullseye! More akin to painting by numbers than true art, and there were people who said that making love was an art. She sipped her hot tea. How irritating of Neil to pitch up at the very moment when Justine was going to tell her something interesting.

'Why must I work with imbeciles,' Patrick shouted as he came in, making her jump. 'These people are morons. It's enough to drive you mad.' He opened a cupboard door then slammed it shut. 'Where's my coffee?'

'Where you left it,' she said, watching him with trepidation. His anger seemed to fill the room. He drummed his fingers on the worktop, then ran them through his hair, which seemed to be sparking with electricity.

'Well, get it,' he said, throwing up his hands as if exasperated beyond endurance by her obtuseness. Obediently she went into the living room and collected his coffee cup, only thinking of saying 'Get it yourself' as she turned to take it back. I mustn't be a doormat, she thought. But she was there with the coffee cup in her hands. And he did seem very angry. She could hear him crashing around in the kitchen, slamming cupboard doors. He'd got angry so quickly, it was like spontaneous combustion. Unexplained and devastating. She went back into the kitchen and put the cup on the table.

Patrick didn't appear to register her return. He was too busy pacing up and down, cursing clients for their infinite stupidity, their total absence of brains, their complete lack of appreciation. He spat out the words with passion. 'And then they have the nerve to tell me – me!' he stabbed his chest with a finger for emphasis, 'that the system doesn't work.'

Isabel didn't know what to say. She shrugged her shoulders and tried what she hoped was a calming smile. 'Never mind. I'm sure you'll be able to sort it out.'

He turned on her, his eyes blazing. 'Never mind? What the hell does that mean? Of course I mind. Of course I fucking mind, you stupid woman. I'm going out.' He swept past her, the swing of his shoulders expressing pent-up energy so strongly that she involuntarily took a step back. The coffee cup on the table must have caught on his jacket because it went flying, smashing onto the floor and splattering shards and black coffee over the tiles, followed by a second crash as Patrick slammed the front door shut behind him. The sound reverberated through the house.

Isabel stood rigid until the house had settled back into stillness. Then she bent down and picked up the broken bits of china. Her hands were trembling. She'd never seen someone so angry, so physically angry, close up before. Neil retreated into a cold shell, teachers at school had been sarcastic, her parents had kept their arguments behind closed doors. She wrapped the pieces in newspaper and put them in the bin.

Should she go? Or was that being hysterical? She hesitated, then started to mop up the coffee, in case the terracotta stained. Neil would be horrified if he knew what Patrick had called her, she thought. What she had said was anodyne to the point of stupidity, maybe. But it was outrageous to call her stupid, let alone with such passion. Neil would want her to go.

Good in bed.

It would be cowardly to go, she told herself. And she didn't want to go back to the weekly trudge through the Situations Vacant and the humiliation of being ineligible even for an interview. She squeezed out the dishcloth and draped it over the sink. She would stay for the moment and see what happened.

She was upstairs in the office, trying to sort out which invoices had been paid and which hadn't, when she heard the front door give a gentle click and footsteps downstairs. She kept her back to the door and her head down.

'Isabel?'

'Mmm?' she said, not turning round, apparently intent on her work.

'I'm sorry. I shouldn't have lost my temper like that.' His deep voice was contrite. A humble rumble, she thought, and smiled inwardly, still checking through the invoices. The nape of her neck felt naked where she'd tied her hair back for work. She could feel his eyes on her and perhaps he sensed her mood because he came and stood next to her.

'I shouldn't lose my temper like that, but I do. It doesn't mean anything. My Italian blood coming out, maybe. My mother is a great one for flying teacups. I hope this won't stop you working for me.' He paused. His voice sounded hesitant and she realised that he was not used to apologising. It made her feel powerful. He lightly touched her arm. 'Isabel?'

She looked up at him and for a mad second thought, he's going to kiss me.

But he didn't.

'Let me take you out to lunch at the pub, to make up for being so foul.' She could feel the blood rush to her face and turned away to hide her confusion.

'I've brought sandwiches.' Her voice sounded tight, as tight as his was relaxed.

'Chuck them. Say you'll forgive me, and come out to the pub.'

She swallowed. 'I do forgive you, and thank you for the offer, but I'm going to eat my sandwiches for lunch. I think that's best.'

'You haven't forgiven me.'

'No, really. Actually, I hadn't given it a moment's thought till now.' She smiled what she hoped was a particularly bland smile at him. The efficient and very respectable Mrs Freeman. 'Now. There seem to be a whole batch of invoices missing. From about 4550 onwards. Any idea where they are?'

'Not really. I loathe paperwork.'

'I'd noticed.'

He looked around the room as if it was the first time he'd seen it. 'You could try in that box.'

He indicated an old photographic paper box, flat and shiny yellow, perched on top of a pile of computer monitors. She started to search for the missing invoices, hoping that her body language would indicate she was busy, although all her senses were alert to Patrick, who left the room after a few minutes.

She sighed and carried on looking through the box. She found old business cards, an Indian takeaway menu, a photograph. She picked it up. Patrick smiled lazily at her, his arm casually draped over a slim brown girl with silver-blonde hair in a white bikini. His ex-wife? Or some other girlfriend? They were on a yacht and the sky behind them was an intense cobalt blue. She turned it over, but there was nothing written on the back, no indication of when it had been taken. She slipped the photograph under the takeaway menu and tried not to think of Patrick looking impossibly glamorous. And good in bed.

She worked upstairs for the rest of the morning having located the missing invoices, scrunched and torn, behind the radiator. When she looked out of the window she could see Patrick pacing up and down the garden, apparently talking to himself, arms waving. He looked absolutely mad, then she realised that he was wearing some sort of headset so he didn't have to hold his mobile phone at the same time as talk.

I was right not to go out to lunch with him, she thought. It was important to keep the lines drawn, not to cross them. He was her employer, after all. Although he shouldn't shout at her. Neil would be furious if he knew about it. She closed the window thoughtfully.

But she liked working for Patrick. The last two weeks

had been absorbing and purposeful. She liked sorting all his stuff out, arranging letters in files and folders, organising the unused filing cabinet, writing headings in the tabs and sliding them on. She liked typing his letters, especially with the spellchecker for her useless spelling. She liked being useful; she liked being defined by her work rather than her functions as wife and mother. She liked answering the phone in her special efficient voice; she liked it when Patrick went out for a meeting and she had the house to herself; she liked it when Patrick was in, and the way he talked to her while she worked. She liked the way he dismissed bills so casually, whatever Neil said about it being completely irresponsible. Sometimes he would lean across her to change a word or two as she typed, close enough for her to feel the heat from his body. She liked that too.

'Right. No excuses. You're coming to the pub with me.'

Isabel jumped. Patrick had come into the office and was handing her her coat.

'But my sandwiches—'

'Feed them to the ducks. You're coming with me.' He helped her with her coat.

'But—' said Isabel, accepting her bag from him, and allowing herself to be gently pushed out of the room.

'No buts. It's company policy.'

'What is?'

'No one's allowed to say "but". And employers who shout at employees have to take them out to lunch in compensation.' He lowered his voice as they went down the stairs. 'Stops all sorts of harassment lawsuits.'

Isabel giggled. 'If I promise not to sue, do I get to eat my sandwiches in peace?'

'Nope, you've got to come to lunch.' He opened the front door. 'After you.'

Isabel hesitated for a second, then stepped outside. 'Thank you,' she said.

The Mason's Arms was at the end of the road. Isabel had passed it often, but never been inside.

'What do you want to drink?' Patrick said.

'Something soft. A bitter lemon please.'

'Have a proper drink.'

'I'm not used to drinking at lunchtime.'

'I insist.'

'A glass of white wine then.'

He went to the bar while she looked around, feeling guilty at being in the dark, traditional interior when it was a gloriously sunny day outside, perhaps the last sunny day of the year. It felt wickedly decadent, like going to an afternoon showing at the cinema in high summer. It wasn't what she had expected to be doing. In fact, she couldn't remember the last time she'd been in a pub like this, resolutely adults only. Before she was married, she supposed. Since they'd been back in the UK they'd tried a few country pubs with the children but this was quite different. No family ghetto in the conservatory, no fenced-off play area outside.

'Let's grab somewhere while we can,' Patrick said, handing her a glass of wine and indicating a table by the fire. They sat down, Patrick opposite her, legs crossed so his left ankle rested on his right knee. He appeared totally relaxed.

Isabel perched on the edge of her seat. She hadn't expected this at all. A pub lunch, with a stranger. Well, not exactly a stranger. Her boss. She shot a glance towards him. Not good-looking, with a crooked nose, perhaps broken in a rugby match, and hooded eyes. Half-closed eyelids should have made him look sleepy, stupid even, not vibrant and alert. She had often wondered what it meant to have 'come-to-bed eyes', and now she thought she knew. It was a phrase that had intrigued her, like 'fuck-me shoes'. What on earth were they? She thought suddenly of the plum suede shoes she'd worn to the interview and blushed.

'It's getting quite full so I think we'd better order food now. Have you thought about what you want to eat?'

Her mind went blank. 'Ploughman's please,' she said, being the only food she could think of.

She watched him weave his way through the other drinkers to the bar, tall enough to have to stoop under the beams. She wondered how old he was. Forty? Forty-two? The pub was filling up with people – office workers, she thought. Men in grey suits with jackets slung over striped shoulders, ties pulled down and slip-on shoes; women in tight skirts and blouses, and high-heels. She remembered Justine saying that Patrick's skeletons were more likely to be drinking with him in The Mason's Arms. Patrick was a regular, judging by the number of people who nodded to him.

He came back with another round of drinks. She fumbled with her purse, but he stopped her.

'My treat.' He settled back in his seat. 'Do you know Justine well?'

'I only met her, what, two weeks ago.' She blinked in the smoky atmosphere, surprised at how her life had changed. 'And you? Do you know her well?' Good in bed, she thought.

'Justine and I go back a few years.' His voice was still deep, still relaxed, but there was a finality about it. 'Tell me about working at the BBC. I know a few people who work there.'

'It was ages ago.' She took a swig of wine, feeling the cool oiliness around her mouth. 'Before I married.'

'And did you stop working the second you got married? How very Fifties.'

'The sort of places Neil was posted, it was difficult for me to do anything. Even in countries where there aren't restrictions on women working it's often difficult: you haven't got the right permit, or your qualifications don't count.' She fiddled with a beer mat, thinking back. 'At the time it seemed logical. Neil was going abroad on a two-year contract, and I could only go with him if we were married. And if we were married the company provided a house, but if Neil was single he had to stay in a hostel. And I wanted to travel so . . .'

'It sounds a very convenient arrangement.' His voice was dry. She didn't want him to get the wrong idea.

'We were madly in love, of course.'

'Of course.' His eyes were half-closed, but she caught a glint of reflected firelight. 'And now?'

Isabel ran a finger round the rim of her wineglass. 'Well, of course. That goes without saying,' she said, conscious of a stiffness in her voice. 'Look, is that our food?' Patrick turned and beckoned the waitress to their table. She put down the simplest ploughman's lunch in front of Isabel and a steaming pie with chips in front of Patrick.

'And another round of drinks on my tab,' he added as the waitress left.

'Oh, no, I mustn't,' Isabel said. 'I've got the school run later.'

'That won't be for ages. And you're not doing anything else this afternoon, are you?'

'Working for you?'

'And this is what I want you to do. You did say at your interview you were prepared to be flexible.' Was he teasing her? Isabel looked at Patrick, but he was busy digging into the top of his pie, letting out clouds of steam.

'That smells good,' Isabel said.

'Guinness and beef. They make them here. Try some.' He speared a chunk of steak onto his fork and held it out to her. Isabel hesitated, then opened her mouth and took it. It was delicious. Their eyes met and Isabel blushed. I shouldn't have done that, she thought. A boundary had been crossed. You simply didn't behave like that with a stranger. An employer, what's more. She reached out for her glass of wine, spilling a little on the table.

'Sorry.'

'Don't apologise,' he said, mopping up the pool with a paper napkin. 'A beautiful woman should never apologise.'

Isabel quickly put down her glass before she spilled more wine all over the place. Patrick ate more pie as if he'd said nothing out of the ordinary. Perhaps to him he hadn't, Isabel thought.

'Help yourself if you want more.' He indicated his plate.

'No, I'm fine,' she said, picking at a crumb of cheese and popping it in her mouth. Her finger tasted salty. Had he called her a beautiful woman? She hugged the idea inside. It was a long time since anyone had said anything about the way she looked. She stole a glance at Patrick who was finishing his meal. As if he could feel her eyes on him he looked up.

'You're not eating. Don't you like it?'

'No, no, it's fine, thank you. I'm not that hungry, that's all.' She tried to think of something to say that would steer her back to safety. 'Have you lived here long?'

'In the area, about eight years.' He used the last chip to mop up the gravy and ate it with relish. 'My wife wanted to move out of London, find somewhere for her horse.'

'Her horse?'

'It was costing a fortune at livery in London.'

'So you moved to the country.'

'Yes. Biggest mistake I ever made.' He leant back on his chair.

'Why, don't you like the countryside?'

'Did I say I don't like the country?'

'Didn't you?'

'I don't think so.'

She waited for him to say more, but he didn't, he just sat there, his crisp white shirt emphasising his dark skin.

'I'm sorry. I thought you said you didn't like the country.'

'No.'

'My mistake. I must have misunderstood you . . .' She drank some more to hide her embarrassment. Patrick fiddled with his fork, frowning.

'I don't dislike the country. Not real country at any rate. I dislike what this sort of commuter-belt country does to people. The men go off to work during the week, while the women stay at home and have babies and run houses. Or they become horsey, and sublimate all the energy they should be putting into their sex lives into some wretched quadruped. Or worse, both husband and wife take up horses and start hunting. And that's the end.' He rolled his eyes.

Isabel wasn't sure what to say. 'You're anti-hunting then.'

"Course. I don't give a stuff for foxes, and nor would anyone else if they looked like rats, but hunting people are the pits, puffed up on snobbery and self-importance.'

'Your wife didn't hunt, I take it.'

'No, she was mad keen on it. Still is, she's always fiddling about with a martingale or polishing her snaffles.'

'Didn't that make life difficult?'

"Course not.' He grinned at her. 'We got divorced.'

Isabel felt very stupid. 'I'm sorry.'

'Don't be. Best thing for us. Except it left me in this dump instead of in London.' He stretched. 'Mmm, that was just what I needed. D'you want something else? What about a brandy?'

'Shouldn't I get back to work?' Isabel pushed her chair back as if to go.

'Don't be silly. Stay and have a brandy. Or a coffee.' She hesitated. She'd had two large glasses of wine and felt distinctly woozy.

'Perhaps a coffee would be a good idea . . .'

He ordered two coffees and two brandies despite her protests. When they came they looked suspiciously like doubles. 'If you don't drink it, I will,' he said airily. He raised his brandy glass towards her, and out of politeness she touched it with her own. It was years since she had drunk spirits and even the little sip she took caught the back of her throat.

'I shouldn't have shouted at you,' Patrick said. 'I wouldn't blame you if you decided to walk out.'

'No, it's fine,' Isabel said, embarrassed.

'Of course it's not fine. You're only being polite.'

'No, really. I didn't take it personally.'

'That's very generous of you.'

Isabel wasn't sure what to say, so she sipped her brandy.

'I'm always impressed by people who manage to stay married,' Patrick said, as if that had been what they were talking about. 'And are happy, of course. It's not impressive to stay married and be miserable.' He finished the rest of his brandy.

'It might be. All marriages have rough patches.'

'That's a euphemism for cowardice. Being too frightened to get out of the cage.'

'No, it's not cowardice,' she said, stumbling over the words in her eagerness to defend. 'It's about being a family, staying together whatever happens.'

'For better or worse?' His voice was cynical. 'Sounds too much like that poem – "And always kept a hold on nurse for fear of finding something worse".'

'That's not my experience,' she said, pushing the brandy glass away from her.

'Then I congratulate you on being one of the lucky ones.'

There was a short, uncomfortable silence. She could feel her heart racing and there was a film of sweat on her skin. I'm not used to drinking in the day, she thought. I shouldn't be here.

Patrick broke the silence. 'You think I'm too cynical.'

'I wouldn't know. I hardly know you.'

'Perhaps I am cynical about marriage.' He leant forward and she realised that his eyes weren't brown, as she'd thought, but a dark green. 'You see, my wife left me.'

'I am sorry.' Her heart went out to him, and she touched his hand lightly to show sympathy, then drank some more brandy so the hand touching looked incidental.

'Yes, she left me,' he said almost to himself, his voice soft and low. 'Left me for that bloody horse.'

Isabel let out a shriek of laughter, which she stifled with her hand firmly over her mouth. 'I'm sorry,' she said when she could. 'It just sounds so funny.'

'Not very funny when it happens to you,' he said, but his eyes were twinkling at her. Isabel tried to be serious.

'Did she really leave you for her horse?'

'More or less.'

'That's dreadful,' she managed, before having to put her hand over her mouth again to stop giggling.

'Glad you find it so funny.' He added lugubriously, 'And it was a bloody mare too.'

I've drunk too much, Isabel thought, eyes watering with laughter. But I haven't laughed like this for ages. Patrick started to talk about Milbridge and the business, and she tried to listen but her brain wouldn't concentrate, it kept skimming over the surface. Patrick ordered two more brandies, and drank both of them but she didn't care. She didn't care about anything. She didn't care if people were looking at her and Patrick, didn't care that Neil would be appalled by her drinking brandy in the middle of the day.

'I'm really enjoying working for you,' she said.

'Despite my terrible temper?'

She nodded happily.

'Well, I suppose we'd better go back and get some work done.' He drained the last brandy. 'Although it's practically going-home time for you.'

'Oh no!' Isabel leapt to her feet, banged her knee on one of the table legs and sat down again sharply. 'I should have gone ages ago.'

'You've plenty of time. I'm glad you haven't been put

off working for me.' He nodded at her, then strolled to the bar to settle the bill. Isabel rubbed her knee, then got up more carefully. Her shoes seemed slippery on the carpet, as if her knees weren't properly connected to her lower legs. Patrick returned and they left the pub.

Isabel blinked as she went outside, hit by fresh air and eye-achingly bright sunlight. She felt she'd had a troglodyte's lunch rather than a ploughman's.

'Are you okay?' He was frowning at her.

'I'm fine.' Isabel squinted up at him, suddenly aware of how much she'd drunk. 'I don't think I should drive, though. But it's okay, I can walk to the school and then we'll take the bus.'

'Sure?'

'Absolutely,' she said carefully, so as not to slur the word. She was conscious that Patrick had his hand on her elbow and was gently steering her down the pavement.

'I'm fine,' she said. 'Really.' She caught her toe on a cracked paving stone and stumbled, wrenching her ankle. Patrick caught her before she could fall, his hands steady.

'Sorry,' she said, out of breath. 'Thank you for saving me.' She smiled up at him, and realised that he was bending towards her. He's going to kiss me, she thought just before his mouth met hers.

Caught by surprise she didn't think to protest, to exclaim, to push him off. Her head buzzed, she felt the blood rush to her cheeks. His mouth felt strange, his hand was warm and rough as he held her head firmly, the other round her back, holding her to him. He tasted of brandy and coffee. She was so surprised she let him kiss her for several seconds before her brain kicked in and she opened her eyes. But before she could react, he released her.

'I shouldn't have done that.' He let his hands drop

from her arms. 'What can I say? I can't keep on apologising to you.'

Isabel stared at him. Her brain seemed to have seized up and the only thing she was able to register was the taste of him on her mouth.

'Look, treat it as a moment of madness. See if you can forget it happened.' He paused and looked at her uncertainly. 'D'you think you could?'

Isabel nodded, then added, 'Could I do what?'

'Forget it happened.'

'Oh.' She straightened her back and slung her bag over her shoulder. 'It's fine, you don't need to say anything more. Well, I'd better be on my way.' She held out her hand.

'Thank you for lunch.'

He shook her hand formally. 'You're welcome.'

'Well. See you tomorrow morning.'

She walked carefully up the street, trying to keep in a straightish line and feeling his eyes on her back, but when she turned the corner and checked, he'd gone.

Isabel kept on losing things in the kitchen later that evening. The wooden spoon in particular seemed to have a life of its own, vanishing and then reappearing in unlikely places. It was tiring having to search for things all the time, especially when you kept on forgetting what it was you were looking for. She tried to have the house reasonably tidy and supper waiting for when Neil came back, but today they'd had to wait ages for a bus and nothing was ready. If Neil wanted a Stepford wife he should have married one, she thought, banging the saucepans. She gave the chicken an unnecessarily vigorous push round the pan so the sauce slopped over the edge and sizzled onto the electric ring. Drat. She knew she should wipe it off immediately before it burnt itself indelibly onto the enamel but all the clean cloths seemed to have disappeared.

What was she going to tell Neil?

Neil, Patrick took me out to lunch and then kissed me outside the pub.

Neil, would you believe it? Patrick kissed me today, but we've decided to pretend it never happened.

Neil, the good news is I'm really getting on with my employer. The bad news is he kissed me.

Neil, my boss kissed me outside a pub and I did nothing to stop him and now I can't get him out of my mind.

She couldn't remember when she had last been kissed like that. If she had ever been kissed like that. She and Neil must have, at some point, surely? But kissing Neil had been like coming home, a safe haven, not the start of a dangerous voyage. Not that this was going to be the start of anything. She replayed the moment, the feel of his mouth pressing down on hers, his arm about her, the way his hand had cupped her head. Her eyes closed, her lips parted.

Bad move. She snapped her eyes open and shut her mouth firmly, heard the television churning in the sitting room and thought of Neil sitting immobile in front of it in his special leather armchair. They'd never watched television abroad – nothing to watch – but since they'd been back Neil had taken to it. Sometimes she thought he was unconsciously imitating his father's behaviour, but that seemed mean. Poor Neil, he was shattered after a hard day working, while she . . .

She filled a pan with water and put it on to boil. Think outrage. Think horror. Think disgust. She played the scene again in her head, this time concentrating on her feelings of outrage. How dare he? The trouble was, she kept sliding back to the shock, the unexpectedness of it, the delicious sensation of melting that started in her toes and flowed up her body. I should have slapped his face. Or done something. She gripped the wooden spoon in exasperation. It was all so sudden, she told herself. You couldn't have done anything about it. Better not to have made a scene. Better to be British and polite and shake hands formally and pretend nothing happened.

She turned the heat down to simmer under the chicken pan and watched the bubbles subside. She knew what she should do. I shouldn't upset Neil, she thought, I should just say I've decided the job isn't what I wanted, and forget about the whole incident. I could get something else, other jobs will come along. After all, I was hardly going to make my fortune doing it.

She stirred the chicken thoughtfully. On the other hand, I could carry on and pretend the kiss never happened. And if it happens again? No, I'd make it clear that it must never happen again. I'd have to tell him. She thought of Patrick's face, could picture the amused smile, could picture her starting confidently on her prepared speech then faltering and then . . . No, she'd have to pretend to be someone else when she told him. Someone bossy. Like that Mary woman, at the new parents' coffee morning. Unconsciously she straightened her back and thrust her chest out. Now look, Patrick. I want to work, but that's all I want. Right? She could imagine Mary saying it. No monkey business. He'd do what Mary wanted, she was sure. She clunked the lid onto the pan firmly. That's what she'd do.

The rice water was starting to boil, bubbles pricking

the surface. She started counting in handfuls of rice. Three per person. Was that four or five that had gone in? Or six? She shook the pan and peered in. She wasn't very good at judging quantity. She added another handful for luck. And then another, just in case. Patrick's hands were long and elegant, tanned with short fingernails. The hands of a sportsman. A sailor perhaps. One had wrapped around her holding her close to him while the other had tilted her head towards him, his skin firm and warm and rough against her neck.

Stop that. She clamped another lid onto the rice pan and turned the extractor fan on full. Lay the table. Get the cutlery. Knives. Forks. Spoons. There wasn't anything for pudding. Put the spoons back, lay out side plates and knives for cheese and biscuits. She moved quickly round the table, putting Michael's precious drawings carefully to one side and bundling the playdough into a plastic bag. A knife sat in an opened jar of peanut butter, like Excalibur waiting for King Arthur. She tidied it away, then laid places for herself and Neil so they faced each other across the table, salt and pepper marking the neutral ground in the middle. Napkins. She rummaged in one of the drawers and found a couple of paper napkins, slightly crumpled but better than kitchen roll. As she smoothed out the creases she had an image of Patrick spreading his napkin over his knee, his fingers strong but delicate. What if she had responded? What if his hand had slipped down into her shirt? She shivered. It was impossible. She couldn't carry on working for him. It would be tantamount to agreeing to – what? She resolutely threw him out of her mind. Concentrate on supper.

She checked the rice, which would be ready in a few minutes. There seemed rather a lot of it. Still, she could

always make a rice salad with any leftovers. Or fry it up
into a paella. Perhaps this time she would actually do it.
She sighed. She used to be able to do it, used not to be
so useless. It seemed so effortless for other women, that
was the problem. If everybody struggled like her she
wouldn't feel so hopeless. Carefully she drained the rice
and arranged it round the edges of the dish, ready for
the chicken to go into the middle. She put the dish on
the table. If she was honest she didn't want to eat, having
finished off the children's tea earlier and had two alcohol-
mopping peanut butter sandwiches at home, but she had
to keep Neil company. She glanced at the clock. It was
nearly nine. How did it get so late: she must have been
dreaming. Dreaming about Patrick. No, don't think about
him. Think about Neil's supper. She started to spoon the
chicken into the dish, making a small but mountainous
island in the middle of a lumpy white ocean.

'So how did you spend your day?' Neil, gin and tonic
in one hand, leant against the doorjamb of the kitchen.

'Oops.' A bit of chicken shot off, skittered across the
table and onto the floor. She stooped to pick it up and
chuck it in the bin under the sink, keeping her face hidden
from him so he wouldn't see her scarlet cheeks.

'Perhaps we should get a dog.'

'You've always said you didn't want one.' Isabel
gripped the edge of the sink.

'It's not been practical before. But if we're staying in
the UK we could get one. A Westie maybe.'

Neil's parents had an ancient Westie with accusing
black eyes and a matted coat, yellowed with age to a pee-
stained shade of white. It would be like having a spy in
the house. She turned round to face Neil. 'A dog would
need walking every day.'

'It'd be company for you.'

'But I'm busy. Working.' I ought to chuck in the job, she thought. I ought to tell Neil what happened. I ought to look around for something else.

Neil sat down and smiled at her. 'Are we going to eat? I'm starving.'

'Help yourself.' She pushed the serving spoon towards him.

'This looks good,' he said, as he said every evening regardless of what it was.

'I made too much rice. Neil, about this job . . .'

'You could never make too much for me. I've always liked rice.' He was spooning great forkfuls in, rice grains catching in his moustache. Isabel looked at her empty plate and reached out to serve herself.

'This job . . .'

'You're finding it too much.'

'I didn't say that.'

'I wouldn't blame you if you found it too much, you know, on top of everything else.'

'It's not that.'

'I expect you're finding it a bit dull. Why don't you chuck it in and find something a bit more interesting.'

'It's not dull,' she said, images of Patrick whizzing through her head. 'Anything but.'

Neil smiled indulgently. 'Ah, I see the novelty value hasn't yet worn off.'

She didn't know what to say to that. She didn't think the novelty value of Patrick kissing her would ever wear off.

'If you don't want to carry on, that's fine by me,' he said.

'You don't want me to work, do you?'

He frowned. 'I thought we'd been through that. I hope I've made it clear that I've no objection to you working, if that's what you want to do.'

'You make it sound as if you're giving me permission to work.'

'Let's not start this up again,' he said in his kind-but-firm headmaster voice.

She pressed her lips together. It was like being fifteen and her father forbidding her to go to some party that she didn't really want to go to at all. She'd snuck out anyway, eyes heavily ringed with black kohl pencil, and had been bored to tears by boys discussing Fender guitars, then drinking too much and being sick. No wonder Neil had seemed so grown-up and sophisticated compared to the competition. She looked at him now, chasing the last few bits of rice round his plate.

'That was delicious. Is there anything for pudding?'

'Cheese and biscuits.' She indicated with her head. 'They're on the side.'

'If you don't mind, I'll take them through. There's a programme I want to watch.'

She sat quite still as he chose some biscuits and cheese, and left. A few seconds later the television kicked into life. She stayed sitting, watching the sauce congeal and the rice form cold sticky lumps. *Is it me, or is it him?*

She got up and cleared the dishes, scraping the remnants of their meal into the waste bin. Kitchen tidy, she went upstairs and got ready for bed. She turned the light off and lay straight under the duvet, feeling the cool cotton settle around her. Downstairs the television went off and the staircase creaked as Neil came up. He undressed quickly in the darkness and got into bed beside her. She stiffened, waiting.

'I've got a headache,' she said as soon as he touched her. The hand paused, then carried on.

'You just need to relax.'

Isabel screwed her eyes tight. Yes was easier than no.

'No,' she said, pushing him away. 'I have a headache.' It was true, her temples were throbbing with daytime-alcohol-induced pain.

'Darling, you'll feel better—'

'I won't.' She said it louder than she meant and paused to regain control. 'I'm tired, I have a headache and I want to go to sleep.'

'But—'

'No!'

A pause. Then, 'All right, keep your hair on. Anyone would think I was about to rape you, instead of just being normally affectionate.' Neil heaved himself over so his back was towards her. In the darkness she could sense his hurt, but also his sulkiness. She knew he expected her to give in, to make amends, to stroke his back and apologise. Two weeks ago she would have.

Instead she buried her head under the pillow and willed herself to sleep.

7

Isabel rapped on Patrick's front door the next morning. Over the last two weeks she'd learnt that the doorbell didn't work consistently and that Patrick was sometimes still asleep when she came round. He'd open the door sleepy-eyed and yawning, with that warm-from-bed smell, hair tousled from a sweatshirt casually pulled over his head. She leant against the side of the house and rested her forehead on the cool brick. She wished she could stop thinking about Justine's parting shot, but it still haunted her. She wished she could stop thinking about Patrick kissing her. I shouldn't be here, she thought, not moving.

'Isabel!'

She looked up. Patrick was leaning out of the window above, his shoulders naked.

'You caught me in the shower. Catch!' He threw the keys down to her, then disappeared back into the house.

Isabel looked at the keys in her hand. Post them through the letterbox and run, her mind said, but that seemed ridiculous. So childish. I'm a grown-up; I can handle this, she told herself. Just act as if nothing happened, and if he mentions it or does anything, just be like Mary. Be dignified. Calm.

'I'm here to work,' she muttered as she turned the key in the lock and let herself into the house. She could hear

Patrick moving about upstairs as she picked up the post from the floor and started to sort through it. Invoice, airmail letter from Italy, electricity bill, computer magazine – what was he doing upstairs? Had he gone back into the shower? No, she could hear a door slam shut. Then footsteps on the landing. She dropped her head down as if trying to decipher the address on a letter so he wouldn't see that she had been watching for him.

Patrick clattered down the stairs. 'Good morning, good morning. Sorry about that. Perhaps I should send you out to get some more batteries for my alarm clock.'

'What?'

'You're right, not your job to do that. I'll get some when I pick up the paper. Hang on to the keys, by the way. Save dragging me out of the shower another time.' He stretched out his arms. 'I should have given you a set before. Mmm, time for coffee, I think.'

Isabel followed him into the kitchen. 'You're in a good mood,' she said.

'Am I?' He spooned coffee into the cafetière. 'Just a good night's sleep, I expect.'

Obviously, he hadn't lain awake half the night worrying about the kiss. Isabel watched him as he made his coffee, quietly humming, his hands deft.

'Anything interesting in the post today?'

'Not really. Maybe this.' She handed him the airmail letter.

'Ah. Mama.' He felt the thickness of the letter. 'New boyfriend, I expect. Anything else?'

'You look.' Isabel shoved the rest of the post at him and stomped upstairs to the office, not caring if she'd been rude. It's too much, she thought. It really is. I don't have to be here. I could be doing something else. She turned on the computer and waited for it to boot up. I could be doing all sorts of things. Not faffing around here with stupid Patrick Sherwin and his stupid business.

'Here.'

A mug of tea was placed on the desk beside her.

'Thanks,' she muttered, not looking at him.

She could sense him standing beside her, not going away.

He cleared his throat. 'Um, is there a problem?'

She looked up at him then, but before she could say anything she was struck by the glaring truth of the situation. He had completely forgotten. He'd completely forgotten the kiss.

'No, no, there's no problem. It's fine. Really.' She stretched down for her bag and rummaged in it, finding a hair-band. As she tied her hair back, she managed a quick smile up at him. 'Thanks for the tea.'

'Anytime.' He paused, then went, shutting the office door behind him.

As soon as he had gone, she dropped her head into her hands. What a fool I've been. She blushed, thinking back to how she had drifted through the morning rush at home imagining this moment, telling Patrick how she had decided to ignore his disgraceful behaviour outside the pub and that it was never going to happen again. Then Patrick would say something like 'But how can I help myself?' And then he would come close and . . . Most of the time she managed to stop herself at that point. The one thing she hadn't imagined would be that he would have forgotten her, forgotten the kiss.

Well, she would forget it too. She smiled wryly to herself, aware of the scratchy lace of her best bra under her striped shirt. No one need know how silly she had been. Or might have been. Her bra straps felt tight, constraining her breasts into rounded hemispheres. She had dreamt of Patrick touching them, hands warm and insistent, cupping them the way he'd cupped the brandy glass. She felt as if she had been close to the edge of a dark place, somewhere very strange where a different Isabel had beckoned. But somehow she had managed to pull away, to come back to herself. And to Neil, of course.

Yes, to Neil, who she'd shouted at last night. I'll make it up to him, she thought. I'll try and be a better wife, try and be more interested in what he's doing. We'll talk more, I'll pay more attention to his work. I can forget the kiss. After all, what did it mean? Nothing. It meant nothing. A boozy lunch, a sunny day. It meant nothing.

She entered the accounts programme and started to prepare customer statements, feeling better. It was natural for her to be thrown by the kiss, she thought, the first time someone other than Neil had kissed her for nearly twenty years. No wonder I was thrown by it, so unexpected. It short-circuited my system and threw me off balance. Thank God, she thought. Thank God I didn't make a complete fool of myself.

The statements took up most of the morning. She'd learnt that Patrick was useless about keeping his accounts up to date, and as she stuffed the statements into envelopes she was certain that at least half of his customers would have already paid him. The question was knowing which half. She shrugged. It wasn't her business. As Neil said, he was completely irresponsible.

Impatient for the computer to finish she pressed the Shut Down button, realised her mistake, tried to go back into the programme to close it down properly. The computer refused to respond to anything she did. She pressed the Escape button several times but nothing happened.

'Drat.' In frustration she thumped the computer and immediately regretted it as the wretched machine gave a high-pitched whine.

'Patrick,' she called. 'The computer's gone wrong.'

'What's the matter?' he said as he came upstairs.

'I don't know. It's gone all funny.'

'Has it had a bang?' He came into the room.

'No,' she lied. 'I pressed two buttons at once or something.'

'Okay. Let's have a look.'

He leant over the desk, one hand casually on the back of her chair, his shoulder just touching hers, watching the screen as he used the mouse. Isabel could smell aftershave and coffee. His mouth was nearly level with hers. She turned her head towards him. Just a few more inches and she could have nuzzled his cheek with the tip of her nose. His mouth was so close. She raised her eyes to his, but he was watching the screen.

'There.' He stood up. 'Not sure what the problem was, but it seems okay now. If there are any more problems, just call me.'

'I will.' She stared ahead at the screen. Was it her imagination or was the mouse still warm from his hand?

Patrick looked out of the window. 'As it's such a nice day, I'm going to work outside. I'll divert the office calls to my mobile.'

'It's supposed to rain later on.'

He peered out of the window. 'Rubbish. It's brilliant sunshine.'

'That's the forecast.'

'What do they know?' he said as he left the room.

What indeed, Isabel thought, alone in the office. What does anyone know?

At lunch she went downstairs and ate one of her sandwiches in the kitchen although she didn't feel very hungry. While she ate she could hear Patrick outside in the garden, talking on the phone. The kitchen seemed very quiet. The flowers she'd picked on her first day, two weeks before, were still on the table, shrivelled and going mouldy round the stems. After she'd finished eating she threw the old flowers away, then replaced them with the last of the nerines from the front garden and a few sprigs of rosemary to add bulk. Rosemary for remembrance, she thought, and immediately remembered the kiss. Forget it, she told herself as she went back upstairs.

But she couldn't settle down to work. The room was too stuffy, too dusty. She started an email to Frances, her friend in Thailand. Help! Don't tell anyone, especially not David, but I'm all confused. I want . . . She deleted the last word. I feel . . . She rested her hands on the computer keyboard, staring at the words on the screen. In a flurry of movement she deleted the message and closed the screen. Stay Connected or Disconnect? the computer asked. She pressed Disconnect then got up and went to the window for some fresh air.

Down in the garden she could see Patrick, leaning back on his chair, legs crossed and feet up on the table, loafers off. He wriggled his toes in the autumn sunshine, oblivious to her watching him. She thought he looked completely at ease.

The air was dense, as if all the oxygen had run out and the world was holding its breath. The light seemed golden, making the brick houses of the town glow a fiery red, grey slate roofs the colour of mercury, white paint glittering so sharply it hurt to look. Lowering over the town was a bank of dense black-purple clouds. She slipped downstairs and went into the garden.

'I think there's a storm coming. Do you want me to give you a hand with bringing in your papers?'

Patrick looked up, annoyance crossing his face. 'It'll pass.' He went back to scrawling notes in green ink over the report he was reading.

Isabel shrugged and went back into the house. Restless with the approaching storm she decided to make some tea. As she filled the kettle the sky darkened and the light took on a greenish hue. The temperature had dropped noticeably. Looking out through the kitchen window she was pleased to see Patrick look up, then leap out of his seat, his shirt showing a few dark splodges where fat raindrops had fallen.

'Christ!' He started to gather the papers on the table together, then bellowed, 'Isabel, where the hell are you?'

Serves you right, she thought. I'm not such a stupid woman after all. She counted to twenty, then went out to help him, ducking her head involuntarily as a crash of thunder sounded. As if that was a cue, the rain started in earnest. They grabbed armfuls of paper and ran with them into the house, dumping them on the kitchen table and going back for more. It took three trips to collect all Patrick's work and bring it into the dry kitchen. Patrick shook his head, spattering raindrops like a dog.

'Christ, this is a miserable country to live in.'

'Would you like a cup of tea?' she said, looking sideways at his bare feet.

'All right,' he said grumpily, shaking his wet papers out onto the clean floor.

Isabel took out two mis-matched but pretty teacups

strewn with cottage roses and reached to the back of the china cupboard to retrieve a teapot, shaped like a cabbage, with a chip in the spout. She poured the boiling water onto the tea and put a tea cosy in the shape of a tabby cat over the pot. Patrick was like a cat, she thought, but not a tabby. Something sleeker, like a Siamese. She looked sideways at him, and smiled to herself. A distinctly wet and cross Siamese with ruffled fur.

She thought of laying the teacups and saucers formally on the table, but decided against it and left them on the side. She couldn't imagine herself presiding over the teapot and asking Patrick 'Shall I be Mother?' The rosebuds on the teacups matched the pink of the nerines, the tight petals loosening to make exotic pink spiders. She stroked them lightly with her fingertips and they quivered at her touch.

'Bugger,' said Patrick, staring out of the window at sheets of rain coming down. 'I've left my shoes outside.'

'Too late now. They'll already be ruined.' Isabel stood beside him. 'Tea?' She turned to look at him and at the same moment he turned and met her gaze and held it. She knew she ought to break away, to pretend nothing was happening. Yet she was caught, suspended in time. Her breathing changed, becoming light and shallow, in the still room. She touched his shirt, feeling the warmth of his chest beneath.

Very slowly he traced his forefinger along the line of her jaw then down her neck. Instinctively she raised her head slightly in response to his touch, turning slightly to one side, leaving her throat vulnerable and open. He paused at her collarbone, then took his hand away, and she ached for its return, the electricity that it had triggered running through her. Her body yearned for him, swayed of its own accord towards him. As if in slow motion she reached out for him, slipping her hand to curl around the back of his neck.

He frowned, pulling away slightly.

'Isabel?' His voice was uncertain, his eyes searching.

The thought of losing the moment made her bold and in answer she pulled him down to her, feeling his mouth on hers, searching, tingling. The strangeness after Neil, the absence of rough moustache, the deliciously different smell of his skin. She pushed herself against him shamelessly, as if she could be absorbed into his body, delighting at feeling him hard. She had never wanted anything as much as for him to touch her, to feel his hand on her bare skin and she tugged at her shirt, not caring what he might think of her boldness, just wanting him. He undid the buttons so her shirt hung open, then bent his head and traced the exposed swell of her breast with his tongue, so her skin goosebumped all over with the teasing. Her head fell back and unconsciously she parted her legs to steady herself. Please, please, she thought, and as if he had heard, he reached under her skirt, his fingers warm and insistent, turning her to liquid in his hand.

She fumbled with the catch of his trousers, any remaining inhibitions lost in the urgency of her need. He pushed her knickers down so they fell to the floor, then he lifted her onto the table, scattering papers everywhere, spread her legs and slipped into her so easily that she realised she had been waiting for this since he had kissed her. No, before that, since Justine had said he was good in bed. And here he was. She clamped her legs around his back, squeezing her hips up to meet his, tightening her grip as the pleasure surged over her body in shades of pink and red as if the world had shrunk to nothing except his body crashing into hers, deeper and further, until she felt she would explode with the intensity. She arched her back, fingers raking across the rough surface of the table, and somewhere someone was moaning, please, please, please, and with each please he went faster and deeper until the red turned to gold and she felt she would die in great shuddering waves that swept over her.

Isabel felt limp, as if her bones had dissolved into the table, her legs dangling over the edge. She kept her eyes shut, aware of Patrick moving beside her, trying not to think about what had just happened. And yet every bit of her was tingling with what she had done. It was impossible to ignore. She felt wonderful, but at the back of her mind she knew she had crossed an invisible line, the line that divided the faithful from the faithless. And there could be no going back. Whatever else did or didn't happen, she would never be Neil's faithful wife again.

Something tickled her stomach. She opened her eyes.

Patrick was watching her, his face about a foot away from hers. He was lying on his side, head propped up by one elbow, the other hand lazily stroking her stomach. His olive-green eyes were flecked with brown streaks turning to warm gold. It seemed a long time since she had been this close to another human being, the long unflinching examination of another pair of eyes as if all the secrets of the other's soul could be revealed if you looked hard enough.

Patrick broke the contact first, kissed her softly then pulled back. His eyes looked more hooded than ever but she thought he looked hugely pleased with himself.

'Well,' he said, tracing circles round her navel. 'That was a surprise.'

'For me too,' she said, then felt herself blush, remembering her private thoughts of the last week. She looked towards him, confused, awash with guilt, happiness, embarrassment, uncertainty, a swirling nebula of emotions. All at once she felt like crying.

'It wasn't that bad, surely.'

'No, it was wonderful. I just feel—' But expressing her feelings was impossible. Instead she clung to him, as if he could provide security from the reality she didn't want to face. She could feel Patrick shift slightly, then he broke away from her, leaving her half-naked and bereft. She realised that he had dressed, trousers in place, shirt buttoned. Overwhelmed by embarrassment she sat up, pulling her skirt down and tugging her shirt across her chest. Her bra seemed to have got twisted under one armpit and she struggled to pull it into place.

'Allow me.' She sat passively, uncertain what to do, while Patrick, his face serious, straightened her out and did up the buttons. It seemed bizarre that a few minutes ago he was an untouched stranger, and now he was doing up her shirt. She hung her head, too shy to meet his gaze.

'You're very quiet.' His tone was conversational.

'Mmm.' She tried to find the words. 'I've not, I mean, I've never done this before.' Patrick raised an eyebrow and she shook her head. 'Never. I've always been . . .' Even saying the word faithful seemed inappropriate. 'I always thought that if I was to . . . well, that it would be more drawn out, that there would be time to think. Snatched meetings and furtive conversations, that sort of thing. More getting to know each other. And lots of agonising and worry.'

'Thank God we missed that bit.' Did he sound bored?

'I don't think I have. I mean, I think it's just beginning. For me, anyway.'

'Yeah, well, I don't go in for much worrying and agonising. It seems a waste of time to me.' Patrick eased himself off the table and went over to the window. 'Still pissing down,' he said, almost to himself. 'Why don't I live somewhere sunny?'

Isabel hugged herself. She didn't like to say that she'd also thought that an affair would involve cuddling and affectionate closeness afterwards. She felt out of place and unwanted.

Patrick leant back against the kitchen units, and looked at her, his face serious. 'So. What do you want to do?'

'Do?'

'About this.'

'Oh.' With an effort she pulled her mind back into the harsh real world. 'I know what I ought to do.'

Patrick made an impatient gesture. 'Forget that. What do you want to do?'

'I can't just forget that. Anyway, you don't know what I was going to say.'

'Let me guess. What you ought to do, is walk out of here right now and never darken my doorstep again. Pretend it never happened.'

Isabel nodded, eyes lowered. Patrick was still leaning back, legs crossed at the ankles as if talking about nothing important at all.

'If that's what you want to do, that's fine by me. I'll go along with you pretending it never happened; a bit of self-deception doesn't hurt. Christ, most of us couldn't function without it.'

Isabel felt devastated by the idea that he was quite happy to go along with her walking out forever. 'Is that what you want?' she said.

'We're not talking about what I want,' he said. 'I don't

have any paraphernalia. I do what I like. Who I screw is nobody's business but my own. I have no commitments, no ties. The only person who gets hurt is me.' He paused and she dropped her head. She felt laden down with responsibility for other people's happiness.

'Still, I'd like to know what you want.' She glanced up at him, feeling shy.

'I can't make your decision for you.' His eyes held hers.

'No, I can see that.' She traced a pattern in the grain of the table.

'An affair would complicate both our lives, but yours far more than mine. So it must be your decision.' He ran his hands through his hair, then grinned at her. 'Don't get me wrong, there's nothing I'd like better than to fuck you repeatedly, but I don't want to push you into something. I don't want you saying later that I made you have an affair.' His voice softened. 'But I would be sorry to see you go.'

'Really?' she said, feeling less depressed.

His lips twitched. 'My filing's never been so well organised. But it's got to be your decision.'

I know what I ought to do, she thought, so why am I hesitating? Why aren't I leaving? 'If I stay—'

'I'm not offering you anything,' Patrick said quickly. 'No romance, no commitment. And I'm famously unreliable,' he added almost as if it was something to be proud of.

Famously good in bed, and she shivered all over at the thought.

'I've been married eighteen years. Half my life.' She felt confused, having this weird conversation, discussing whether or not to continue with an affair. Did Patrick want her, or not? She remembered him saying he'd like to fuck her repeatedly. It was a good thing the coil she'd had fitted after Katie's birth meant she didn't have to worry about pregnancy. She sat up straight, suddenly registering that nowadays there were other things to worry about apart from pregnancy. How awful if she'd caught something from him.

'I hope you don't mind me asking, well, I'm not sure how to ask, but . . . well, we didn't use anything. I know I'm okay, I mean, I've been in a monogamous relationship for eighteen years.'

'How do you know your husband hasn't—'

'Neil? Oh, no, never. He wouldn't.' Patrick raised his eyebrows and Isabel was compelled to defend Neil. 'He just wouldn't.'

'Hmm. I'll take your word for it. As for me, I'm clear.' He smiled. 'I'm usually extremely careful. Unless the unexpected arises. And you, Mrs Freeman, were very unexpected.'

An image ran through her mind, herself spread-eagled over the table, arms flung out wide in abandon. She turned away from Patrick, not wanting him to see the blush she could feel rising.

'We knocked the flowers over,' she said. The jam jar had smashed on the floor and the nerine stems were twisted among the broken glass. The spilt water on Patrick's papers had turned his scrawl to green smudges.

'We?'

'Me, then.' She couldn't remember knocking them over. Her insides contracted, aching with remembered pleasure. There's nothing I'd like better than to fuck you repeatedly, he'd said. But he wanted it to be her decision. She realised she'd made her decision long before, without knowing about it. No discussion, however rational and dispassionate, could change that. She had made the decision when she had touched him during the rainstorm. The line had been crossed then, and there was no going back. Now she turned and touched him again, hesitating, unused to taking the initiative, excited to be making the first move.

He stood still, waiting, his breathing shallow, not touching her. 'Take your hair out of that stupid band.'

She pulled the band off and shook her hair out.

'Better. You shouldn't tie it back.'

'It's more practical.'

'Practical!' He touched her hair. 'Who wants to be practical?' He stood very close to her, his hands stroking the little hairs at the nape of her neck, stirring up the nerve endings. His fingertips caught the tiny whorls at the edge of her hairline, moving down to stroke the hollows of her collarbones. She let her head fall back, giving in to the feeling, letting the sensation flow from his fingertips and down through her. She felt her body was like an acupuncture chart, meridians flowing and connecting, linking neck to breast to centre in one tingling universal line.

Feeling very daring she ran her hand further down, feeling him pressing hard against her hand. Her breathing had changed, become heavier, deeper. With her other hand she undid his top trouser button. He put his hand on hers to stop her.

'Sure?'

'Yes.'

'No regrets. No falling in love. No tears when we part?'

'No.'

'Two adults enjoying each other with no strings on either side?'

'Yes.' He released her hand, then slid his own up her thigh. It was almost painful when he touched her, sudden, all-absorbing, wonderful pleasure. 'Oh yes, yes please.'

'And what do you want?' he murmured.

'This.'

'Say it.'

'I want . . . I want . . .' It was hard to say the words, hard to concentrate on speaking. Each word came out on a rush of breath. 'I want you to fuck me.'

'Ah,' he said. 'That's better.'

And this time it was better. Slower, deeper, longer. They went upstairs to the bedroom where Patrick carefully removed the rest of Isabel's clothes. She had always thought that the embarrassment of exposing her body would be enough to stop her having an affair, yet here she was allowing Patrick to cover her with kisses, running his tongue over her skin, apparently unfussed by the stretchmarks and imperfections. No, unfussed was the wrong word. He made her feel that these were glorious, sensual emblems of a woman in her prime, not middle-aged, and that her body, for all its flaws, was beautiful. Encouraged by his appreciation she relaxed, and without shame opened herself to him in a way that she had always been slightly embarrassed to do with Neil.

And afterwards he held her close as her mind drifted, half-asleep but listening to the rain falling outside in a continuous murmur. She nuzzled his skin, feeling the tang of salt on her lips.

'Which do you prefer,' he said, running a lazy hand over her body, 'fast and furious on the kitchen table or slow and sensual in bed?'

'Both. I want both.'

'Exhausting. You'd better pass me the water; there should be a glass on the floor on your side.'

Isabel rolled over and looked on the floor. She saw Patrick's water glass and alarm clock. She was an hour late for the school pick-up.

'Help! The children!' Isabel jerked upright, then subsided back down beside Patrick, heart still beating fast. 'No, it's all right; Michael's late tonight and Katie's at a friend's house.' It felt strange, to have forgotten them, the same sickening jolt in the stomach as when you think there's an extra step on the stairs only there isn't one, but magnified by so many times it hurt to think of it. How could she have forgotten the children for one second? She sat up, pulling away from Patrick's encircling arms, and swung her legs over the side of the bed.

'I trust Madam found the service satisfactory?'

'Oh, yes. It's just I feel—' she hesitated, uncertain of what to say.

'Delighted? Exhausted? Shagged out?'

'All of them. Bruised mostly. I'll be walking like John Wayne for the next few weeks.'

'Mmm. Wasn't he the strong, silent type?'

'Oh dear. Was I—?'

'Let's just say it's a good thing the neighbours on both sides go out to work.'

She smiled to herself, remembering, as she fished her clothes off the floor and started to get dressed. Drat, my knickers must be downstairs in the kitchen, she thought. Patrick knelt behind her and kissed her neck.

'Don't tie your hair back again.'

She turned to him with a shy smile, feeling as if against all odds she had pulled off some clever trick.

'I won't.'

'Happy?'

'Oh, yes.' She remembered Patrick saying 'No falling in love' and kissed him, to stop herself from saying anything more. Kissing Patrick made her realise how rarely she and Neil progressed beyond a friendly peck on the cheek. She remembered reading something about prostitutes never kissing their clients, that it was too intimate, but the thought frightened her and she kissed Patrick with more intensity. Finally she separated from him.

'We've not got much work done this afternoon,' she said.

'And whose fault is that?'

'Yours.'

'Really?'

'Mine then.' She couldn't stop smiling at him.

'I'll dock your wages.'

'I'll work harder tomorrow,' she pretended to grovel.

'You'd better,' he growled, 'or I'll take the whip to you.'

'I'm not sure I'm into S&M.' She took a deep breath. 'I ought to be going.'

'Off into the real world.' He smiled, then patted her behind. 'Go on, scoot. No guilt trips though, promise?'

'Promise.' She smiled at him, then eased herself off the bed. 'My legs are all wobbly.'

Patrick put a navy blue dressing-gown on. 'C'mon, Bambi, let's check you're all ready to go home to your family.' He tilted her face. 'Mmm, I think you're presentable.'

'I've got no knickers on.'

'Don't tempt me, or you'll never get home.'

Isabel went down the stairs, very conscious of her nakedness under her skirt and Patrick behind her. She went to pick up her knickers, which were curled in a heap on the kitchen floor. Patrick bent too and, with a swift sweep of his hand, beat her to it.

'These are mine.' He smiled at her. 'An incentive for you to return or a souvenir to comfort me in case you don't come back.'

She thought about saying something, but decided against it. It seemed odd, almost perverted, but then again, with her limited experience, what did she know? Her legs did feel most peculiar. She collected her bag from the sitting room and went to the door. Patrick stopped her.

'Isabel.' She looked up at him and saw him suddenly look uncertain and vulnerable. 'Will you come again tomorrow?'

A slow smile spread across her face. 'Oh yes,' she said shyly. 'I do hope so.'

Isabel was convinced that one of the other mothers would notice something different about her, but they appeared oblivious. And if she had told them, would they have believed her? Come to that, did she believe what had happened? That she, Isabel Freeman, devoted wife and mother of two, could have spent – or misspent – the afternoon in the arms of one Patrick Sherwin, employer, now lover. It couldn't have happened. It shouldn't have happened. But it had.

As she stood outside the gym, waiting for Michael to finish Cubs, she could feel her nakedness under her skirt, the cool rustle of the fabric against her thighs. It seemed extraordinary that no one should notice; she felt surrounded by a glowing halo of scarlet wickedness. The heat given off by her body alone should have been enough to generate a few raised eyebrows. And the smell. She must reek of sex. She casually raised one hand to her face, as if she was going to push back a wayward strand of hair, and surreptitiously sniffed. The scent of Patrick brought back the afternoon's activities in a rush. It was wicked, it was wrong, but, oh, it was wonderful. She hid a smile behind her hand.

Michael came out, grumpy about some argument over badges. Isabel nodded and made soothing noises without listening as she drove to Helen's to collect Katie. She was thinking about Patrick, the unhurried way he stroked her skin, the way he knew without telling when to be slow and when to be fast, the skilful way he—

'Why are we going this way, Mum? I thought we were getting Katie.'

Isabel looked around her. 'Oh dear, I've overshot the turning.' She reversed into a gateway, narrowly missing the post, and set off again. She collected Katie from Helen's house, declining a cup of tea. Helen seemed disappointed and kept Isabel chatting on the doorstep about the PTA committee. 'You ought to join,' she kept on saying and Isabel, conscious of a breeze trying to lift the edge of her skirt, kept trying to leave. Finally she managed to escape. Her naked bottom felt round and cold as she walked back along the path to the car.

Back home she quickly made Michael a sandwich, then charged upstairs into a hot shower. She had just finished dressing in clean clothes when she heard Neil's cheery 'Hello' downstairs.

'Just coming,' she called back, twisting a towel around her wet hair. Neil's footsteps on the stairs. She bundled her clothes into the dirty linen bin, just in case some lingering scent of Patrick remained on them, then checked her face in the mirror. Was this how she normally looked?

Eyes bright, cheeks flushed. She had to be normal. Neil came into the bedroom.

'Sorry, didn't mean to disturb you. I was just going to change.' He looked at her curiously, as if surprised to see her upstairs.

'No, you carry on. I've finished here. I forgot to wash my hair yesterday,' she added. 'I thought I'd do it now so it'd be dry by bedtime.'

'No need to explain.'

No, no she didn't have to explain. Stop explaining, she told herself. Be normal. She felt as though someone had placed stereoscopic glasses over her eyes so her depth of vision was heightened into super three-D. Every little bit of fluff had heart-piercing definition. She smoothed the bedspread nervously, seeing her hands as if for the first time.

'How was work?' she asked. 'Busy?'

'Same as usual.' He shrugged. 'Meetings, meetings and more meetings.'

'Sounds a bit dull.'

'Office politics.' He got out of his jacket and dropped it on the bed. 'What about you?'

'What about me?' Isabel froze in the middle of reaching for the jacket.

'Your job.'

'Oh.' She picked the jacket up and put it on a coat hanger, like a good wife. 'It's just me and Patrick so there's not much opportunity for office politics. We'd have to have factions of one and gossip to ourselves in corners.' She paused. Perhaps it wasn't a good idea to stress that it was just her and Patrick in the house. 'Of course, Patrick is out a lot. Most of the time. In fact, almost all the time. Seeing clients, that sort of thing.'

'So how are you finding it?' Neil's face was politely inquiring, rather than challenging. He hardly appeared interested, and she relaxed.

'Fine. A bit boring in fact. I just answer the phone and do the filing.' It wasn't a lie. That was all she had been doing. Until today.

'Doesn't sound very stretching.'

Isabel brushed imaginary fluff off the jacket, trying not to think of being stretched out across Patrick's bed. 'You'd be surprised. Chuck me your trousers and I'll hang them up.' He tossed them towards her, sensible grey from M&S, with a touch of hard-wearing polyester to prevent knee and bottom sag, although on Neil they did have a marked resemblance to loose covers on an old armchair.

A drip of water slid down her neck, tracing a cold path where Patrick had run his tongue over her collar-bone. She felt herself go scarlet.

'When's supper?' Neil asked, now dressed in old cord trousers and a lambswool sweater, both an indeterminate shade of khaki.

'I don't know. Soon. About an hour.' How could he not have noticed her face, flaming with desire and longing? She hoped her voice at least sounded casual. 'You can have some pâté on toast if you can't wait.'

'That'd be nice.' He yawned and stretched, rotating his shoulders and neck to ease the tension. 'That's better. I think I'll go and watch the News.'

'Send Katie up for her bath, would you?'

He nodded and left the room. Isabel sank onto the bed, her legs threatening to give way for the second time that day. Then it had been the trembling reaction to sex, now the reaction to deceit. Although, she salved her conscience, she hadn't actually lied to Neil. She frowned.

She hadn't needed to lie to Neil; he hadn't asked any awkward questions, hadn't noticed anything different about her. Which was strange as she felt gloriously, rampantly different. Every molecule tingled, every atom glowed. She flopped back on the bed, arms wide. Patrick, Patrick, Patrick. Fourteen hours until she saw him again. Would it be as good tomorrow? She smiled to herself. He was quite right. She didn't feel guilty. She felt great.

8

Helen and Isabel arrived at the church for Harvest Festival at the same time so it was natural for them to sit together. Isabel was pleased, as she still didn't know many of the other mothers, at least, not well enough to go and sit next to them. And the fathers with their camcorders and serious cameras were completely unknown. Helen, on the other hand, seemed to know lots of people. Isabel commented on that.

'It's the PTA committee,' Helen said. 'I've met loads of people through it. I told you, you should join. They're always on the lookout for new blood.'

'You make them sound like vampires.'

'Seriously. Why don't you join?'

'We were always having coffee mornings when we were abroad. I'm not sure I can take many more.'

'It's not just coffee mornings,' Helen laughed. 'And all the meetings are in the evening. Not everyone's a lady of leisure, you know.'

'Nor am I any more.'

'Of course, you're working now. How's that going?'

'Fine.' Five weeks of work, three weeks of them as Patrick's lover. It seemed incredible to Isabel. She realised that Helen was looking at her.

'I had to take the morning off to come to this and it didn't go down well.' Patrick had been furious when she had told him. They'd had a row which had ended up with them tearing at each other's clothes and having sex on the stairs. Isabel smiled to herself. Perhaps they should have rows more often. She was brought back to the present by Justine slipping into the pew next to her.

'Can I join you?'

'Of course,' Isabel said, moving up.

'I was telling Isabel how she ought to join the PTA committee,' Helen said, leaning across Isabel. 'She was saying that she thought it was too much on top of her job.'

Justine gave her a sidelong glance. 'Is working for Patrick that tiring?'

Isabel stiffened inside. Had Justine guessed? Or did she know? Had Patrick said anything? She made herself smile. 'Not tiring, but time-consuming.'

Justine settled back in the pew while Helen persisted, talking about what the committee did and pressing Isabel to join. 'Look, it's a bit difficult at the moment because Neil's had to work late at the office recently, but I promise I'll think about it, all right?' Isabel said at last. Helen flushed with pleasure, and Isabel was touched that it mattered to her. In a sudden flash of insight she wondered if George was always nice to Helen. Helen was rearranging one of her hair combs, and her sleeve fell back from her wrist. Was it Isabel's imagination, or was there a shadow of a bruise on the inside of her arm?

'If you want me to come onto the committee, I will,' Isabel said. 'But can I join just like that? Wouldn't I have to be elected?' She turned to Justine.

'Being elected implies that there are lots of people who are just dying to join,' Justine said. 'I can't see Mary, but she'll be about somewhere. Probably organising the vicar. We'll catch her at the end of the service.'

'I've not been to a Harvest Festival service before,' Isabel said, thinking how alien it was after all the desert countries she had been living in. 'I was expecting enormous marrows and baskets of apples.' She craned her neck to see the pile of tins and other non-perishable goods such as nappies and cotton wool. More useful, perhaps, but decidedly less romantic.

There was a stirring among the pews, a ripple of shushing and heads turning to try and see. The children came in singing 'All Things Bright and Beautiful', the smallest first, then the older children. They put their gifts down at the front, then were shepherded by the teachers to sit cross-legged in untidy lines. Isabel spotted Katie, wide-eyed and sucking her thumb. She looked very young. Rachel sat up straight beside her, her hands folded in her lap, unlike Millie who was picking her nose in the row behind them. Isabel could sense Helen wince.

Michael strode along, his hands in his pockets, his head cocked as he took in the strange surroundings. Once seated his eyes sought hers in the audience. Then he saw her. He didn't smile – that would be utterly uncool – but he condescended to remove one hand and give her a minimal wave, so slight that only a sharp-eyed observer would have noticed. Isabel felt her heart swell with love for him, and his determined masculinity that had banned all maternal displays of affection except in private when he was her cuddly, loving little boy.

The children sang a lilting melody in praise of the harvest, most of their faces beaming with sincerity, mouths opening like baby birds. Isabel was pleased to see Katie was singing, although Michael appeared more interested in the back of his neighbour's shirt. His mouth opened occasionally, but Isabel could tell he was la-la-la-ing along to the music. After the song the vicar gave a speech of welcome and thanks for the generous gifts. Isabel immediately felt guilty that she hadn't given more. He invited the congregation to rise to sing 'We Plough The Fields and Scatter'. Isabel was singing the words unthinkingly when an image of Patrick ploughing her fields and scattering his good seed came into her head. She dropped her hymn-book, pink-cheeked with shame to be thinking such thoughts in church, and had to scrabble round Justine's polished shoes to retrieve it. She recovered herself just in time to hear Katie's single line, which she had practised to distraction.

After the service the parents swarmed out and stood in clusters talking loudly. It was rather like the new parents' coffee morning all over again. Helen found Mary, who was wearing a tweed hat complete with jaunty pheasant feather, and explained that Isabel had volunteered to join the PTA committee. Mary was pleased, then set off to accost the headmistress, leaving Isabel feeling that she had just had a close encounter with a steamroller.

'Don't worry, you'll get used to it.' Justine was standing next to Isabel, her eyes sparkling with amusement.

'I think being on this committee might be exhausting,' Isabel said.

'Now Mary's eldest three have been packed off to boarding school she's got time on her hands. And she does get a lot done for the school.' Justine walked beside Isabel as they made their way out of the churchyard. 'I meant to ask you earlier, but have you lost weight? You look terrific.'

'Thanks. I have lost some.'

'What's your secret?'

Isabel blushed, thinking sex, sex and more sex. 'I've taken up swimming,' she said. Not for the first time,

Isabel wondered exactly what Patrick and Justine's relationship was. He said they were friends and, when she pressed him, that Isabel shouldn't pry. 'You wouldn't like it if I talked about you, would you?' he'd asked. Which was unanswerable.

'I must dash,' she said. 'I promised Patrick I'd be back to cover lunchtime. I'll see you soon, if not at school then later on.'

'The next committee meeting is on Monday,' Justine called as Isabel escaped to the security of her car.

Isabel swam steadily, eating up the lengths and letting her mind roam. She hadn't lied entirely to Justine; she was swimming regularly. Swimming at lunchtime was her cover for the frequent afternoon showers and hairwashing needed to wash the scent of sex away. If caught with wet hair she just said 'I've been swimming', and two days out of the five it was true. At first she had been puffed after a few lengths but to her surprise she had quickly got fit enough to swim for half an hour non-stop. She loved the feeling of efficiency, trying to power along with making the smallest of ripples. She despised the flashier swimmers, the splashers and flailers, the goggle-wearers. After a quick burst of front crawl, squandering energy along with the arcs of water, they loitered at the shallow end, maybe doing a few stretches while their heaving lungs recovered. Isabel swam serenely, enjoying the feeling of being suspended in the water, of her muscles working, legs kicking, arms scooping, stomach holding the energy together and propelling it forward, while her mind wandered.

Sometimes she replayed scenes with Patrick, or excuses with Neil, lies that she had got away with. Other times her mental cinema scrolled up images from a possible future, a future as different as possible to her present: perhaps a modern apartment in London, somewhere trendy like Notting Hill, with a glass staircase and American walnut floors, the sole decoration being a solitary butterfly orchid arching gracefully from a matt black raku pot. Or there was the Italian fantasy; dark glasses and cappuccinos in the Piazza Navona in front of the Bernini fountain, watching the passeggiata, or strolling through the urn-filled inner courtyard of a crumbling palazzo. Patrick lounged elegantly in these settings, but she couldn't put herself there. She kept slipping out of the frame.

In the changing rooms Isabel showered, washing the chlorine away in rivulets of hot water. She soaped her body, feeling the new firmness, the definition around her waist where once there had been flab. It had only taken a few sessions before she had started noticing the difference. On her non-swimming days she would take a bath at his house before the school run, Patrick running slippery hands over her. The thought made her weak with longing for him and she hung her head, letting the water pound onto her skull.

There was a camaraderie among the women swimmers that she loved, especially among the older women. Bunioned feet, pendulous breasts, arthritic hips, padded thighs that had moved beyond cellulite into a world of cushioned rolls and deep dimples like lunar craters. It wasn't just that Isabel felt young and slim in comparison. She felt accepted. After three weeks, every Monday and Friday, she had become a regular, someone who would share a grumble about the shower temperature, or the splashers who were now safely ensconced in the male changing rooms. She had started coming for an alibi, but stayed for the enjoyment of the gossip with strangers. Problems with neighbours and the planners came up most frequently; acquaintances' past histories were comprehensively filled in with eyebrows raised and lips pursed.

She wondered what they would say if she told them about Patrick.

But Patrick was tucked away in the house with the parrot-green front door and didn't belong in the outside world. She recognised that she had drawn lines across her life, slipping Patrick into a neat little box, while the real world carried on outside. The school run, the meaningless conversations with other mothers, preparing Neil's supper, going to bed. Nothing had changed.

Sometimes, standing in the schoolyard waiting for the children at the end of the day, she felt like shouting 'Guess what I was doing an hour ago'. Would the mothers be shocked, or would some say smugly, 'Me too'? Because if they couldn't spot Isabel, then could Isabel spot anyone else? She washed herself thoroughly, scrubbing away the chlorine, just as on Tuesdays, Wednesdays and Thursdays she scrubbed away the scent of Patrick and sex. The smell of guilt is soap and water, she thought. Cleanliness is next to adultery.

And then there was Neil. She had wondered what to say, but in the end said nothing. She had wondered how she would feel, but in the end felt nothing. It was easy to deceive someone when they trusted you absolutely. But was it really trust that Neil felt – or arrogance? He trusted her because he thought she was incapable of such a betrayal, not because she was a good, upright person of unimpeachable morals. He thought she would be inept at deception, incapable of deceit because that required mental agility and confidence. Stuff the morals, he thought she lacked the nerve. And wasn't there an element of self-satisfaction in his arrogance? That he was enough and she would never feel the desire to go elsewhere. Then she thought how unfair that was to him. After all, she assumed that he was faithful to her. Would she notice the signs, or was she blind too?

As she dressed she thought more about Neil. She didn't want to be unfair to him. There was the distinct possibility that she took Neil for granted in exactly the same way that she felt he took her for granted. Before Patrick she had felt that she was invisible to him. Look at me, she sometimes wanted to shout. See me as I am. Did he feel that about her? But she had tried to talk to him. She could think of all too many occasions when he had snubbed her approaches, treating her like a loved but wayward child who really shouldn't bother the adults. She couldn't think of a time recently when he had reached out for her in any but the physical sense. And now, now she was convinced that she was invisible to him. Otherwise, surely he would have recognised her mistakes, the lies, the slips of the tongue?

She combed her hair through, feeling the wetness seep across her back. She was brought back to the present by one of the women saying a cheerful goodbye to her.

'Bye,' she said quickly. 'See you Friday.' A whole new week lay ahead, and three blissful days of Patrick. But she'd got the rest of Monday to get through first. Her heart sank, remembering that tonight she had agreed to go to the PTA meeting. She thought about not going, but then, what would her excuse be? She sighed. Neil was right in his assessment of her; she was a useless liar. It was only that he was worse at spotting it.

After swimming she walked into town. She thought about having lunch at one of the cafés, but that seemed totally extravagant when there was a whole house filled with food only ten minutes away. Patrick usually went to a pub for lunch, if he bothered with lunch at all, and she did think of drifting past The Mason's Arms but stopped herself. You'll see him tomorrow, she told herself. Instead she strolled down the High Street, looking into shop windows. She thought about buying some new clothes – the ones she had were getting loose around her middle – but decided to wait and see if she would drop down another dress size. One of the advantages of an affair, she thought, swinging her bag happily and giving a little skip. The pleasurable way to lose ten pounds. Perhaps she should start a club. Instead of counting calories, you'd get points for the number of times you made love. And there could be variations, like the Mediterranean Diet with lashings of olive oil liberally smeared all over, or the All-Protein Diet (a firm favourite with the men). The sun was bright, lemon-sharp but the wind was cool on her wet head and she felt cold. She ought to get inside.

Isabel turned into the bookshop and started to browse. Books were laid out enticingly on tables, covers as glossy as sweets. And entirely non-fattening. She sighed. Adulteresses in fiction ended badly, like poor Anna Karenina, losing her children and dying under a train. Or Madame Bovary. Isabel couldn't remember what happened to her: it was hard to empathise with a heroine whose surname you weren't sure how to pronounce. Did it rhyme with ovary (which would be apt) or carry? Or perhaps it was something completely different, one of those unlikely French spellings that pronounced Reims as Rance and d'Oex as Day. Isabel put down the book she was holding and moved to the children's section where she chose a book for each of the children, on kittens for Katie and racing cars for Michael.

She paid and left the shop. In the street she looked up and down. Left to collect the car and go back home, right to walk into the heart of town. She checked her watch. If she went left she'd have an hour or so at home before picking up the children. Just enough time to hoover everywhere. It didn't seem enticing. On the other hand, she was fed up with looking in shop windows. She shifted from foot to foot, trying to decide. Left looked unenticing, right looked – was that Patrick? She peered. At the end of the street, at the point where it became pedestrianised, a tall dark man was talking to a woman with shimmering blonde hair. Justine? Isabel couldn't tell at this distance. The man threw his head back and laughed and Isabel became almost certain it was Patrick. Then he kissed the woman. It was brief, the social kiss of casual acquaintances, but something about it – the tilt of her head, the placing of his hand on her upper arm maybe – made Isabel freeze. They parted and the woman turned and was swallowed up by shoppers. The man came towards Isabel, and as he came closer she saw that it was indeed Patrick.

She waited for him, questions buzzing in her head like a hive of angry bees. I mustn't ask him, she thought. I promised I wouldn't make demands on him. He seemed oblivious to her until about twenty feet away, then his face lit up.

'Isabel,' he said. 'How nice to see you.'

'What are you doing here?' she blurted out.

'I do live here, remember.' He leant forwards and kissed her cheek, a cool friendly kiss.

'You smell of garlic and booze,' she said, trying to sound playful.

'Been out to lunch.'

She couldn't stop herself from asking, 'With a client?'

'Mmm.' He reached and took the bookshop bag from her. 'Now, what have you been buying? A present for me?'

'No, for the children.' She took the bag back from him, strangely disturbed by the thought of him handling Katie and Michael's books, as if by handling the books it confirmed that Patrick would spill out into her domestic life. He hadn't answered the question about the client.

'Your hair's wet,' he said, fingering a strand.

'Who were you with?' There. She'd said it.

'You ought to dry it. I don't want you off work because you're sick.' He smiled at her, his hair ruffling with the breeze, his eyelids heavy.

'Was it Justine?'

He paused, looking up at the sky as if deciding what to say. Or what lie to tell. Isabel bit her lip, feeling slightly sick. He looked at her, his face serious.

'I told you at the start. No strings. No commitments. No falling in love.'

She tried to laugh lightly, the laugh of a cool, sophisticated person. 'I'm just curious.'

'I see.'

'Please?' She registered that she sounded neither cool nor sophisticated, but she didn't care.

'You know I don't discuss people, and especially not one woman with another. You really ought to get that hair dried, you know.'

She stared at him. Would he suggest going back to his house? Her heart beat faster, and she realised it didn't matter if he had been out with another woman, been out with Justine. She wanted him. Wanted him so badly that if he'd suggested going up an alleyway and doing it against a rough brick wall she would have followed.

'Patrick,' she said, touching his hand, feeling his skin warm and alive. He moved his hand away, brushing back his hair.

'This is a small town, darling,' he said quietly. 'Let's be discreet.' He kissed her cheek and she had to stop herself from clinging onto him. 'I'll see you tomorrow.'

She watched him saunter up the street, turning up his jacket collar against the wind, which had sharpened, tossing dead leaves and litter in the air. Her head was freezing, the strands of wet hair whipping around her face. Patrick turned up a side street that led towards his house. He didn't look back.

'Sorry I'm late,' Isabel mouthed at Mary, squeezing into the last empty place in the school library. Mary glanced towards her, obviously annoyed, then majestically turned away and listened to the woman on her left. Isabel shifted on her uncomfortable child-sized chair and grimaced as she sifted through the loose bits of paper in her bag – receipts, notes, cards, petrol vouchers. She was sure she had the agenda somewhere.

'Here,' muttered her neighbour, passing a copy over to her. 'We're on number three.'

'Thanks.' She looked round the table. Again, like the coffee morning, it was all female. She wondered what all the fathers were doing while the mothers were out at PTA meetings. Of the twelve women there she recognised only a couple, apart from Helen and Justine. She looked at Justine. Had it been her with Patrick? As if aware of Isabel's gaze, Justine looked up and smiled at Isabel, her pussycat smile brimming with secrets. Flustered, Isabel looked down at her agenda. Numbers one and two were apologies for absence and minutes of the last meeting. Item number three was school uniform and a woman she didn't recognise was getting very agitated about the service at the school shop.

'The school shop is run by volunteers. You can't expect Harrods,' Mary was saying, impatience fighting with gracious tolerance on her face.

'I daresay, but—' The woman was determined to say her piece. Mentally Isabel switched off, although keeping an alert, listening look on her face. When she had taken Katie and Michael to the shop to be kitted out she had thought they were amazingly efficient. She looked around. Most of the rest of the committee were fidgeting, playing with pencils. School uniform was obviously a regular item. Justine sat still, her manicured hands resting lightly on the table in front of her. I mustn't be jealous, Isabel thought. I don't own Patrick, and anyway, Justine knew him before I did. What if they did have lunch together? It doesn't mean anything. Does it? It might not even have been Justine. It could have been some other woman. Isabel couldn't decide if that would be worse.

Mary, obviously sensing the restless mood of the women present, decided to bring things to a close.

'It's a subject on which we all have plenty to say. I suggest that we form a subcommittee and they can report back to us. Agreed? Fine, then we need some volunteers.' Mary looked round the table. Most of the women present had become very interested in doodling or finding something in their coat pockets but the woman who had been talking had her hand raised.

'Lucy and . . .' Much fiddling in handbags and checking of Filofaxes. Isabel felt guilty about not volunteering, although not guilty enough to stick her hand up.

'Oh, I'll do it,' Justine said suddenly.

'Thank you, Justine. You two can report back at the next meeting. Now, next on the agenda is the Fireworks Party. Rebecca, perhaps you'd like to tell us how things are going?'

Isabel found it difficult to follow exactly how things were going as Rebecca assumed that everybody already knew what was going to happen. It was a long time since Isabel had been to a Guy Fawkes party, complete with poor Guy on his bonfire. In some countries where they had lived, burning effigies was a dangerous political act. Isabel gathered that the committee brought hot dogs, baked potatoes and mulled wine – made to Mary's special recipe – and sold them along with sweets, fizzy drinks and sparklers. She volunteered to be a roving sparkler seller, a job that she hoped meant she would be able to keep an eye on how the children were coping with the noise. In Syria the rattle of gunfire had been an everyday occurrence, sometimes for a wedding, sometimes more sinister. The company provided cars and drivers so their employees never got involved in an argument over jumped red lights. On a trip out into the desert their driver, Hamid, had shown them the gun he kept in the glove compartment. 'Don't worry, Madam, I won't let bandits take you or the children.' He grinned reassuringly, gold tooth gleaming. 'I shoot you all first.' Isabel knew what he meant: there was said to be a market for European women and children, especially blue-eyed boys like Michael, brown hair streaked to blond in the sun. That evening she had asked Neil to apply for a transfer back to the UK. Perhaps the children wouldn't remember the sound of guns, or if they remembered, wouldn't associate them with fireworks. She wanted to be near them at the bonfire party, just in case.

She listened to the discussion, which had moved on to how they were going to ensure the sausages were cooked through, without leaving them hanging around in a lukewarm state for hours, given that they couldn't use any of the cooking facilities at the school. It seemed extraordinary that something so simple could require so much organisation. Isabel started to doodle. She shaded in all the spaces in the word 'Agenda', then added in the top right-hand corner a large 'P', surrounded with lines, frilled round the edges with small picots. Then in case anyone was looking she added two more bumps so the 'P' was converted into a trefoil. 'Lucky clover' she wrote underneath, then started filling in the bumps. She thought of Patrick's eyes, green and long-lashed. She closed her own eyes, scrolling through images of Patrick: Patrick on the phone, Patrick searching for some vital bit of paper and getting crosser by the second, Patrick looking at her and saying 'Come to bed'.

'Wake up!' Her neighbour elbowed her in the ribs. 'It's you.'

'Sorry.' There was a small ripple of amusement from the rest of the women.

Mary did not look amused. 'As I was saying, we'd like to welcome Isabel Freeman, who is a new mother and I'm sure she will be an asset to the committee.'

Isabel, hunched in her chair, felt that she was going to be anything but an asset.

The meeting dragged on for what seemed like ages. Isabel got home after ten to find Katie in the middle of a complicated game involving all her stuffed animals and Michael still in the bath, his fingertips wrinkled into white prunes. Quickly she hustled them into their respective beds, kissed

them and turned the lights off, all the time inwardly
seething at Neil, who couldn't even be bothered to put
his children to bed.

'They kept saying they wanted you,' he said as if that
explained Michael's everlasting bath, the unwashed dishes
downstairs, and Katie's unread bedtime stories. He had
managed to get himself to bed, she noticed sourly, and
was halfway through a gold-embossed thriller. He was an
intelligent adult with two arms and two legs who professed
love for his children, she thought. Was he deliberately
incompetent because he thought she wouldn't ask him to
manage the evening again, or was he just incompetent?

She loaded the dishwasher and tidied up downstairs,
then came back up and got ready for bed. As she slipped
under the duvet Neil looked up from his book.

'By the way, my parents rang.'

'Oh, yes? Are they well?' she asked, polite as ever about
Neil's parents, safe in Scotland. Far enough away for her
not to have to think about them.

'Fine. I've invited them down for the weekend.'

'Neil, no, you haven't.' It was an appalling thought.

Neil appeared distinctly put out.

'They haven't seen the house yet.'

Isabel swallowed. 'When are they coming?'

'Two weeks' time. Ma's got some basketweaving course
that she doesn't want to miss.'

'Two weeks.' She mentally ran through their diary. 'I
don't think we're doing anything that weekend. I suppose
I'd better ring Moira up and confirm.'

'No need, I've already said it's okay.'

'But I might have arranged something else.'

'Have you?'

'It's the first weekend of half term. We could easily

have been doing something – going away, even.'

'But we're not.'

'No, but don't you see—'

'What?'

'You should have asked me.'

'You weren't here. You were off at your PTA meeting.' He went back to his book, making what sounded like a little grunt of satisfaction deep in his throat.

'I can't win, can I?' She closed her eyes. Everything seemed so difficult with Neil at the moment. All conversations ended up in antagonism, the grit in the shell rasping against the side. Only there was no pearl to soothe the irritation. Did being with Patrick make it better or worse? Better, because she had her other, secret life to dream of, or worse because it emphasised the contrast with her life as Neil's wife?

Did she love Neil? Underneath the irritation, was there love? She couldn't imagine her life without Neil being in it, but that could be habit. She had favourite books that she felt the same way about, dusty paperbacks she hadn't read for ten years or more but had lugged from one country to the next. She could never throw them away. They were part of her, in the same way that Neil was part of her.

'I'm sorry I was sharp,' she said. 'Just tired, I suppose.'

'Perhaps you should give up work,' he said. His voice sounded neutral but she thought she could detect a spike of something else, like guacamole laced with chilli. She decided to ignore it and settled herself down to sleep, her back towards him.

'By the way,' he said, 'speaking about work, I know you said you weren't earning much but the accountant needs to know. Give me your payslips and I'll pass them on to him.'

'I don't get payslips.'

'What then, cash stuffed down your bra?' He sounded amused and for a second she hated him.

'No, of course not.' She hunched the duvet over her shoulder. At the end of the first week she had asked about her wages. Patrick had looked surprised, and said they were having a four-week trial period. He'd pay her at the end, and if both wanted to continue the arrangement, at the end of every month thereafter. It had sounded reasonable; after all, she might have been useless or got bored. But she wasn't useless, nor was she bored. The afternoon of the storm had come before the four weeks were up. Since then, Patrick had not offered her any money, and she hadn't liked to ask. Neil made an irritated 'tsk' noise.

'I've told you before that it's important to keep proper records. It doesn't take much to go over the tax threshold. We'll have to do a certain amount of juggling.'

'We?'

'Gordon and me. Our accountant, yes? We've been minimising my tax bill through using your allowances as a non-earner. You know that.' Well, yes, she did know that. Or at least, Neil told her what he was doing and she let it pass cleanly through her head without touching the sides. Dealing with the money was what Neil did, like she looked after the children. Occasionally she felt guilty, thinking of the great campaigners like the Pankhursts who had struggled to gain independence for women. On the other hand, if Neil wanted to do it . . . She rolled over and looked at him. He was still talking.

'Now you're making some money, however little, we'll have to look again. And there's National Insurance to consider.' He smiled at her, as if metaphorically patting her little head. 'But you don't have to worry about it. Just make sure he gives you a proper payslip.'

'I don't think I can.'

'Don't look so dismayed. If you like, I'll give him a ring and sort it out for you.'

'No!'

'All right, don't bite my head off.'

'You're not to phone.' Her nerve ends jangled at the thought of Neil ringing Patrick. It suddenly seemed too much, Patrick and Justine, money, the PTA, and now Neil. Anger flared. 'What are you doing, talking about my business to some stranger?'

'Gordon's hardly some stranger, darling.'

'He is to me.' She covered her mouth with her hand, as if she could keep the words inside.

'Now, come on, that's not fair.'

They lay beside each other in the bed, letting the hot, red silence between them dissipate. Neil picked up his book.

'We'll talk about it in the morning when you're a little less tired.'

'I promise I'll ask, just please don't phone. Please.'

'There's no need to look so tragic. I only want to make sure you're not taken advantage of.'

Oh, to be taken advantage of by Patrick, she thought. After a whole weekend without him her body was taut with longing. She wrenched her mind back to Neil and his wretched payslip.

'Promise you won't phone?'

'I promise. Just bring back a payslip.'

9

'He wants a payslip.' 'Mmm?'

'He wants a payslip.' Isabel looked at Patrick stretched out on the bed stark naked, eyes closed, as unself-conscious as a cat. She pulled the sheet more tightly around her. Patrick opened one eye and squinted at her.

'What are you rambling on about, darling?' he said on a yawn.

'Neil. He wants me to have a payslip to give to his accountant.'

Patrick considered this for a moment then shut his eye. 'Prat.'

'Patrick!'

'Man's a complete arse.'

'He's my husband.'

'I rest my case.' Patrick rolled over and twitched the sheet away from her. 'Look at you. *La bellezza.*' He ran his hand over her outline. 'You must let me photograph you one afternoon.'

Isabel reached for the sheet again; too hard to concentrate on holding your tummy in and talk at the same time.

'Seriously, what am I going to do?'

'Ignore him. Let me teach you Italian. This is your *pancia*, your *ance*, your lovely *coscia* and down here, down here is your *figa*. C'mon, relax.'

'I can't,' said Isabel, sitting up and swinging her legs over the side of the bed.

'Don't go. I was going to teach you about my *erezione*.'

'I can guess what that is.' Isabel started to get dressed.

'For a mistress you're being very boring.' Patrick flopped back on the bed. 'I wish I hadn't given up smoking. This is just the right moment for a lungful of tar.'

Isabel paused from doing her new jeans up. 'Is that what I am? A mistress?'

Patrick shrugged. 'What else? Employee, if you prefer. What's wrong with mistress anyway?'

'It's just—' Isabel paused, trying to work out in her own mind what she felt. All these labels defining her with reference to someone else. Wife, mother. Now mistress. She watched a shaft of sunlight filter through the curtains and light up a slice of shimmering dust motes. There was hardly any furniture in the room, just a chest of drawers and a chair as well as the bed. Several heaps of clothes were dumped on the floor.

The phone started to ring and she crossed the landing into the office room, tugging down her sweatshirt as she went. 'Patrick Sherwin Associates . . . yes, I'll just see if he's available.' She held the phone to her chest. 'It's Andrew. Are you available?'

'No. Damn, I should speak to him. Tell him I'm coming.' Patrick started to pull his trousers on. 'Make me a coffee, would you, hon?'

'He's just coming,' Isabel told the long-suffering Andrew, then put the phone down on the table and went downstairs to the kitchen.

Only three weeks, she thought, staring out of the window and waiting for the kettle to boil. Three weeks ago I was standing here watching Patrick get wet in the rainstorm. And now I'm his mistress. Mistress. Such a loaded word. She smiled, picturing herself on a chaise-longue, dressed in a frothy negligée, waving one white arm languidly in a come hither fashion, half-eaten box of chocolates lying discarded on the floor. That sort of mistress probably wore high-heeled mules with puffs of pink swansdown on the front, and satin French knickers and stockings, and simply existed for sex. It had a certain appeal, she admitted to herself as she put the cafetière together. She couldn't see Patrick being attracted to it though; he was far too restless. No, the soothing geisha-like passivity would be more attractive to the tired businessman, popping into his *nid d'amour*, after a long day at the office, for a few hours of pampering and fluffing up of the male ego. Someone like Neil. She pushed him out of her mind.

Perhaps she was closer to the modern mistress, the businesswoman who managed her life, her lover, her husband, her children and her personal trainer with consummate ease and a Psion Palmtop. She could see herself successfully playing that role for about ten minutes. She smiled. I don't think I'm very good at bossing people around; I'm too worried they might say no, she thought. Perhaps I should be more decisive, more assertive. She pushed the cafetière plunger down hard, too hard. The cafetière broke and scalding coffee spurted out, splattering across her top and jeans.

'Shit!' She grabbed a tea towel and scrubbed at her front, leaving hot, dark coffee splodges. Her jeans were burning her legs. 'Why am I such a mess?' A vision of Justine's perpetually neat bob and self-contained expression passed across her mind. She took off her sweatshirt and saw that the coffee had gone right through to her white shirt. Bugger. Now what?

'Problems?' Patrick was leaning against the door, half-dressed.

'I've stupidly managed to get coffee all over me.'

'Bad luck.' He didn't sound very sympathetic and she felt put out.

'But I've got nothing else to wear.'

'Just how I like you,' Patrick leered at her, then relented. 'Grab one of my sweaters from upstairs.'

Isabel went back up to the bedroom and stripped off her steaming clothes. There were red marks on her legs where the coffee had scalded, but they weren't painful. She rummaged through Patrick's clothes, choosing the largest sweater she could find – one hundred percent pure cashmere, she noticed, and the thick, expensive kind. She rubbed her cheek against her shoulder, feeling the softness and inhaling his smell. He's selfish and he doesn't love me, she thought. He might even be seeing someone else. As a mistress I have no rights, no claims. I can't even ask. This relationship is about sex, and that's all there is. Falling in love is out of the question.

She came back down to the kitchen and bundled her coffee-stained clothes into the washing machine.

'Why don't you chuck some of my stuff in while you're at it?' Patrick said, slipping his arm about her waist and planting an affectionate kiss behind her ear. She twisted round to face him.

'Yeah, and I expect you think I could do a little bit of housework while I'm at it.'

Patrick ran a lazy hand down her spine. 'I was hoping you might . . .'

'You must be joking,' Isabel laughed. 'I'm famous for being the untidiest person in the world.'

'Really?' Patrick looked surprised. 'You seem very organised to me. You're brilliant at sorting my stuff out.'

Isabel thought about it. It was true that since she'd been working for him she'd put Patrick's papers into some sort of order, persuading him to use his filing cabinet and bookshelves, and devising a system that he could follow. There were no more papers strewn around the sitting room and the office looked positively professional.

'Perhaps it's different when it's someone else's mess. Easier to deal with than one's own.'

'I need you to sort me out.'

'No, you don't. I don't mind doing the office stuff, but your dirty washing is your own. Don't sulk.' She kissed the palm of his hand, thinking, is this really just sex? 'Wives get the dirty socks, mistresses don't. Even I know that's the deal.'

'I see . . . And what do you think mistresses should get? Apart from payslips, of course.'

'It's not me that wants a payslip, it's Neil. And his bloody accountant.'

'I hope you don't mind me saying this, but your husband seems a complete buffoon.'

'I do mind you saying it, and you still haven't given me a payslip. Actually, you haven't given me any pay.'

'How much do you want?'

'What I've earned, of course.'

'Ah. Now that's an interesting issue.' He was very close to her. 'Are you charging me for services rendered, or am I charging you?'

'How much do you think your services are worth?' she murmured.

'It's what they're worth to you.'

'Why don't we just say they're mutually beneficial.'

He kissed her. 'Shall we go and be mutually beneficial upstairs?'

'Not until I've got some money.' The washing machine clunked on and started to vibrate against her backside.

'You're a hard woman, Mrs Freeman.'

'You're a hard man, Mr Sherwin,' she said. 'In several senses of the word.'

'Are you blackmailing me?'

'No, I'm going on strike.'

'Do you think you can?'

'Um.' She tried to ignore his hand on her. 'To be honest, I'm not sure.'

'I'd hate you to have to suppress yourself.' He reached into his back pocket, brought out his wallet and shook it out, coins spilling onto the floor, notes fluttering down. 'Every penny I possess I give to you. All I have.' He nibbled her ear.

She put her arms round his neck. 'Everything?'

'Of course. Will everything be enough for Madam?'

'Mmm, s'pose so. It'll do for now. For the moment,' she said, kissing him back.

'Then turn around, you gorgeous creature, and bend over.'

Afterwards she said, 'In some ways the money's not really important, but in other ways it is. Let's face it, I'm not your kept woman, I'm somebody else's kept woman. So in that way I don't need the money. But coming to you was, in a very small way, a chance to do something with my life, to have a little money of my own. Keep myself, rather than be kept. So it is important.' She sipped her tea.

'Money's the most important thing there is.' Patrick leant back on his chair and stared up at the ceiling.

'More than love?'

'Oh, yes. Love comes and goes, but the bills have to be paid.'

'I don't believe you're really that cynical.'

'Perhaps not. I don't know, Isabel, I'm as confused as the next man. I just know that if it's a choice between love or money, money will win every time.'

'That's not true.'

'Look around you. Look at all these empty marriages.'

'They didn't all marry for money.'

'But they stay because of it. Don't you?' he asked very softly.

Isabel paused, pushing back the sleeves of Patrick's sweater.

'If I say I stay for things like security and stability and company, you'll say that's just the same as money, won't you?' She clasped her hands in front of her, trying to disentangle her thoughts. 'I do love Neil. Perhaps not in the same way I once did, but . . . we've shared so much. That matters. And then there are the children.'

'The clinching argument.'

'At the end of the day, yes. Why not? Don't sneer; just because you're not interested, it doesn't mean that other people aren't. Anyway, it's all right for you. In ten years' time, if you decide to have children, you'll still be able to pick up some girl and have children, no problem.'

'Perhaps.' He looked out of the window, his face sad.

'I suppose that what it comes down to in the end is, I'd never leave my children, they want to be with both me and Neil, and so we stay together.'

'So romantic.' He looked back at her, as if in contempt.

'What about us? Is that any more romantic? Sex without love? Without a future?' She spoke more bitterly than she had meant and the atmosphere became as brittle as icicles. There was a slight pause, then Patrick got up.

'I'm going to do some work. As for your husband's payslip, as far as I'm concerned you're self-employed and therefore you can sort out your own tax and National Insurance. Just invoice me for the hours you've done.' He touched her shoulder lightly and said more kindly, 'I'll show you how to lay it out later.' He hesitated. 'Isabel, don't forget what I said. No falling in love.'

After he'd left the kitchen Isabel pressed her hands to her face. I don't love him, she told herself. I don't. I can't. I mustn't. But without love all it becomes is sex. Perhaps I should be like Patrick and say that sex is enough. No strings, no ties, no commitment. Isn't that what modern women are supposed to be able to do, say 'I like sex' and not be ashamed?

The money was still scattered over the floor and she bent down to pick it up, retrieving coins where they had rolled under the washing machine – £85.76, and sixty-five euros. She wasn't sure how much they were worth; about forty pounds she thought. Even if she said she spent half the day in bed with Patrick it wasn't enough to cover all the hours she had worked. I have earned this money, she thought. I have worked for it. It should be mine to keep. So why do I feel like a prostitute if I take it? She stacked the money into two piles on the table, unwilling to put either in her bag. Perhaps she should work out what she was owed, prepare the invoice he mentioned and then ask him directly. She'd seen enough invoices now to copy the format; she didn't need Patrick to help her.

There was a knock at the door and she got up, her

bones aching as if she had flu. Why did life have to be so complicated? Patrick's sweater came halfway down her thighs, making her decent enough not to give anyone a thrill. More knocking.

'Coming,' she called and opened the door, expecting to see a deliveryman with a box of computer peripherals to be signed for. What she saw was Mary Wright, her eyebrows shooting upwards as she registered Isabel in Patrick's sweater.

'Isabel, good morning.'

Isabel nodded, speechless. Of all the people she expected to see, Mary was as likely as Nelson Mandela. What was she doing there?

'May I come in?'

'Of course.' Isabel opened the door wider and stepped back to allow Mary through. Mary came into the house and wrinkled her nose.

'Do I smell coffee?'

'Yes, in the kitchen . . .' Mary started to move through into the kitchen and Isabel trotted after her, very conscious of her bare legs and naked feet padding on the cold floor. 'But you'll have to have tea. I smashed the cafetière and got coffee everywhere, which is why . . .' Her voice trailed away. Mary didn't seem to be listening.

'What did you make of the meeting last night?'

'Um. Very interesting.' Isabel tried to think of something to say. 'The Bonfire Party sounds fun.'

'Yes, people seem to enjoy it.' Mary ran her fingers along the top of the work surface. 'Anyway, I just thought I'd pop in to make sure everything was fine.'

Isabel stared at her. Why was she there? What business was it of hers to check if everything was fine. And what did she mean by that anyway?

Mary gave Isabel a quick up-and-down, sniffed, then carried on. 'I haven't seen Patrick for ages. You know what men are like; they're useless about staying in touch. Unless they're gay, of course.' The phrase hung in the air. Isabel wasn't sure what to say. Any comment on Patrick's sexual preferences was beyond her, especially when some evidence was drying on her legs. She could feel herself blushing.

'Oh, look, my clothes have finished washing.' She hoicked them out of the machine, and shook them out. 'I'll just hang them up. Help yourself to tea.' She pulled the airer out of the cupboard and escaped to the living room, calling to Patrick up the stairs.

He stuck his head over the landing. 'Who is it?'

'Mary Wright.'

'Mary? Good.' He clattered down the stairs.

'What's she doing here?' Isabel hissed at him as he passed by, but he didn't seem to register the question before going through into the kitchen.

'Good to see you,' she could hear him say as she draped her damp clothes over the airer in front of the fire. 'And how's Richard? And the children?'

Her ears strained to catch Mary's response, but she couldn't distinguish the words. When she felt she couldn't arrange her clothes any longer she hesitated, then decided to go upstairs to the office like the good employee that she was. Back in the office she studied her list of things to be done, but none of them appealed. She wanted a soothing job, like untangling paperclips. A burst of laughter from downstairs. What could Patrick and Mary be talking about? She dithered between working and blatantly hanging over the banisters to eavesdrop. The decision was made for her by the phone ringing.

She skipped downstairs and hesitated in the kitchen doorway.

'Sorry to disturb you, but it's Andrew on the phone again. He says it's important.'

Mary was leaning against the washing machine, just as Isabel had been not so long ago. The thought that Mary might have turned up a little earlier made Isabel's stomach do an internal somersault.

'I'll have to take this call,' he said to Mary. 'Can you hang on for five minutes? Isabel will look after you.'

He left the room. Mary looked at Isabel in the same way that her formidable headmistress had done at school. It had the same effect on her heart, the sinking sensation of being scuppered by an iceberg.

Isabel tried for a beaming, welcoming, 'I'm not bothered' smile, but had a horrible feeling her lips had formed a sort of 'I'm as guilty as sin and please don't tell me off' simper.

'More tea?'

'No, thanks.' Mary heaved herself away from the washing machine. 'Patrick told me he'd got someone in to work for him. He didn't say it was you, however.'

'He's very discreet,' Isabel said, then thought it was the worst thing she could have said as Mary's eyebrows shot up again. 'I mean, he never talks about people. Only work,' she added, inwardly wincing, trying to sound more businesslike.

'I see.' Mary hesitated, then lowered her voice. 'I hope you know what you're doing.'

'I don't know what you mean,' Isabel said, heart pounding.

'I don't know you very well, but I know you have a husband and children.' Mary carried on, inexorable. 'I am very fond of Patrick but he is, how shall I put it? Unreliable.'

Isabel felt her face flush scarlet. 'Patrick is my employer,' she said, gripping the edge of the table. 'That's all there is to it.'

'I dare say,' Mary said, examining her gardener's nails, cracked and short with ingrained dirt. 'When I think what poor Caro had to put up with. Words fail me.' She lied, because words continued to roll out. 'I feel partly responsible. It was my idea that they move to Milbridge in the first place. Then there was all the trouble with Justine.'

'Justine?'

'Didn't you know? Caro found them in bed together – in her bed, what's more. It was the last straw and she chucked Patrick out.'

'I didn't know about . . . not for sure.' Isabel held her hand to her mouth, seeing Patrick and Justine together, her blonde hair swinging against his darkness.

'Not that Justine stayed with Patrick for long – if I were gossiping I'd say she discovered that the money was Caro's and not Patrick's. How she kept it from her husband I don't know, but she managed to get a good settlement from him when they finally divorced. Justine's a clever girl, but greedy. Always one eye on the cheque-book, though I think she'd settle now for a good provider,' Mary added, her tone that of the dispassionate observer.

'And Patrick?' Isabel asked, despite herself.

'You're not the first and you won't be the last. I'd hate to see another marriage break up because of him.'

'I work for Patrick, and that's all,' Isabel said, trying to keep calm. 'There is no question of anybody's marriage breaking up. He means nothing to me.' She could feel her lower lip quiver and her eyes fill with water. 'Nothing,' she repeated.

Mary looked at her, a steady, appraising sort of look. 'I really don't want to know. Just be careful.'

Isabel felt her spirit shrivel up. Lying to Neil was one thing, lying to Mary another. She tried desperately to think of something that could deflect Mary's clear-sighted gaze. 'I don't know what business it is of yours, anyway. What right have you got to come here and say these things?'

'There's no need to get upset. It's common knowledge. You should know what you're getting into.'

'Know? I don't want to know all this – this gossip. That's all it is. Gossip, and jumping to conclusions. Just because I spilt coffee over myself and had to wash my clothes, you've decided I'm having an affair with Patrick.'

Mary paused. She stared at Isabel's feet and then let her gaze travel up her bare legs and over Patrick's sweater until she was looking Isabel straight in the eye. 'I am only warning you. Patrick has made a lot of women very unhappy. It's up to you if you're one of them.'

'You hardly know me. Why should you care?'

'I don't, particularly. But I do care for Patrick.'

'You're jealous, aren't you?'

Mary snorted. 'Hardly.'

'You must be, or why else would you be saying this?'

'Hasn't he said?' To Isabel's surprise, Mary suddenly laughed. 'Well, I can see it might look a bit peculiar to you, as you don't know. Not that there's any reason why you should know, of course.'

'Know what?'

Mary smiled. 'Why, that Patrick's my brother.'

IO

'Why didn't you tell me that Mary was your sister?'
Patrick shrugged. 'No reason. It never came up.'

They were sitting opposite each other at the kitchen table the following day. Isabel had left the money, unable to bring herself to take it, and now it was gone. She knew she wouldn't ask for it again. After Mary's visit, Patrick had disappeared to deal with the importunate Andrew, so this was the first opportunity Isabel had had to ask him. Patrick appeared nonchalant, but Isabel knew him well enough now to detect the tension lines pulling at the corners of his eyes. The more tense he got, the more controlled his movements. She had seen him like this with clients on the phone, his words becoming slower, as his natural inclination to explode fought with his need to be calm and polite. Then, finally, the eruption. He usually managed to contain himself until he could put the phone down, but occasionally a hapless client was treated to clearly enunciated invective and then wild threats. He had promised to see so many people in court that it was astonishing the legal system hadn't ground to a halt – except that as far as Isabel knew he never carried out his threats. They would make love roughly, passionately and then Patrick would lie back on the bed and phone the client to apologise, his deep voice dripping honey and charm, one hand casually stroking Isabel's spine. It usually worked.

Now he sat sipping coffee, his lids drooping, hiding his eyes from her. Isabel put her head in her hands. 'It was so embarrassing.'

'So what? She won't say anything. She's already ticked me off and given me the usual lecture about being irresponsible.' He gave a snort of laughter. 'I don't know why she bothers; I know that one off by heart.'

'Did you tell her about us?'

'She knew not to ask. Don't worry. Whatever she knows, or thinks she knows, she'll keep to herself.'

'I do worry.' Isabel chewed her thumbnail.

'Why?'

'Is what Mary said true? About you and Justine?'

The tension lines tightened. 'It depends what she said.'

'You told me Caro left you for her horse.'

'And so she did.'

'Mary said Caro discovered you in bed with Justine.'

Patrick stood up and looked out of the window. He ran his hand through his hair but it immediately flopped back against his forehead. 'Caro wanted to come out to the country,' he said at last. 'She wanted somewhere to stable her horse. I didn't want to leave London, but Caro's father gave her the money to buy a farmhouse with a bit of land. Her family's well-off,' he added. 'Anyway, we moved down complete with quadruped. I swear she loved that animal more than she ever loved me. So she took up hunting and left me to different sorts of country pursuits.'

'With Justine.'

'Sometimes.' He smiled, as if at a private joke. 'Not exclusively. There are quite a lot of bored married women out there.'

'You mean, like me,' Isabel said flatly.

'No. Not like you.' He frowned. 'I don't know. Perhaps.

If the cap fits . . .' He smiled charmingly at her as if to take the sting from his words, however lightly spoken.

Isabel felt sick. He had told her to expect nothing from him, but now she realised what nothing might be. All those little caresses, the affectionate kisses, could they really mean nothing?

'I don't understand how you can do it. I mean, sleeping around like that, saying it means nothing. You were married.'

'Look who's talking.' She looked up at him, startled. 'Look, I don't know what arrangement you have with Neil but I can't imagine he's said, "Fucking Patrick are you? Excellent idea, old girl."' He spoke clearly and Isabel hung her head. 'You're doing now exactly what I was doing.'

There was a slight pause before he continued. 'I told Caro that I couldn't promise to be faithful to her. She knew that, right from the start. Same as you did. I haven't lied to you.'

'And you think that lets you off the hook,' Isabel said slowly, turning the idea over in her mind. 'You tell people – women – that you're going to be unfaithful and unreliable, then when you are, you turn round and say, "But I told you it was going to be like that." I don't think it works that way. I don't see how you can pretend that it doesn't matter.'

Patrick shrugged. 'If Caro didn't mind, I don't see why you should. After all, you have Neil. I'm the one who's sharing you, and you expect me to put up with it. He gets all your loyalty, your commitment, all your—' He pulled himself up sharply and Isabel wondered if he had been going to say 'love'. He drummed his fingers on the kitchen worktop, then turned on her. 'I ask nothing from you. Nothing,' he said, his voice silky, smooth and dangerous.

'But it doesn't have to be like that,' she said, her own voice trembling, as she got up and stood by him. She reached out for his arm. 'Patrick? It doesn't have to be like that.'

He flung her arm away from him. 'Yes, it does,' he shouted, his face dark. He stalked out, slamming the door behind him so hard the house shook.

Isabel mooched around the house aimlessly waiting for Patrick to come back. Every now and then there were phone calls for him. 'I'm not sure when Mr Sherwin will be back,' she said politely. 'I'm sorry, I couldn't say,' and the caller would ring off, frustrated, although not as frustrated as Isabel. She watched the enormous wall clock she had installed in the office in an attempt to get Patrick to appointments on time. In ten minutes I'll go to the pub and see if he's there, she thought. When ten minutes were up she waited for another five, not wanting to go, but not wanting to stay. When the second tranche of five minutes was up she went downstairs to collect her coat. At the foot of the stairs she paused, hearing a noise. A key in the lock, then Patrick came in. They stared at each other, Isabel trying to read in his eyes what he wanted from her. Then they moved closer, like magnets being drawn to each other and Patrick was kissing her and stroking her hair, and saying 'I'm sorry' over and over. She felt miserable and happy and confused because all that mattered was that he had come back.

'I—' she started to say, but he put his hand over her mouth as soon as he heard the start of the word 'love'.

'Don't say it,' he murmured. 'Don't say it. Come to bed.'

'Yes,' she said, arms around his neck, and he picked her up and carried her upstairs.

* * *

'Teach me Italian?' Isabel said, snuggling under Patrick's arm.

'*Ciao bella,*' Patrick said sleepily. Isabel could feel the sound rumble as she pressed her cheek against his chest.

'I thought *ciao* was goodbye.'

'Hello and goodbye. Both.'

'Say something else.'

'*Mi piace questa donna. Mi piace i suoi occhi, il suo naso, la sua bocca,*' he said, kissing her eyes, nose and mouth. He moved further down to her neck, and then beyond. '*Mi piace la sua gola, le sue tette, la figa,*' he mumbled, his voice muffled.

Isabel languorously stretched her arms out across the bed. 'I'm not sure how much Italian I'm going to learn if you carry on doing that.'

'Should I stop?'

'No.'

Later she said, 'Will you teach me some Italian every day?'

Patrick picked a hair off the tip of his tongue and examined it. 'If you like. If you're a good girl. *Una buona ragazza.*' He settled back against the pillows.

'*Una buona ragazza,*' she repeated happily, running her fingers over his chest. 'I'll try. Is it your father or your mother who's Italian?'

'My mother.'

'Does Mary speak Italian?'

'A little.' He sighed. 'My father had three children by his first marriage. Then his wife died leaving him with Anna, June and Mary. My mother came over from Italy to help look after them. He had that tweedy English gentleman sort of charm and I suppose my mother thought it exotic. Anyway, they had me. But after a bit my mama discovered that he wasn't exotic, in fact he was just like any other Nigel or Henry you might meet at the Golf Club or at the annual Conservative Summer Garden Party. And then there were the girls.' He raised his eyebrows. 'If you think Mary is bossy, you should meet Anna and June. I don't really remember, but I get the impression that Anna especially thought my mother was taking *her* mother's place. Usurping the blessed memory, and all that. It can't have been easy.'

'So what happened?'

'My mother ran off with a Tunisian airline pilot.'

'Did you go too?'

'No. She left us all.' Patrick sat up. 'I ought to get some work done. Lord knows why I'm telling you all this, you're probably bored to tears.' He gave a little laugh.

'No, I'm not. How old were you?' She moved up so she was beside him.

'Mmm? About seven.'

Isabel kissed his shoulder. 'Poor boy.'

'Yeah, well, that's the way it goes. Besides, I wasn't really badly off, I had three splendid surrogate mothers in my sisters. I went to live in Rome with her in my teens, after I was chucked out of school. I was persona non grata at home, as you can imagine, and Dad had remarried and got a new family, so he wasn't really interested anyway.'

He spoke lightly, but Isabel could sense the hurt behind the words. She could imagine him as a small dark boy, perhaps already tall for his age, bewildered at his mother's departure, then a sulky teenager rejected by his father.

'What about you?' Patrick surprised her by saying.

'Me?'

'Yes. You've had the Sherwin tale of woe, now you tell me something about your family.'

'Um. Well, I'm an only child – so no sisters to surprise you with – and my father was a businessman. My mother didn't work, although I think she would have liked to, but she had my father to deal with. Sometimes things would go well with the business, and sometimes they wouldn't. You never knew what would happen next. He would arrive at school in a helicopter for Sports Day, but then the next minute the deal would have fallen through and we'd be living on soup. We moved around a lot, depending on the money, everything from a caravan to an Elizabethan mansion, ending up in a terraced house in East Sheen. I've still got that. My poor mother, she was always waiting for the bailiffs to turn up. I promised myself that I would give my own children a proper home and that we'd stay there. Not that I've managed that very well so far: Michael's already lived in four different countries. But here we are.'

'Your father sounds quite a character.'

'He was. He looked a bit like Errol Flynn, but shorter and without the muscles. Or the tights.'

'Tights?'

'You know, Robin Hood. And a cigar. He always smoked a cigar, even when he was broke.' Isabel smiled, remembering him talking expansively, cigar in hand. 'He would have loved mobile phones,' she said, looking at Patrick. 'You'd have got on.'

'Did he get on with Neil?'

Isabel shifted in the bed. 'He encouraged Neil. With hindsight, I think he thought Neil was responsible and would look after me. You see, my mother had died a few years earlier, and he knew he was ill, although he didn't tell me. He was only trying to protect me, but I wish I'd known. He died three months after we married. I was stuck in Saudi with Neil. He didn't let the hospital tell me he was so ill; he knew I'd be on the first plane back. So he died alone, without me.' She pressed her lips together. 'Still. Nothing I can do about it now.'

Patrick stroked her hair. 'Poor little girl,' he said gently.

Isabel rubbed her cheek against his chest. 'Makes two of us then.'

She was thinking about Patrick and that exchange when she and Neil were driving over to Helen and George's house for dinner on Saturday night. She had quite forgotten about the invitation until Helen had phoned her on Friday to change the arrangements slightly. The invitation had been for supper but Helen said that George had decided he didn't want supper, but a proper dinner party. Wednesday had been the best yet, with Patrick tender and considerate. She had felt stroked all over, inside and out. Loving, she would have said of anyone else, but that word was banned. She stared sightlessly out of the window at hedges and trees going past in a blur, while in her head she and Patrick talked, their voices low and contented. The next day he'd been irritable, as if she'd come too close, and he had to put up the barriers again. She sighed. If she'd learnt anything in the six weeks she'd known him, four as his lover, it was that he was unpredictable and edgy about any emotions.

George and Helen's driveway was blocked by two cars so Neil parked their car hard against the verge to allow for any other passing traffic, but it meant Isabel couldn't open the passenger door and had to clamber out over the gear-stick. There didn't seem an elegant way of achieving this, but she felt particularly inept, clutching a box of chocolates in one hand, and getting her legs stuck under the steering wheel. She prayed that the plum suede high-heels, worn for the first time since meeting Patrick, wouldn't catch and ladder her tights.

'No stars tonight,' said Neil, looking up at a sky brought close by a dark bank of cloud. 'D'you want to grab a torch?' Isabel thought about climbing back over the gear-stick to get at the glove compartment.

'No, we'll be fine. The drive's not that long.'

At night the yew trees were distinctly menacing, rustling with malice. Isabel walked close to Neil. It would be childish to say she was scared of the trees, but she found his solidity reassuring. They turned the corner and could see the house, the windows lit up and low-wattage lights feebly illuminating the pathway to the front door. It looked absurdly formal.

'I bet you anything that Helen will get the women to withdraw after dinner while George dishes up the port,' Isabel said, remembering the Victorian dining room. 'It's just the sort of thing he'd insist on.'

'Don't be ridiculous. No one does that nowadays.'

They had to step carefully up the flagstone path that was slippery with evening mist. Isabel kept catching the heel of her shoes in the cracks and slipping, so Neil put a steadying arm around her. It felt odd to be held by Neil, almost as if he was a stranger.

'Just you wait,' she said, aware of the pressure of his hand.

'You don't like port anyway.'

'But I want to be offered the choice. And I bet he's stingy with the booze. Let's hope Helen will have made something alcoholic for pudding.'

'Sherry trifle,' Neil suggested.

'Tiramisu.'

'Syllabub.'

'Um . . . um . . . um.' Isabel could only think of things like spotted dick and Sussex pond pudding. 'I know, rum truffles.'

'Nearly got you there.' He gave her a gentle push.

'Didn't.' She pushed him back.

'Did.'

Isabel stuck out her tongue at him. 'Know-it-all.'

'You're just jealous,' he said, giving her shoulder a squeeze.

'You're in a good mood,' she said, suddenly realising that it was ages since they had gone out together. Perhaps if we did things together more often, just us, there would be more life in our marriage, she thought. Neil rang the doorbell, then, as they heard steps coming to answer it, pinched Isabel's bottom hard so that she was caught by George with a grimace of surprise on her face.

'Isabel! You look surprised to see me.'

'George, of course not, it's lovely to see you.' She kissed him lightly on the cheek. 'I was just going to murder Neil.'

'Well done. Neil, good to see you alive and in one piece. Come on in and have a drink.' He led them into the drawing room and indicated the other guests. George rubbed his hands together.

'Now, who do you know?'

Four faces turned towards her. Mary Wright's was as welcoming as a slab from Stonehenge and Justine was looking as bland as if rain had washed all expression away. The two men were unknown to Isabel, though not for long.

'My husband, Richard,' Mary said, social graces presumably beating private misgivings, introducing a portly man with hair sprouting from his ears.

'And this is Quentin Anderson,' Justine added. Isabel shook his hand, which was disturbingly soft and cool. His face was plump and slightly pink as if his razor had newly scraped his skin. Perhaps he's rich, Isabel thought, and was ashamed of her meanness.

Isabel introduced Mary to Neil. 'And you remember Justine, don't you?'

'Of course,' he said, rather stiffly. Isabel was surprised; she'd thought he'd quite liked Justine when they'd met. As far as she could remember Justine had put herself out to be entertaining. Maybe it was just meeting all these new people at once. It was a long time since they had been to a formal dinner party rather than a casual barbecue in someone's back yard.

'So, you're working for Mary's little brother,' Richard Wright said, swaying backwards on his feet to counterbalance the weight of his paunch. 'Quite a handful, I'd have thought.' Isabel prayed Neil hadn't heard.

'I really couldn't say. I just do the paperwork and answer the phone.'

'Pretty young thing like you, thought he'd have difficulty keeping himself to himself, if you know what I mean.' He leant closer, so Isabel got a good view of the network of spidery red veins that webbed his face and the flakes of dandruff along the parting of his corrugated hair.

'No, I don't know what you mean,' she said as coldly as she could.

'Terrible reputation the boy's got.' Richard shook his head. 'Terrible one for the ladies. But I expect you can handle yourself.' His eyes twinkled at her in a way that should have been avuncular, but which Isabel found sinister. Had Mary said anything?

'If you'll excuse me, I must go and say hello to Helen,'

she managed to say before escaping into the hall, ignoring Neil's questioning turn of the head. She stopped by an elaborate flower arrangement in front of a mirror and pretended to sniff a rose, breathing deeply to regain some equilibrium, gripping the front edge of the side table. The marble top was cold and unyielding to her hands. She relaxed her fingers and straightened up, de-smudging her eye make-up as best she could. Pull yourself together, she thought. It's only natural that people ask about Patrick. She gave herself a bright smile in the mirror that didn't reach her eyes and moved to the kitchen to find Helen.

'Hello, I came to see if I could help.'

Helen looked up, her fair hair flopping over pink cheeks. 'You couldn't give me a hand to take these out of the oven?'

'Sure.' Isabel looked around and found a pair of oven gloves. 'They smell delicious.' She pulled out a tray of scallop shells piped with mashed potato, some of them burnt around the edges.

'I wish I'd never started them,' Helen said vehemently. 'They're fiddly, take ages and they don't look anything like the photograph.'

Isabel immediately felt better. 'Never mind,' she said consolingly. 'I'm sure they'll taste wonderful.' It was so reassuring to know that other women weren't perfect cooks.

'I wanted to have a kitchen supper, just simple food and friends,' Helen was muttering to a bowl of whipping cream. 'But, oh no, George wants to make it dinner. Well, it's all right for him. He doesn't have to do any of the work.'

'Let me give you a hand.'

'That's sweet of you, but it's more or less under control.' Helen looked around the kitchen rather wildly.

'I know what you mean about kitchen supper, but it's fun to dress up. You can have kitchen supper anytime.' She realised that Helen was waiting for her to go so she could scrape off the burnt bits and make the food more presentable. She wanted to tell her that it didn't matter, that it was mad to expect anyone to produce restaurant-quality food at home. But she thought that if she said it, it implied that all Helen's efforts had been worthless.

'Are you sure there's nothing I can do?'

'Absolutely,' Helen said, her hands obviously itching to pick at the burnt edges. 'Go and grab a drink.'

Isabel left the kitchen and slowly went back into the hall, thinking about how difficult it was living up to standards set by other people. Her shoes made a pleasant click-clack on the wooden floor, her skirt swished around her legs. Poor Helen, she thought. I bet George has no idea how hard it is to produce a dinner party like this. Come to that, she herself didn't know much about it. Most places they had been to abroad it had been easy – and cheap – to get domestic help. The doorbell rang just as she crossed the hall. She hesitated, then called out, 'I'll get it.' One less thing for Helen to worry about, she thought. She opened the big front door.

Patrick stood there, with his arm around a woman with short blonde hair who looked familiar. With a start Isabel recognised her. The woman on the yacht, in the photograph she'd found in the office.

11

'Patrick!' She was so surprised to see him, her legs felt as if her knees had just taken a trip to the Bahamas. 'What are you doing here?'

'What do you think? Gate-crashing, of course. Are you going to let us in or just stand there?' She could tell from the way his head was tilted back that he hadn't expected to see her, and was on the defensive. His arm was no longer round the woman-from-the-photograph's shoulder.

Isabel realised she was hanging onto the door like a crutch. She let go and stepped back to let him and his companion through. 'Would you like me to take your coat?' she said, aware that she sounded too formal, too polite.

'Thank you.' The woman slipped her coat off and handed it to Isabel, who chucked it over the banisters. She was dressed in a simple shift dress, navy but with a glittering thread running discreetly through it. It was low-cut with slim spaghetti straps that crossed over her beautifully tanned back. Isabel, who had been feeling quite sleek and attractive, immediately felt fat and frumpy.

'What a lovely dress.'

'Thank you.' The woman smiled politely showing even, white teeth. She wasn't as young as Isabel had first thought, nearer to thirty maybe.

'This is Victoria,' Patrick said. 'And this is Isabel, who works for me.'

Isabel's ego plummeted into the slippery soles of her plum suede shoes. 'Come into the drawing room and get a drink.' She walked forwards trying to act nonchalantly, feeling as if her head was spinning round. She'd always known that, logically, she was bound to run into Patrick at some point. It was just that, somehow, she didn't expect it to happen. What went on in Patrick's house was so far removed from her daily life, it was like some private fantasy world, unknown and separate from the normal round. And now there was Victoria. She wondered when the photograph had been taken, and she realised it could have been taken that summer and not some years before. Patrick and Victoria, together, on holiday. Possibly just before Isabel started working for him. The thought made her feel sick and cold.

'Are you all right?' Neil was at her side. 'You seem a bit . . .'

'What? No, no, I'm fine.' Fine, that useful word, so handy for masking anything meaningful or honest. She smiled broadly at him. 'I'm just fine. Don't worry.'

He patted her shoulder. 'We can always go—'

'Oh no, really, I'm fine.' He looked uncertain. 'Really. How's your drink?'

Neil shrugged, then looked down at his glass where a bit of soggy lemon sat in a puddle of ice water. 'It's all right.'

'You're doing better than me. I haven't managed one at all yet. Do you want me to drive?'

'It's my turn.'

'I wouldn't mind.'

'No, no, darling. You have a good time.'

She tucked her hair behind her ears several times then went up to where George was fussing with ice cubes and tonic water. Have a good time, Neil had said. Right.

'Could I have a drink please, George?'

'Isabel, I'm sorry, did you get missed out?' He made her a drink, measuring the gin carefully, and handed it to her. Keeping an eye on George she steadily drank it, feeling the cold liquid glug, glug down her throat. His eyes got larger and more distressed as she finished it. 'Delicious. Another please,' and she held out the glass, empty but for the ice cubes. George seemed as frozen as the ice cubes, so she shook her glass a little, hearing them chinkle softly. 'George?'

George poured her a small measure of gin and a lot of tonic water, his face rigid with the strain of his innate meanness fighting against the code of hospitality. Isabel thought about asking for more gin, but decided not to push her luck. Neil, watching her, shook his head slightly, but amused rather than censorious. Perhaps she would get very drunk tonight. Yes, very drunk. Mind-numbingly, brain-freezingly drunk. She raised her chin, went to the armchair furthest from Patrick and Victoria and plonked herself down. She crossed her legs, so her skirt fell back over her thighs, and studied one of her plum high-heels, twisting her foot for a better view. The snakeskin glittered in the firelight. Fuck-me shoes, she thought. Fuck me.

Over the edge of her glass she studied the room. Neil and Richard stood in front of the fire, hogging the heat. Mary, feet firmly planted on the ground, was talking to Quentin. He, poor man, was leaning backwards as if to escape contact, but Mary's gravitational pull was stronger than his desire to escape her orbit. Justine was talking animatedly to Victoria and Patrick. Victoria kept touching Patrick, and looking up at him.

Isabel fidgeted with the bead buttons that held her top together. What if she stood up and said 'Excuse me, but I just thought you'd like to know that I'm sleeping with Patrick Sherwin'. No, not sleeping. Anything but sleeping. Screwing, fucking, shagging. Hard-edged words, not soft, sweet ones. She hoicked out a bit of ice cube from her glass and popped it in her mouth, wrinkling her nose with the sudden cold. Wake up and feel the ice water, she thought.

'Have you forgiven me for being here?' Patrick was standing before her, his crotch level with her eyes.

'I was startled. You didn't say you'd be here.'

'Nor did you.' There was a slight pause. She fiddled with the top button of her cardigan, and to her horror it came off in her fingers, exposing more cleavage than she wanted. 'Buggeration.'

'I'm sorry you're upset,' he said, not looking at her.

'Upset? Who said anything about being upset?' She stood up from her chair, but even with her high-heels on she had to look up to him.

Patrick touched her arm. 'Isabel—'

'There nothing to be upset about, is there? I expect she's just an old friend.'

'She is.'

'And as you have pointed out to me on many occasions, there is nothing between us beyond what goes on in the office.' She could hear her voice was brittle, and looked around to see if anyone had noticed, but they all seemed deep in conversation.

'I'm sorry.' He ran his hand through his hair. 'If I'd known you'd be here I would have said something. I didn't expect—'

'Obviously.' She felt herself bristling and glared at him. He looked down at her, his lips twitched and involuntarily she almost smiled back at him. But he was aware of the internal smile, and smiled broadly himself.

'Oh, Isabel, what shall I do with you?'

He made her sound like unwanted baggage, she thought. She hung her head, not wanting him to see how aware she was of his presence, the very scent of him, his warmth beside her. She felt confused at her emotions – anger, jealousy, love swirling round together like primeval soup – but knew that she must control them. No one must know how she felt. She straightened up.

'Hadn't you better introduce me properly to your girl-friend?' she said.

'If you wish.'

They crossed the room together, Isabel careful not to let her hips sway and bump into him accidentally, as once she would have done deliberately. Justine's eyes flickered over Isabel as she and Patrick joined her and Victoria.

'I feel I haven't seen you for ages,' she said.

'Since the PTA meeting,' Isabel answered, proud that her voice was steady. 'I'm so pleased to meet you at last,' she said to Victoria. 'Patrick has a lovely photograph of you in his office.' She sensed Patrick react although he said nothing.

'Patrick, I'd no idea. That's so sweet of you,' Victoria said, wrinkling her nose and blowing him a kiss. Old friend my arse, thought Isabel.

'Now, Patrick, I can't let your ego get even bigger by having three adoring ladies surrounding you,' Justine said gaily. 'I'm off to seduce your husband, Isabel.'

'Be my guest,' Isabel answered, equally gaily.

'Now, which is your husband?' Victoria asked, following Justine with her eyes.

'The one talking to Richard. You know Richard, I expect.'

'Gosh, yes. I adore Mary and Richard, don't I, darling?' Victoria slipped her hand around Patrick's arm, clearly staking her claim and warding off intruders. Patrick looked harassed, Isabel realised with amusement, slightly surprised that she could feel amused in the situation. Poor Victoria, she thought. If she's only half aware of Patrick's activities she probably feels every woman she meets must be either a past, current or future mistress of his. Perhaps that's why she's so clingy.

Helen saved her from having to make any further conversation by coming in and announcing that dinner was ready. They all trooped through to the candle-lit dining room. Helen had even gone as far as to put copper-plate place-name cards in little silver apples and pears around the table. Isabel found her place, sandwiched between George – at the head of the table of course – and Quentin, who seemed to have wilted after Mary's monologue. Directly opposite her was Mary, with Patrick on her right and Justine to his right.

Isabel pushed burnt Coquilles Saint-Jacques around her scallop shell. She glanced round the table. The men were eating solidly, shoving forkfuls in their mouths. No burnt bits for them. Or for Mary. She thought that Justine's and her own piped mashed potato were equally burnt, while Helen had given herself the most squidged and burnt one. She couldn't see what Victoria, on the far side of Quentin, had got. Isabel smiled to herself. It was interesting to know that Helen ranked her as equal status to Justine in the burnt food stakes. Either that or Helen thought she would be less likely to mind.

'This is delicious, Helen,' Justine said, leaning forwards so she could smile sincerely at her. Helen looked flustered but pleased.

'I'm afraid it got a bit burnt.'

'Oh, no, it's wonderful to have something hot to start with, especially now the evenings are drawing in. I don't know how you manage with so many people.'

There was an echoing chorus of congratulations. Isabel asked Quentin what he did.

'I'm a dermatologist. That's skin problems. Eczema, psoriasis and so on,' he explained. 'The skin's the largest excretory organ of the body, you know.'

'Really?' Isabel said, looking at her scallops and trying not to think about excretory organs. 'Fascinating.'

Encouraged, Quentin started to talk about dermabrasion, the new PUVA light treatments available and Chinese herbal medicine. It must have been murder for him to have to listen to Mary's monologue. Isabel nodded and interjected a suitable word every now and again. She could see why Helen hadn't put Quentin next to herself when she did her seating plan. George joined in, asking serious questions about acne treatments.

Isabel tried to switch off, repulsed by the thought of George's teenage problems. Instead she watched Mary and Patrick across the other side of the table. Mary was talking, and judging by the look on Patrick's face she was telling him off. He prodded a bit of scallop around his plate, then looked up and saw her watching him. His face went from miserable to happy in one second and despite herself Isabel's heart contracted with longing for him. Mary sensed his change and turned her head swiftly as a striking hawk. Isabel felt herself blush and turned back to Quentin.

'What an interesting area of medicine,' she said faintly. 'I had no idea.'

'I certainly enjoy it. Aside from the work, it has its advantages.'

'Really?' Isabel said, thinking 'Private practice' and wondering if money would make up for him being a bore with such creepily smooth hands. She found it hard to believe that Justine would think so.

'You get to work fairly regular hours, and not much at weekends,' Quentin carried on. 'Unlike so many of the other specialisms, you don't get paged when you're off duty.'

'Mmm. I can see that you're not going to be dragged out of bed in the middle of the night over a case of raging pimples.'

'It's a most important area of medicine.' He looked affronted.

'But it's not exactly ER, is it?' She saw Helen pick up her plate and clutched at the chance of escape. 'Can I help you take things through?'

'No, no, sit down,' Helen responded. Isabel slumped back in her seat. She wanted to go home and be safe from all the undercurrents. She felt confused. She knew what Patrick would say. You have a husband, what's wrong with me having a girlfriend? She shifted in her seat. She didn't like being deceived herself, but she was deceiving Neil without too many qualms. Wasn't this what she deserved? And what about Victoria? Funnily enough, she felt as uncomfortable about deceiving her as she did Neil. Neil was content, as far as Isabel could see. He had no idea about her affair with Patrick. Yet there was something desperate about Victoria, clinging onto Patrick. She winced at the idea that it was some-how all right to cheat Neil. She knew it was wrong, that

Neil deserved a good and faithful wife who was loyal to him alone. Oh Patrick, she thought. Life was so much easier before you kissed me.

He was now having a conversation with Neil and Richard, something about a mutual acquaintance, and a deal involving preference options. Patrick was animated, while Neil seemed slightly withdrawn.

'You've got to admit he sailed pretty close to the wind,' Neil said.

'All perfectly legal,' Patrick shrugged. 'And think of the profit margin.'

'He made a lot, certainly. But as for being perfectly legal . . .'

'Maybe a little bending of the rules. But hey, what are rules for if not to be bent a little from time to time? After all, if God didn't want them to get fleeced, he wouldn't have made them sheep.' He leant back on his chair and grinned across at Neil, his face brimming with mischief. Isabel found she was praying that he wouldn't say anything outrageous.

'They said that after Lloyds, and I don't think many people found it funny then either,' Neil said quietly.

'Hear, hear,' Justine said, and Patrick flashed her a look of annoyance. Isabel felt annoyed with Justine too, for showing her up. It should have been her backing Neil, not Justine.

'Lloyds is still a sore point round here, Patrick, old boy. As you well know,' Richard said heavily. 'We shouldn't talk business anyway.'

'The first rule of civilised behaviour, I've been told,' Neil said. Patrick looked as cross as a cat when it's been caught out doing something stupid.

Richard swivelled his attention to Neil. 'I understand

you have children at St Joseph's too. How are they finding it? Settling in all right?'

'Yes, thanks to Rachel,' Neil said, to Isabel's surprise. She wasn't aware that Neil had known anything about Justine's daughter. She supposed Katie must have told him. He added, 'Those girls seem to have hit it off from the first.'

'How nice for her,' Victoria said. 'School can be hellish without a friend.'

'Send 'em all off when they're seven, if not earlier,' Patrick said leaning back on his chair.

'You don't really mean that,' Victoria frowned.

'Sure, why not. Get rid of the ankle-biters until they're old enough to appreciate a good Burgundy and have a decent conversation.'

Justine smiled very sweetly at him. 'Perhaps you say that because you don't have any children.'

'Don't intend to either.'

Isabel was aware of Victoria fiddling with the cutlery.

'Bet you will.' Justine was leaning back in her chair too, challenging him.

'No,' Patrick shook his head. 'I'm far too selfish.'

'At least you know yourself,' Justine said.

'Don't you want to feel that your genetic material is continuing down the line?' Richard asked.

'Look, my father had six children over three marriages, my mother managed three over two, and most of those children are spawning like newts, me being the exception.'

'You're the only boy,' Mary said stiffly. 'And I don't consider four children is exactly comparable to a newt.'

'Whatever. I reckon there's quite enough Sherwin DNA floating around the world without my help.' He shifted in his seat as if bored with the conversation. 'Hey,

Isabel,' he called across the table. 'Why don't you get Justine to do her colour thing on you?'

Isabel froze at the sound of Patrick's voice, caught in the spotlight of attention. Patrick's eyes held hers as they had done once, years ago it seemed, during the thunderstorm. Then it had been dangerous, but she had been a willing participant in the danger. Now he was challenging her, and she had nowhere to hide.

'Sorry?' she said, stalling for time and suddenly horribly conscious of Neil further down the table. Why did aliens abduct people on deserted country lanes when if they came at moments like this, they'd be welcomed with open arms?

'Justine does a colour thing – what's it called?' He turned to Justine.

'Beautiful You,' she said quietly, but her face was alert, eyes darting between Isabel and Patrick.

'You're kidding.' He laughed then swung back to Isabel. 'Why don't you let Justine turn you into a Beautiful You?'

'I don't know,' she said, trying to sound casual and thinking wistfully of the mother ship. Everybody was looking at her. Mary was stony-faced. 'I don't think it's my sort of thing.'

'Quite beautiful enough already,' said Richard gallantly, which made Mary's face go granite.

Isabel smiled at him. 'Thank you, Richard.'

'You really ought to have it done,' gushed Helen suddenly. 'It's wonderful. We had a session, didn't we Mary, with Rebecca too – you know, from the PTA – just the three of us and it was such fun. You can really see which colours suit you and which don't, and then you get a little book with all the colours which are right for you so you can go shopping and always choose something that suits you. It was fun, wasn't it Mary?'

'Yes, I'd certainly recommend it.' It conjured up an image of the three of them having a wonderful time together and Isabel felt excluded.

'Thank you, Mary,' said Justine. 'I'm glad you enjoyed it.'

'I bet you didn't get Mary to chuck any clothes out,' Patrick said, and Isabel remembered the ancient sheep sweater.

'We made a pile to go to charity,' Justine said smoothly.

'But you're not sure how much will end up there.' Patrick's eyes glittered and Isabel could sense the tension in his body.

'Thank you for that, Patrick,' Mary said, obviously offended.

'I had it done in London,' Victoria said. 'Not with Beautiful You, but with one of the other ones.'

'Did you do the one with seasons?' Justine asked.

Victoria nodded vigorously. 'I'm a Summer.'

'Beautiful You doesn't work quite like that; there are more categories so the colours are more subtle—' Justine stopped. 'But I mustn't pitch for business at a dinner party. Isn't that the first rule of civilised behaviour?' She looked towards Neil.

'That hardly counts.' Isabel couldn't see Neil's face beyond the dumpling that was Quentin's body but she could hear the smile in his voice.

'Why don't you have it done, Isabel?' Patrick interrupted.

'Oh, I don't know,' she muttered, hoping he would go no further.

'You're not very interested in that sort of thing, are you, darling?' Neil's voice, well-fed and indulgent. Isabel wanted to shout 'Yes, I am' although she knew that she wasn't really.

'Do it for Isabel,' Patrick said to Justine. 'I'll pay.'

Isabel felt that all eyes swivelled to her. Forget crop circles, she sent her thoughts to the aliens, just beam me up now. But she stayed where she was. What would Neil think? She couldn't see him beyond Quentin and Victoria, but she hoped that he had somehow not heard Patrick's challenge.

'No. Thank you,' Isabel added, hoping that she seemed at least vaguely natural despite the stiffness in her voice.

'In lieu of wages, if you prefer.' He was laughing at her, daring her to respond. 'It might even be tax-deductible.'

'I hardly think that's necessary.' Neil's voice was firm as he cut across. 'I'm sure Isabel can make whatever arrangements suit her.'

Patrick shrugged, sitting back in his chair. 'If she doesn't want to . . .'

No, I don't want someone rummaging through my wardrobe, Isabel shrieked inside her head, but she could see that Justine was staring down at her plate, shoulders hunched in embarrassment.

'I'd love to do it, Justine. I've always meant to.' She hoped no one could spot the insincerity in her voice. 'Let me give you a ring and we'll make a date,' she said quickly.

'I'm sure you'll enjoy it. Although it seems a pity to throw away perfectly good clothes,' Mary said, her interjection defusing the atmosphere round the table.

'Now, Mary, you know you don't have to throw anything away. Just make sure that everything new is in the right colours.' Justine had perked up. Great, thought Isabel. What have I let myself in for? I could murder

Patrick. She looked up and caught him staring at her intensely. He ran the tip of his tongue over the edge of his teeth in a tiny movement. Oh, for heaven's sake, thought Isabel, it's like being with John Malkovich in *Dangerous Liaisons*. Grow up, she mouthed at him.

She didn't care if she looked like an alcoholic, she needed a drink. 'George, some more wine, please.'

George removed his gaze from her cleavage and looked as wide-eyed as Bambi in a panic. 'I'll have to open another bottle.'

'Great. Carry on. Wield the corkscrew.'

She realised Patrick was looking at her, his face unreadable. What did he want from her, blowing alternately hot and cold like an erratic April day? He held her gaze for a moment then turned his attention to Justine. Isabel watched him smiling and being his most charming. She became aware that Quentin was also watching Justine and Patrick, the fair hair close to the dark.

'D'you know him well?' he asked. Isabel knew immediately who he meant.

'He's my boss.' And my lover, she thought. 'Sometimes I think I hardly know him at all.'

Quentin looked at her sharply and opened his mouth to speak, then shut it. When he spoke, Isabel got the impression he had changed what he was going to say. He leant towards her and spoke conspiratorially. 'I've heard a rumour Justine's seeing someone here in Milbridge.'

'I thought you were—' Isabel was startled into saying.

'Oh no. I'm Justine's fallback position, you could say. She thinks I don't realise, but I do.'

Isabel didn't know what to say to that.

'Justine told me that there's been nothing between

them for years,' Quentin continued. 'But you don't suppose . . .'

'No,' Isabel said sadly. 'I don't suppose anything where Patrick is concerned.'

She hardly managed to eat any of her Poussin Provençale, pushing chunks of courgette around the plate. As Helen cleared the plates away she excused herself and slipped out to the loo. She ran cold water over her wrists and wiped the back of her neck with her cold hands. Her face in the mirror was wide-eyed. She flicked water at her reflection, letting the droplets run down her face and blur her features. Patrick was pushing her boundaries, seeing how much she could or would take, but she didn't know why. She prayed that Neil hadn't noticed.

Patrick was waiting in the hall for her when she came out of the loo.

'Why are you doing this?' she said, keeping her voice low.

'What?' he said, his voice caressing her. 'What am I doing?'

'You know. The colour thing. And Victoria. No, don't touch me,' she said, putting her hand out to ward him off.

'Don't? That's not what you usually say. Normally it's please, please, please, Patrick, fuck me.' He imitated her voice, his eyes hard.

She tried to go past him, but he stopped her. 'Why so standoffish, sweetheart? You're normally much more accommodating.'

'My husband is in the next room. Along with your girlfriend.'

'Are you jealous?'

'No,' she said, not looking at him.

'But I have to share you, so it's only fair that you have to share me, don't you think?' He kissed the top of her head. 'You smell delicious,' he murmured. She could feel his breath hot against her ear. 'When I was little my mother would dress up and go out smelling delicious. I thought it was for me.' He kissed her neck. 'You know, Victoria doesn't make any difference to us.'

'But—' she started to say, when he stopped her by kissing her mouth. He held her tightly and she clung on to him, even though she knew it was complete madness.

'I want you,' he said when they pulled apart. He put his hand under her elbow as if to steer her to some corner but she resisted.

'No, I must go back. Someone will notice we're gone.'

'Forget them.'

'I can't. Neil might—' At the mention of Neil's name Patrick dropped her arm. He shrugged.

'So, no chance of a fuck then.'

'Patrick.'

'Or inter-course intercourse.'

Isabel took a deep breath. 'Look, we can't talk here, we'll talk on Tuesday.' She started to move down the hall towards the dining room.

'Isabel—' He had caught up with her and taken her upper arm in a tight grip.

'I must go back,' she said pushing him off.

'Back to your hubby,' he sneered. 'No wonder you're like a bitch on heat, the man's a patronising bore. You'd be better off with me.'

'Don't you dare talk about Neil,' she hissed at him. 'He's worth a hundred of you.'

'I love it when you get angry.' He was close, she could

smell his scent, feel the warmth of his body, the danger of being with him. His eyes held hers and she felt she was falling, falling. 'Bitch,' he whispered before kissing her. '*Carissima.*' His hand was on her breast and she could feel him against her. She felt as limp as a puppet, where sex was the puppet master and Patrick pulled the strings. She wrapped her arms around his neck and kissed him back, almost lost to the moment.

Almost. With the tiny corner of her brain not curling up under Patrick's caresses she registered a noise, the scrape of a chair, and a man's voice. George. The horror of being caught by George acted like an ice shower. She tore herself away from Patrick, and scuttered down the hall, heart racing. She met George at the door.

'Excuse me,' she said, slipping past him, head down so he shouldn't see her flushed cheeks. She quietly sat down next to Quentin, hoping no one had noticed her absence.

Patrick didn't come back into the dining room, which flustered Helen as she doled out profiteroles.

'D'you think he's all right?' she said. 'Perhaps I should . . .'

'Please don't worry,' Mary said. 'My brother's manners are atrocious and I apologise on his behalf.'

'Not for the first time,' Richard muttered.

'If you'll excuse me,' Victoria said, standing up and leaving the room.

The next ten minutes were hard for Isabel. Patrick and Victoria's absence divided the table in half – Neil, Helen, Richard and Justine at one end, Mary, George, Isabel and Quentin at the other. Mary was talking to George, a conversation Isabel definitely didn't want to get involved with. Quentin tried having a conversation with her, but she found she kept on thinking of Patrick and then realising Quentin was waiting for her to reply. 'Sorry,' she kept saying. 'Sorry.'

She lost her bet with Neil. Helen didn't expect the ladies to remove themselves from the dining room leaving the men to port and cigars. Instead she served coffee in the drawing room.

Justine came to sit next to Isabel.

'So, what do you think's going on with Patrick?' she said, tucking her slim legs neatly underneath her.

Isabel's heart flipped but she thought she managed to look unruffled. 'Who knows?'

'Bit of a surprise him turning up with Victoria. I thought that was over ages ago.'

'Oh?' Isabel tried not to show interest.

'Poor girl, she's been dangling after him for years, and every now and then he deigns to notice.' Justine shrugged her elegant shoulders, as if to show contempt at any woman who could be so foolish. 'He really does treat women badly.'

All at once Isabel felt angry with Justine. 'Speaking from personal experience?' she said as lightly as she could.

'No,' Justine purred sweetly. 'I don't believe in letting men treat me badly. Especially not men like Patrick.'

'What do you mean?'

Justine paused. 'You can divide people up into cats and dogs. Dogs are loyal and dependent and trustworthy and look at you with big doggy eyes. Cats are independent and think for themselves. They can bestow affection, but they usually demand it.'

'So?' said Isabel, trying to work out if she was a cat or a dog on Justine's scale. Dogs sounded better people, but cats were more glamorous.

'So cat people can be happy with other cats but they're happiest with the uncritical attention of a dog. And dogs can be happy with other dogs, but they're happiest with a cat to worship. Patrick and I are both cats, so we're better off with dogs.' She drew out the word and Isabel wondered if she meant to be insulting.

'You don't really want me to do your colours, do you?' Justine said, disconcerting Isabel with the abrupt change of subject, as if she had tired of a game that Isabel had not even realised they were playing. 'I got the impression that you weren't too keen.'

'Well, it was a bit embarrassing, the way Patrick brought it up over dinner.' Isabel winced inwardly, thinking about it. 'It's probably a good idea. My wardrobe is stuffed with things I don't wear.'

'Did you want to do the wardrobe sort-out as well? It's quite expensive.'

'In for a penny, in for a pound,' Isabel said. 'I expect I need the whole lot chucking out.' She picked up her bag and fished out her diary.

Justine got her diary out too. 'When's a good date for you?'

'It's got to be a Monday or a Friday in term time. What about the Friday after half term?'

'That's the Bonfire Party night. I'll be busy setting up.'

'Help, I'd forgotten. I'd better write that in, I don't want to forget and get into Mary's bad books,' she added, knowing she was already in them. 'The Friday after, then – the morning would be best for me, I think.'

'That's fine by me. I look forward to it.'

That's more than I will, Isabel thought as she wrote the date in her diary. As she replaced the diary in her bag there was a clatter and Victoria came back in, her face glowing. Patrick behind her looked impassive, his eyes inscrutable. They sat together, near Mary.

'You found him then.' Mary was good at stating the obvious.

'Yes,' Victoria said, a bubble of laughter escaping. She turned round to Patrick. 'He'd gone outside for a cigarette.'

'I thought you'd given up,' Mary said.

'I have.' His expression was bland.

Isabel heard Justine, sitting next to her, snort with amusement. She looked up quickly, but Justine was watching Patrick and Victoria, a wry smile on her face.

Victoria smoothed her dress down over her hips. She had lowered her head, but Isabel could see the blush spread over it, the satisfied smile. One of her hands lay casually on Patrick's thigh. Patrick looked almost sleepy, sleek and well fed, the look he had after—

Isabel took a sharp intake of breath. Patrick looked across at her, and very deliberately smiled.

12

Isabel let herself into Patrick's house on the Tuesday after the dinner party. From habit she bent down to pick up the post. As she straightened up she realised that Patrick was dressed and sitting on the sofa.

'Good morning,' she said. Usually she would have taken off her coat and slung it over the banisters, but today she stood there, fingering the middle button. 'You're up early.'

He stood up. 'I was waiting for you,' he said.

'We need to talk,' she said. She hesitated, then started to take her coat off, turning her back on him. He came and stood behind her.

'Isabel.' He pressed his mouth to her neck, ran his hand down her shirt. Once she would have swooned back against him, but today she felt cold, with no more interest than if he was tuning a dodgy radio. 'I've been waiting for you all weekend.'

'We need to talk,' she said again, moving away from him. 'About Victoria.'

'She's irrelevant,' he said, following her.

She spun round. 'And what about me?' All the emotion that she'd been feeling flooded her mind, anger melting the cold indifference she had been maintaining. She hit him, and then again, her fists pounding into his chest. 'Am I irrelevant too?'

He grabbed her wrists and kissed her though she struggled against him, his mouth on hers, and suddenly she was kissing him back, and they were snatching at each other's clothes, desperate for each other, and all she could think of was how much she wanted him, and then he was inside her and her back was pounding against the cold flagstone floor.

Afterwards she lay on the floor, her back aching, energy leaching out of her. She felt too feeble to move. She turned her head towards Patrick lying beside her.

'What do I mean to you?' she whispered.

He kissed her neck, her hair. His voice was muffled but she heard him clearly. 'Everything,' he said. 'You mean everything.'

'And Victoria?'

Patrick sat up. 'What about her?' he said, and started to get dressed.

'You're sleeping with her.'

'So what? You sleep with your husband, don't you? Every bloody night, and I don't complain.'

'We haven't for ages,' Isabel said, starting to get dressed herself in her cold and crumpled clothes.

'Oh, sure,' Patrick said, shrugging his shirt on and stalking off to the kitchen.

'No, really,' Isabel said, wriggling into her skirt. She couldn't remember the last time, wondering if the night when she had shouted at Neil was really the last time he had approached her. She'd become so absorbed in her affair with Patrick that she'd lost track of time. Her clothes felt horribly uncomfortable, twisted and damp, as she followed Patrick to the kitchen.

Patrick seemed on a mission to slam all the kitchen cupboard doors while taking out the new cafetière and a single mug.

'I don't know why you're so cross,' Isabel said. 'If anything, it's me who should be cross. Doing it under my nose like that.'

'I asked you first: you wouldn't, she would.' Crash. Any minute the new cafetière would be following its predecessor into the dustbin. 'I think the word is prick tease.'

Isabel was shocked by his crudeness. 'That's a horrible thing to say.'

'It's true. Isn't it?'

'I didn't know you could be so cruel.'

'Perhaps we don't know each other very well.' He fiddled with the signet ring on his little finger, then sighed. When he spoke his voice was quieter, more measured. 'You were waving your husband under my nose. How do you think I felt?'

'I don't know. I don't know how you feel.'

He stared out of the window, his mood unfathomable. Isabel felt confused, trying to understand why he was so angry. Her lower back was sore.

'You've always known I was married,' she tried, 'so why does it make a difference now?'

He hunched his shoulders and turned away from her.

'If you won't talk to me, how can I understand?' she cried. She wanted to go to him, to touch him, turn him round to face her. But his back was rigid.

'I'm going to start working upstairs. There's a lot to do,' she said, although she knew that the only job with any urgency was locking herself in the bathroom and crying. Just as she was through the kitchen door he called her name.

'Yes?' she said from inside the living room, not wanting to appear at his beck and call by going back, but longing for him to come to her, for this not to be the beginning of the end.

'Do you love me?'

Isabel stared at the ceiling to try to keep the brimming tears from overflowing. How can he even ask me this? she wondered. She didn't know how she felt. 'No falling in love. That's what you said. No strings, no ties, no responsibilities, no nothing.' She kept her voice level as if it didn't matter, and it flashed into her mind that she'd become good at deceit.

'So I did.'

Isabel waited for him to say more, or to come out from the kitchen, but there was nothing but silence. It was ridiculous for them to be in separate rooms but she didn't move and neither did he. After a while she collected the post from where she'd dumped it on the stairs and went up to the office, her feet heavy on the treads and her whole body aching as if she were climbing Mount Everest without oxygen. This is it, she thought. This is the beginning of the end.

Patrick was irritable for the rest of the day, shouting at her for losing some vital telephone number, shouting again when she told him she wouldn't be in next week because of half term. Later in the afternoon, she looked up from the computer to discover him watching her, but she couldn't read his expression and he left the room before she could ask him what he wanted.

The next day Patrick was out most of the time with a client. At least, that was what he said, although she wasn't sure if it was true. He kissed her gently before leaving, but a kiss could mean anything, she thought. Or nothing. She started to think about money. She hated the idea of discussing it with Patrick, especially in his present mood, but she couldn't work for nothing. She began to flick through her diary to check the dates she'd worked and caught sight of Frances's address and phone number in Thailand.

Her hands shaking, she dialled the number. They're seven hours ahead, she thought, she's bound to be in, perhaps making tea for the children.

'It's me, Isabel' she said, when the phone was answered. 'I can't talk long, I'm using the office phone.'

'Naughty girl,' Frances said, her familiar voice distorted by heavy crackling. 'But lovely to hear you. Is everything okay?'

'Yes, fine.' Isabel hesitated. How to start? 'I'm thinking about giving up my job.'

'Is that why you're calling? I thought you were loving working, you lucky thing. God, it's so boring out here at the moment, I wish I were you. And the humidity! Is it raining in England?'

'I'm not sure . . .' The hissing noise on the phone sounded as if Frances was in the middle a tropical storm.

'I've been nagging David for us to go back home, but no luck so far.'

'I thought you were having a good time,' Isabel said, confused at the direction the conversation was going. Frances started to talk about living in Thailand, chattering as if she hadn't spoken to anyone all day, which Isabel knew from her own experience might be true. The loneliness of the ex-pat wife. But she couldn't concentrate on what Frances was saying.

'I've had an affair but it's breaking up,' Isabel blurted out across the stream of talk.

'Breaking up? Am I? The line's not good this end either.' Above the background hiss Isabel could hear other voices. 'Look, love, I've got to go and feed my ravening hordes. Send me an email and tell me all about it. Love to Neil and the children. Bye!'

Isabel put the phone down, feeling lonelier than she'd ever felt before.

On Thursday morning first thing, before she had time to lose heart, she laid the envelope containing her invoice in front of Patrick, who was working at the kitchen table.

He looked up at her, and reached out an arm to pull her towards him. 'What's this?' he said, with a smile in his voice as if it might be an invitation to a party or some other pleasant function, as he ripped open the envelope and pulled out the invoice. His expression changed. 'What's this?' he repeated, in quite a different tone.

'An invoice for the work I've done,' she said, faltering. He took his arm away from her.

'You said that's what I was to do,' she added, standing on one leg in embarrassment. She'd only invoiced him for half the hours she had been at the office, on the grounds that they might have been making love for the other half. It didn't come to very much, but it was something.

Someone rapped at the door. 'I'll get it,' she said, glad for an excuse to escape.

A deliveryman stood outside, almost hidden behind an enormous bouquet of flowers.

'There you go, love,' he said, pushing the flowers into Isabel's hands.

'No, that can't be right. You must have the wrong address,' Isabel said, pushing the flowers back.

'Freeman? Number forty-five, Downton Road?'

'Yes, but are you sure?' Isabel took the flowers from him.

'Someone loves you, sweetheart. Don't knock it.' He winked at her before going down the path.

There must have been at least a hundred flowers in the bouquet. Isabel had to cradle it, almost overwhelmed by the scent from the lilies and freesias – freesias, at the end of October. Isabel looked for the card with trembling fingers.

'*Mi perdone, carissima*' it read.

Patrick. She looked up from the flowers. He was leaning against the kitchen door, watching her.

'They're amazing. Thank you.'

'The timing was interesting.' His voice was cold, his face withdrawn. He had the invoice in his hand.

'Patrick, I can't work for nothing.' She hugged the preposterous flowers to her. 'We agreed this is what we'd do.'

'I'll write you a cheque,' he said, turned abruptly and went back into the kitchen. She hesitated, then followed him in.

'There you are.' He held out a cheque to her. She disengaged a hand from the flowers and took the cheque.

'Thank you.'

He sat down at the table and started to read as if she wasn't there.

Isabel put the flowers in the sink.

'Patrick.' She touched his shoulder. 'What does the card mean?'

'Nothing.' He shook her hand away. 'Absolutely nothing.'

On Friday morning Isabel consulted the 'to do' list she'd made late on Thursday evening. Drat, she'd forgotten to remind Neil about coming home early. She thought about phoning him at work, but decided against it. He'd probably have remembered and there was something offputting about phoning the office on such a wifely task. Her at home. The little woman. She pulled a face. She was sure he would remember.

She'd meant to start cleaning the house in anticipation of her parents-in-law's visit during the week but each evening she'd felt dragged down with worry about the situation with Patrick. For the first time in weeks she'd eaten her way through a packet of biscuits, not tasting them but finding comfort in the rhythmic munching, the sweetness.

Cleaning the house in anticipation of the in-laws worked off some of her spare energy. Isabel scrubbed at floors, dusted the tops of the curtains and wiped dirty fingermarks off the woodwork. Pictures that had been lying against walls cocooned in bubble wrap were hung on the walls, Isabel whacking in picture hooks with an oversized hammer that made a satisfying thud. The company paid for transporting a container and a half, so their belongings were edited with each move, but she'd filled this permanent home quickly: toys waiting to be mended and spare legs from the new kitchen units saved 'just in case'. She opened a new roll of bin bags.

At midday she thought wistfully of swimming, of lying suspended in cool water, but there was too much to be done. Windows were washed, flowers arranged in vases of aspirin-laden water, toys put in graded ranks – big at the back, ranging down to the front row of tinies. A bit like war, she thought. The most vulnerable go over the top first while the big guns lie in safety deciding which way to jump.

She paid particular care to the guest bedroom, putting out new geranium-scented soap. There were so many flowers in Patrick's bouquet that each room could have a bunch. She'd have to tell Neil that she'd bought them in honour of his parents' visit, although he was unlikely to notice. More likely his mother would comment on the unnecessary extravagance. Still, the alternative was to put them in the bin. She popped some freesias, alstroemerias and a few fern fronds into a small milk jug. She hoped her mother-in-law wouldn't notice the chip. Fat chance. As she worked she listened to Radio Four, turned up loud to drown out the continuous murmur of dissent in her head. Miserable old cow. Coming to interfere. Not fair. Not fair.

Her lower back was still sore from Tuesday, the desperate coupling on the sitting-room floor. At the beginning of the affair she'd been excited by the roughness; common sense and rationality overcome by a more urgent force. Lust, she supposed. She felt as if she'd been sleepwalking and Patrick had woken her up. And there was no doubt that once you started thinking about sex, you became more interested. It was like buying a new car; suddenly the same model seemed to be everywhere, cruising down the street, popping up in advertisements.

But at the dinner party everything had changed, become complicated and dark. Poor Victoria. She'd looked so happy, her face lit up. Isabel wondered if that was how she'd looked after the first time with Patrick, and was amazed yet again that Neil hadn't noticed. She felt dishonest, sordid even. Oh, Patrick. Was he thinking of her, as she was of him? *Mi perdone* meant forgive me. She couldn't work out what he meant. Forgiveness for what he had done, or what he was going to do? He had been difficult on Thursday, irritable and cold, hardly speaking to her all day.

She plumped up the pillows on the guest bed, shaking them out and thumping them so they looked temptingly soft. The sheets were her best ones, properly ironed and put away with lavender bags. The dusty scent irritated her nose and she sneezed. One for sorrow. It seemed an easy prophesy. Why were mothers-in-law quite so irritating? Everyone she knew was driven mad by their mother-in-law. Except for the smug few who cooed over how wonderful theirs was, winners in the ma-in-law stakes. What was the problem? She had older women friends, got on well with the swimming-pool crowd, so it wasn't the generation gap. Perhaps it was the forced intimacy with strangers, the feeling that you had to get on. Or perhaps it was the power issue, suppressed for the sake of family harmony; like dogs, sniffing, circling, growling, but unwilling to fight outright.

Why do I feel the need to compete with her? she thought. The tidying, the cleaning, the Stepford wife stuff? It's so dishonest. Suddenly she laughed. Imagine what she'd say if I announced that I was being unfaithful? 'Whore, slut, always knew my Neil was too good for the likes of her.' She smoothed the bedspread with slow strokes, then straightened up, wincing as the pain in her back caught. And she'd probably be right. Neil doesn't deserve someone like me. Isabel looked about her. The room was ready, immaculate as a magazine set, a gleaming shrine to the benefits of Mr Sheen and dusters. There was no more she could do.

Neil stuck his head around the kitchen door just after Isabel brought the children back from school. She was trying to feed them without making any mess in the kitchen, an enterprise that was successfully tightening all her nerve endings.

'Hello, everybody.'

'Daddy!' Katie leapt up, knocking over her milk, and attached herself to Neil, clinging like a gibbon. Isabel mopped up silently, lips compressed into a straight line. Neil unpeeled Katie.

'No need to break my neck, poppet. Hi there, Michael.' He kissed the top of Michael's head, which Michael ducked with an embarrassed shrug of his shoulders. Isabel pushed a loose strand of hair out of her face with the back of her hand, and offered her cheek to be kissed.

'Any chance of some tea?' he said. 'I'm knackered.'

She made him a cup while he listened patiently to Katie explaining about some dreadful act of injustice at school. She desperately wanted him to look after the children so she could have a bath and wash her hair in preparation for the arrival of his parents. Her skin felt covered by a thin film of dirt that she longed to soak away. She put the mug of tea down in front of him.

'Look, would you mind if I had a five-minute lie down before I help?' he said.

'Is everything all right?'

'I'm fine, just a bit tired that's all.'

What's the point of coming back early if all you do is go to bed? she wanted to scream at him. And what about me? Don't I get to be tired too? But she suppressed her irritation. When all was said and done, her tiredness came from having an affair that was disintegrating whereas poor Neil was having to spend three hours a day commuting as well as often having to stay late at the office.

'It's fine,' she said, gently touching his shoulder. 'I've got everything ready. Go and relax.' He looked relieved.

'If you really don't mind . . .'

'Go on, before I make you wash the kitchen floor.'

He grimaced, kissed her cheek then went, taking his tea with him. Isabel could hear his feet treading heavily up the stairs to their bedroom. So much for helping. Never mind. Just so long as they didn't come early.

Whatever time they arrived it would have been too soon. But Isabel hadn't reckoned on their appearance before seven. At five thirty-five she registered the sound of a car engine outside, but ignored it, assuming it must be the neighbours. The front doorbell didn't ring, after all. She carried on mopping the kitchen floor, squeezing the grey water out with energy. It's a bad idea for me to do housework, she decided. It just makes me think mean thoughts. A puncture, exhaust dropped off, tragic accident on the motorway? The nice bit of her brain stopped there, deterred from continuing by thinking about how Neil would be upset. The wicked bit snuck in an image of her dressed in black, being wonderfully supportive, holding Neil's hand at the funeral. She slapped the mop back onto the terracotta tiles. She was just wondering if the police would telephone or call round in a car with flashing lights when a loud rap startled her. She clutched the mop in surprise as the very alive face of her mother-in-law loomed through the kitchen window.

'Cooee,' Moira said, her Exocet eyes pinpointing immediately the bit Isabel had missed. 'Sorry, I didn't mean to make you jump.'

Liar, thought Isabel, whose heart was pounding as if she had seen Frankenstein's monster. Still, two can play at that game. She put her perfect daughter-in-law face on.

'Moira. How wonderful to see you. And so early, too. The traffic must have been good.' She opened the kitchen door. 'Where's Ian?'

'Getting the luggage out of the car.' Moira ran one pearlised pink fingertip over the window sill, and sighed happily at the sight of dust. 'I thought we might be a wee bit early, so I came round the back to check you were here first.'

Isabel tried casually to tidy the mop and bucket away, a difficult task as it was full of soapy water. 'I didn't hear the front doorbell.'

'Och, I didn't want to bother you with that. Shouldn't you empty the water out before putting that away?'

'I will later.' Only two minutes and Isabel could feel her cheeks aching with the effort of keeping a welcoming expression on her face. 'I'll go and help Ian with your things.'

Neil's father was ponderously taking luggage out of the boot of the car, hampered by his walking stick, and the dog, a West Highland terrier, yapping at his heels. Isabel rushed to help take out a matching pair of suitcases, a travel rug and a carrier bag that clinked as she put it down. Please, Isabel prayed as she embraced Ian, not more whisky. Isabel took the two suitcases and went into the hall followed by the dog sniffing the corners suspiciously.

'Perhaps Buster can stay in the kitchen?' she asked, worried, as the dog seemed about to lift his leg against her Korean spice chest.

Moira shooed Buster into the kitchen and shut the door.

'I know you don't like dogs, Isabel,' she said.

How to say, I do like dogs, just not yours? Isabel decided it was best to say nothing and led the way upstairs to the guest bedroom, Ian hauling himself up as if the stairs were a rope ladder.

'I expect you'd like to wash and relax for a little,' she said hopefully. 'Come down and have a drink when you're ready.' She escaped without waiting for their reply. She carried on down the landing and gently opened the door to her bedroom.

'Neil? Your parents have arrived.'

He was lying on the bed fully clothed as if he had just decided to rest for a second before being overcome by sleep. His face had sagged with the weight of sleep into a younger, more relaxed Neil, closer to the man she remembered under wide African skies. Isabel carefully undid his laces and eased his shoes off, lifted his lower legs so they were properly on the bed, then covered him with the bedspread, and drew the curtains. He was snoring slightly when she left the room. Isabel ran downstairs to the sitting room where the children were watching television, the toys Isabel had so carefully tidied earlier spread out all over the carpet.

'Quick, quick, pick everything up,' she hissed. 'Granny and Grandpa are here.'

'Now?' Michael said, not looking up.

'Yes, now. We've only got a few minutes before they'll be down. Thank you, darlings, that's brilliant,' she added to encourage them as the children, faces turned towards the television, started to collect their toys up in slow motion. She nipped into the downstairs cloakroom and quickly brushed her hair. She wanted to wash her face but heard the sound of heavy feet on the stairs so contented herself with moistening a bit of loo paper and wiping the dust streaks off before going into the sitting room.

'What can I get you to drink?' She smiled at them, using her best hostess smile, and surreptitiously tried to push one of Katie's plastic ponies out of sight behind the sofa with her foot. The children had half cleared up and then scarpered.

'We've brought you a little gift,' rumbled her father-in-law, holding out the carrier bag.

'Whisky! How super.' I'll be saying jolly hockeysticks in a minute, Isabel thought in desperation. 'Is that what you'd like?'

'Well, now, that would be an idea,' he said, as if he didn't have a whisky and soda at six o'clock every evening without fail. Isabel poured him a drink from the bottle she'd opened the last visit but three. The intervening bottles she'd given away. She realised that Ian thought it was a great treat for them to have whisky, as so often they were living in countries where alcohol was banned, even though they'd explained that the authorities usually turned a blind eye to drinking within the ex-pat community. She'd given up wondering if they would ever notice that neither she nor Neil drank whisky.

'Moira?' She noticed Neil's mother scan the drinks tray. I mustn't be paranoid, she told herself. She couldn't possibly be deliberately choosing something that was not there. She was.

'A gin and tonic, please. If it's no bother.'

'None at all.' Isabel answered just as sweetly. 'I put the gin and tonic water in the fridge to keep them cool.' One up to me, she thought, as she went to fetch them, inadvertently letting Buster out as she did so.

'When does Neil get in?' Moira's expression was as sour as the lemon in her gin as she fondled Buster's ears.

'He's here already, but went upstairs to lie down.'

'Is he ill?' Moira looked concerned.

'No, just a bit tired I think.'

'The poor boy. And to think I'm sitting here drinking.' She glared at Isabel as if it were her fault and stood up.

'He's sleeping.' Isabel stood up too.

'I'll just take a wee look.'

'I really think it would be better if—' Isabel started, but Moira had stalked out of the room, leaving her to talk to the back of her retreating twinset. It struck Isabel that, from behind, her mother-in-law's silhouette was just like the symbol of a woman on loo doors – tiny upper body with broad, spreading skirt and tapering legs. Isabel shrugged apologetically at Ian, trying to think of a conversational starter while Buster sniffed round her ankles as if choosing the best place to bite.

'The traffic wasn't bad on the way here then? You made good time.'

It wasn't much, but Ian was off, front runner in the traffic relay stakes, describing the route they had chosen, others that had been considered and discarded, and the bad driving encountered on the road. The rot had set in during the Sixties, apparently, which opened up whole new conversational avenues: homosexuals, hippies, asylum seekers, all of whom deserved to be shot.

As he sat his jacket fell open, revealing braces pulling his trousers up towards his armpits, like an old man. But he is an old man, Isabel reminded herself. Old and set in his ways. His voice resonated around the room, bouncing off the ceiling as if he was summing up in a council meeting or boardroom, both arenas in which he'd had considerable experience. His complete confidence that she would listen attentively mesmerised her into sitting still. But, but, but, she wanted to say. That's just not true. But then, what was the point? He was hardly going to change his opinions because they so dismayed her, a mere woman. Just be thankful that the bile had bypassed Neil, who was miraculously a normal human being.

Fortunately, before she'd bitten her tongue off with the pressure of holding it between her teeth, the children created a diversion by coming in. Ian embraced them stiffly, tweed suit rough and unyielding. Isabel often thought that he would have been good with children, if only he knew where to start. But distance was ingrained from an Edwardian-style childhood, confirmed with his own children, and then the accident that had made him nearly bedridden for two years when Neil was in his early teens. Neil had ended up playing head of the household while his father recovered. Ian was left with a pronounced limp and a sudden ageing that moved him from his prime into old age.

Now Ian held a protective hand around his glass as Katie lolled against his armchair, her shrill voice explaining exactly how chocolate Labradors were bred while her grandfather pressed against the seatback in unconscious alarm. He found Michael easier, his passions for fishing and racing cars safer topics for masculine conversation than Katie's innocent twitterings on dog breeding. From the comfort of his chair he promised the boy grand fishing trips on lakes near his home. Isabel twitched. She knew from past experience that his promises were easily made, equally easily forgotten. It seemed dishonest, somehow, to make the child promises that would never be fulfilled. But then, who was she to accuse another of dishonesty? She felt her cheeks go red.

'I'll just go and start seeing about dinner,' she mumbled and escaped to the kitchen where she tripped over the forgotten mop and bucket. Dirty water splashed over the clean floor. She slopped at the grey tide ineffectually, sloshing water back into the bucket with angry jerks, her lower back creasing in pain as she bent over the mop. Tears pricked at her eyes. Damn. She stood for a second, clutching the mop, a latter-day Cinderella. But no ball in prospect, no Prince Charming, no Fairy Godmother. She started to work more methodically. Perhaps that was what Cinders found, that happily ever after just meant more of the same. Finished, she poured the water down the outside drain, watching it swirl away under a froth of bubbles.

Back in the kitchen she turned the oven on ready for their meal. Smoked salmon roulade, then pheasants in apple and cream sauce and Pommes Dauphinoises, followed by lemon tart. Too much cream, too much stodge for everyday, but just right for drowning bad feelings in calories and carbohydrates. And it was easier to cook well with lots of butter and cream: everything tasted good, if heavy on the cholesterol. Still, one meal wouldn't matter. They can sleep it off later, she assuaged her conscience.

She took the pheasants out of the fridge. At this time of year they were cheap, the area being rife with shooting estates. The last two weekends Michael had collected spent cartridge cases found on walks – green, yellow, red, the occasional black. Isabel kept finding them in pockets and behind cupboards. The birds looked unappetising, a mottled mixture of grey and purple. She draped them with flaccid strips of streaky bacon, drizzled them with oil, chucked a few onions into the roasting dish around the birds and shoved it in the oven, slamming the door shut with her foot.

Halfway through beating the salmon mousse for the roulade, Moira came in, shoes clacking like tongues.

'Is Neil up yet?'

'He's poorly.' Moira's mouth compressed.

'Really?' Isabel blinked. 'I thought he was just tired.'

'The boy's exhausted,' Moira said. She obviously felt it was all Isabel's fault. 'And going down with flu.'

'Poor Neil,' Isabel murmured, concentrating on spreading mousse over the roulade base. If you didn't get it even, it squidged out of the sides and bulged ominously. His mother sniffed loudly.

'I'm going to make him a hot toddy.'

'Oh. Help yourself. Just ask if you need anything.' She started to roll up the roulade, manoeuvring the greaseproof paper carefully and ignoring the sounds of slammed doors and wrenched drawers as her mother-in-law progressed round the kitchen cupboards.

'Do you not have a lemon squeezer, Isabel?'

'No, I usually use a fork. Easier to wash up.'

'I see.' More cupboard rummaging. 'What's this?' Moira pulled out an electric citrus press.

'I'd forgotten I had that. Sorry.' She must think I'm mad, Isabel thought. Still at least she'll be pleased to have a bit more evidence of my hopelessness. She finished the roulade. 'There.' She poked a bit of filling back in, then took a step back to admire the roulade, plump as a pillow. The decoration in the book had involved skinning cherry tomatoes, but she didn't feel that she had the time, now or ever, to fiddle with tomato skins and boiling water, however easily they were supposed to slip off. It'd have to do as it was. She glanced at her watch. She ought to peel some potatoes – they really should have gone in with the birds – but she needed to get the children ready for bed. Executive decision. It'd have to be mashed potato. She called the children to her and went upstairs.

Once Katie was in the bath, Isabel slipped in to see

Neil, still lying on the bed with the curtains drawn. Isabel noticed that the hot toddy, now cool, was undrunk on the bedside cupboard. He was awake.

'Your mother thinks you're dying.'

'I am.' He flopped his head back and rolled his eyes.

'Mmm. I need a potato peeler.'

He started to get up. 'I'm sorry, I'll come and help.'

Isabel pushed him back down.

'Don't worry. If the worst comes to the worst we'll have instant mash and frozen peas. I only have to boil a kettle for that. Your ma thinks I'm hopeless as it is, so I might as well prove it.' She could see that he was torn between two loyalties, and felt guilty again. Why should he feel loyal to her, when she— She kissed him on the forehead, wincing at the pain in her back as she leant forward.

'Are you really ill?'

'No. She just likes to fuss. A bit under the weather, maybe.' He rubbed one eye and yawned. 'It's been a tiring week. Office politics.'

'I'm sorry.' She realised how little she knew about his work at the moment. 'Do you want to talk about it?'

'Do you want to listen?' The question hung in the air between them.

'Of course,' she said finally. 'I always want to listen.'

'You seem rather preoccupied at the moment.'

'Sorry. I don't mean to be.'

'No.' He smiled and took her hand. 'Never mind.'

Isabel felt like crying. Her hand in his felt useless as if, although it touched, it could not connect. There seemed a huge chasm between them, completely impossible to cross. So many things to say, which could not be said.

'I've had a lover, but I think we're breaking up,' she wanted to tell him, and have him comfort her. 'I'm confused, I don't know what to do. It was exciting at first, but now it's something else. I'm so unhappy.' And Neil would cuddle her and say 'There, there, never mind, I still love you'.

But that wasn't going to happen, was it? However tolerant Neil might be, he was hardly likely to tolerate that. How appropriate that the punishment for adultery under sharia law was stoning. She could imagine the weight of the stones, heavy as lies, crushing the spirit. So many deceits, pressing down like stones, the only possible release being confession. But why should Neil share the burden of her guilt?

'I'm sorry,' she repeated, shaking her head.

The evening was a disaster. Michael and Katie, oblivious to their grandparents' belief that children should be seen and not heard, refused to stay in bed. Isabel would gently return them to their rooms, read them stories, see eyelids droop, lips relax, breathing become softer. Then she would tiptoe out, at which point they would catapult up, wide awake. Katie was the worst, impossible to reason with. Michael at least was bribable, negotiating successfully for five pounds in exchange for staying in bed. Katie kept on appearing at the door wanting a drink, a biscuit, a story. Wanting a good smack, according to Moira.

'When Neil and Heather were little—' she started, but Isabel had ushered Katie out and escaped upstairs. Pointless to even think of getting into a conversation about the rights and wrongs of smacking. Bad wife, now bad mother.

On Saturday the children were up bright and early despite the lack of sleep. They ran out of energy in the afternoon, halfway round a nearby stately home that

Moira wanted to visit. They all squeezed into Isabel's car because Ian, having secured prime position right outside the front door, didn't want to move the car in case he missed the space on the return. Isabel surveyed a half-empty street and kept her mouth shut yet again.

It was the last day the house was open that year and the grounds had a dead look, a few shrivelled rosebuds forlornly clinging onto leafless bushes. Katie clung to Isabel's arm, weighing her down like a floppy anchor, while Michael became disobedient and surly, scuffing his shoes on the gravel drive. They squabbled over who was going to walk Buster around the grounds and their crossness transmitted down the lead to the dog, who became crotchety, finally nipping Katie on the ankle.

Back home, ankle kissed better and suitably covered in plasters, Katie decided to eat her tea in front of the television. Michael tripped her up – an accident or on purpose? Who knew? Certainly not Isabel, who had to try to maintain both the peace and a smile on her face. Katie had dropped her plate so Buster eagerly devoured the food to Katie's accompanying wails.

'He's on a special diet,' Moira said, as if Isabel had spilt Katie's food deliberately. 'You have to take on the responsibility when you look after a dog, you know. Being with people keeps them like puppies, stops them growing up and fending for themselves. You have to look after them, or they won't manage.'

Isabel privately thought that Buster was managing pretty well. At least he had enjoyed his supper, because she was sure no one at the table had. It seemed pointless having Ian and Moira there: they moaned on the phone that they were longing to see their grandchildren but once there, they either ignored or criticised them and, by default, Isabel. She wondered what her own parents would have been like as grandparents.

Sunday morning, and yet another meal. Neil was downstairs cooking bacon and eggs, judging by the aroma permeating the whole house, when she heard his voice.

'Bel? Can you get the phone?'

She stopped putting Katie's clean clothes away.

'Sure,' she called back, making for the hall phone and picking it up. 'Hello?'

'Isabel,' said a familiar deep voice. Patrick. She pressed the receiver close to her ear as if any stray words might escape into the house.

'What do you want?' she muttered.

'To see you.'

'Why?'

'To say sorry. I behaved like a complete shit on Thursday.'

'Yes, you did,' she whispered, turning around to face the wall and wrapping the phone cable around her body.

'Can you get away?'

'Now?' He'd never asked to meet up outside office hours before. 'I've got the in-laws staying.'

He laughed. 'All the more reason to come.' His voice changed, became serious. 'Please, just for a few minutes. I've got something I want to talk to you about.'

'I don't know . . .' She twisted the cable round between her fingers.

'Meet me at the Italian café in half an hour.'

Neil's voice. 'Who is it?'

'No one,' she called back to him. She waited but Neil made no reply. 'Okay, in half an hour,' she whispered to Patrick, and put the phone down.

She went into the kitchen. Neil was in an apron,

pushing bacon around a frying pan while Ian and Moira read the Sunday papers.

'Who was that?' Neil said.

'No one,' she said. 'Someone selling double-glazing.'

'It's outrageous, badgering people in their homes,' Moira said. 'And on a Sunday too. You ought to go ex-directory.'

'You're right,' Isabel said, sidling up to stand next to Neil. 'I've forgotten to get anything for pudding,' she said to him in an undertone. 'I'm just going to pop out to the supermarket, okay?'

'I thought you'd done apple crumble.'

'It went wrong,' she whispered, hoping he wouldn't think to look at the back of the fridge. 'And I haven't got enough apples to make another.'

'I'm sure they won't mind not having pudding.'

'No, no. You know how your father loves apple crumble,' she said, hating herself for the lies.

'What's the problem, Neil?' Moira said.

'Nothing,' he said, automatically covering for her. 'Isabel just needs to go out for a bit.' He tilted his head at her, telling her to go. Feeling horribly guilty Isabel ran upstairs, grabbed her make-up bag, and then escaped from the house. Once round the corner she stopped the car and did her face, obliterating the dark shadows under her eyes with foundation.

It had started to rain by the time she had parked, the sort of fine rain that deceives you into thinking it isn't wet, until you're drenched to the skin. Patrick was sitting with an espresso inside the Italian café opposite the bookshop.

He looked up and smiled at her.

'You came.'

'You said you wanted to talk to me about something.'

'Can I get you a coffee? No,' he stopped himself, 'you'll want a tea. You see, I do notice.' He went up to the counter and ordered. 'Would you like something to eat? A *palmieri*? Or a *bombalone* – that's an Italian sort of dough-nut; they're very good.'

'No thanks,' Isabel shook her head, and a scatter of raindrops fell from her hair. She took off her mac and draped it over the back of her chair. She'd not been here before, although she knew it was one of Patrick's regular places. The only decent espresso in town, according to him. It was surprisingly busy for a rainy Sunday morning, the tables half-full, tinny music blaring out with the man operating the espresso machine singing along. Condensation was dribbling down the plate glass window at the front. The walls were covered with bright posters of crumbling ancient monuments against cobalt blue skies. Sicilia – Roma – Napoli. Patrick brought over her tea and she had a moment of déjà vu. Of course, she remembered, Patrick bringing over the drinks that first time in the pub, when he'd kissed her. That had been the beginning of everything. It came to her then that this might be the end of everything, that this might be what he wanted to talk to her about.

What had he said? 'No regrets, no falling in love, no tears when we part.' Well, she could manage the last part. She sat up straight in her chair, shoulders back.

Patrick settled next to her. 'There's a *pasticceria* round the corner from Santa Maria del Popolo in Rome that makes marvellous *bombalone*. I used to go with my mother on Sunday mornings, the first year I was with her. I'd grown about a foot in two months and was always hungry so she filled me up with *bombalone* and *suppli*.'

'*Suppli?*'

'They're fried rice balls, with a lump of mozzarella inside. When you bite into them you find runny mozzarella. Delicious, but they must be fresh.'

'I can't stay long,' she said.

'No.' He reached out and took her hand, his thumb stroking hers. They sat in silence, while the staff greeted other customers and took orders with a clatter of cutlery. The music moved on to grand opera, and the man sitting on the next table turned the pages of the weekend papers in a flurry of newsprint. He seemed vaguely familiar to Isabel, but he disappeared from her mind as she stared at Patrick's hand holding hers. She felt she could have stayed like that forever. His hand was warm, still tanned. Immediately she thought of the photograph at the office of Patrick and Victoria, set against cobalt blue skies.

She disengaged her hand. Patrick hardly seemed to notice, he was looking at the window. 'Patrick? What do you want to tell me?' she said.

'When I was a child, it always seemed to be raining, just like this,' he said, still looking at the window where the condensation had made rivulets down the inside.

'That's so sad,' she said, thinking of the little boy, abandoned by his mother. 'I think that's one of the saddest things I've ever heard.'

'I don't mean it to be. It's just a fact. It is wetter in the North West than in the South East.' He gave himself a little shake. 'Still, I didn't want to see you just to talk about the weather, although that does play its part.'

'What do you mean?'

'As you know, I hate the English weather. Here we are, end of October, it's pissing down, and there's probably another six months of it to come.' He sipped his coffee. 'I'm thinking of moving back to Italy.'

Isabel was so surprised she could have fallen off her chair. 'When?'

'I don't know. Soon, possibly. It depends.'

'On Victoria?'

'Partly.' He swirled the black coffee round the cup, watching it as if hypnotised. When he spoke his voice was so soft Isabel had to lean forward to hear him. 'I was so angry with you at that stupid dinner party. I still am angry.'

'Why? What did I do?'

'Nothing. Everything. You were beautiful and desirable and married to someone else. It's funny, but I've never minded before, never felt bothered by sharing. That side of it is usually dead anyway within the first few years of marriage.' He looked at her directly. 'But you seemed to be very much a couple.'

'You know that . . . We've already talked about this,' she said.

Patrick drained his coffee cup then gestured with it to the man behind the counter. '*Senta*,' he called, '*encore, per favore*.' He turned back to Isabel and spoke briskly. 'I could stay here and marry Victoria. She's good-looking, rich and for some strange reason, keen to marry me. I think she thinks that she can change me.'

'And can she?'

'No.' It was a bald statement, spoken so flatly that Isabel knew it was true. He paused, cleared his throat. 'Someone else could though.'

He paused and she wondered if he meant her. But after the dinner party that seemed unlikely.

'Ah, *grazie*,' he said to the waiter who replaced his

espresso cup. 'Anyway, she wants to move to the Midlands, which is where her family come from. I want to give up the business: it's not making any money and I hate dealing with clients, they're all so stupid, and the paperwork bores me to tears, as you know. Victoria will support me while I look around for something else to do. Rather a modern arrangement, don't you think?' His voice was harsh.

'And the alternative?' Isabel whispered.

'The alternative is to move to Rome. I could do something in computers but I'm fed up with them. My mother's current husband wants to start exporting into the US; he could use an English-speaking partner. I could try it out, see if I liked it. If not, there'd be other opportunities.'

'It sounds a bit uncertain.'

'Life's more fun without a safety net.' He grinned at her, his eyes teasing her. He looked like Michael looked when he was planning some adventure. Then he shrugged. 'But if you insist on being practical I have a flat in Rome that I've had for years. It's let out at the moment, but I could move there, sell up here and live off the capital for a while. What do you think?'

'Me?'

'Yes, you. What do you think?'

'I think,' Isabel said slowly. 'I think I'd hate to be Victoria.'

'D'you think she'd be unhappy? Mmm. Possibly.'

'You really are a shit sometimes. Don't you think of anyone else's feelings?' She felt on the edge of tears. 'Look, I must go. I've got to get back.' She started to stand up but he held her arm.

'Don't go yet.'

'Why not?'

'I haven't said . . . I haven't told you . . . Sit down, just for a minute. Please.' She perched on the edge of her seat, hardly able to breathe.

'I said I was angry with you that night. I still am angry. Angry because . . . I don't find this sort of thing easy, Isabel. Talking about things. You know that.' He looked up at the travel bureau posters, all bright and sunny, while the rain fell outside. 'I've been very happy these last months with you. Happier than I can remember.' His hand shook as he picked up his coffee cup. 'I'm good at taking. Take what's offered, that's what I've done. Take and you don't get hurt.' He smiled at her, and she felt as if her heart had melted. 'It's asking that's hard.'

She clasped her hands in front of her to stop herself from touching him. 'What do you want to ask me?'

'I want you to leave Neil. I want you to leave Neil and come to Rome with me.' He sat very still. 'Will you? Will you come with me?'

13

Isabel and Neil stood in the doorway, waving goodbye to Moira and Ian. Through the car window Isabel could see Moira waving maps about, her lips moving as she gave instructions to Ian. They were going to see Neil's sister, Heather, breaking the long journey back North. Isabel waved her arm mechanically, a fixed smile on her face like a mask. Neil had one arm around her as they stood in the doorway of their suburban house, with their two children – one boy one girl, neatly separated by two years – in front of them. The perfect family. Except instead of stormy skies and sodden leaves in the street, the mother was seeing blue skies and grape vines.

'Well, that's that,' Neil said, as they finally left. 'I think they enjoyed themselves.'

Isabel was jolted back to raining reality. 'Do you think so? All your mother does is complain.'

'She likes complaining,' he said. 'Gives her something to think about apart from Dad's health.' They went inside and Neil offered to give Isabel a hand clearing up.

'There's no rugby on this afternoon then,' Isabel said, not quite succeeding in keeping her voice neutral. If Neil heard the touch of acidity he didn't notice.

'No, there was flooding in Widnes.'

The detritus of Sunday lunch was stacked in the kitchen. Isabel started to fill the dishwasher, scraping plates into the bin, sorting cutlery. She worked quickly, wanting to get upstairs and be on her own at last. What was she to do about Patrick? Rome sounded glamorous and exciting, but terribly hand-to-mouth. If she took the children it would mean giving them the same sort of childhood she'd had. Neil stripped the remaining meat off the roast chicken and put it in a dish.

'I find them difficult too, you know,' he said as he covered the dish with foil and put it in the fridge. 'It's not just you.'

Isabel looked up, amazed. She had never heard Neil utter a word of criticism about his parents before. 'But they're always saying how wonderful you are.'

'All those digs about the business.' He picked up the tin containing the remainder of the vegetables.

'Your father's business? I didn't think you had anything to do with it.'

'Exactly. But I was supposed to take it over. Fourth generation and all that. Founded by my great-grandfather, got to keep it in the family.' He leant back against the counter. 'All my life I've done what they wanted, been responsible. I don't think it occurred to them that I wouldn't come back and take over. So when I said no . . . The irony is that Heather would have jumped at the chance, but it didn't cross the old man's mind to ask his daughter. So he sold up instead.'

Isabel frowned. 'I don't remember this. When was it?'

'When you were expecting Michael. They'd assumed we'd come home when we had children.'

'You didn't say anything to me.'

'No.' He looked sheepish. 'I was worried you might want to come back.'

'You decided not to tell me?'

'I had to make the decision on my own. Decide what I wanted.'

'You didn't tell me.' Isabel couldn't believe that he would have kept such a thing secret.

'I didn't want to worry you.'

'It's like you've got a secret life.'

'Don't be ridiculous.' He shoved the tin in the fridge and slammed the door shut. 'It's water under the bridge, now. Except Mum keeps on going on about Dad's health as if it's my fault.'

'Why should it be?'

'Oh, he could have sold up and retired years ago, he was only hanging on until I came back to the UK, and now his health is ruined. That sort of thing.'

Isabel thought back over the weekend. Moira certainly did go on a lot about Ian's health, but she'd never thought it was directed at Neil. If anything she had assumed it was directed at her for not looking after Neil properly, who worked so hard.

'I'm not sure coming back was a good idea,' he said abruptly. 'Life's more complicated here.'

And how, thought Isabel. Then she became wary. Did he know something about Patrick? She started to stack the glasses. 'In what way?' she said as casually as possible.

'Things. People. We seemed happier abroad. Things were settled.'

'Perhaps too settled.'

'Maybe.' Neil looked at the floor and jangled the change in his pocket.

'I know you don't like me working—' she started to say, picking her words carefully, but Neil cut across her.

'Someone said something about that man the other day. They said he has a dreadful reputation.'

'Which man?' She knew what he was going to say before he said it.

'Your boss. Patrick Sherwin.'

'Oh, him,' Isabel said as if she knew thousands of men with dreadful reputations. To her surprise she was completely calm and in control of herself. She felt like an actor who knew all the lines by heart, and all she had to do was say them for the play to carry on.

'Yes, I've heard that too. Who was it who said it to you?'

'It doesn't matter; it was just in passing. I'm sorry, I shouldn't have said anything.' He looked so guilty that she felt sorry for him. Poor Neil, always trying to do what was best.

'No, it's fine. I don't mind, really. He does have a dreadful reputation, I understand.' I bet it was George, she thought. It's the sort of mean thing he'd do, telling Neil about Patrick. She could just see him, nudge, nudge, wink, wink, old boy, better watch the wife. But he didn't know anything. He couldn't. And no one knew anything about Patrick's plans, except her. She managed to squeeze a last mug into the top rack and closed the dishwasher. She still felt completely calm. 'Patrick's going out with that girl, Victoria. You met her, remember? At Helen and George's last weekend.'

'I know.'

'Well. There you are then.' She looked around the tidy kitchen. 'That's about it here. I've got a slight headache; I think I'm going to have a lie down for ten minutes.' She left the kitchen and went upstairs, adrenaline starting to pump into her system so her hand trembled on the banister rail. She made the bedroom and fell onto the bed, hands over her face. It was true she had a headache, her brain bulged with information: Neil with secrets, Neil asking about Patrick, Patrick asking her to go to Rome with him. She closed her eyes tightly and rolled herself up in the duvet.

Rome.

She'd had fantasies about going off to Italy with Patrick, but she had never really thought he would ask her to leave Neil and go with him. The last week in the house she had thought he almost hated her. There was no tenderness in the way he took her. But did he love her? Last week she would have said not. But now? She remembered him that morning, sitting in the café with his hand trembling as he asked her to go with him.

She thought back to the kiss outside the pub, the first time during the thunderstorm on the kitchen table. She stretched out, feeling her toes spread out, her fingers extend. Her body felt strong, tight around the middle, muscles firm from swimming. Use it or lose it, she thought, forgiving herself for the smugness. She spread her hand out on her stomach and could feel the heat of her palm, the skin of her stomach not stretched flat between her hip bones admittedly, but still smooth and soft, with the fullness of a ripe nectarine. Not something flabby and bloated. She closed her eyes thinking of the moment, that first time, when she had wrapped her legs around him and pulled him in deeper. It had been good. No, more than that. Wonderful.

She stretched out again, luxuriating in her body. The physical side of her affair with Patrick would be hard to give up if she stayed behind. But if she went with him, the physical side might dwindle, as it had with Neil. She and Neil had been happy when they first married, apparently well matched in their needs and desires. And if the physical side diminished with Patrick, what was left? I hardly know him, she thought. I know a bit about his background – all those sisters – but I don't know what films he likes, or which books. She imagined each room in his house, trying to remember if there were bookcases or, more likely, cardboard boxes full of books. She couldn't visualise any. Perhaps Caro had taken them all after the divorce, although Caro didn't sound like much of a reader either.

All we have in common is sex. Sex, with no expectations, no demands, that's all we've offered each other. What we agreed to offer each other. Until now. Now he wants me to leave Neil and go to Rome with him. No, he asked me. She shut her eyes remembering his face, lined with anxiety, as he asked. It had cost him a lot to ask. Perhaps he did love her.

And then there was Neil. Steady, reliable Neil who had kept a secret from her for nearly ten years. Except that he didn't think it a secret. It was a decision he'd had to make on his own, he'd said. She could see the logic, but that didn't stop it hurting. He should have told her; they were supposed to be partners, equals within the marriage. She should at least have known. A bubble of resentment floated into her brain, jostling for space with all the other thoughts and emotions.

She struggled out of the duvet, pushing it away, and sat on the edge of the bed. If she went now she could catch one of the swimming-pool lane sessions, she saw, glancing at the little alarm clock. She changed into a T-shirt and tracksuit, and slipped down the stairs. She met Neil coming up, with a cup of tea.

'I'm going swimming,' she said. 'Is that all right?'

Neil looked surprised. 'What about your tea?' he said.

'I'll have it when I come back.' She kissed his cheek. 'If I don't go now I'll miss the session.'

The pool was not busy, each lane occupied with one or two swimmers. As she swam she turned the arguments over in her mind. You're safe. Neil doesn't know. Finish it now and it'll be as if it never happened. But I can't, she wanted to cry. I can't give him up. But was it Patrick or the sex that she couldn't give up? She thought about this as her arms and legs worked. Perhaps she could find what she wanted in Neil. Take the initiative, show him what she liked. Stay with Neil, stay with the children. If I stay with Neil I know what I'll be doing every day from here to the grave. Then make more of a life for yourself outside the house. Forget Patrick. I can't forget him, a small voice wailed in her head. I want him. But what about the children? You can't leave the children. They can come with me. It'll be fun. A new country, yes, but a European one. A new father, one who says he doesn't want children, a man of whom you know nothing except for the way he makes you feel.

She swam until the last possible moment. Everybody else had gone, and the new session had yet to start. She could hear voices echoing around the pool, drifting in from the changing rooms. But for a few minutes she had the pool to herself. She swam trying to disturb the water as little as possible. Her movements became slower and slower. The only sounds were the gentle slap, slap of water on the tiled sides. Treading water she reached up and released her hair from where it was piled up on top of her head. She rolled onto her back and floated, feeling her hair streaming out. She moved her head gently, and the mass of hair slowly moved and swirled around. She closed her eyes and lay suspended, arms and legs outstretched, mind clear of all thought.

* * *

Over half term Isabel arranged to walk with Helen and the children in the arboretum. Most of the leaves had fallen, making a scarlet and orange carpet of the ground. The women sat shivering on a bench made out a tree trunk while the scarlet-cheeked children whooped and played in and out of the trees.

'They'll be too old for this, soon,' Isabel said suddenly, watching Michael sprint and catch his sister, then dart off again in a swoosh of fallen leaves.

'Oh, no, don't say that,' Helen said. 'I hate the way children have to grow up so quickly nowadays.' Isabel said nothing. She knew Helen was quick to give way to her own children, that they had televisions in their bedrooms and CD Walkmans. Michael had told her that Rufus was going to get a DVD player for Christmas. No way, Isabel had told him, ignoring eyes as full of pleading as a hungry spaniel. You're not getting one. But, Mum, he had whined. Don't set your heart on it, she had said, because it's just not going to happen.

'Guess what?' Helen looked excited. 'George has agreed to us having a swimming pool.'

'That'll be nice. When do you start building?'

'We have to wait until his Christmas bonus comes through, and there's planning permission of course, so I think round about Easter. Then it'll be ready for the summer.'

'That'll be nice,' Isabel repeated, unable to get much enthusiasm up at the prospect of their swimming pool.

'You'll have to come and swim. Anytime you like,' Helen added graciously. 'It will save you having to use the local pool.'

'Thanks.' Isabel smiled tightly. I like the local pool, she thought, with the ladies on the OAP's lunchtime special

– a swim, a cup of tea and a hot meal for £1.50. It was anonymous, but friendly. Women stripped bare and past caring what others thought of them. Not like the competitive people-watching of private pools, eyes swivelling under the latest Dior or Chloe sunglasses. Or worse, George eyeing you up. She hated the way he only spoke to her chest; it'd be even worse in a swimming costume. She pulled her coat more tightly around her.

'That's kind of you to offer, but I like doing lengths,' she said, in what she hoped was a diplomatic voice. 'And you can't really do them except in a big pool.'

'Whatever.' Helen sounded cross.

Isabel stood up. 'Shall we make a move? It gets dark so early now, and I'm freezing. Let's have tea at my house.' They called to the children and started to make their way to the car park, feet scrunching on the path. Isabel kicked at the leaves with each step, making little puffs and flurries of action. If yesterday had been a normal day, not half term, she would have been in the house with Patrick and today she might have been unable to walk without feeling sore, swollen from making mad passionate love on the hearthrug in front of a flickering fire. She smiled at the cliché and felt a stirring of excitement. If she gave Patrick up she would never experience that particular cliché. She couldn't imagine Neil in front of the fire, Neil with his gentleness, his tentative touching that sometimes made her want to scream.

All week she had been thinking about life with Neil and Patrick. There was something so exciting, so alive, about being with Patrick. Dangerous. But a comfortable danger, contained within the walls of the house. Since the dinner party it threatened to spill out into her life. Victoria, Neil, the deceit like stones, crushing the life out of her. And now Rome. It was impossible, of course. She couldn't leave Neil. Or could she? Swish, swish, went the leaves on the path. Helen started to talk about schools, the usual refrain. Isabel had heard this monologue before. She wanted to talk, to say I'm at a crossroads. Which way should I go? She wished she could have a proper talk to Frances, like they used to, not a brittle exchange of banalities.

She turned her attention to Helen, who was agitating over whether Rufus would pass Common Entrance.

'But that's not for another four years, isn't it?'

'You have to be prepared,' and Helen was off, bemoaning how the stupid league tables meant that schools were taking entrance exams much more seriously, and not caring if the parents were Old Boys or not. Isabel hardly bothered to listen, but watched Michael dashing about, head back, laughing at the other children. He ran fast, twisting and turning to escape outstretched arms, with an agility that was surprising in a child who often seemed quiet and sedentary. Stolid even. He ran towards her, dancing on the path in front of her, teasing her to join in the game but she shooed him away, laughing. He clasped his hands around her waist and for a second leaned into her, woolly head on her chest. Isabel hugged him, bending down to kiss the top of his head, awash with maternal feelings. And then he was off, detaching himself with a shout. 'Race you round the lake!' and the two boys hared off, splitting up and running in different directions on the encircling path.

'Boys! I don't know where they get all that energy from,' Helen said.

'We feed them too much, I expect,' Isabel murmured absently. She wanted to be left alone with her thoughts, trying to work out what to do. It was confusing being different people, reconciling the woman she was with Patrick to the mother she was to her children. To the wife she was, or wasn't, to Neil, even. By sleeping with Patrick she had added another dimension to her life. An exciting, dangerous dimension for sure, but her life was the same. She was still playing the same roles, still walking down the same rutted pathway. Still talking about schools and domestic trivia as if that was all there was to life. Perhaps the time had come to move on, do something mad.

What would she do in Rome? Apart from learning to like espresso. Patrick had talked of the vibrant market in the Campo dei Fiori and she could imagine herself shopping, a huge straw hat shading her face from the strength of the Roman sun, sniffing honey-scented pomegranates and tucking her purchases into a raffia bag. It sounded romantic, but perhaps it would pall and become as ordinary as going to the supermarket. It would probably be easy to find work as a TEFL teacher as she was an experienced, native English-speaker. She could teach privately and help Patrick with whatever he was doing. The trouble was that all this sounded ordinary, and she had no experience of Patrick and ordinary. They had never gone window-shopping together or shared a takeaway in front of a video. Could Patrick change a tyre or mend a fuse? Perhaps Patrick didn't do 'ordinary'. Once she had made the leap, given up the safety net of Neil, there would be no going back.

So, a very different life in yet another new country, and possibly – no, probably – insecure financially. A life like her childhood, always moving, never knowing what would happen next. But she had survived that. It hadn't been ideal, but then whose childhood was? A stable and secure home for my children, she had promised herself then. But it was silly to let yourself be swayed by a childish vow.

'I couldn't leave the children,' she'd said in the café and Patrick had said she could bring them. Patrick, the man who had made it very clear that he didn't want children, had no interest in children. Had he hesitated before saying they could come too? It was hard to remember, she was so agitated at the time. And all too easy to think you remembered what you wanted to remember. But why would he want to take on another man's children? Come to that, would Neil let her take the children away? She couldn't leave them. She thought about Patrick's mother. She imagined her to be dark-haired and elegant, small hands and feet. She'd left her tweedy husband to his comfy leather armchair and run off with her glamorous lover. She'd left her little boy. Could Isabel do the same?

She stamped her feet, but the fallen leaves, quietly decaying down into sludge, muffled the noise. Katie and Millie trotted ahead of her on the path, lifting their knees in unison, and holding their hands up in front as if holding reins. Katie carried a long leafstalk that she flicked against her thigh from time to time. Giddyup, giddyup. Every now and then she tossed her head and gave a little whinny. Fantasy worlds. Isabel smiled.

'There's the Bonfire Party coming up. And soon it'll be Christmas,' Helen offered.

'Christmas!' The thought appalled her. She felt life was being doled out in a series of school holidays and events: Christmas, Easter, half term. On and on, until suddenly the children would be gone, and then—Then there would be nothing, just her and Neil stuck in their box of a house. No, not nothing. Then there were lectures from the Decorative and Fine Arts Society, bridge parties and art courses, dabbling in watercolours or messing around in oils for the Summer Exhibition at the local library. She felt like Katie's hamster, running for its life on a tiny treadmill that was getting smaller every year. Was this the price of a stable childhood?

'Are you all right?' Helen was looking anxious.

Isabel clenched her fists inside her pockets, squeezing them so tight she could feel her nails making tiny crescents of pain on her palms through her leather gloves. The lake was still, its surface rippled by a few ducks paddling half-heartedly towards them in search of bread. The trees on the far side were reflected with luminous clarity. She searched her mind for something to say, something that would show she was 'all right'.

'Do you ski?'

If Helen heard the wobble in her voice, she chose to ignore it. 'Mmm,' she nodded. 'We're taking a chalet in Meribel with George's sister and her family.'

'That'll be nice.' Isabel, Queen of the Platitudes. 'Have you been there before?'

'Yes, we went last year with the Fowlers; they live the other side of Milbridge. He was at school with George.' Helen lowered her voice, although there was no one to eavesdrop. 'But it was ghastly. They kept on getting drunk and having arguments.'

'How awful for you.'

Helen started to talk rapidly, detailing the horrors of sharing a small chalet with the Fowlers. Isabel tried to appear interested in the gossip. This could be me, she realised with piercing awareness. If any of them finds out about me and Patrick . . . She pulled the belt of her coat tighter. It would be intolerable. Then she thought, but I could go and leave it all behind. I needn't know what people say about me. In fact, I need not see any of these people ever again. I could be sunning myself on the Italian Riviera, with Patrick lounging beside me, his body lithe and tanned. She realised it had been a very long week since they had made love, or rather, had sex, because Patrick had been angry with her. That week had not been good, and she had felt used. But she wanted him now.

She screwed her eyes up with longing, and when she opened them she saw Rufus loitering ahead, at the point where the path that circled the lake joined with the path to the car park.

'Where's Michael?' she called to him, cutting across Helen's stream of gossip and speculation.

Rufus shrugged. 'Dunno.'

'What do you mean, "Dunno"? Isn't he with you?' Her voice was sharper than she had intended. Rufus shrugged again, put out. She walked faster, past the girls, and up to the boy. 'Where is he?'

'He raced me round the lake,' he said, pointing to the far side. Isabel strained to conjure up Michael's figure, but couldn't see it. The path on the far side didn't follow the lake edge all the way round, but looped into a small shrubbery, good in the summer for playing cowboys or robbers. Drat, Isabel thought. That's all I need now, Michael to play up.

'Sorry, Helen. I expect he's hiding in the shrubbery waiting to jump out at us. I'll go round and get him.' She set off briskly thinking, if I call him, he'll only sit tight, so I'll let him jump out at me.

The shrubbery was very still. Isabel walked through, feeling like a decoy and expecting at any moment to be leapt on with bloodcurdling yells. But the rhododendrons

and laurels remained undisturbed. She reached the end.
Looking back across the lake she could see Helen and
the children gathered at the far side. For a moment she
thought there were four small outlines, but no, only three.
He had to be in the shrubbery. She turned and walked
back, calling out to Michael this time. The walk became
a run as panic grew in her.

'Found him?' Helen's face was anxious.

Isabel shook her head, not wanting to say the word
no.

'Maybe he's gone to the cars?'

Isabel half walked, half ran up the path to the car park
where their cars stood alone by a solitary oak tree. She
scanned the car park. No sign of him there. She ran back
to the others.

'Not there.' She bit her lip, unwilling to say more in
case the jumble of fear spilled out. Helen patted her arm.

'Don't worry. He'll be around, somewhere.'

'Yes.'

They walked back, calling his name. Michael, Michael,
Michael. The sound reverberated around the trees,
bouncing off the glassy surface of the lake.

'He can swim okay?' Helen said softly.

'Like a frog.' Michael at the swimming pool, thin legs
and arms working, head bobbing up and down, his
expression one of concentration in order to beat the
others to the side. Michael the fisherman, leaning over
the edge for a better look at the water, Isabel looked at
the reeds around the edge, reeds that even a competent
swimmer could get entangled with. But the lake wasn't
deep, everybody knew that. 'A child can drown in a few
inches of water' popped into her head. But not Michael.
Not my Michael.

'He must be hiding,' Helen said firmly. 'There's nowhere else he could have gone. Don't worry.' She put her arm around Isabel's shoulders and gave her a quick hug. 'We'll find him.' She bent down to Rufus.

'Rufus, when you were running round the lake, did you see anyone? Or hear a car?'

Rufus shrugged. 'I don't think so.'

Helen knelt down in front of him. 'It's really important.'

'Maybe a car.' Isabel's heart froze. Rufus screwed up his face with effort, trying to squeeze out something helpful. 'Mike runs much faster than me, that's why he went the long way round. I didn't see him.'

'I didn't hear a car when we were walking.' Helen hesitated, then turned to Isabel. 'Did you?'

'No.' I was too wrapped up in my own stupid thoughts to be paying attention to what Michael was doing. Please God, let him be safe, she prayed. She looked around, scanning the paths and trees as if willpower alone could conjure him up. But there was nothing. She could feel panic rising in her throat and put her hand over her mouth to keep it in. This can't be happening, this isn't happening. Please, don't let this happen. No. Stay calm. Think. She steadied her breathing.

'You go and check the car park again. I'll go back to where we were sitting.' She meant to walk calmly, but her feet broke into a run. The light was closing in and the shrubbery looked menacing, shadows and leaves merging, rustling as she ran past. Once she skidded on the slimy leaves, and instinctively grabbed at a branch for support. It felt hard and unforgiving. She ran on into the clearing, reached the bench where they had sat. No Michael slipped between the trees. High in the branches a pheasant cackled, let out for the shooting season. The noise echoed round the clearing like a ghost. Isabel swung around for a last look. Michael wasn't here. She started to run back, heart thumping, lungs bursting. She saw herself talking to the police, then pleading for Michael's safe return. Another missing child, another headline. His school photograph on the front page, hair neatly brushed, tie straight, gap-toothed smile, the innocent eyes. How long had it been since he had disappeared? Ten minutes? Fifteen? This isn't happening. Not to me. This happens to other people. Past the lake, the surface a dark glass reflecting the looming trees behind, back to the hedge where the others huddled in a small group.

'Any luck?'

Isabel shook her head, out of breath, gulping down the evening air. She hugged herself, clutched at her sides as if trying to stop herself fraying as the world disintegrated around her.

'What do you want to do?' I don't know, Isabel wanted to wail. I want my baby back. The other children were silent, faces white in the twilight, eyes dark sockets. 'I think we need to get help,' Helen continued. 'I don't have a mobile. Do you?'

Isabel shook her head again. 'No, I lost it. Stupid of me. Perhaps we can call from the village.' She said it reluctantly. To accept the need for help, for the police, meant that this was real, that it was happening. She felt in her pocket for her car keys. She didn't want to go, to leave Michael here. 'Stay where you last saw your mother and she will come and find you', that's what they always said to children. But she was going. She was at the car. She couldn't leave. She had to. She put the keys into the lock when:

'Yah!' Michael leapt out from behind the tree trunk

and jumped at her back. She spun round, clutching her heart.

'Oh! Michael!' The shock of seeing him, the relief, made her knees buckle. He danced in front of her, delighted with himself.

'I got you, I got you!'

Isabel's arm swung back and clouted him across the side of his head so he staggered under the blow. 'Don't you ever do that to me again,' she shouted. 'Don't you dare.' Then she grabbed him to her, and hugged him, ashamed of her violence. 'I'm sorry, I'm sorry,' she murmured to him over and over again. 'I was so worried. I didn't know where you were. I thought . . . I thought . . .' His hair smelt musty, his cheek hot where she had hit him. His body was compact, so precious, the only thing that mattered. She started to cry, sobbing into his anorak, wordless sobs that came from nowhere. Crying because he was with her, in her arms and safe, and crying because, in losing Michael, she had found the answer to Patrick's question.

14

Isabel creamed the butter and sugar together until the mixture was smooth and pale, almost white. She could remember being a small child and stealing pieces of the mixture from her mother's mixing bowl, letting the intense sweetness melt on her tongue. But her mother had never beaten the mixture enough, never carried on until the right shade of paleness had been achieved. Isabel broke the eggs into a mug and beat them lightly, then slowly, drop by drop, added them to the creamed butter. By the end the mixture was stiff and foamy, not slack and floppy. She sifted in the flour, letting it fall in a soft covering. Then, using a metal spoon, she sliced and folded the mixture, minimising the number of air bubbles exposed with each cut. Finally she spooned the mixture into two tins, smoothed the surface and put them in the oven. The door closed with a satisfying clunk.

She cleared the utensils away, running a finger round the mixing bowl to take the last smears of mixture. Uncooked cake tasted nicer than cooked cake, she thought, but you couldn't eat as much. Still, millions of calories with every lick. She quickly put everything into either the dishwasher or the sink, pouring on water to prevent herself from stealing any more. She'd weighed herself that morning and discovered that she'd lost nearly a stone. It must be the swimming – swimming and sex.

And she wasn't eating as much. While looking for the self-raising flour she'd come across a half-eaten packet of KitKats. Unheard of. And she hadn't immediately finished the pack off, just gently closed the cupboard door.

It's funny, she thought, but the more I have to do, the less I need to eat. It occurred to her that she wouldn't have a job anymore. Not that working for Patrick could count as a proper job, as she hadn't been paid. Partly her own fault, she knew: she hated to take money from him. His cheque, written in anger, was still folded in her purse. I should get a proper job, a real one. I can't sit around at home getting fat and depressed again. Or maybe I should do a degree. She pictured herself walking around a sunny campus with a pile of books under her arm. Then sitting under a tree with other students with shiny faces and beaming smiles discussing— What? Kierkegaard and Nietzsche? She wasn't sure how to pronounce them, let alone discuss them. Politics? History? Eng. Lit.? She loved reading, devouring classic novels as a child then rediscovering them as an adult.

She put the kitchen scales away. They were expensive ones, a present from Neil for her last birthday, Victorian-style but with polished silver pebbles for weights. She considered the balance: Patrick, sex and excitement on one side, Neil, Michael and Katie on the other. In her heart she knew that there wasn't any contest but she toyed with the idea of shifting the weights around to make the decision more clear-cut. The children couldn't go onto Patrick's side, but could sex and excitement go onto Neil's side?

She straightened up from putting the scales in the cupboard and looked around for something else to do. Restlessness, assuaged by vigorous cake mixing, began to creep over her again. Her fingers drummed on the

immaculate worktop. She realised that as well as having
dieting benefits, the more she had to do, the more she
somehow managed to get done. The house was far cleaner
and tidier now she had to squeeze the housework into
two days a week. Perhaps I should study physics, the
strange expansion and contraction of time according to
how much you have to do. She had even got around to
making chicken stock from the carcass the weekend
before and poured it into ice cube trays so she could add
little frozen cubes of concentrated flavour to recipes, just
like the cookery programmes advised.

'I wondered where you were.' Neil stuck his head
round the door.

'Making cake.'

'I'll look forward to that. You haven't made cakes for
ages.' He leaned against the edge of the table, looking
genuinely pleased at the prospect. She suddenly felt shy,
as if seeing him for the first time. That first time, when
he had saved her from the embarrassment of the disintegrating dress. She could remember him quite clearly,
coming across the dance floor to her, taking off his jacket,
his freckled face serious with concern.

'I felt like trying again.' Isabel filled the kettle with
water, more to give herself something to do than from
any overwhelming desire to make tea. Her overwhelming desire was for something quite different. It had been
a long time since she'd been at Patrick's house. Nine days,
to be precise. Could she show Neil what she wanted?
She looked sideways at him, noticing that the paunch he
had started to develop had vanished. He looked fit and
well, full of energy. The children were still watching the
video they'd hired as the solution to entertainment on a
wet Saturday afternoon.

'Fed up with the ants?' she said.

'I expect you need a really wide screen to see the animation properly. Still, it's keeping the children happy.'

She went past him to get milk from the fridge, lightly brushing against him on purpose. She wasn't sure if he had noticed. She took out the milk and put it on the table. He seemed very close. Very masculine. Very different to Patrick's smoothness.

'Neil, the catch of my necklace seems to be caught in my hair. Can you look?' She turned her back to him, lifting her hair up and exposing the nape of her neck. She felt slightly guilty, as if Neil was forbidden to her, as if she was betraying Patrick. But excited too, and her breath quickened. His fingers touched her skin lightly.

'Seems fine.'

'Are you sure?' She leant back slightly so their bodies were close.

'Yes.' His voice was more alert. She twisted around and kissed him, running her tongue over his lips, rubbing her aching body against his. Against her cheek his skin felt rough, his moustache tickling her soft upper lip, then travelling over her face with butterfly kisses, cheeks, eyes, forehead. She licked the base of his throat, salty to the tip of her tongue. A real person, known yet strange. The strangeness was exciting. They kissed, more urgently, losing awareness of their surroundings, concentrating on being together, now. She took his hand and pressed it to her.

'Touch me,' she murmured. His hand was tentative so she pushed herself harder at him. 'Like this.' She kissed him hungrily, deeper, more thoroughly, all the while pressing herself against him. She reached down and felt him hard, wanting her. She slipped her hand down the front of his trousers, heard him sigh as she clasped him firmly, moved up and down. He pulled away from her.

'Upstairs.'

Hand in hand they sneaked past the door to the sitting room, like teenagers stealing past disapproving parents. Then up the stairs, Neil's hands burning on her hips. She turned to him, wanted to do it there, but he pushed her on into their bedroom and shut the door.

Isabel kicked off her shoes and started pulling at her clothes, at his clothes, reaching for him, rubbing herself against his body as if she had a desperate itch all over. She could feel she was wet, aching for him, just wanting him to take her. They fell onto the bed, clothes scattered around the floor, hands touching, stroking, probing, mouths joined, sharing breathing, gasping. He slipped his fingers inside, and she yelped with surprise and pleasure, for it was unusual for Neil to touch her like that. His hand on her was delicious, but not enough. Fuck me, she ordered, fuck me now. He paused, as if surprised, but wordlessly he slipped into her and she opened for him, and for a moment they were still, suspended in time, caught on the moment, the rightness of what was happening. Then he started to move, slowly at first, withdrawing to infinity, hanging there like on the edge of a rollercoaster, then plunging back in. She shifted her position in the bed, as Patrick had taught her, bringing him deeper, making him move faster and faster, her fingers convulsively gripping his arms, as she lost all sense of self, of time, just alive to the sensations that were juddering over her, making her cry out as if in pain, awash with love.

They lay, their faces inches apart, sharing breaths, arms around each other, skin glowing under a slippery layer of sweat. Quiet voices, murmurs that buzzed softly around the still room, spoke of little things, trivia, inconsequentialities. Eyes fixed on each other, clear blue examining brown depths, searching and finding answers to unspoken questions. Gradually the world reasserted itself, colours losing intensity, outside noises returning, a child's voice calling. Slowly, reluctantly, they broke the magic circle that held them and returned to the mundane life of getting dressed. But not without flip comments and giggles as they remembered what they had done, smiles suddenly breaking out, bodies leaning towards each other.

Isabel took her cake from the oven, a little too brown, but not much, only enough to make a slight crunch against the teeth as the crust was broken. She spread it generously with raspberry jam that oozed out in glistening drizzles, dredged the top with icing sugar. At teatime they sat round the table, mother, father, munching children, boy, girl, lovers. Now and again Neil and Isabel's eyes would meet, sharing secret smiles. What's so funny, the children kept asking, and Neil and Isabel would smile again and say happily, nothing. It's nothing.

Isabel posted the video through the letterbox of the video store, hearing it drop onto the mat with a clunk. Now it had gone she had to face up to her decision. The Sunday papers were on the passenger seat, along with milk, golden syrup for making treacle tart and a bunch of supermarket alstroemeria, 'Specially selected by us for you', bought on impulse, guaranteed to last seven days. She wished it was seven days later.

Yesterday it had seemed clear. Her place was with Neil. But now she had to tell Patrick of her decision. She shrank from making any contact at all, just wished he would vanish into thin air so she could pretend it had never happened. But he wouldn't vanish; he was all too real.

She had seen this happen to women getting divorced. Having ditched their irritating husbands they breathed a sigh of relief, thinking that they could move on and leave the wreckage behind them. But ex-husbands were not like flotsam and jetsam, floating away on the tides; they had their own agendas, their own grievances. Grievances to be vociferously aired until so-called civilised behaviour degenerated into bitterness, ripping open half-healed scars so the wound was left knubbled and twisted in a livid streak.

But we have no shared history to squabble over, she argued, trying to convince herself that there was no reason to fear Patrick's reaction. He has Victoria and we're grown-up people. She jangled the car keys. She'd never felt particularly grown-up. It was Neil who'd been the grown-up, she realised, letting her remain a child. She didn't think Patrick, erstwhile playmate, was very grown-up either. He'd said 'no tears when we part', but she knew he fully expected that it would be him who would be doing the dumping, not her.

Earlier, before anyone was up, she'd written him a letter. Should she drive to the house now and risk knocking on the door? Or slip it silently through the letterbox, to glide onto his nonexistent doormat? She bit the side of her thumbnail, running her teeth along the edge, gaining some comfort from the familiarity of her own smell. What to do? Face to face seemed the only honest way of breaking off the affair, but she didn't feel like being honest. She could imagine Neil in the same circumstances being sad, but accepting. She didn't think Patrick would be either. She felt stupid, standing in the street umming and ahhing, so she got in the car, and stuck the key in the ignition. She had to make a decision, and quickly. It only took so long to return a video and pick up a few things at the supermarket.

It would help if she knew whether he would be in or not, she thought. If she knew he was out, she could knock on the door and then, when he didn't respond, drop the letter off and drive away fast with a clear conscience. Clearish, anyway. But if he was in . . . He might be angry. Worse, he might take no notice of her, and stop her talking with a 'Don't be stupid, woman', then screw her. And if he did, she wasn't sure that she could withstand his confidence. She saw herself, stumbling explanations, getting confused under his amused stare. And would her body, so used to him, swing into action before she could stop herself?

No, she didn't want to see him alone inside the house. But it seemed so awful to write, a coward's way out. Don't be silly, she told herself. The reason it seems bad is that it gives the other person no chance to respond, to put their side. And that's what you want, isn't it? No comeback. She glanced at her watch. He often went away at weekends, she knew. Perhaps he was with Victoria. Even if he were at the house, he probably wouldn't be up yet. A brief vision of Patrick, unshaven, hungover, answering the door bleary-eyed with his skin warm from bed, came into her head. She resolutely pushed the image away, slid the car into gear and drove off.

The house looked deserted, curtains closed at the upstairs windows. She parked and got out of her car, closing the door carefully so it didn't make a noise. She looked around but couldn't see his car. She opened the gate carefully and stepped up the path to the front door. She listened for a moment but heard nothing, so tapped the door softly. Her heart was thumping as she listened, but nothing disturbed the silence on the other side of the door. Either asleep, or not there, she thought. She slipped back to the car and read her letter through.

Sunday morning

> Dear Patrick,
> I've been thinking really hard over half term and have decided that I can't come with you to Rome. I can't leave the children, and I can't take them with me. So I must stay here and make the best of things. I expect you'll be angry, but hope you can forgive me. You told me from the start, no regrets, and we both knew it was never going to last. I've had a wonderful time but I can't risk the children's happiness. It's too high a price to pay for my own.
> Love, Isabel

She found a biro gathering dust in the footwell and crossed out the sentence about it being too high a price to pay for her own happiness. If she made the break it had to be final. Patrick mustn't know how difficult it was for her to leave him. She read the letter again and as she did so, she remembered her father saying, be careful what you put in writing. He was a great one for never putting anything in writing.

She tore the letter up, ripping it into tiny pieces. Scrabbling around the car she found a piece of lined paper that had strayed from Michael's homework bag. She paused, sucking the end of the biro, then started to write.

Sunday morning

> Dear Patrick
> I came over to tell you in person, but you're not

in so I'm writing this letter. Please forgive the grotty
paper and biro. I have decided that, due to family
commitments, I can no longer work for you. I'm
sorry to leave you in the lurch, but I'm sure you'll
find someone else soon.

But will they work for no money? she thought and she
suddenly wondered if Patrick had started the affair so as
not to pay her. But no, she couldn't accuse him of that.
Although he had kissed her, it had been she who had
initiated the affair on the afternoon of the storm. It
seemed a very long time ago. She sucked on the end of
the biro for inspiration. Grimacing, she wrote:

> I'm giving no notice in lieu of wages.
> With best wishes
> Isabel Freeman

Not very good, but it would have to do. She folded the
note into four and wrote Patrick's name on the front. At
the door she hesitated for a second. Was this right? What
she wanted? She pushed the note through quickly. There.
It was gone. Too late to change her mind. As she got back
in the car she felt light-headed. It was good to have
chosen, to have made the decision. She slipped Mozart's
horn concerto into the CD player and sang along to the
resolutely cheerful music as she drove the few miles home.

15

The euphoria of Sunday morning had vanished by Monday morning when Neil left for work, leaving her alone in the house, depressed and without energy. She spent the day in a state of anxiety, fearing for Patrick's phonecall. In town, hair damp round the edges from swimming, she walked nervously along the pavement, expecting to see Patrick emerge and accost her. Sick with nerves, she loitered in the bookshop, half looking at the books and half watching out of the shop window to see if he went into the Italian café opposite. Once she looked up from Organise Your Life Forever! and thought he was peering in at her, dark face in shadow, but it was only some stranger who didn't even look like him. She realised the man at the till was watching her, presumably because he thought she looked shifty. A potential shoplifter, probably. Flustered, she bought a book called Rekindling the Passion: Rediscovering the Joys of Marital Sex, blushing slightly as the man at the till gave her a sideways look, having read the title. She hid it in the depths of her shopping basket in case she bumped into Patrick and his eyes might see through the paper bag.

She swam every day that week. On the way down the pool her eyes were fixed on the entrance to the men's changing rooms, just in case, and on the way up she could feel his eyes burning her back through the water. But he was never there. It was never him who emerged and surveyed the pool as if he owned it, pulling at his swimming trunks as if too tight, like all the other men. Some of the swimmers had beautiful bodies, broad-shouldered, tapering to slim waists and long legs so firm that the calf muscles threw arcs of shadow towards the ankles. Their smooth movements through the water made her think of Patrick lying languorously on the bed, sated and contented as a cat. But cats have claws. She waited for Patrick to flex his.

On Tuesday, when she should have been at work, she started writing the Christmas Round Robin letter they sent every year to friends. It was a good way to stay in touch when your friends were like you, working all over the world. But what to write?

> *Dear Everyone,*
> *The year's been an interesting one. We moved back to the UK – Neil's now a big cheese at company HQ – and I got a job and took a lover, but I've chucked them both in now.*

Perhaps not, although it would make a change from the usual litany of minor successes. She struggled for a while with anodyne phrases before giving up. Instead, she read the book she had bought and tried rekindling the passion, or rather, tried kindling with Neil the passion she'd had with Patrick. But although they had made love satisfactorily at the weekend, Neil now seemed wary of her advances, almost embarrassed as if that Saturday afternoon had been an aberration. He did what he usually did and seemed thrown when she tried whispering suggestions or showing him what she liked. She felt ashamed, as if she'd been caught doing something wrong. Which in a way she had, because she had learnt how to ask, and what to ask for, from Patrick. After her second attempt she gave up and they each retreated to their own side of the bed.

She thought of Patrick a lot. Patrick laughing in the garden, Patrick pacing the room talking rapidly into the phone, Patrick getting angry and crashing through the house slamming doors then fucking her. Bedroom, kitchen, stairs; it didn't matter where. She knew the quality of the floors and furniture in that house better than a surveyor. He would be angry when he got the letter. She was sure of it. She kept thinking about him being angry, anger turning to passion.

At the pool she swam fast. Her arms and legs trembled as she got out. Twice she had to sit down in the middle of changing, limp and exhausted, legs flopping open, arms hanging uselessly by her side, waiting for her pulse to settle down and her chest to stop heaving. I'm just not used to all this swimming, she thought. I'll be more careful tomorrow. But the next day, although she might start carefully, after a few lengths her pace quickened. She ploughed up and down the lanes, counting the lengths in her head, repeating the number on each inward breath. She had always swum by time before, twenty minutes, half an hour. She'd heard sixty-four lengths equalled a mile so she aimed for that. She counted lengths obsessively. It shut out thoughts of Patrick.

By Friday she had got used to feeling sick when the phone rang, and fed up with standing beside it, agonising about whether to pick it up or let it carry on ringing merrily. It rang again and she realised she was bored with jangling nerves. She picked the phone up.

'Yup? Oh, Mary. Hi.' She hated herself for saying hi. She never said hi. Cringing inwardly, she listened to Mary reminding her about the Fireworks Party. Her name was down for selling sparklers. She had to admit, she had forgotten completely, although she realised the children had been talking about it only that morning. It was information that hadn't stuck inside her brain.

'I hear you're not working for Patrick any more.'

'No.' Her hand gripped the phone, as she thought back to Mary coming round to Patrick's house, when she'd told her that Patrick meant nothing to her. She realised it would sound odd if she didn't say anything else so she added, 'It just didn't work out.' She waved her free arm airily, even though Mary couldn't see her. There was a slight pause. Mary was obviously running through all the things she could say, but decided against any of them.

'Well. See you tonight,' was all she said.

'Tonight, that's right.' Isabel nodded furiously.

'And, Isabel? Don't be late.'

'We mustn't be late,' Isabel said, bundling the children into layers of coats and sweaters and searching for matching gloves among the newly acquired supplies. It was strange how a person could so consistently lose the right-hand glove of any pair. She found a pair of gloves on a string which would fit Katie, and had to get her out of her coat, thread them through and then put Katie back in. It all took time.

'I don't need a hat,' Michael said, tossing his head away from a blue wool job, the plainest Isabel could find.

'It'll be freezing,' Isabel said, jamming it down. 'You're not used to the cold. C'mon, we've got to go.' She nipped back into the kitchen to collect her car keys and checked Katie's note was still there for Neil.

> *Dear Daddy we have gone to the Fireworks Party.*
> *Here is a tikket for you if you get home in time.*
> *Love Katie.* XXXXXXXXXXXXX

Isabel had dictated the words but the Xs were all Katie's. Such love, she thought. So many kisses to be squeezed into such a small space. She sighed, then squeaked at the sight of the kitchen clock and grabbed her shopping basket.

'Yikes. Quick, everybody in the car.'

The children, excited about being out in the dark, chattered in high-pitched voices as she drove through the streets. How many hot dogs, how many sparklers, how many sweets were they going to have? Millions, billions, trillions, squillions. They topped each other, squealing with delight. The children's excitement was infectious, and Isabel felt excited too, even though the weather was poor, threatening rain, clouds hiding the early stars. The moon was a thin sliver of diffused light hanging suspended on the horizon.

Isabel's wasn't the only car in the car park but she was one of the first. She presented herself at the classroom they used as HQ on Bonfire Night, slightly puffed from the hurry. The fluorescent lights seemed horribly bright after the darkness outside. She waved her basket.

'I'm here. Where are the sparklers?'

Justine detached herself from a group fussing over the heated trolleys.

'In this box. And the matches are here. Mary's got all the float money.'

'Everything going okay?'

Justine grimaced. 'Helen forgot to come in early and turn the trolleys and the urn on. So the mulled wine is lukewarm and we're selling tepid, not hot, dogs.' She lowered her voice. 'Food poisoning apparently threatens the entire school community. Mary was furious and shouted at Helen, then stormed off.'

How like Patrick, Isabel thought, her insides turning over just thinking of him.

'Stupid, really; it's not the Ritz,' Justine drawled.

'I seem to have missed the action,' Isabel said, matching Justine's cool tone. She looked across, and saw the high colour still on Helen's cheeks. 'Poor Helen.' She decided against commiserating with Helen now; it would only draw attention to her. She'd say something later. She crammed as many packets of sparklers and matches as she could into her basket and went outside. It was very dark, lit only by the light from the school buildings, and she wished she had remembered to bring a torch. That was the problem with rushing about, trying to be early: you ended up forgetting things. The children had joined Rufus, Millie and Rachel and several others and were running about, bodies criss-crossing the dark lawn. She called Katie and Michael to her.

'They'll be lighting the bonfire soon.'

'Where?' Katie looked around her, eyes big under her hat.

'Right up at the very top of the field, as far from the school as possible.' Isabel pointed into the darkness, although it was impossible to see anything. 'And then the fireworks will be in half an hour. Be careful.'

'Remember, remember the fifth of November,' Michael chanted.

'Here's some money for hot dogs and sweets. Rufus's mother is dishing up; she'll help you. Please watch out for Katie, Michael. I won't be far away if you need me, or if you're frightened.'

Michael snorted with derision.

'You may be fine, but Katie might get scared,' she said quickly. 'I'll be wandering around outside but if you miss me, go into the classroom where the food is.'

She gave them a packet of sparklers each and lit the

first. They streaked off up the lawn towards the top field, which was hopefully called the athletics track in the summer term, sparks of light emitting from their sparklers so they resembled boisterous Tinkerbells.

Car headlights started to flash up the track to the car park, at first irregularly, then in a steady stream. Isabel sold sparklers to children and parents, having brief, meaningless conversations with most of them – 'Let's hope the weather holds' and 'When do the fireworks start?' Children wrote their names in sparkler fire, or swung great swooping arcs of flashing neon that burnt out the darkness, after-images lingering in the air before dissolving into the night. Parents talked loudly, fuelled by mulled wine, while their children ran wild. The bonfire blazed beyond the lawn in the top field, a beacon that people gradually drifted towards. The first firework went up, a large rocket that exploded into a chrysanthemum head of green petals with a thunderclap of sound, and everybody oohed.

Isabel sold the last of her sparklers to the crowd in the top field, and thought about going back to get fresh supplies. She looked down towards the school buildings. Through the big windows she could just make out the PTA women, shadowy figures chatting in the warmth. They would be clearing up and making ready for the next bout of frenzied feeding and drinking after the firework display was over. Standing alone in the cold night air, she felt torn between staying with the crowd and watching the rest of the firework display or continuing her duty by trudging all the way down to collect the rest of the sparklers. I want to be with my children, she thought, oohing and ahhing with everybody else. But the children were at the front of the crowd, unfussed by the noises that had made her duck involuntarily. They didn't need her and she couldn't reach them even if she wanted to. She looked at the empty basket. She knew what she ought to do.

Reluctantly she started to walk down, turning her back on the crowd and the fireworks. The darkness pressed in on her, making her stumble, and the money she had taken nearly fell out of the basket. She stopped and gathered it together, putting it into a plastic bag in her pocket. Her hands were cold, and she fumbled tying the top of the bag. When she reached the school buildings, she decided, she wouldn't go back up to join the crowd but would stay for a chat, perhaps have some mulled wine to warm herself up. There weren't many packets of sparklers left in the classroom to sell.

As she passed the cedar of Lebanon, part of the trunk detached itself and turned into a figure, making her jump.

'God, you gave me a shock,' she said, hand on heart.

'I didn't mean to make you jump.' A rocket exploded in the black sky above and flooded Patrick's face with lurid green light. 'Mary told me you'd be here. I've been watching you.' His voice was steady but in the brief flash of light she saw that his face was set in deep lines. Then the light faded and all was darkness again.

'What do you want?' She could hear the fear in her voice and clutched the empty basket in front of her.

'Why, you, of course. What else would I want here?' He took a step towards her and involuntarily she stepped back. There are hundreds of people all around me, she thought. There's no danger. But all she could see was darkness and the nearest people were fifty yards away behind windows.

'You can't have me.' She tried to make her voice cool. 'I'm not available.'

'Aren't you?' he said, his voice almost purring as he came closer. She stood her ground.

'No. Not anymore. I told you, in my letter.'

'Ah, yes, that charming document.' He was close now, his outline dark against the school. She'd always loved his voice. 'Do you know, I don't believe you.'

'What do you mean?' Run, her mind screamed at her. Run. But she stayed put.

'I think you are available.' He removed the basket from her hands and dropped it on the ground. His hands cupped her face, fingers rough against her skin. She tried to keep her body stiff and unyielding as he kissed her, keeping her lips clamped shut. She tried, but she could feel herself responding. He steered her back to the tree, ignoring her stumbling feet, and pushed her against the trunk. He leant against her, pinning her down with his weight, while one hand undid her coat and fumbled with her clothes, yanking her underwear down.

'No,' she said, twisting away from him. 'I don't want . . .'

'But you do. I can feel. You're dripping wet for me.'

'Oh God, no.' Involuntarily her back arched, body trained to respond to him. 'Please don't . . .' Her breathing was heavy and she turned her head, battling inwardly with the reactions his fingers were bringing. Her hands gripped his shoulders. She couldn't, not here. But it felt so good. So good. Especially after Neil's rejection.

'Please . . .' she said, and she didn't know if she meant please, no or please, yes.

He was undoing his zip. She had to stop. Had to. 'No,' she moaned.

'But you want me to.' His voice buzzed close to her ear.

'Not . . .'

'. . . here?' His voice in the darkness was triumphant.

'They won't be finished for another ten minutes. No one will catch you.' He settled himself between her legs, hands on her hips, ready to take her. If I do this now I am lost, she thought, and in reaction cried out.

'No. I said no.' She jerked herself away from him.

He missed and swore. 'You fucking bitch.' Seizing her chance she slid sideways from under him and ran for the school, coat flaring out, feet stumbling in the darkness, hobbled by her clothes. Her breath made puffs of white mist in the cold night air, while behind her the air erupted with shooting stars and screechers.

The classroom lights were on, and she could see the committee chatting, oblivious to her mad flight. She swerved away from them and headed for the side of the building, which was in total darkness. She ducked behind a bay window and crouched down, hugging her knees to her. If he found her she would not be able to break away from him again. She felt her body was imprinted with Patrick, like the after-image left by the sparklers. She squeezed her eyes tight shut. She had to regain control over herself. Her breathing slowly returned to normal. Voices started talking nearby, getting louder, and she guessed that the display had ended. If Patrick had been looking for her he must have given up.

She stood up slowly, knees creaking. Her skirt was rucked up, tights torn. She adjusted her clothes, smoothing them down. They would be hidden under her coat. Isabel retraced her way, back to the party. She noticed that her shoes were caked with mud and tried to scrape some off on the path, standing on each wobbly leg in turn. There seemed to be hundreds of people standing around while shrieking children threaded their way between them. She listened and realised that Mary was drawing the raffle.

There seemed no point in trying to push her way through the crowd so she leant against the building, suddenly exhausted with the effort of staying upright.

'Mum, Mum, where've you been?' Michael came zooming out of the crowd, followed closely by Katie. He ducked away from her attempt to caress his head. 'Gerroff. Where are our tickets?'

'Oh. In my pocket, I think. Hang on.' He jiggled up and down while she felt in her coat pockets.

'Hurry, Mummy,' Katie pleaded. Isabel felt very stupid and slow, as if her hands were disconnected from her brain. 'There.' She took out several strips of blue paper, which he snatched from her hand and studied intently.

'Blue, thirty-six. They've had that.'

'Oh dear.' She tried to concentrate. 'Never mind.' Michael was having none of it. He grabbed her wrist and pulled.

'Come on.' He pushed through the crowd heading for Mary, Isabel following meekly. 'Sorry,' she kept saying as she bashed into people. Her legs didn't seem to work properly. 'Sorry.'

The draw finished, the crowd started to disperse, peeling off in clumps. Michael didn't hesitate but marched straight up to Mary, dragging Isabel in his wake.

'Excuse me,' he said politely. 'But my mum's got blue, thirty-six.'

Mary turned with a smile. 'Isabel. You're a bit late.'

'Better late than never,' Isabel was stung to respond. 'Michael thinks he's won something.'

'Blue, thirty-six?' Mary looked at the list in her hand. 'Yes, it did win something. It'll have been set aside for you, in there.' She indicated the classroom.

Michael's face lit up and he rushed off to see.

'Thank you, Mary,' Isabel said, matching her son for politeness. She took Katie's hand and they went through to the classroom. Michael was standing by a small table laden with boxes and bottles of whisky, and beside him was a man. A man with a basket on his arm. Isabel stopped dead on the doorstep. Among the noise of women clearing up, clattering dishes and chatting, she could hear their male voices but couldn't make out the words.

Katie pushed past her. 'What is it? What have we won?'

Isabel followed her with reluctant steps, as if treading on broken glass.

'Here it is!' Michael's voice was triumphant. He waved a small wooden box around. 'Look, Mum.' He turned to her, then added, 'What is it?'

'Cigars, I think.' To her surprise her voice sounded quite normal. Patrick turned, his face tinged with triumph. She walked up to Michael and took the box, turning it over. 'No, cigarillos. They're little cigars.'

'Very useful.' Patrick's voice was sardonic.

'I'm sure they will be. Come along, children.'

'So these are your children.'

'Yes.' She took Katie's hand. 'Come on, Michael. Daddy'll be at home waiting for us.' She willed Michael to come to her.

'Oh, Dad won't be home for ages, he never is.' He was busy examining some of the other prizes. 'Look at that big bottle of whisky. It's just like the ones Grandpa brings us. You'd get very drunk if you had all that.'

'I should have guessed they were yours.' Patrick crouched down so he was Katie's height. 'Hello.' Katie leant into Isabel's coat, half hiding her face. He reached out and touched her hair. 'Pretty,' he said. 'Like her mother.' He stood up. He was very close to her.

'Michael, come now,' Isabel called, failing to keep anger from her voice. Michael reluctantly came to her, clutching his box of cigarillos.

'May I see?' Patrick held out his hand, and Michael handed them to him. 'These are very good. You'll enjoy them.'

Michael rolled his eyes.

'Don't be silly, I'm too young to smoke.'

'So you are. Do you know who I am?' Michael shook his head. 'Your mother works for me.'

'Worked. I worked for you. I don't anymore,' Isabel hissed. Patrick ignored her.

'My name's Patrick, and you are?'

'Michael.' They shook hands, Michael's hand looking small and trusting in Patrick's.

'Michael, we're going. Now.' Isabel set off, dragging Katie with her, praying that Michael would follow. She walked fast up the path that led to the car park, Katie having to trot to keep up. Another family was ahead, strolling along so Isabel had to slow down. She heard footsteps and panting behind, and then Michael was with her, puffing exaggeratedly from having run.

'Last one to the car is a big fat twit,' he shouted, and he and Katie took off into the darkness. Isabel increased her pace and overtook the dawdlers, anxious that the children might decide to hide. But they were leaning against the car when she arrived. She unlocked it and they scrambled in. She was about to get in herself, when she heard Patrick's voice.

'You forgot this.' He was holding out the basket.

'Stop following me.' She felt wedged in between the parked cars. She shut the car door so the children couldn't hear.

'You might say thank you.'

'What for?'

'Why, returning this of course.'

'I wouldn't have lost it if it hadn't been for you.' She took the basket from him, opened the driver's door and slung it onto the front passenger seat. She started to get in, but he stretched his arm across the door to prevent her.

'You shouldn't have run away from me.'

Furious, she faced him.

'You practically raped me,' she whispered angrily.

He laughed. 'Don't be ridiculous. You want me as much as I want you.'

'No.'

'Why tell lies to yourself?'

'I must go.'

'Why? Daddy won't be back for ages.' His voice was mocking.

'Go away. Just go away.' She pushed past his arm and got into the car, slamming the door shut. Her hands were trembling and it took two attempts to get the key into the ignition. She shot out of her parking space without checking her rear-view mirror, earning her an outraged honk from the car she had just missed, and accelerated away from the school.

Neil was at home when they got back.

'Had a good time?' he called from in front of the television.

The children ran in to greet him while Isabel hung back, uncertain if she could face Neil now. The phone rang and she answered it without thinking.

'I must see you.' Patrick said.

'No. Leave me alone.' But she didn't hang up.

'Don't be so melodramatic. I just think we should talk.'

'There's nothing to talk about.'

'You know there is. It's not fair to leave me like this.' He let the words hang in the air. It's not fair. He sighed.

'I asked you to come to me, offered you everything I have, and you sent me that letter. I think you owe me some explanation. Let's meet up for lunch and talk.'

'I go swimming at lunchtimes.'

'Not every day, surely. We could go to the pub if you like.' He must have heard her sharp intake of breath and quickly carried on. 'Or somewhere else. You choose.' She pressed the phone closely to her ear as if she could pick up his thoughts through the skeins of wire that connected them, but she said nothing. She was thinking of being against the tree and letting him spread her legs apart.

His voice continued, seductive and low. 'I never took you out to lunch properly when we were together. Let me do it now.'

She hesitated. 'I don't know.'

'You owe me that much.'

'I owe you nothing after tonight.' She made her voice harsh, cold even.

'I'm sorry. I thought you wanted to as much as I did.' He paused, and she knew she ought to say, no, you're mistaken. But the words wouldn't come.

'The house seems empty without you,' he said. 'I miss you.'

I miss you too, she thought. Despite everything, despite her decision. She could hear Michael and Katie's voices, high-pitched and laughing as they told their father about the fireworks. She leant her head against the wall.

'I can't be with you anymore, Patrick. It's impossible.'

'Let's be friends. Let's not end badly, not like tonight.'

'All right.' Her voice was little more than a whisper. 'But not the pub.'

'No, that's fine. What about that new place in town? The one off the market square.'

'Bentham's?'

'Tomorrow? At twelve thirty?'

She swallowed. 'Just to say goodbye properly. Nothing more.'

'Nothing more.'

There was a pause. Then he said, 'I'll see you there.'

'Yes.'

He put the phone down gently and after a few moments, so did she.

Isabel drove past Bentham's, looking for a parking space. She passed Patrick's car and felt a stab of recognition. A few cars on there was a space and she reversed into it, pulling hard on the steering wheel to get her estate car to fit in. It was difficult to concentrate, she was in such a hurry to be there. She checked her make-up in the mirror. Her eyes were bright, cheeks flushed like a woman going to meet her lover.

She examined herself more closely. Low-cut cardigan, buttoned down the front and no shirt underneath so it clung to her breasts, worn with a wrap-around skirt. Dressed for action. She closed her eyes, and rested her head on the steering wheel. Who was she kidding? This wasn't to say goodbye, this was to start up all over again. She had even arranged for the children to go to Helen's house for tea that evening so she could dawdle over lunch. Dawdle all the way to bed.

I've made my decision, and it's the right one, she thought. I must stick to it. I can't leave the children, and the children need to stay here, so I have to stay here. Going to Rome with Patrick is impossible. But it's what you want, her internal voice answered. To be with him, starting out again, the excitement.

I am addicted to him, she thought. And he was waiting for her. She had only to get out of the car and go to him. The alternative was cold turkey. Hard, but not impossible. Not slow withdrawal. The words, slow withdrawal made her stomach contract, thinking of Patrick, that agonising, delicious moment just before he plunged back in. No. She sat up. Don't think of it. Think of the children. Think of Michael and Katie. I have to get away, she thought. I can't be with him. Get away. Get away now. She started the car and shot off, heart pumping, turning off at random. A sign to the station caught her eye and she turned into the road, parked and went to the ticket office.

'When's the next train?'

'Where to?'

'Anywhere.' The ticket man looked at her as if she was mad.

'The Intercity to London should be here in five minutes.'

'Fine. A cheap day return please.' She fumbled with her purse, handed the money over, took the ticket. Milbridge station was old-fashioned, complete with waiting room. She stood in it, pretending to flick through ancient copies of *Country Life*, her heart thumping. She half expected Patrick to turn up and drag her off, although she knew that was impossible. She'd be safe on the train, safe from Patrick. Safe from herself. The train pulled in. She stepped up into the carriage then paused, one foot on the platform, one in the carriage. She could go back;

she'd be only a little late. She thought of Patrick waiting for her, how he'd feel at being stood up. It seemed wrong to just run out on him. She wavered, half in, half out. The guard came up, peaked cap jauntily on the back of his head.

'All right, love?' She looked at him blankly. 'Need a hand there?'

'No, thank you. I can manage.' She moved forwards into the carriage, and the door slammed shut behind her.

Isabel aimlessly trawled down Knightsbridge looking in shop windows. There was so much stuff, but everything either looked like something she had anyway or so radically different she knew she wouldn't wear it. She had a bulging wardrobe full of clothes she didn't wear anyway. It seemed wasteful to add to it. She suddenly remembered that she'd arranged for Justine to come round and 'do' her wardrobe at the end of the week. She stood looking at a red bias-cut dress, head on one side. Now she had lost some weight and had firmed up it might look good. It was certainly different from everything else she had.

The shop was not the sort she usually went into, thinking it too young for her. It struck her that for most of her married life she had been trying to look older than she was, to make up for the fact that she was younger than most of Neil's colleagues' wives. And now she was older. Somehow she had missed out on being young. She went into the shop and tried the dress on. She tried to look at the back view, peering over her shoulder. It looked good on her, clinging with a low back. Too good, in fact. It was a fuck-me dress, to go with the fuck-me shoes. And the fuck-me attitude. Don't think of Patrick, she told herself, which immediately made her yearn for him.

It's only sex, she told herself. An addiction. Lust not love. Oh dear. She sat down on a little stool, the red dress swirling round her. Her hair frizzed out in a halo around her face. All that swimming's doing it no good, whatever it's doing to my body. She examined one lock, bursting with split ends. Perhaps I should cut it all off. She put her hair up, holding it with one hand and turning from side to front to get the full effect. She couldn't imagine herself with short hair.

She stared at her reflection. She looked sexy in the dress, felt sexy. But what was the point when you can't have sex? Or at least, you can't have sex with the man you lust after. It was so unfair. She loved Neil, she would never leave Neil and the children. But it was . . . She bit her lip, thinking. It was safe. Dear, darling, reliable Neil. Safe as houses. But she wanted more. Perhaps if I'd slept around, had more boyfriends, become more experienced I wouldn't feel like this. I'd be content to settle down. I'd know that the grass isn't greener. She sighed.

'You all right?' An assistant stuck her head round the curtain.

Isabel jumped up. 'Yes, fine.' The assistant gave her a swift, calculating look.

'That looks good.'

'Yes.' Isabel sighed again. 'But when would I wear it?'

'At parties, out to dinner, clubbing. Whatever. It's a great dress on you. You ought to get it.'

Isabel looked at the sexy Isabel reflected in the mirror. It was nice to know that she could look like that. If Patrick saw her in it . . . But Patrick wasn't going to see her in it. 'I'm not going to take it. I love it, but I can't see when I'm going to wear it.'

'Pity.' The assistant withdrew with a shrug and a rattle of curtain rings, while Isabel slowly took off the dress and put her own clothes back on again. She left the shop and carried on, stopping at the corner by the tube. She didn't want to go back to the station to catch a train home, but nor did she feel like going into Harvey Nicks and risking more depressing sessions in changing rooms. Besides, she should go clothes shopping after Justine's visit, not before. What was the point, though, of looking sexy, feeling sexy, when your husband didn't care? She turned the corner into Sloane Street, thinking she'd walk down and go to Peter Jones and look at kitchenware. Her shaggy-haired reflection marched alongside her, past expensive dress shops and a hairdresser's. On impulse she turned in.

'Have you got a free appointment?'

'When for?'

'Now.'

The receptionist looked surprised. 'I'll check the book. Let's see.' She ran a perfectly manicured finger over the appointments book. 'I suppose Karl could do you a cut and blow-dry in about twenty minutes. Any good?'

'Okay,' Isabel nodded, hoping her nerve would last. 'I'll wait here.' She sat on a squishy black leather chair, and nervously flicked through a copy of *Vogue*. She was halfway through *House & Garden* when Karl, a willowy young man in trousers that matched the chair, collected her.

'And what can I do for you?' he asked, combing through her hair.

'I want it all off.'

'All of it?' He looked so horrified that Isabel back-tracked.

'Well, perhaps not all. But most of it. It's too long. I feel it's dragging me down.'

He started to play with her hair. 'Well, we could take the weight off here and here and . . .'

Isabel bounced up Sloane Street towards the tube station, watching her reflection bounce along with her, tossing its head and running its fingers through a mass of short curls. She felt as though a huge weight was off her shoulders, literally. Her hair had dropped to the ground of the salon in great hanks, more hair than she realised she had. It felt strange to feel the wind tickling the back of her neck, the way her fingers went through her hair so quickly. She was light-headed and light-hearted, young, free and sexy.

At the entrance to the tube she hesitated and checked her watch. She had a few minutes to spare. She ran down to the shop.

'The red dress I tried on,' she panted. 'Have you still got it?'

'Wow. Your hair.' The assistant did a gratifying double-take. 'Looks good.'

'Thanks. The dress?'

'Sure. Here it is.'

Isabel ran her fingers over the silky fabric. 'It's beautiful.' Why shouldn't she look attractive? If she could change, why shouldn't Neil? She gave the assistant a big smile and nodded. 'I'm going to take it.'

'Pretty Mummy!'

'Your hair. It looks amazing. Where did you go?'

'Ugh, what have you done, Mum? It looks awful.' Michael pulled a face, but both Katie and Helen were open-mouthed.

'Tough. I like it.' And she did. Like a girl with a new

engagement ring that she keeps on spotting on her hand, Isabel kept tossing her hair. She supposed it was a rather coquettish gesture but she enjoyed the feeling of it swirling against the nape of her neck. And the fringe made her feel she was peering out of a jungle, a sexy wild animal with big eyes. Helen and Katie had been approving, Michael's comment was only to be expected. She had been a little nervous of Neil's reaction; after all, he had once said he would divorce her if she ever cut her hair, but he seemed to like it, walking round her, making appreciative noises.

'Just you wait until you see my new dress,' she promised. She chucked a ready-made meal from the freezer into the oven, laid the table for their supper adding a couple of candles as an afterthought, then got the children to bed. She slipped on the red dress. It seemed very bare about the shoulders now her hair wasn't there to cover it up. She thought of putting on a cardigan, but that seemed to be missing the point of the dress. It was meant to be revealing. She came downstairs and leant against the door to the sitting room where Neil was watching television.

'Dinner is served.' He turned, and his face told her what she had wanted to know.

'That's some dress.'

'D'you like it?'

'Very much.' He got up and followed her through to the kitchen. She could feel his eyes watching her back and swinging hips. She bent down to get the food out of the oven and one of the straps slipped down her shoulder exposing even more breast. She held the hot dish in the oven mitts and went to Neil.

'You couldn't put that up for me, could you? My hands are full.'

He hesitated as if reluctant. His fingertips lightly touched her skin as he pulled the strap up.

'Thank you,' she said politely, and he bowed slightly and said, 'It was nothing.' But she had scented his interest, and the knowledge made her feel powerful. It could work. She could make it work.

They ate the food and drank their wine and talked, Isabel teasing Neil with jokes and pretend misunderstandings. At the end Neil patted his lap.

'Come here, you.' Isabel sashayed over to him. Instead of perching demurely on him she swung her leg over so she straddled him, hoicking the swirling skirt of her dress up over her thighs. Neil ran his hands up under her dress.

'What a sexy girl you are.' They kissed, Isabel cradling his head in her hands. It was like Saturday afternoon again. Perhaps this was the answer, not wait until they were in bed, laid out side by side like medieval effigies on a tomb, but catch him unawares, before his Protestant angst could react. The phone started ringing, and she pulled away from him.

'Let it ring. If it's important they'll call back,' Neil mumbled, his voice thick as he kissed her shoulders.

Isabel paused. The ringing tones were urgent. She knew it was Patrick.

'It's probably a wrong number,' she said. She put her mouth to his again, willing herself not to listen to the phone as it rang on and on, determined and insistent.

16

'**B**ut I love this,' Isabel said, holding the dress up to her and hugging it.

'Is it your size?' Justine said.

'No.'

'Your colour?'

'Mmm. Not according to you.'

'Is it your colour?'

'I suppose not. Oh, all right, no.' Isabel pulled a face.

'Have you worn it in the last two years?'

'No.'

'Five years?'

'No.'

'Ten years?'

'Help. No.'

'So is it out of date?'

'Yes. But it might come in again,' Isabel added brightly. Justine ignored her.

'Do pleats round the middle do anybody any favours? And are you ever going to fix that missing button?' She pointed an accusing finger and Isabel looked down as if she hadn't noticed it before. Which she hadn't.

'No.'

'So where does it go?'

'The charity-shop pile?'

'Or the chuck pile. Whichever.'

Isabel started to put the dress on top of an already large heap of clothes on her bed, then paused. 'Can't I keep it just because I like it?'

'No.'

'Gosh, you're hard,' she said, impressed by Justine's decisiveness as she laid the dress down.

Justine laughed. 'You'd keep everything otherwise.'

'But I'm going to have nothing left.'

Justine sat down on the bed and leant back on her elbows. 'You had plenty to start with. Don't worry. You'll have less, but what you have will suit you and you'll wear it all the time. All I'm doing is getting rid of the clutter that drags you down and stops you seeing what you really do have.' Isabel looked at the pile of clothes. Justine said, her voice sharp, 'After I've gone, you can shove it all back into your wardrobe if you like and carry on as you have before. Or you can move forward and—'

'I know, "buy less, buy better". I can see it makes sense, it's just—'

'Hard to get rid of perfectly good clothes?' Isabel nodded, fingering the belt of the discarded dress. She could remember buying it on the last trip to London before she was pregnant with Michael. They'd gone to the theatre.

'But they're not perfectly good clothes,' Justine said. 'They're out of date, they don't fit, they may not even have suited you in the first place.'

'But what about memories?' She couldn't remember the play, just remembered laughing until it hurt. They'd been so happy.

'Cut a bit out of each dress and make a patchwork quilt or a collage. Or get someone to do it for you,' Justine added. 'That way you have the memory without cluttering up your wardrobe.'

Isabel looked at the piles of clothes, some for charity, some destined for the dress agency. She flicked through the clothes left in the wardrobe. It was embarrassing how many clothes she had that had only been worn once, or sometimes not at all. Things bought in the sales because next month she would have lost the weight and would fit into them, but now she could fit them they were out of date. Or dull, respectable clothes bought on the grounds that they would be useful one day, except that they still languished unworn, the labels hanging from buttonholes. She didn't like respectable clothes very much, she decided, looking through the things that were left. From now on she would only buy clothes she liked, not ones she thought she ought to have.

'You're not working for Patrick anymore, I hear.' Justine's voice cut across her thoughts.

'No, that's right.' Isabel was glad Justine couldn't see her face. 'It was too much hassle and as I don't really need the money . . .' Her voice trailed away. What money. She had finally put Patrick's cheque into her bank account, where it had promptly bounced. She wished she'd torn it up instead.

'How are you doing?' Justine stood up and went to Isabel. Her voice was pleasant. Professional. Just as it should be.

'Oh. I'm fine.' Isabel made herself smile. 'You're right, of course. It all needs to go.'

'Look on it as an opportunity to go shopping.'

'And now I know what to buy. Thank you so much, it's been good. If a bit traumatic.' It felt strange, going through all these old clothes that had ended up at the back of the wardrobe and at the bottom of drawers, carted around in bin liners from one country to the next.

Strange, but good, she thought. Liberating, even.

'Is that your doorbell?' Justine said, her head turning.

Isabel frowned. 'Probably someone collecting for the RSPCA or something. Hang on, I'll be back in a second.' And Isabel went out, leaving Justine in the bedroom.

Isabel skipped down the stairs. First her hair had gone, now all those old clothes. Excess baggage, she thought. Got to get rid of it all. She grabbed her bag, ready to give some money to the collector, and opened the front door.

'Oh.'

Patrick stood in front of her. She had been so deliberately not thinking about him that to see him in the flesh was shocking. He looked equally surprised.

'What have you done to your hair?'

Without thinking she touched it. 'Cut it.'

'You look different.' He frowned. 'Older.'

'Thanks.' You look older too, she thought. His face was strained and for the first time she noticed lines of white in his hair. He'd always been elegant, despite his dishevelled house, but today his jacket looked crumpled and his shirt wasn't properly ironed.

'I didn't mean it like that. More sophisticated. It suits you.' He cleared his throat. 'Aren't you going to invite me in?'

'What do you want?' She could feel her heart thumping.

'I don't want to discuss it in the street. Ask me in.'

'No.' She clutched her bag in front of her, as if he was a bag-snatcher. It had never occurred to her that he'd come to her house. 'Go away.'

'That's not very friendly, is it?' He smiled at her as if she was welcoming him in.

'I don't want to be friendly. I want you to go.' She

started to close the door, but he pushed it open. She caught the scent of stale alcohol.

'Don't you want to hear what I've got to say?'

'No.'

'It's a shame you've cut your hair.' He put his hand out to stroke her head, but she turned away from him. He sighed. 'I thought we were going to be friends.'

'No. It's not possible.'

'I don't want us to finish on bad terms. We have to talk.'

'There's nothing to talk about,' she managed to say. 'Go away.'

'Make me.' His voice teased, but his eyes were hard. She suddenly thought of Justine upstairs, Justine possibly listening. She closed the door as far as she could without shutting it completely.

'We can't talk here,' she said quickly, trying to conjure up a way to be rid of him as soon as possible. 'Somewhere else. Wherever you like, I promise I'll be there.'

'I'm afraid it has to be here, right now. I don't want you standing me up again.'

She dropped her eyes. 'I'm sorry about that.'

'Let me in.'

'No.'

'What do you think I'm going to do? Rape you?'

The question hung in the air. He reached out as if to touch her cheek but she twisted her head away. He dropped his hand.

'Why did you cut your hair off?'

Isabel said nothing.

'You look different. Sexy.'

Isabel bit her lip. She wondered what Justine was doing upstairs, whether she was aware of Patrick's presence.

She checked the front door was on the latch then stepped outside, closing the door behind her.

'Say what you have to say, right here, then bugger off. I'm not interested in playing games.'

'Makes a change.' His attitude changed from playful to businesslike. 'So. On the doorstep it is.' Patrick pulled out of his jacket pocket a brown manila envelope. 'Now this is the sort of deal I really like,' he began confidently. 'Everybody wins. You, me, Neil. Everybody.' Isabel folded her arms in front of her, trying to look as uninterested as possible, so any casual onlooker might think he was trying to sell her life insurance or washing-up liquid.

'Now, what do you want?' Patrick continued. 'You want your nice house, your nice children and your nice husband. It's all a little dull of course, so you also want a bit of excitement. A lover. But then your lover asks you to come away with him, and you discover that you're not really brave enough. Or, you don't love him enough.' He paused, but she wouldn't meet his eyes. 'But I think you do love him. I think that if he hadn't asked you to leave your husband you'd have been happy to carry on. Isn't that so?'

She looked at the path, refusing to answer him.

'Isabel. Forget Rome. If I stay here, will you come back to me?'

'I can't.'

'I'll ditch Victoria.'

'It doesn't work like that, Patrick,' she cried. 'I don't love you.'

He flinched. 'You're lying.'

She wanted to tell him about promising a stable home for the children, how she'd felt when Michael disappeared. She wanted to tell him how Neil had provided stability for her, the safe haven she had needed, her feelings of obligation to him. How all these things mattered to her, were intrinsic to her sense of self. But it was impossible.

'It's too late. I can't go back.'

'I see.' He licked his lips as if nervous. 'So, you think you can't have the lover and continue to have the nice house et cetera.'

'That's not what it's about.'

'No? I think you're wrong there, but we'll come to that later. Now, what does Neil want? Well, he wants the nice house scenario too, and he likes the idea of having his wife all to himself. Yes, the last thing he wants is to know he's having to share her with someone else.' He looked at her, his expression serious. 'Trust me, I'm a man, I know this. I don't want to share you either.'

Isabel's mouth felt dry. 'And what do you want?'

'Let me tell you what I don't want. I don't want to be stood up, I don't want to be dumped by a pathetic note, I don't want to be pissed around, I don't want to be treated as if I don't matter, as if I have no feelings.' His voice rose until he was almost shouting at her. 'I don't want any of this shit you've been giving me.'

Isabel leant back against the door to stop her legs giving way. 'I'm sorry—' she started, but Patrick cut her off.

'I'm sorry,' he mimicked. 'I'm sorry.' His face was contorted with rage. 'Well I'm sorry, but it's not bloody good enough.'

Isabel pressed herself into the door. All she could think of to say was I'm sorry, which she didn't think would go down very well a second time. If I scream, she thought, Justine will hear and come and help me.

'So, what do you want?' Her eyes challenged his. He

took a few steps away from her, breathing heavily, gaining control over himself, smoothing his hair away from his forehead, the normal Patrick, sleek and controlled, reasserting himself.

'I hope I didn't frighten you. I find these constant apologies somewhat . . . irritating. And intrinsically untruthful. But never mind.' He looked at the envelope as if the next words he was to speak were written on the blank face. Suddenly Isabel was really frightened, chilled to the bone. 'What I want is for you to come back to me, of course. That's what I want; if you are honest with yourself, it's what you want. We both know that. All this,' he gestured at the house, 'however nice and cosy it is, is never going to be enough for you.'

'That's not true,' she whispered.

'You might kid yourself for a bit, but you need more. If you had been happy you'd never have come to me at the start.'

'It *is* enough,' she cried, spoiling it by adding, 'and there are other things.'

'Like what?'

'I could get a proper job. One where I got paid, for a start. Or do a degree.'

'Isabel,' Patrick snorted. 'Why sublimate all that sex drive when you could be having the real thing? With me, preferably.' He fingered the flap on the envelope. 'Don't lie to yourself; if it's not me it'll be someone else, sooner or later. Now you've woken up, you can't go back to sleep. It'll be one man after another.'

'It won't.' He looked at her, one eyebrow raised in disbelief. 'It won't because I don't want to. I *am* happy, this is enough for me. I love Neil and I don't want anything more. And certainly not you. Patrick, it is over.

I can't pretend it's been easy for me, but I've decided what I have to do. And today has just confirmed that it's the right decision. I'm not coming back.' She stared at him defiantly, but was surprised when he just shrugged.

'We'll see.'

'Is that it?' She couldn't believe that he was going to leave it at that and, strangely, felt almost disappointed.

'You said you didn't want to play games anymore. So, no more games. I had hoped that it wouldn't come to this.' With one hand he lifted her chin so she had to look him square in the face. 'I would never, never hurt you. You know that, don't you? But I can't let you destroy what we have. Here's the deal.' Tucking the envelope under his arm he pulled from his inside breast pocket a scrunched-up bundle of cloth. He spread it out and she recognised—

'You wouldn't. Patrick, you wouldn't.' She felt as if her world were crumbling.

'A bit old, but definitely yours, I'd say.' He stuffed the knickers back in his jacket pocket.

'You have a choice. Either your husband knows by, let's say, next Tuesday evening. Or you're round at my place on Tuesday morning, just as before. Don't look so worried, darling. I'm making it easy for you. You get what you really want, and you needn't feel guilty about it. Just blame it all on beastly Patrick.' He kissed her softly on the mouth. 'And just in case you're thinking "I'll say they could belong to any one of a million women", I'm giving you something else.' He pushed the envelope into her frozen fingers, then leant close and whispered.

'Do you remember that little session we had with the camera, one rainy afternoon? That day when you loved me properly?' She could remember clearly, how she had felt gloriously sensual, and then giggling at the photographs with Patrick under the duvet together before making love, excited by her audacity.

His voice was very soft against her ear, his mouth nuzzling her neck.

'That's what I want back. It's what you want too. Don't throw all that away on a man who doesn't appreciate you. And don't think he's going to change; it's either in your nature or it's not. I know you. If I just run my hand down here . . .'

'No.' Isabel pushed his hand away and he stood back from her, his manner suddenly businesslike.

'I'm leaving a set of photographs here to remind you, and I've got another set for me which I really don't want to send to your husband. But if need be . . .' He tried to kiss her again, this time more forcefully, his tongue pushing against her clenched teeth. Isabel shoved him away.

'Why are you doing this?' she cried. 'You have Victoria—'

'But I don't want her, I want you.'

'You can't expect me to come back because you're blackmailing me.'

He stopped as if it hadn't occurred to him before to call it blackmail. 'I don't want you to leave me,' he said after a pause, his face lined and heavy.

'But I have, Patrick, I have left you.' There was a pause, both of them breathing heavily. Finally she spoke, amazed at her self-control.

'It never occurred to me that you could do this. That you could be like this.'

He looked shame-faced, like Michael when he'd done something wrong. 'I want you back,' he said, looking at the Welcome mat, not her.

'Isabel?' It was Justine's voice from inside the house. 'Hello? Are you there?'

'I'll be with you in a minute,' Isabel called back. She turned to Patrick. 'Tell me you won't do this.'

'Not if you come back to me.'

She shook her head.

'Then I have no choice. It's what we both want, darling.'

'Please go.' She pushed the front door open with a shaking hand.

'You'll be back,' she heard him say as she shut the door behind her. 'You'll be there for me on Tuesday.'

'Isabel? Are you okay?' Justine was leaning over the landing banisters.

'Yes, fine,' Isabel said on autopilot. 'I'll be with you in a minute.'

She took the envelope through into the kitchen and took a quick look at the first photograph. Her legs gave way and she sat down abruptly, her stomach heaving in response to the shock.

'Isabel? Can I come in?' Justine peered round the door. She'd got her coat over one arm and her bag on her shoulder as if she was on her way out. Isabel quickly shoved the photographs back into the envelope.

'Are you all right?' Justine's face was anxious.

'No. No, I'm not.' Isabel's lower lip quivered and she blinked rapidly, trying to stop herself from crying. 'I'm sorry. It's just – I've had a bit of a shock.' She opened the cupboard under the sink and buried the envelope in the rubbish bin, then turned round, hand over her mouth.

'Sit down. Let me get you some tea.'

Isabel was hardly aware of Justine as she started to bustle about, boiling the kettle, pulling out mugs from the cupboard. She could feel herself shaking and clung onto the edge of the table with both hands. Justine came and sat next to her, putting her hand tentatively on Isabel's shoulder.

'What's the matter? Was it someone at the door?'

'Yes.' Isabel opened her mouth, gave a hiccupping sort of gasp, and then began sobbing. She couldn't help herself, she cried and shook, the shock devastating her nervous system, while Justine patted her on the back, saying, there, there, never mind and other soothing noises.

'Would you like to tell me about it? Would that help, mmm?'

'He says . . . he says . . .'

'What?' Justine's voice was soft but insistent.

'He says he's going to tell Neil unless . . .'

'Tell Neil what?'

Isabel felt constricted as if her skin had suddenly become one size too small, stretching taut over her cheekbones, making her chest feel as if it could explode outwards if too much strain was put on it. She didn't think she could bear it. She had to share it with someone.

'Tell Neil what?' Justine repeated.

'I've been having an affair with Patrick,' Isabel cried, 'and he says he's going to tell Neil unless I go back to him and I don't know what to do.'

'I see.' Justine's face seemed rigid, as if she was controlling herself with great effort. But her voice was calm as she said, 'You need some tissues.'

Isabel waved her hand. 'Kitchen paper. Over there.'

'Right.' Justine got the kitchen paper and handed the roll to Isabel. Isabel started to mop herself up, talking in-between sniffs.

'I haven't told anyone about it, no one knows, and now he says he's going to tell everybody.'

Justine sat down. 'When did it start?'

'Beginning of term,' Isabel began, slumping down onto another chair. 'Not long really.' Oh, God. She pressed her hand to her mouth, biting her knuckle to stop herself from crying again. 'I finished it over half term. But now Patrick says that unless I go back to him, he'll tell Neil.'

'Do you love him?'

'Neil? Of course.'

'No. Patrick.'

'I could have done, but he wouldn't let me. I don't know. It was so exciting, I couldn't think.'

'And now?'

Isabel sighed. 'I wish it had never happened. No, I don't, it was wonderful, but now . . .'

'Now it's not so simple.'

'No. You know Patrick.' She remembered all at once exactly how well Justine knew Patrick. She wanted to ask Justine how it had ended, once Caro had found them, how Patrick had reacted. Instead she said simply, 'Do you think he'll tell?'

'Even if he does, Neil might not believe him.'

Isabel went scarlet, and looked down at the table. Neil probably wouldn't believe Patrick if she insisted he was lying. Neil, who believed his wife would tell the truth, had always told him the truth. 'It's not that simple. He's got—' Isabel swallowed, and traced a pattern with her finger on the wooden table. 'He's got evidence. Photographs.'

'Oh, Isabel. No. How could you?' Justine's face was a mixture of horror and glee.

'It seemed a good idea at the time.' She raised her

shoulders in a gesture of apology. Justine laughed at that, a short bark of a laugh. Then she became serious.

'What a stupid thing to do.'

'I know.' Isabel put her head in her hands. 'I don't know what to do.'

Justine stood up and walked round the kitchen. She seemed to be working something out, turning over the options in her head. Or at least, Isabel hoped she was. At last Justine said, 'I think you should tell Neil.'

'I can't.' Isabel shook her head. 'You don't know him; he'd never forgive me.'

'What about going back to Patrick?'

'Never.'

There was silence. Isabel felt so angry that tears came, hot and desperate. 'I hate him for doing this,' she cried. 'He's ruined everything. How could I go back?'

'Then the only option left is to call his bluff and hope he won't tell Neil.'

Justine's voice sounded distant. Isabel snuffled, trying to stop crying. After all, she hardly knew Justine. 'I'm sorry. All this stuff. It's so embarrassing. I haven't even offered you a coffee or a tea.'

'No, thanks, I'm fine.' Justine looked at her watch. 'I ought to be getting back. We've finished with the wardrobe sorting.'

'Oh, yes, that,' Isabel said vaguely. Clearing out her wardrobe seemed to have taken place a very long time ago.

'Could I have a cheque now? I know it's a bad time but . . .'

'I'm sorry. Of course you can have a cheque.' Isabel looked around her. 'I must have left my bag in the hall. Hang on a second, I'll just go and get it.' At the door she stopped. 'Justine. Thanks for being here. I'm sure it must have been very embarrassing. You will—' she paused, searching for the words. 'I'm sure you will be, but obviously I'd rather no one knew about this. You will be discreet, won't you?'

'Of course,' Justine said. 'Don't worry.'

'Thanks. For everything.' Isabel smiled at her, then went out to find her bag, which she had dropped by the front door. She opened it and searched through the jumble to find her chequebook. The everyday action caught her unawares, and with a pang she realised that everything she took for granted might disappear if Patrick carried out his threat. Neil, the children, down to her usual surroundings: the chest, the plates, the fraying rug. She didn't know if she could carry on pretending everything was all right, waiting for the bombshell to hit. Then she remembered Justine, waiting in the kitchen for her cheque. Isabel wrote the cheque out, hoping that the bank would pass her signature although it was all over the place, and went back into the kitchen.

'Here you are.'

'Thanks.' Justine took the cheque and left.

Isabel watched her climb into her trim little car. 'I shouldn't have told her,' she thought. Anxiety, as sticky and unpleasant as cold rice pudding, came over her slowly. She felt completely alone. 'Too late now to worry about her when there's Patrick to deal with,' she thought.

Isabel spent the rest of the day going through the options. She thought about ringing Patrick up and pleading with him, but decided against it. She knew what would happen; he would suggest she came round and discussed it. Which was impossible. The children, sensing her preoccupation, became demanding. They fought all the way home, bickering at best, thumping each other at worst.

'For Pete's sake,' she screeched. 'Can't you just stop it for once? You'll have enough of it when you're married, so why do it now when you're children?'

'I'm not going to get married,' Katie said. 'Boys are disgusting.'

'Girls are aliens,' Michael replied. 'They're not human at all.'

And they were off again, squabbling and niggling, until Isabel thought her head would implode from the constant barrage.

'Stop it. You're driving me mad.'

'But, Mum . . .'

'Stop it. Or you can walk the rest of the way home.' Never threaten what you won't carry out, all the child-care books said. She would never let them walk home from this point; they were too young and unused to heavy traffic. Fortunately the children subsided into small grumbles. She drove on, wondering if Patrick had read any childcare books. Would he carry out his threat?

Back at home she wandered aimlessly round the kitchen, burning the first batch of fish fingers, while the children squabbled over the television remote control. She longed for Neil to come home, yet dreaded his appearance. If she told him, would he be kind and under-standing? Or stern and unforgiving? It occurred to her that she had never seen him really angry. Tired, pissed-off, annoyed, yes. But not filled with rage. The thought made her feel sick.

How would she feel if he told her he had a mistress? She tried it out, but the only emotion was complete disbe-lief. She simply couldn't imagine Neil doing such a thing.

Would that be how he would feel about her? She hadn't felt like a faithless wife before, because somehow, in her mind, the sexual side had been paramount with Patrick; the rest of her had continued to be a dutiful wife and mother. More so, in fact, as the affair had given her more energy and direction than before. And although their sex life had dwindled, Neil being too tired from commuting during the week, she felt she was a better wife and mother because of the affair.

She sighed. She didn't think that that argument was going to appeal to Neil. The loss of trust would hit him badly, as it would do her if she had been in his position. While she thought about faith and trust a sneaky sliver of a thought crept into her mind. Perhaps there was a chance that she might bluff her way through, use Neil's faith and trust, say that Patrick was a fantasist, that of course she hadn't had an affair. But then there were the photographs. She blushed to think of the photographs. They had shocked her. She had looked so naked. Stripped of shame, of inhibition, of reserve. She could remember posing, feeling free and empowered, the old uncertain Isabel left behind. Empowered. Liberated. She could weep at her naivety.

The children had their baths, taking advantage of her absentmindedness to have a splashing fight, which left more water outside the bath than in it, then went to bed. Isabel read them their bedtime stories, all the time her mind churning over whether she should tell Neil. It dawned on her that Neil might forgive the affair – a moment of madness, ended almost before it had started – but he would never forgive the photographs. Because the Isabel they showed was an Isabel he had never seen.

Neil came back late, after the children had settled for

the night, grumbling about the trains, and stomped off upstairs to change. She heard him shouting and rushed up.

'What the hell is this?' He pointed to the mounds of clothes heaped up over the bed. One of the mounds had tumbled onto the floor, spreading over discarded shoes in a colourful lavaflow.

'Sorry, Justine came over and did her colours and wardrobe thingy. I had forgotten all about it.' It seemed like years ago. 'I meant to put them into bin liners.'

'What, all of them? Seems a bit of a waste.'

'I haven't worn most of them for years.' She found a space on the bed and sat down, sending more clothes tumbling to the floor. She felt as if she were a hundred and thirty-six, shrivelled skin and fragile bones. 'Apparently these are the wrong sort of colours for me.'

'What should you be wearing?'

'Light, clear colours. I've got a little book of swatches.' She flopped backwards ignoring the clothes and stared at the ceiling. There was a thin diagonal crack running to the edge of the cornice that she had not noticed before. Or perhaps she had noticed it before, staring at the ceiling while Neil made love to her, but each time she had closed her eyes and forgotten about it. It's all very well having your husband as your best friend, she thought, but what happens when you want your best friend's advice on whether to confess to your husband that you've been having an affair? She closed her eyes.

'Isabel. How the hell are we going to sleep here tonight?'

'I'll sort it out,' she said, not moving.

'I see.' She could hear him moving around as he changed out of his suit, showing his irritation by wrenching drawers open and muttering under his breath. She heard the familiar creak of the wardrobe door. 'The wardrobe looks better at least. Perhaps I might get some of my things in there.' He paused. 'Do you want me to help put all this stuff away?'

His words were willing but she could tell from the tone it was an empty offer.

'No, no, I'll do it. Honestly.' She opened her eyes and levered herself off the bed. 'You go down and have a drink. Supper'll be ready in about ten minutes.' She started to shovel clothes into bin liners – charity, jumble, second-hand shop. This morning I felt as if I was getting rid of my old life, like a butterfly emerging from a chrysalis, she thought. And now, just half a day later, here I am, trying desperately to think of a way to save it. She went downstairs, dragging two of the bags behind her, letting them thump their way over the treads, then left them in the hall while she went to serve Neil his supper.

The weekend passed. Isabel did the things she usually did: cook, clear, tidy up, take the children for a walk, chauffeur Katie to her ballet class and sit on the canal next to Michael fishing, the dreary water suiting her mood. She began writing an email to Frances, then stopped when she realised that it could become yet another thing to incriminate her. Even supposedly deleted material could hang around on hard drives and Neil was so much better at computers than she was. It would be ironic if Patrick didn't carry out his threat, only for her to be caught by an explanatory email to Frances.

On Saturday night Neil and Isabel drove into Fordingbury to see a film. Billed as a romantic comedy it struck Isabel as neither romantic nor funny, but Neil seemed to enjoy it. Isabel sat in the darkness holding

Neil's hand while twenty-foot-high heads talked and kissed and laughed, and things went wrong, but it all worked out in the end. The weather was appalling as they drove back, wet and cold. Isabel sat in the car, windscreen wipers swishing back and forth efficiently, and thought that, if this were a film, she would tell Neil now, while the light from the instrument panels made strange dark shadows over their white faces. The closing shot would be of the windscreen wipers, back and forth, back and forth. She said nothing.

On Monday morning she knew she had to decide, and soon. Would Patrick really go through with his threat? Perhaps it would be better to go back to him and wait for him to get bored with her. She couldn't imagine wanting to have sex with someone who didn't want you. But then Patrick didn't believe that she didn't want him. He thought that he was helping her to make the decision she really wanted to make, but was prevented by conventional morals from doing so. Or so he said. Did she want him? She had, but not now. Not just because of losing Neil and the children, but how could she want a man who would blackmail her?

She swam up and down the pool at lunchtime, trying to work Patrick out. Funny, wilful, spoilt? Yes. Spiteful? Possibly. He had been furious when he came to the house and shouted at her, although he had quickly regained control over himself. Control. Perhaps that was it. He didn't like the fact that he couldn't control her. Blackmail was the only way. But would he go through with it? If he went to Neil he would lose the only power he had over her. By length twenty-four she was starting to feel that he might not go through with his threat; by length thirty-three she had convinced herself that he wouldn't do anything. She usually got out at this point, but anxiety drove her on. By length forty she was thinking about being in the house with Patrick, the good times, the first time, that first kiss. She swam, tears flowing, the salt mixing invisibly with the chlorine, until she was thrown out to make way for the school swimming lessons.

She was very sweet to Neil that evening, aware that it was possibly the last one when he still believed in her. Unconsciously she treated him as though he were an invalid who would be told terrible and terminal news the next day. While Neil slept, Isabel stayed awake in the darkness, staring at the invisible crack in the ceiling.

On Tuesday morning she drove the children into school as usual. At the exit to the drive she hesitated. Left to Patrick, right to home. She hesitated. The woman behind her tooted her horn and Isabel decided which way to turn.

17

Isabel sat in the kitchen waiting for Neil to come home. When the woman behind had sounded her horn she had let her unconscious mind make the decision and the car had swung to the right, towards home. The house was quiet, just the faint hum of the fridge. Around midday she heard a car pull up, then footsteps. Hands hammered on the door. She could hear Patrick shouting.

'Let me in, you bitch. Let me in.'

She let him shout, while she stared at bland kitchen units. I think I'll paint them, she thought, paint them in cheerful colours that make me smile. She felt drained, beyond anger, beyond hatred, curiously detached. She didn't care what the neighbours thought. Eventually she got up and went to the front door.

'Why aren't you at work?' Some of the aggression had gone now she had opened the door and he sounded plaintive, a small boy who has been thwarted. She used the voice she used sometimes with Michael and Katie: ultra-reasonable but firm.

'I'm not coming.'

'I'll ruin you.'

She nodded. 'Maybe.'

'I will.'

'Oh, Patrick.' She looked up at the overcast sky, trying

to find the right words. She looked at him directly. 'Why won't you let me go? You don't love me.'

He flinched. 'I want you back. Now.'

'No.'

He turned his face away from her. 'Why did you leave?'

'You told me not to fall in love with you,' she said softly. 'I can't separate out bits of myself, and you don't want the children.'

'And if . . . ?'

'It's too late for that,' she said quickly.

'I want you back.'

'I'm sorry.'

'For Chrissakes, why do you have to complicate things?'

'Goodbye Patrick.' She started to close the door, but he stopped her.

'Isabel, you will come back.' She shook her head and closed the door. She heard him shouting at her. He threw something at the house, gravel or soil judging by the angry pattering against the windows. Then he drove off, his tyres squealing in protest. She sat still in the kitchen while the silence closed in around her again.

She was still sitting when she realised that it was time to collect the children. On autopilot she drove to the school, thinking about Patrick and Neil, about what might happen. Her brain felt heavy, lopsided with worry. She felt she was driving too fast and slowed down, but she had only been doing thirty to start with. She crawled all the way into school, other cars overtaking, other mothers on the rat run. Her bones ached as if she was going down with flu. She had called Patrick's bluff, and now she felt sick, sick at heart, sick with worry.

But going back would have been intolerable. What had Patrick imagined? That she could pretend nothing had happened? Or that she would lie back and passively accept him, until he tired of the game? For a second she thought of Neil rummaging under her nightdress in the dark while she let her mind wander elsewhere. But that was different. She loved Neil. Didn't she?

She tried to park the car, seesawing backwards and forwards to manoeuvre it into a large space. Her ability to judge distances seemed to have vanished. In the end she gave up and left it eighteen inches from the kerb. Her legs felt uneven, and she had to lean against a wall to stay upright. When Katie came out she hugged her tight, as if she wanted to absorb her back into her body, swinging her up off the ground, and smelling the elusive sweet scent of her warm, living neck. Katie allowed herself to be hugged, too young to reject such displays. Then she tired and pushed herself back. Isabel set her down, but kept hold of her hand. Someone tugged her other arm, and she looked down. She saw, almost as if at the end of a microscope, another child. She found it hard to focus, then realised it was Rachel, Justine's daughter. Rachel had to repeat herself before Isabel could take in what she was saying.

'Please, Mrs Freeman, could Katie come to tea at my house today?' Her face with its neat small features was pleading. Isabel looked past her and saw Justine. It was the first time they had met since Patrick's visit. Isabel suddenly remembered herself confessing, and the blush rose. Justine's face seemed avid.

'How did you get on?' she whispered. 'What did you decide?'

'I'm sorry?' Isabel stammered, suddenly conscious of

all the other mothers standing about, waiting for their children.

'About Patrick? Did you go back?'

'Please Mummy, I want to go to Rachel's house.'

'Please Mrs Freeman, can Katie come?'

'What did you do? Did you tell Neil?' Justine seemed excited, her sleek hair swinging forwards. Isabel was horrified at her eagerness, the implied intimacy of shared secrets.

'I . . .'

Faces loomed up at her, everyone was looking at her. She felt naked, exposed, and twisted round looking for escape, looking for someone to rescue her. But Rachel held her arm. She shook her off.

'No,' she gasped. 'She can't come. We've got to get home.' She registered the child's face crumpling, Justine's becoming hard and angry. Isabel turned and ran, not caring who saw her, Katie held tightly by the hand. Safe inside the car, Isabel let Katie's complaints wash over her: how her hand hurt, how unfair it was and why couldn't she go to Rachel's house for tea.

When her breathing had calmed, Isabel turned to Katie and asked her to go back and collect Michael.

'Why should I? It's not fair, why do I—'

'Just do it,' Isabel shouted at her and then felt terrible as Katie burst into tears.

Isabel rang later to apologise to Justine and Rachel, not very successfully as she was unable to keep the stiffness out of her voice. Justine sounded polite but distant as if she had been mortally offended but wasn't going to say anything. Isabel hated to think that she could have upset a child and kept saying how sorry she was, but didn't have the strength to try and win Justine round.

She wished with all her heart that she had confessed to someone else. Even better, kept it to herself. Every time she saw or thought of Justine she remembered that dreadful Friday, and Patrick with the photographs.

Wednesday improved, Thursday got better. She didn't hear anything from Patrick, and neither, presumably, had Neil. She allowed herself to relax a little, the tightness in her jaw eased and the persistent pounding of a headache subsided. She had been right about Patrick; he might threaten, but he wasn't going to follow through.

One week after Patrick's visit, life was almost back to normal. Neil off first thing, school run, another trip to the supermarket. This time, in an attempt to reassert normal life, she'd devised a menu plan for the coming week, and written out a complete shopping list so she would only need the one trip. Isabel got back from the supermarket, tired but flushed with efficiency, to see Neil's car parked outside the house. She hoicked the shopping bags out of the boot, one eye on the house in case he came out. It was unusual for him to forget something, although it did happen. She let herself in, laden with bags.

'Neil?' No reply. She went into the kitchen and started to put the shopping away. It was satisfying: full cupboards, food squirrelled away for winter. All the time she was stacking tins of baked beans and cartons of cereal, she expected Neil to come through. When she had finished she went to look for him in his study, but he wasn't there.

'Neil?' she called again. It felt peculiar to be in an empty house when you thought it wasn't empty. Rooms waited to be filled like empty stage sets. She went up the stairs and looked down the landing. If this was a horror film, she thought, we'd be yelling at the heroine to switch the lights on. But it was the middle of the day. Instinct drew her to their bedroom.

'Neil?' He was lying on the bed fully dressed, eyes closed, hands resting on his chest. He didn't answer so she leaned over the bed and reached out for his hand. 'Are you all right, darling? I saw the car.'

In answer he handed her the envelope he had been holding to his chest. Redundancy, was her immediate reaction. She took the envelope, uncertain what to do with it.

'Look inside.' His voice was croaky, and she wondered if he might have a throat infection. She pulled out the contents of the envelope. It only needed an inch for her to see what they were, and she pushed them back as if hiding them could make it better. Her heart was beating fast and the air seemed thin, as if all the oxygen had been sucked out of it. Her legs gave way and she sat down abruptly on the bed, hand to her mouth.

'Don't be shy, let's have them out.' Neil took the envelope from her and sprinkled the contents on the space separating them. 'After all, you weren't shy then.'

He spread them out on the bed. 'At first I thought it was a mistake. Someone had sent me dirty pictures by mistake, I thought. I almost didn't bother to look and see who it was.' He pushed them so they made two neat lines of three. 'A little note came with them. I've torn it up so I can't show it to you unfortunately, but I can tell you what it said. "Your wife is having an affair." That's all. "Your wife is having an affair."' His voice was controlled. Too controlled.

'I'm sorry,' Isabel whispered.

'I expect you are.' The photographs lay between them, as effective as a mile-high wall. She glanced down and saw herself, legs and arms splayed out in abandonment. Mouth willing, fingers nimble. She looked away.

'It's over. The affair, I mean. It didn't last very long, only a few weeks. I realised I'd made a mistake.' Her voice trailed off as Neil didn't seem to be listening to her. He was looking at one of the photographs, turning his head to one side.

'It's funny, I haven't looked at this sort of thing for years. I suppose by today's standards in pornography this is pretty tame.'

'Neil, I know you're angry, but you must listen to me, please.'

'Why? Why should I want to listen to anything you say ever again?'

'Because I'm your wife. I love you.'

He recoiled from her outstretched hand and went to stand by the window. She followed him.

'Neil? Please, I'm so, so sorry.'

'Go away.'

'Please. I love you.' She touched his shoulder and he spun round, anger flaring.

'Get out, you whore. Go on, get out. Don't come near me again.'

'But Neil—'

'None of that. I want you out of the house.' He advanced on her, pushing her away from him with hard, sharp jabs to her chest. 'How do you think it feels? To see your wife like that. Your wife, who you trusted. The mother of your children. Huh, some mother. How do you think I feel? Did you think of me at all while you were prancing around, of the children? You were the one who insisted on coming to live here and look what happens.'

'That's not fair.'

'Fair? Fair?' His voice rose alarmingly and Isabel stepped back. 'None of it's fair. Was it fair when you spread your legs for him, you bitch? Was it fair when you fucked him? Look at them.' He grabbed her hair and forced her down on the bed. 'Look at them. Look at you. Is that fair?'

'No.' Her nose was squashed against her open-mouthed image, she could feel the hard glossy surface sticking to her cheek. His fingers were laced in her hair, his weight pressed down on her, squeezing the breath out of her. 'You're hurting me,' she managed, her voice a thin squeak. He pressed down harder. Her mouth filled with bedspread, tongue smothered by cloth, blocking her airways. She gasped for breath, her inhalation a ragged, rasping jerk. She struggled, arms waving feebly. Then he released her, and she slid down off the bed, hand to her chest, sucking the air in. He sat on the armchair, shoulders hunched.

'I want to kill you,' he said, his voice thick with defeat.

He put his head in his hands to hide his face, pressing his palms tight over his eyes. She could see his body shake with the effort of controlling himself. Tears came from her own eyes, hot salty trails that brimmed over and slid down her face. She crawled over to him, tried to put her head on his knees but he pushed her off, twisting away from her.

'Leave me alone.'

She slumped against the side of the chair, longing to comfort him, to put her arms around him. Her face crumpled with the effort of repressing her sobbing. Why had Patrick done it? She had become so sure he would do nothing, that he would accept her leaving, and let her go.

The only thing he gained was revenge. Tears seeped out of her swollen eyes. She had come so close to loving him, and for what? For it to end like this, her and Neil crying together, alone in an empty house. She shuffled round, and put her hand on his knee.

'Neil?'

He twitched his leg, though not enough to shake her off. He sighed deeply and rubbed his eyes with his hands. She reached out and grabbed the box of tissues from her bedside cupboard. 'Here.'

He took the tissues from her and blew his nose, still keeping his face turned away from her. Then he got up and went into the shower room. She heard the taps being turned on full, water splashing everywhere. Then silence. She wondered if he was looking at his face in the mirror, seeing a new self, a man whose wife had betrayed him. Slowly she got up, her body shaking and uncertain. She mopped her face with a tissue, wincing as she touched her sore eyes. She gathered up the photographs, trying not to look, and put them back in the envelope. Then she slumped down on the bed and waited for Neil to come back.

At last he emerged from the bathroom, and went back to the window, avoiding her eyes by looking out at the view. Finally he spoke.

'Who was the man?'

'Patrick.'

'So when I asked you about it . . .' he stopped, then started again. 'When I was warned about him . . . they were telling the truth.'

'Yes.'

She could see this came as a shock, as if he hadn't been able to believe it was true, despite the photographs.

He had needed her to tell him. There was a pause while he digested the information.

'Will you go to him?'

'No!' She was horrified. 'I told you, it's over. I finished it ages ago, at half term. That's why he's sent the photographs to you.'

'I see. I hadn't taken that in.' He sighed, still looking out at the hills beyond the town, which were shrouded in rain clouds, and ran one hand through his hair. 'It doesn't change anything. The photographs exist, whether you are still . . . still with him or not. I can't pretend I haven't seen them.' He rubbed his hands, feeling the knuckle joints as if they were sore with arthritis. 'I can't bear to be with you. I want you to go.'

'What do you mean?'

'Leave. Go.'

'I can't.'

'I don't want you here anymore.'

'But . . . the children . . .' Isabel shook her head in bewilderment.

'I've been lying here, thinking about it. At first I thought that I would go. That's what usually happens. The husband moves out. The wife gets everything, the house, the children. Whatever she's done, she still ends up with everything. Then I thought, why should I go? I haven't done anything wrong. It's not me who's wrecked this marriage. So it has to be you.'

'But why does anyone have to go? Can't we talk about it?'

'What is there to say? You disgust me.'

'Neil, no.'

'I want you to go. Now.'

Isabel stared at him. 'But what about the children?'

'I rang my mother before you got back. She's willing to help for the time being until I can make other arrangements.'

'What do you mean, other arrangements? You can't throw me out and pretend I don't exist.'

'Just go,' he said, clenching his fists. 'I can't be with you. Take what you like and go. The lawyers can argue about it later.'

His eyes had filled with tears and a nerve jumped in his jaw. Isabel realised he was very close to breaking down and she felt overwhelmed with guilt that she should have brought him to this.

'How can I go? You can't expect me to.'

He shrugged, refusing to look at her.

'I haven't got anywhere else to go. The children, you, this house. You're everything.' She felt the tears start again, and tried to stop them, feeling her mouth shake with the effort.

'You should have thought of that before.' His voice was hard, his body turned away from her.

'Neil, please. Think of the children.'

He looked at her then, and his eyes were now as stony as pebbles.

'I have thought of the children, which is more than you seem to have. Why should they have to suffer because of your . . . your . . . antics?' He spat the word out. 'If you go now there's a chance the scandal will die down.'

'But there needn't be any scandal. No one knows about it; they couldn't.' She guiltily thought of Justine. Thank God she had thrown the photographs away and not shown her. She wiped her face with her hand, but the tears kept coming. She tried to control her breathing but could only gasp jagged breaths. 'Millions of people have affairs and they don't split up. Why should we be any different?'

His voice was very cold. 'Because I expect the whole area is already buzzing with the news. There's no way we can keep it quiet.'

'What do you mean?' she stammered.

'I told you. I opened the envelope on the train. I didn't realise at first it was you— My God, who'd imagine that they'd see their wife like that?' Isabel hung her head.

'I'm sorry, I'm sorry.'

Neil shot her a sharp look, then carried on. 'I was sitting with the others, George, Richard, the usual crowd.'

Isabel's heart missed two beats and she looked at Neil with horror. 'Oh no. Oh please, no.'

'Unfortunately, oh yes. They saw. Not their fault, they couldn't help but see. We were laughing and joking, guessing what the person who was supposed to get them might have got instead, when one by one they went quiet. Then someone, Richard I think, said I should put the photographs away.' He rubbed his hand across his forehead as if he was easing a headache. 'I hadn't looked at them. Not properly. It's not my sort of thing. I just looked enough to see that they weren't for me – or so I thought.' The lines in his face were etched deep, thrown into relief by the grey light coming from the window. 'Not my sort of thing, you see. Never has been. Well. Obviously, you know that. Silly of me to say.' He bit the side of his thumb. 'I got off at the next station. They're good chaps, but they won't keep this quiet. They'll go home and tell their wives, and the wives'll tell just one really good friend, and so on.'

She bowed her head, already feeling the weight of the gossip lying on top of Neil's pain.

'It'll be hell, of course, but people will rally round. Keep an eye on the children, help out, that sort of thing. If you're not here.'

'I see.' She could see too, see the way people they knew locally would rush to help Neil, the innocent victim, and how the gossip would die down sooner if there wasn't an object to vilify. He was right. Her not being around would make it easier for the children. She looked round the room as if seeing it for the first time.

'I can't just leave.'

'Why not?'

'Because . . . the children need me.'

'Really? I can't say the evidence points to you giving them any thought at all.'

'That's not fair, and you know it.'

'If you do think about them, then you'll want to spare them pain. What's it going to be like, everybody pointing and whispering? Go now and you save them from that.'

She couldn't think. She couldn't do what he was asking. She couldn't leave the children. Couldn't.

'I can't . . .'

'This isn't about you. It's about what's best for the children.' His words burnt through her head. 'If you loved them you'd go.'

'No,' she said, pressing her fists into her eyes. 'I can't leave them.' But what if he was right? What if it was better if she went? It wouldn't have to be for long, just until the gossip had died down a bit, a week at the most. I must do what's right for them, she thought desperately. Tell me, someone, tell me what to do. But there was no one. I have to think for myself. She tried to control her breathing, tried to calm down, tried to stop the swirling thoughts. If I stay, it'll be like this all weekend, fighting, crying, recriminations. And they shouldn't see us like this. Perhaps Neil was right. She was thinking of herself and not the children. Perhaps it was better to go. Better for them.

'Maybe for a short time. Just the weekend,' she said, the words stumbling out.

'I don't care.' He looked tired and grey, nearer sixty than forty.

'Neil, I'm so sorry.' She moved towards him but he put up his hand to stop her. She couldn't go. But if she stayed . . . she thought of Neil pressing her face down into the bed, so hard she couldn't breathe. If Michael saw that, would he rush to rescue her? And then what? She had to protect the children from seeing the ugly consequences of her affair. Finally she spoke.

'I'll pack some things.'

He pulled down a weekend bag from on top of the wardrobe and handed it to her. Their fingers touched briefly and he pulled his hand away from the contact. She felt tired and defeated. She started to pack at random, unable to think properly, flinging clothes into the bag. I can't believe I'm doing this, ran through her brain incessantly, but her hands continued to pack. She went into the shower room and filled a bag with toiletries, adding them to her case. When it was full she picked it up, and let out a gasp, surprised by its heaviness.

'I'll take it down for you.'

'Thank you.'

'No problem.'

They spoke quietly, politely, as if they were strangers.

'I haven't said goodbye to them. I can't go without saying goodbye.' She could feel panic rising inside as she thought of leaving.

He shrugged. 'What would you say?'

'That I love them.'

'Ah.'

Isabel caught sight of the envelope lying on the bed. 'What are you going to do with that?'

Neil looked at it in surprise, as if he had forgotten it was there. 'I hadn't thought.'

'I'd like them destroyed.'

'I'm sure.'

'Please.' He hesitated. 'They've done enough damage,' she added.

In answer he rummaged in the drawer of his bedside cabinet and found a dusty book of matches from a restaurant. He tipped up the metal waste-paper basket, scattering tissues over the carpet, then lit a corner of the envelope. It burnt with a glowing golden flame, turning lurid green as the fire flickered over the photographic paper. As the flames caught hold, leaping up, Neil dropped the blazing envelope into the bin, and they watched in silence as it burned brightly then subsided into smouldering charcoal and ashes. There seemed to be nothing to say.

They walked down the stairs, Isabel going first, Neil following behind with her bag. She had the feeling she was wading through treacle. 'What are you going to say?'

'That you had to go away suddenly. I hadn't thought.'

'It's only for a few days, I'll be back soon. You will tell them that? You will tell them that I love them, that I didn't want to go?' She hugged herself, trying to keep the sobs inside. 'Please, Neil, let me stay.'

'No.' He stopped. 'I am trying hard to be civilised. If you stay I will . . .' His voice trailed off while he regained control. 'I don't think you understand how I feel. I can't . . . I can't . . .'

She hugged him, feeling his body stiff and unyielding. She let her arms fall, limp with embarrassment and remorse. He wouldn't meet her eyes.

'Please. Just go.'

'Neil, it's all wrong.' She couldn't go. It was impossible. Her chest ached, her brain was spinning. Impossible.

'I can't bear to see you. Every time I look at you I see . . .' He shut his eyes as if shutting out pain. Isabel couldn't bear to look at him and stared at the floor. I should have got that rug mended, she thought wildly. If it doesn't get fixed soon it'll collapse into threads.

'Neil, please . . . I'm sorry—' She started to shake at the prospect of going. But she had to, she had to protect the children.

'Don't.' The expression of pain on his face stopped her from carrying on. She took a deep breath, then picked up her bag and opened the front door.

'Neil, I'm only going for a short time. Not for ever. You will tell them?'

Neil nodded, lips pressed tightly together. She stepped out of the door.

'Isabel?' She turned back. He looked so tired, she wanted to hug him again, but instead she stood there, conscious of the heavy bag weighing down her right arm.

'The photographs. Is that what you . . . I mean, do you like . . . did you want . . .' He looked embarrassed. 'I'm sorry, I shouldn't ask.'

'It's all right.' She shifted the bag to her left hand. 'It was different. Exciting. Fun. Eighteen years is a long time. You know.' She shrugged. 'I didn't love him. I never loved him.'

Neil didn't say anything so she walked stiffly on shaking legs to her car, dumped the bag on the passenger seat and got in. She couldn't believe she was just going to drive away. She swivelled round in her seat and caught Neil watching her. Please, she said to him with her eyes. Please. But he turned his head and refused to look at her. He looked old and shrunken, the family resemblance between him and his father very strong. He went back into the house and shut the door. Isabel stared at it, unable to really believe that it had closed with her on the wrong side. Finally she started the engine and drove off. She felt totally alone.

Isabel drove aimlessly, circling the lanes around Milbridge until the third near miss made her realise that she wasn't safe on the roads. She turned the heater on full blast to try and warm up, starting with her feet, which were so cold they kept slipping off the pedals. She needed to find somewhere to stay. A little way further on was a village sign, and she realised that she wasn't far from Helen's house. She could see Helen's people carrier, so she knew she was back from the school run. There was another car in the drive, an expensive saloon she suspected might be George's. It must be later than she thought.

The driveway seemed scarier than usual, the big yews whispering in the wind, their branches reaching out to snatch. She rang the doorbell.

'Isabel!' Helen looked surprised to see her.

'Helen, can you help me out? I've got a problem.'

'I heard.' Helen looked embarrassed and despite the cold Isabel blushed. Did everybody know?

'Can I come in for a while? I'm freezing.'

'I don't know.' Helen bit her lip, her face anxious.

'Please, Helen. I don't have anywhere else to go.'

'Who is it?' George's voice, obviously in the sitting

room. Isabel could hear the television in the background.

'It's nobody,' Helen called back to him.

'If it's that bitch, tell her she's not welcome.' Isabel flinched as his voice echoed in the stone hall.

Helen looked shamefaced. 'I'm sorry.'

'No, it's my fault, I shouldn't have come.'

'I can't go against George.'

'I know.'

'Where will you go?'

'Don't worry, I'll find a B&B or something.' Isabel turned away.

'Hang on.' Helen came out, closing the door behind her. 'Are you okay for money? I've got some you could have.'

'Don't.' Isabel screwed up her face with humiliation. She should have known not to ask. 'I'm fine,' she said, trying to smile.

'Look, come round tomorrow. George always plays golf on Saturday mornings.'

But I need help now, Isabel thought.

'I want to help. Let me give you some money.'

'No, I'm fine, really. I shouldn't have come.'

'Come round tomorrow and you can tell me all about it.' Helen's face looked eager, excited by the prospect of vicarious thrills.

'Oh no, Helen, I couldn't possibly make you go against George.' Isabel stomped off down the path back to the car. The interior had cooled down dramatically in the few minutes she had been absent. She drove off smartly, trying not to register the tears in her eyes. If Helen wouldn't help her then no one else would. Or rather, they might, sneakily and behind their husbands' backs, in exchange for salacious details and a sense of being at the

heart of things. I'd have done the same, she told herself,
trying to forgive them. I wouldn't have gone against Neil.

Thinking of Neil, his distress, made the tears start to
roll down her cheeks. She tried to blink them back but
they wouldn't stop coming, making driving dangerous.
She was near the escarpment of the Downs so she headed
up the next track that led to the summit. The metalled
section petered out quite soon leaving a muddy farm
track rutted from tractors and motocross bikes. She
pulled the car over, worried about getting stuck in the
mud, and then got out. Stumbling, she made her way to
the brow. There was a clump of trees and she settled
down with her back against the largest of them. The
ground was crisp with fallen leaves: scarlet, terracotta,
yellow-blotched green. She carefully shredded one of
them, removing what was left of the fleshy part, leaving
nothing but the skeleton. Michael was doing flower parts
in school. Stamen, sepal, calyx. The sex life of plants,
dissected and drawn in section. Stigma, style, ovary. Busy
bees, buzzing to and fro. The light started to fail.

The valley was stretched out before her, shrouded in
twilight. In the villages around the town people were
putting their lights on, making pinpricks of yellow warmth
among the misty grey haze. She watched, ignoring the
cold wind that drove its way through her coat, her sweater.
Milbridge itself was a cluster of lights, gold and silver,
creating an aura of dark orange in the darkening sky. In
one of those houses Katie and Michael were eating their
tea, and asking where she was. She hoped they were,
anyway.

She sat there a long time, letting the wind whip her
hair onto her face, the chill creep in and age her bones,
the damp penetrate to the marrow. The valley became

dark, lit only by the twinkly fairy lights that showed where people lived. A vixen screamed, a high-pitched shriek. On the ground there were little rustlings in the leaves and an owl swooped by on silent wings. She realised that she was cold, really cold.

Thinking vaguely that she should find a B&B she staggered down the escarpment, slipping in the mud and getting caught by brambles. It seemed a long way and for a horrible moment she thought she had made a mistake and had missed the farm track. The thought of being stuck up on the hills late in November concentrated her mind and she became more alert to the signals that she was going in the right direction. She followed a hedgerow, went over a stile and there was the car.

She opened the door to the driver's seat. As she stood there she changed her mind, closed the door and clambered into the back. Anything was preferable to going back into the harsh real world, even a night in a freezing car. There was an old blanket that the children used on frosty mornings, their thermostats still not fully adjusted to the cold after the heat of a Syrian summer. She wrapped herself in it, finding some comfort in the traces of their presence, arms folded across her lower stomach, trying to hold in the pain. Perhaps if she lay perfectly still nothing would hurt her again.

But the loss of the children was like a dull ache that filled her mind, blocking out any other thoughts and even awareness of the cold, despite her shivering. She could picture them now: Michael, leaping amongst the windswept leaves, faun-like in long-limbed exuberance; Katie, serious and intent, puppy-fat cheeks curving over the planes of her face, star-fish hands unfurling to show some discovered small treasure. If someone said to her, you may have the children back, but you must lose your right arm, she would instantly hold it out, hack it off herself, if need be. Nothing mattered except them.

She hugged herself tightly, a hard twisted knot of pain piercing her inside. She thought of Michael, lost in the woods, the way the branches had clawed at her, holding her back. She had thought then that she would die if he had been lost, yet here she was, through her own fault, without him. The world outside the car was cold and dark. She shifted position on the back seat, stretching her legs out before curling them up again. There was no escaping from her thoughts: it was entirely her fault. She should have been faithful, and if not that, then at least more careful. Oh, Patrick, why? Jagged emotions caught at her, confused and indistinct. She tried to unravel the strands: love, hate, anger. Anger. If only he had not carried out his threat, she would be safely at home with Neil and the children. Would Neil know that Michael liked seven kisses before being tucked into bed, that Katie couldn't sleep unless the bathroom light and not the landing light was left on?

She scrunched her face up, trying not to think about them, but it was overwhelming. She longed for them, every molecule in her body yearning to hold them. But they were gone.

18

Isabel woke to someone thumping on the car window. She half sat up, bleary-eyed, and squinted at two faces peering in at her through windows covered with condensation, one face black and white and hairy, the other red and blue and fluffy. Was she hallucinating? She wiped the window with her sleeve and looked more carefully. The faces transformed into a border collie and a woman in a woolly hat, well wrapped up against the morning chill. God, she was cold. And stiff. Her face felt pressed to one side, probably imprinted with the pattern of the rear seats. She screwed her face up to try and bring some life back into it. The woman in the woolly hat was mouthing something to her. Isabel pulled herself into a sitting position and gingerly opened the car door.

The collie jumped up at her, healthy pink tongue lolling amid clouds of hot doggy breath. She disentangled herself a bit more from the blanket to fend him off. The collie's owner was speaking, one gloved hand to her chest, as if she'd had a shock.

'I thought you were a suicide.'

'No.' Isabel's mouth felt strange as if she had sealed it when she had withdrawn to the comfort of the children's blanket. She licked her dry lips, feeling the raw cracks at the corners with her tongue. 'Not dead yet.'

'You do get them up here. They put bricks on the

accelerators so the car goes until the petrol runs out.'

'I'll know another time.'

The woman looked horrified. 'I didn't mean . . .'

'It's all right; neither did I.'

Isabel ran her hands through her hair, feeling it stick up in tufts. The woman lingered, obviously itching with curiosity, but too polite to ask. Once Isabel would have tried to allay her concerns, asked the dog's name, chatted about the weather, but now she was too tired to bother. Whatever reserves of social good behaviour she possessed had vanished over the last twenty-four hours. She leant back against the seat, eyes closed.

'Do you need help?'

'I'm fine. Just fine.' She kept her eyes shut.

'I'll be on my way then.' Isabel made no response. She could sense the woman teetering on the brink of departing. 'Well.' A deep intake of breath. 'It's a beautiful day. Come on, Tan.'

Isabel listened to them go, stoutly shod feet crunching the ground, dog rustling through the hedge, the sounds fading. She sat still, absorbing the silence. Then other sounds began to impinge. Birdsong in short snatches, three repeated notes ending on a rising note, like a question. A blackbird's whirring warning call further away. Rustling in the hedgerow, a fieldfare searching for hawberries. She opened her eyes and saw a spider had made a web between the car and the wing mirror. It glistened with ash-white dew strung like beads along the silvery threads, the sunlight passing through the dew, prisms converting the light into sparkling rainbows. She could feel the warmth of the sun on the car, see it melting the frost on the muddy track. Slowly, with her joints feeling as rusty as the Tin Man's, she pushed the door open and stood up, her lungs aching as she breathed in the sharp, thin air. The sky was high, a clear pale blue floating over ploughed fields, earth rich as chocolate, and the escarpment of the Downs, sweeping across the horizon. The dog walker had been right. It was a beautiful day.

It was a beautiful day, so what was she doing, loitering up on the Downs when her children were waiting for her? Neil wouldn't know the routine, getting Katie to her ballet class, Michael to football practice. She was part of the fabric of their lives; Neil couldn't throw her out or banish her to the furthest corners of the kingdom like a king in a fairy story. Anna Karenina and Emma Bovary had no option but to kill themselves because they were created by nineteenth-century men. They had to pay the price for their adultery regardless. But she didn't.

Suddenly it struck her how easily she had accepted Neil's demand that she left. Throughout their life together she had always deferred to his decisions. She might make requests and state her opinions, but in the end it was Neil who would decide, Neil who would weigh the evidence and pronounce his verdict. They had married quickly because of another country's rule and it seemed as if that rule had stuck: she had become his property to dispose of as he wished. And she had complied. She thought back to that time, the excitement of a new country followed by her father's death. Neil had dealt with the arrangements and she had been grateful, a habit that had continued. It had seemed a fair deal at the time: he looked after their external lives, earning a living and so on, and she looked after the domestic side. For ex-pats that was often the only possible arrangement but now, for the first time, she wondered if she had exchanged her independence because it was easier.

Easier to let Neil handle the money, organise their lives.

Easier, maybe, to surrender autonomy, but look where it had got her. No more, she thought, staring out at the wide valley sprawling below her. No more. It's time to go home.

The children were pleased to see her, clinging tight as she knelt to greet them.

'Daddy said he didn't know when you'd be coming back,' Katie said, nuzzling into her shoulder.

'Did he?' Isabel said lightly, her eyes meeting Neil's as he stood in the hall open-mouthed. 'Silly Daddy. He must have misunderstood me. Now, run and get your ballet things.' She eased Katie away. 'Quick, or we'll be late. Michael, hurry up and get dressed. Your kit should be ready for you by the back door.'

Michael looked confused. 'But Dad said Granny was coming to look after us.'

'Don't you worry about that. You just get dressed as quickly as you can.'

She went up the stairs after him. No time for a shower, but she quickly washed her face and changed, grimacing as she peeled off the dirty clothes. Newly spruced up, she went back into the hall where Neil was still waiting, hands on hips, mouth tight under his moustache.

Checking the children were out of earshot she faced Neil. 'I'm not going. I'm sorry for what's happened, but I can't just walk away and let you pretend I don't exist.'

'I don't want you here.'

'I am here, and I intend to stay. I'm not going to be separated from my children.' She heard Katie skipping down the stairs and spoke in a more normal voice. 'We'll be out for the morning and back at lunchtime. We'll talk this evening.'

'My mother's coming.'

'I didn't marry your mother, I married you. You'll have to deal with her.' Isabel gave Katie a hug. 'Ready sweetheart? Good girl. Is Michael ready?

'Dunno.'

Isabel called up the stairs. 'Michael, hurry up.'

Michael's voice wailed, 'Can't find my trainers.'

'They should be by the back door.'

She managed to get the children out of the house and off to their respective classes, all the time her heart thumping. As she dropped Katie off at ballet there were a few sidelong glances, conversations that stopped suddenly, but none of the other mothers said anything except Justine.

'I'm surprised to see you here,' she said, raising carefully plucked eyebrows.

'Oh, really? Why?' Isabel said, as casually as she could, as she fiddled with Katie's ballet slippers.

Justine flushed slightly. 'I heard—' She stopped as Isabel looked up with the blandest expression she could muster.

'You shouldn't believe everything you hear,' Isabel said. 'I think you need some new elastic on those, Katie. I'll get some in town while you do your class.' She flashed a smile at Justine. 'Must dash,' she said, and ran to the car and the waiting Michael.

She dropped him off at football practice. Where would we be without the weather? Isabel thought, having called 'What a beautiful morning' with a forced cheeriness to several parents. She tried not to register who had raised their eyebrows or who had been startled. Her luck held and she found a parking space immediately in the town centre.

Elastic bought, she wondered what to do next. She

had been surprised at how easy it was to breeze back
into the house and tell Neil she wasn't going, to take
control of the situation. What would happen next was
less predictable, depending on Neil's reaction. Guilt overwhelmed her for a moment. But remorse wouldn't help
her now. She needed to know her legal position. The
papers were full of aggrieved men complaining how the
courts favoured the mothers, even when the fathers were
blameless innocents and the mothers wicked women, but
she didn't know if that was a true reflection of the current
situation. Any lawyer could tell her but she wanted to
know now, before seeing Neil again. She went to the
library and quickly looked through their legal section but
the books she wanted were out on loan. Obviously she
wasn't the only person with marital problems.

So she went to the bookshop, trying to creep in without attracting any attention in case Patrick was sitting in
the Italian café opposite. To her surprise the shop was
busy, and although the Legal section was quiet she kept
bumping backs with people browsing in Cookery. The
subjects were serious: criminal law, contract law, company
law, constitutional law. There seemed a lot of Cs. She
scanned faster. Tort, equity, property, business. There
wasn't book on matrimonial or even family law. She
thought about asking an assistant, but the shop was full
and she didn't want to risk anyone overhearing her.
Besides, what should she ask for? *An Uncertain Woman's
Guide to the Implications of Separation* was what she
wanted, but she doubted such a book existed. She moved
round the corner into the Self-help section. She picked
up a book on helping children cope with divorce and as
she held it in her hands she felt the rush of tears, as if
the mere fact of the book's existence meant that yes, this

was happening to her, yes, this was real. But only if I let it, she thought, putting the book back on the shelf.

She found another book that seemed to favour a dry, factual approach, rather than an emotional one. She flicked through, looking at the chapter titles. Mediation and reconciliation. 'Many couples who attend mediation sessions decide against divorce', she read. She didn't like the idea of mediation sessions. Too many opportunities for humiliation, although at least Neil had burned the photographs so he couldn't produce them. Blame. Guilt. Adultery. The book had it all. She moved onto the section about children. It seemed the aggrieved fathers were right: the courts were generally reluctant to assign primary responsibility for the children away from the mother, even if she was the motivator, as they called it, in the divorce. She sighed. It did seem unfair that a man should lose his house, wife and children just because he was out at work all day making the money to pay for it all. On the other hand, the needs of the children had to come first.

She decided to buy the book, but had to wait to be served.

'You're busy today,' she said when she got to the end of the line.

'Christmas,' the man said. 'That'll be ten pounds ninety-nine.'

Isabel handed him the money. 'I'd forgotten about Christmas.'

'Busiest time of the year,' he said, counting out her change. 'Next four weeks we'll be heaving. If you know someone who wants a job . . .' He tapped the top of the counter.

Isabel took her change and looked where he was

pointing. A notice taped to the counter read:

> Temporary Sales Assistant required from now until
> Christmas.
>   Apply to the manager.

'Me,' she said, to her own surprise as much as his. 'I need
a job.'

'Seriously?' He handed her a plastic bag containing
the book.

'Yes.' She realised that she was serious, that she did
need a job, now more than ever before, and nodded.
'Seriously.'

The woman behind her cleared her throat and Isabel
saw that the queue had grown.

'Look,' the man said, scratching his head. 'Come in
on Monday morning, first thing. It won't be so busy then.'

'That'll be great. Monday morning, then. Thanks.'

Outside, she ran to her car. A traffic warden stood by
it, peering in at the windscreen.

'I can't have run out of time, can I? The queue was
enormous.'

'You have run out of time, but you're in luck,' he said.
'I haven't started to write the ticket.'

She was so relieved she could have kissed him.
'Thanks,' she said, and got in. She drove off to pick up
first Katie, then Michael, scarlet-cheeked from running
about in the fresh morning air. Moira's car was on the
drive when they got back.

'Granny's here,' she said to the children. 'Be good.'
She wondered what Neil had said to Moira. It flickered
through her mind that if she and Neil got divorced she
would never have to speak to Moira again. 'Be good,' she

repeated, even though the children had got out of the car.

Moira was in the hall, being accosted by the children.

'And this is the mermaid position,' Katie was saying as Isabel came in. She was sitting on the floor like the Little Mermaid statue in Copenhagen, legs to one side, arms outstretched.

'Very nice, dear,' Moira said, 'but do get up or you'll get dust all over your pretty clothes.'

'Katie, darling, go and change,' Isabel said. 'You too, Michael. And put your tracksuit in the dirty linen bin, not under the bed, this time,' she called after him as he scampered upstairs, closely followed by Katie.

At the sound of her voice Moira turned, hands on hips.

'Good journey down?' Isabel said cheerily, determined not to be thrown by her mother-in-law.

'Yes, thank you,' Moira replied tersely. 'Though rather an unexpected visit.'

'Couldn't agree more,' Isabel said. 'Very unexpected.' She looked Moira straight in the eye, challenging her to say more. But to her surprise, Moira hesitated, then looked away. Her hair was messy and Isabel could see a bare patch on her skin where she had failed to blend in her foundation. The exposed skin looked waxy white, deadened by age. In comparison Isabel felt young and strong, and she was ashamed.

'Moira. You've driven a long way. Why don't you go and sit down, and I'll bring you a coffee.'

'Will it be real or the instant?' Moira said, straightening up into her usual belligerent posture. But her messy hair and slapdash make-up spoilt the invincible effect. She looked more like a tired old turkey hen, scrawny-necked and flightless, but defending her chicks to the last.

Isabel laughed. 'Instant, and if you don't want instant, you can have tea. Take it or leave it, it's all I have.'

'Instant then, if you haven't real. And cream?'

'I don't know, but I doubt it.' She spoke quietly but firmly, too tired herself to play games of one-upmanship.

Moira looked uncertain, as if puzzled by an Isabel who didn't respond. Perhaps that's the secret, Isabel thought. All these years I've been striving to be the good daughter-in-law, when the careless one would have served better. Not that careless was the right word. More, unconcerned, unruffled by the little digs and niggles. Looking back it seemed ridiculous, two grown women squabbling over dust.

She wondered again what Neil had told his mother, both on the phone the day before and this morning, when she'd arrived. Even if he'd left the details out she must be aware that something had happened. So pointless to quarrel over trivia when there were real battles to be fought.

She smiled and said gently, 'You look tired. Go on, sit down. I'll bring the coffee to you.'

'You're very kind,' Moira said stiffly.

'It's no trouble.' Isabel went into the kitchen. Neil wasn't there, and she wondered where he had gone. On the side was a large dish covered in foil. She lifted a corner. A pie of some sort, all the way from Moira's freezer she guessed. Moira had written something on a label in quavery writing but it had smudged and become unreadable. An image of Moira diligently stocking her freezer with family-sized pies, slaving on an eternal domestic treadmill even though her children had grown up and left twenty years ago, came to Isabel's mind.

Isabel remembered that yesterday she had come back from the supermarket with her shopping, all bought according to a weekly meal planner, the start of her new, organised life. She'd planned pizza for lunch. Instead she turned the oven on and put Moira's pie inside.

She went back into the sitting room. 'Here's your coffee,' she said.

Moira sat up, as if startled from sleep, and took the cup from Isabel. Her hands on the cup were frail, knotted dark-blue veins on the backs of her hands, wedding ring embedded in her finger.

Isabel cleared her throat. 'Moira, do you know where Neil is?'

'He said he had to go out and make some arrangements.'

Arrangements. It sounded a horribly cold word. Isabel sat down beside Moira. 'I don't know what Neil's said to you but—'

'He said you'd gone, and he needed my help with the children.'

'I see.' Isabel ran her hands through her hair. 'I don't know how much detail he went into—'

'Enough.' Moira sipped her coffee, mouth pursed like a cat's bottom.

Isabel counted to three, then ten. 'Neil's very angry with me,' she said. 'And he has every right to be. But he can't just chuck away all those years together because of one mistake.'

'Some mistake.'

'Yes,' Isabel said simply and the two women sat in silence. One mistake. But it was more a series of mistakes. Neil hadn't wanted her to work for Patrick from the beginning. He'd been suspicious about the lack of a proper office address. If only she hadn't gone to the interview, if only she hadn't worn the purple suede shoes, if only Patrick hadn't kissed her. If only she hadn't been so stupidly naïve. From now on, Isabel thought, I shall only work for people with proper business addresses. Then the guilt rushed in again. She had been more than naïve, she had been wilfully oblivious to the hurt she might cause.

Moira broke the silence first. 'I suppose you think I'm on Neil's side.'

Isabel thought of Michael. 'Of course.'

'I may love my son, but that doesn't blind me to his faults.' Moira sniffed. 'Not that he says much to me. He always was a secretive little boy. Keeps it all bottled up. I can see that might be hard to live with.'

Isabel opened her mouth in surprise.

'Not that I'm condoning your actions,' Moira continued briskly. 'A fine way to carry on. But I can see you're a good mother, even if we don't see eye to eye. And we don't go in for divorce in our family.' She made it sound as if divorce was a minor social solecism on a par with putting ketchup bottles on the table.

Moira lay back in the armchair and closed her eyes. 'All this rushing around isn't good for me at my age,' she said. 'And don't those children need their lunch? I brought one of my specials down with me.'

'I've put it in the oven.'

The eyes snapped open. 'At what temperature?'

'One hundred and eighty, I think.'

'It'll be ready in half an hour then.' The eyes closed.

Isabel stood and waited but it was obvious her interview with Moira was over. She went back into the kitchen to begin organising lunch, counting out knives and forks. Strange that Moira, who she had assumed would be a fearsome enemy, might turn out to be an ally.

But where was Neil? He hadn't come back for lunch.

'Did Neil take anything with him when he went out?' Isabel asked. Her throat was tight with anxiety.

But Moira thought not.

They played Monopoly in the afternoon. Moira amassed a fortune quickly, built an empire and beadily collected her rent. Isabel kept on being sent to jail. She drove Michael mad by forgetting which properties were hers. He, like Moira, was playing seriously and was obsessed with getting Mayfair and Park Lane. Katie didn't mind: she had the Scottie dog – just like Buster – to push around the board, making a little yapping bark as she counted out each square.

Neil came back at teatime, his presence indicated by a resounding crash of the front door and heavy footsteps up the stairs. Isabel followed and found him packing.

'What are you doing?' she said.

'If you won't go I must,' he said, stripping shirts off their hangers and flinging them into the case.

'Where are you going?'

He didn't answer.

'Neil, we need to talk.'

He looked at her then. 'You might want to talk, but I don't.' He went to close the case but she put her hand out and stopped him.

'You can't just walk out.'

'Watch me.'

'What about your mother? She's driven all this way.'

He shrugged. 'You've come back; you deal with her.'

Isabel was astounded at his callous attitude. This was not the Neil she knew. Or thought she knew. 'Neil, please stay. Stay until you've calmed down and we can talk.'

'If I stay, it could be construed that I condone what you've done.'

'What? Have you been speaking to a lawyer?'

He turned his back on her and zipped up the case.

She thought of the book that she'd bought, that must be still in the hall. She'd bought it to find out her rights, discover ammunition that could be used. Why should she assume that Neil would do any less? She felt tired, the disturbed night catching up on her. Her skin felt heavy, dragged down by fear.

'Where are you going?'

'It doesn't matter.'

'But what if there was an emergency? How would I reach you?'

He paused, then took out his diary, scribbled on a page, tore it out and tossed the scrap to her.

'My mobile phone number.'

Isabel stared at the number, confused. 'I didn't know you had a mobile phone.'

'The company gave me one.' He picked the case up and left the room. Isabel dropped the piece of paper and ran after him, stopping him on the landing.

'Stop being so melodramatic,' she hissed at him, conscious of the children in the sitting room. 'First you throw me out, now you're leaving. People have affairs all the time and yes, it does break up some marriages. But it doesn't have to.'

'So I'm supposed to pretend nothing's happened, that everything's fine—'

'Of course not. I'm not asking you to do that, I'm asking you to stay until we can talk about it and decide what's best for the children. I know I've hurt you, and I am so, so sorry for that. But it's happened and we've got to deal with it. It's no good going because that won't make it vanish, it won't make the past any different. All it'll do is make it hard for the children.' She realised she was gripping his arms so she dropped her hands and stepped away from him. 'I'll move into the spare room, I won't get in your way, you could pretend I wasn't here. Please don't go.'

'I've made arrangements,' he said abruptly without looking at her.

'Un-make them.' She watched his face intently as he paused, as if weighing up his options.

'I can't.'

'You mean you won't. Not even for your children,' she said, unable to keep the anger from her voice. He turned on her and pushed her against the wall.

'Stop using the children as a weapon, you selfish cow,' he spat, his face looming large, so close to hers. 'You're the one who's wrecked everything. This is all your fault. I did everything for you and you've thrown it away. And now you're making me leave.'

'That's not true,' she protested.

'The truth is I despise you,' he said and picked up the case. Isabel watched him go down the stairs, then turned as the children came into the hall, presumably drawn by the raised voices. She fervently hoped they had not been able to hear any of the row. Moira stood behind them.

'Where are you going?' Michael said.

Isabel held her breath.

'I'm going to stay with a friend for a while,' Neil said easily, despite having been hurling abuse at her a few moments before. 'Nothing to worry about.'

'Can I come?' Katie asked.

'Not right now.'

'When?'

'We'll see.' He bent and kissed Moira's powdery cheek. 'Sorry, Ma.'

'I should think so,' Moira said tartly, but she clung

onto his arm. 'I hope you've thought about what you're doing, Neil.'

'Of course.' He picked Katie up and buried a kiss in her neck. 'I'll see you soon.'

Katie had obviously decided this was an unexpected business trip. 'Will you bring me back a present from where you're going?'

'What do you want?'

'A cat.'

'And what do you want?' He tousled Michael's hair.

'A tank. Or a racing car.'

'I can't make any promises, but I'll see what I can do.' He kissed Michael, who didn't duck away as usual. 'Bye.'

He didn't look at Isabel as he left.

Isabel, Moira, Michael and Katie stood in the doorway and watched him drive away.

'He is coming back, isn't he?' Michael said, his voice uncertain and high-pitched.

'Och, of course,' Moira said, giving him a hug. 'D'you know, when your daddy was a wee boy he packed his case and walked out. He was off to Australia, he said, to see if they were all standing upside-down.'

Katie removed her finger from her mouth. 'Did he get there?'

'He was back by teatime. Now, I expect it's time for your baths and bed.' She looked up at Isabel.

Isabel felt unable to think. Her brain had seized up, leaving her incapable of thought. But she mustn't cry in front of the children.

'Granny's right,' she said, her voice hoarse and cracked. 'Upstairs for your baths.'

'It's not time yet,' Michael whined, scuffing his shoes. 'Only babies have baths this early.'

'None of that, young man,' Moira said, taking his hand and marching him up the stairs. 'There's been quite enough temperament in this house.'

Isabel watched them go up the stairs. 'Be a good boy.'

'I'm a good girl, aren't I?' said Katie.

Isabel hugged her. 'You are indeed. *Una buona ragazza*,' she added, remembering.

'What's that?' Katie asked as they went up the stairs, Katie's hand hot in hers.

'It's Italian for a good girl.'

Moira stayed until Sunday afternoon and although Isabel had flashes of exasperation they were less extreme than before, despite her lack of sleep the previous night. She had just dropped off when Michael had come through, scarlet with embarrassment and distress having wet the bed for the first time in years. Making reassuring noises, she changed the sheets and settled him back down. When Katie came through later Isabel was too tired to take her back to her own room even though she knew that the presence of Katie's hot little body would disturb whatever sleep was left to her. In the morning she changed the sheets on Katie's bed, but left her own untouched, unwilling to lose the familiarity of Neil's smell.

Neither Isabel nor Moira mentioned Neil, as if chary of admitting his absence. With the children they both maintained the idea that he had gone on a nebulous business trip. In fact, Isabel couldn't quite believe that he had gone. She kept thinking she heard him around the house, and was surprised when the room was empty. Deprived of Ian and Neil, Moira fussed over Michael, who was torn between embarrassment and pleasure. Katie meanwhile clung to Isabel. She followed her round the house, one finger firmly in her mouth, a babyish gesture that Isabel thought she had abandoned months before.

Isabel didn't think about the bookshop until she was putting out the children's coats, bags and PE kits for Monday and came across her bag with the book on divorce. She had said she was interested in working there as an automatic response, but now she was unsure. On Sunday evening, however, she read the divorce book, making notes as she went. One thing was quite clear: however it was divided, Neil's income was not enough to support two households in the way they had been living. Working was no longer an optional extra.

So much else had happened over the weekend that the photographs had almost slipped from her mind. Not so the other parents at the school. Parents normally dropped their children and left promptly, especially on a chilly late-November day, but that Monday morning there were small knots of mothers talking and a hum of conversation and quickly suppressed shrieks. Complete strangers felt free to stare and there were whispers and snickers of laughter as she passed by. She gripped Katie's heavy PE bag tightly and tried to look as if she couldn't hear, her eyes fixed on a point just above people's heads. For once Katie was reluctant to leave Isabel. Isabel had to prise her clutching hands off and push her into the classroom, terrified in case Katie registered any of the whispers.

She hung Katie's bag up in the cloakroom, trying to remember who had been there when Neil had opened the envelope. George was one, she could remember that, along with him saying clearly, 'If it's that bitch, tell her she's not welcome.' She hoped Helen wasn't the source of the gossip, buying a few moments centre stage with juicy morsels of scandal.

Not that she blamed the other mothers for passing the gossip on. She knew so few of them that the gossip would have distance, like hearing of some tragic accident halfway round the world. But if you were the one whose house had been swallowed up in a mudslide then the accident had a nearly unbearable reality. She shoved her hands deep into her coat pockets and curled them into fists. Don't let them know you mind, she told herself. Don't let them see you care.

Isabel left the cloakroom and headed for her car, trying to make an unobtrusive escape through the entrance hall full of gossipers. She knew logically that not every mother at the school could have heard about the photographs, and that some were probably talking about their own weekend activities, but the knowledge didn't stop her feeling exposed and friendless. She tried not to look at anyone directly, to avoid the sliding glances and raised eyebrows. Then, in front of her stood one unavoidable figure.

'Isabel, the very person.' Mary's voice dominated the hall, and Isabel was conscious of a hush of anticipation. She raised her chin ready to respond, but to Isabel's surprise Mary linked arms and walked with her to the car, talking loudly. 'I was sending out the invitations to our Christmas party, and I couldn't find your address. So stupid of me to mislay it. I do hope you and Neil will be able to attend.'

Isabel could see that Mary's friendliness to her was noticed, that it was silencing the whisperers. She knew she should be grateful for the support. She was grateful, but she was also angry at the fact she needed rescuing.

They reached Isabel's car, Mary having talked pleasantly all the while.

Isabel unlinked her arm. 'Thank you for the invitation but I doubt we'll be able to come to your party. You were quite right to warn me about Patrick breaking up marriages. At least, he has been very successful at breaking up mine.'

Mary lowered her voice. 'I've heard. That toad George Weedon-Smith was full of it, Richard said. Yakking on for hours at the Golf Club.'

Isabel felt sick and put out a hand to steady herself. 'No wonder everybody seems to know.'

'Never mind. It'll be a nine-day wonder, you'll see. People will forget.'

'Neil won't.'

Mary patted her arm. 'My dear, in my experience, what men say in the heat of the moment and what they actually do are two quite different things.'

'Oh, but that was exactly where I went wrong,' Isabel said, her voice shaking with suppressed fury. 'Patrick said he'd use the photographs and I didn't think he would.'

'Patrick has behaved very badly, but he says he didn't send them.'

Isabel flung open the car door. 'Then he's a liar as well as a shit,' she said, 'because who else could it have been?'

Her hands were still trembling as she knocked on the bookshop door and she had to take deep breaths to try and steady herself. The door had a closed sign on it, but there were lights on inside. The tall, thin man she'd seen on Saturday appeared behind the counter and saw her waiting outside. He unlocked the door and let her into the warmth.

'I've just made tea. D'you want some?'

'Please,' Isabel said, thinking she would need some caffeine to get her through the interview. Behind the counter was a stairway that led down to a narrow corridor, made even narrower by stacks of books. She'd expected the office to be untidy and shabby, with more books and a good layer of dust, but to her surprise it was functional and modern with a stunning glass-and-steel desk.

'Sit down,' he said, indicating the black leather armchair opposite the desk. 'I realise I don't know your name.'

'Isabel,' she said. 'Isabel Freeman.'

'Adam Rockcliffe. I'm the owner.' She was surprised; he seemed too young to own a bookshop. He must be about her own age. She'd imagined bookshop owners to be older – it was the sort of thing people did when they retired. But then she also thought the office would be untidy and cluttered, yet here it was, gleaming and new.

Adam handed her a clipboard. 'Now, while I get you some tea, perhaps you can fill in this form.' He left the room.

Isabel's heart sank as she tried to fill in the form. Adam Rockcliffe came back in with a mug of tea, put it down beside her then leant on the edge of the desk, long legs stretched out in front of him. Silently she handed the clipboard back and he quickly scanned it.

'You've not filled in much,' he commented, rolling up the sleeves of his thick, ribbed jumper.

Isabel felt anger rise in her, anger at everything and everybody. 'You've not asked the right questions,' she said, standing up. 'I've done lots of things but none of them fit your boxes. No, I haven't worked in a shop before, but it can't be that difficult, even though my only qualification is irrelevant and out of date. And the last job I had went wrong. I can't give you a P45 or a proper reference, and all my friends live on the other side of the world. So what am I to do? Lie? Or what?' Her body was shaking but she carried on. 'And you might as well know, because everybody else in town seems to, that my lover wanted me to leave my husband and go with him to Rome but I wouldn't so he blackmailed me, and my husband first of all threw me out but I wouldn't go so now he's left me, and all I wanted was a job where I could earn some money and support myself, and I don't think that's much to ask, is it?'

She stopped, horrified that she could have blurted all that out.

Adam blinked, but that was the only sign that anything untoward had happened.

'Seems reasonable,' he said mildly.

'I'm sorry,' Isabel said, picking up her bag. 'I've wasted your time.'

'No, don't go. Please, sit down.'

Isabel perched on the edge of the chair and stared at the floor in embarrassment.

'Look, I have two full-time assistants and a Saturday girl. Maria's had a threatened miscarriage and has been told to take things easy, so she's not here and Angela's father had a stroke on Friday so she's had to go back home. My Saturday girl would come in, but she's still at school. It's the busiest time of the year for me and frankly, I'm desperate. I don't care how many boxes you can tick so long as you're willing to work.'

'I need the money,' Isabel said.

At that he looked sharply at her, but merely said, 'I pay twenty percent above the minimum wage, which isn't great, but better than most shops. Hours are nine thirty to five thirty although I'll probably stay open later a few nights closer to Christmas. You get an hour off for lunch and two tea breaks of twenty minutes each. Can you do Saturdays?'

Isabel shook her head, reeling from the quickfire information.

'Pity. Well, do you want the job?'

'Yes,' she said instinctively.

'Then you're hired. Could you start today?'

'What, now?'

'Yup. The shop opens in half an hour so there'd be time to run through some of the procedures before we open.'

'I suppose I could start today. I couldn't stay as late as five thirty, though. I'd have to go at three.' She could book the children into the After-school Club for the rest of term, but it would be unfair to sign them up without warning.

Adam quickly showed her round the basement of the shop, most of which was used for stock, and then gave her a crash course in using the till. His instructions were clear and logical. There was also a file full of neatly typed procedures, and Isabel had a pang remembering Patrick's chaos. No need for her so-called organisational skills here. Adam was obviously far more organised than she could ever hope to be.

The first customer came in ten minutes after opening and from then on she was busy all day, muddling change, checking customer orders, taking deliveries down to the stock room and unpacking them. She found the day exhausting and was thankful to be finishing early. She wasn't sure if she – or her feet – could cope with standing all day. She collected the children from school and drove back. It would have been wonderful to have been greeted by a smiling face and a large drink, and have nothing else to do except put her feet up in front of the television. But there was no one to do the things she had once done for Neil. She made the children supper, supervised their baths and dozed off while reading to Katie. She left the kitchen untidied and went straight to bed herself, having her first undisturbed night's sleep for the past four days.

The next two days were worse, the physical tiredness dragging at her body. The shop was busier too, which meant more pressure to get the till right and not to mislay any vital documents such as delivery notes and invoices. But it was a blessing to be so tired that she couldn't think.

By the end of the week her body had started to adapt to the rhythm of the job and she'd found a pair of shoes that didn't pinch. She had thought that the work would be boring, hours spent standing with nothing to do except wipe down the counter top. But there were few opportunities for standing around. When not working at the till there were piles of books to be straightened and queries to be answered. These usually meant having to ask Adam, but she was beginning to learn the answers to some of the more straightforward questions. Overall she realised she enjoyed working there. The bookshop had a warm, comfortable glow to it, a safe haven from the darkness outside.

Neil rang each evening to speak to the children. The first evening she was so tired from work that she couldn't think straight and forgot to ask him where he was staying and what his plans were. Over several stilted conversations she discovered that he had moved out of his friend's house and into a B&B.

'I needed the space to think,' he said, and then stopped as if he had revealed something too personal.

'You can come back here,' she whispered.

'Don't let's go there,' he said, and asked to speak to

the children. Later she thought that that was a very un-Neil-like thing to say and wondered where he'd picked the expression up from.

On Friday, as she was going, Adam put a brown envelope into her hand.

'What's this?' she asked, and he gave her a surprised look.

'Wages, of course. If there's any way you can work the next two Saturdays let me know. Even a couple of hours over lunchtime would help.'

'I'll let you know,' she said, holding the envelope. It felt solid and she could feel the edges of two coins. Once outside the shop she couldn't resist looking, her fingers trembling as she carefully tore across the top of the envelope. A small wad of notes with a larger piece of folded paper. She took it out and unfolded it. A payslip with her name on it, hours worked, National Insurance number, tax deductions, everything exactly as it should be. There was even an extra amount in lieu of holiday pay, something she'd never thought to ask about. She thought of Neil demanding she get a payslip from Patrick. How angry she'd been with him, and yet she should have been given a proper payslip, just like this one. She hadn't thought of Patrick for days. He occupied an angry, sore place in her mind that she didn't want to explore in case it exploded in a deluge of accusations.

She looked up and saw Adam looking at her through the window, his thin face curious. She smiled and gave a little wave. He'd not referred to her outburst on the first day, but perhaps one day she'd know him well enough to tell him why a humble payslip could make her both laugh and cry at the same time.

19

Michael and Katie agreed: it had to be buttercup yellow. Katie had first gone for purple and Michael wanted camouflage green, but Isabel steered them towards lighter colours.

'Don't you think it's a bit bright?' she asked, blinking at the depth of colour. The night before she had drunk a bottle of wine and stumbled to bed and oblivion, but not before deciding that she couldn't live with a magnolia kitchen any longer. The small square of egg-yolk brilliance was enough to give anyone a headache, even without a crashing hangover, but Isabel still bought the paint, along with brushes and rollers. She paid in cash – her cash – and then took the children for a pizza as a treat. In the market she bought sunflower-printed fabric to make curtains, guessing at the quantity, and yellow gingham for a tablecloth.

When they got back to the house the air smelt different and she realised that Neil had been there. She ran upstairs and, yes, he'd taken more shirts, a suit and some weekend clothes. It seemed infinitely tragic that he'd chosen a time when he knew they would be out at Cubs and ballet, that he felt it was preferable to sneak like a thief into his own house rather than meet her. And she wondered how he could bear not to see the children. She rang his mobile but a metallic voice informed her that the number was unavailable.

The kitchen, with all her bits and pieces piled haphaz-ardly on the kitchen table, was so bland that the yellow paint was like an all-out assault. Perhaps I should have started with something like wheat, or even primrose, Isabel thought as she rollered dramatic arcs of colour over the walls. Luckily they were in good condition and didn't need preparing. Michael got bored quickly and drifted off to play on the computer but Katie diligently worked away in her corner, spattered with yellow freckles, clutching her paintbrush and letting the paint drip over her hand. Isabel hoped the room would look better with another coat.

She did the second coat of paint early on Sunday morning. It was still dark outside but the room shone under the electric light with a nuclear glow. The muscles in her forearm ached, then settled into a dull pain. She finished just as Michael emerged, sleepy in pyjamas, so she laid out breakfast for him in the sitting room and left him watching cartoons with instructions to feed Katie when she came down.

'You'll have to eat on your laps,' she said, looking at the piles of things evacuated from the kitchen. Then she went back to bed herself and slept, for what seemed like hours but merely lasted the duration of children's television.

After a picnic lunch she dragged the reluctant children out for a walk in the country. The fields looked sodden and miserable, stumps of cornstalks flapping stiffly in the bitter wind, the light flat and grey. The children managed a ragged cheer when Isabel announced that they were turn-ing back for home. They were walking into the wind now, the hedges providing little shelter. The wind made her eyes water and her voice wavered as she jollied Katie along.

Michael lagged behind, splashing through muddy puddles, kicking black water over the track.

'I want my Daddy,' Katie whispered and Isabel's heart contracted as she knelt in the mud and hugged her little girl so tight.

On the way back they picked up a video and Isabel settled the children down with cocoa to warm them. The kitchen was aggressively yellow, a challenge to depressives everywhere. Isabel moved her possessions back in: the string of Mexican chillies, the Moroccan copper pots. She paused at the photograph of Neil in the Empty Quarter, the desolate sands stretching out behind him, the distant mountains touched with gold. He looked so young. She touched his face and the image of Neil carried on smiling confidently, frozen in time.

Back to work on Monday. Saturday had been a good day, Adam said, and Isabel spent much of the morning helping him put out replacement stock. It was fascinating what people read. Adam said that each year there were books that were bought specifically as presents, usually inoffensive books with a celebrity or television connection, or the latest hardback blockbuster from an established author.

'Even a small shop like this, which can't do much discounting, will shift those.'

'Don't you worry about the big chains taking away your business?' Isabel asked.

Adam shook his head. 'Milbridge is too small for a big chain. And although people can go to Fordingbury for their books we're on their doorstep. It's just a question of playing with the numbers, guessing what will sell at what price, at what point it's worth someone's while to go elsewhere.'

He glanced round the shop, which had one solitary browser ensconced in the Popular Science section. 'Speaking of which, as it's quiet now, I'm going to finish processing Saturday's figures and work out what we need more of, then do the orders. Give me a shout if you need help.'

He clattered down the stairs to his office, leaving Isabel behind the counter. A young mother with a baby in a pushchair came and bought a cloth picturebook. The browser bought a book about gene therapy and placed an order for another. As she handed the book over the shop bell rang and she looked up to see a familiar shape duck his head as he came through the low door. He politely held the door open for the browser to leave, his manners as polished as his shoes.

'Hello, Isabel,' he said as he strolled past the Biography table and came to stand before her.

'Patrick.' It felt strange to see him, his hands resting lightly on the counter. Hands that she had once known well, that she had kissed, that she had let explore her body. She folded her arms across her chest, tucking her own hands out of sight and curling them into fists.

'As you won't come to me, I have come to you.' His voice was as deep and smooth as ever, but controlled as if he knew its power and was searching for a way to find her weaknesses.

Isabel swallowed. 'I suppose Mary told you I was working here.'

'No, Justine. Mary isn't speaking to me at the moment.' He gave a rueful grin. 'Or rather, she has said so much to me that we're both exhausted. Apparently it's all my fault.' He looked at her in a way she'd once found charming, voice confiding.

'And isn't it?' Her own voice sounded metallic.

'C'mon, we're both adults. You knew what you were getting into.'

Isabel turned her head and stared up at the ceiling. Yes, she'd known at the start: he'd made his limits for a relationship clear. And yes, she'd known that she had far more to lose than he did. But he was the one who had said 'No tears when we part'. He was the one who had tried to blackmail her. She hadn't known about that.

He was leaning forward now. 'Poor baby, you've had a rough ride.' His finger traced the line of her jaw, touched her lips. 'My offer still stands,' he said, his voice a resonant whisper insinuating itself into her being.

She took a step back, out of reach. 'I must have been mad to get involved with you,' she said slowly.

'Darling, I know you're angry with me and I accept things got a little out of hand—'

'Out of hand? Out of hand?' Isabel ran her fingers through her hair. 'My God, have you any idea of the damage we've done?'

He had, at least, the grace to look a little shamefaced. 'You knew the risks. Nobody made you have an affair.'

'So it's all my fault. Is it my fault for making you black-mail me?' The shop bell clanged as the door opened, and a shopper started to look through the books on the front table. Isabel kept her voice low as she said, 'I should have thought more about what I was doing. Not just let myself get swept up into it.'

'But it was fun, though,' Patrick said and their eyes met.

'Expensive fun.'

'Then come with me. You don't have to stay here.'

Isabel gripped the edge of the counter and tried to stay calm. 'I can't just run away, I still have responsibilities, and you are the last man in the world I would run away with. Patrick, it is over. Whatever I may have felt for you has been wiped out.' She stopped to try and control her breathing, pressing her hand to her upper chest as if she could squash down what she felt. If she let him make her feel angry it meant he could still control her feelings. When she felt able to carry on she said, 'When you sent the photographs to Neil you knew what was likely to happen, and you did it anyway, without thought for me or the children or anyone except yourself.'

Patrick straightened up. 'I didn't send the photographs.'

'Oh, sure.'

'It wasn't me.' His face was a sullen red.

Isabel turned away in disgust. 'Do you really expect me to believe you?'

'I don't lie. You should know that.'

'Go away, Patrick. Just go. I really don't want to see you anymore.'

'No.' He reached across the counter and grabbed her arm. 'I didn't send them.'

Isabel tried to twist away from him. 'Let me go.' She pulled at his hand but he was too strong. She looked around for help and saw the shopper, an elderly woman, looking up from the biographies, her face a picture of genteel horror. In desperation to get free she bent her head and bit his wrist as hard as she could.

Immediately he released her. 'You fucking bitch,' he spat, holding his wrist. 'I offered you everything—'

'I don't want it. I don't want you,' she shouted back. 'Leave me alone.'

'What's going on?' Adam's voice behind her.

Isabel turned, unable to speak. Her stricken eyes met

his and he put a reassuring hand on her shoulder.

Adam looked across at Patrick. 'Well?' he said.

Patrick swept his hair back, his eyes narrowed as he looked from Adam to Isabel. 'My, my,' he drawled, 'you are a fast worker, aren't you?'

Isabel gasped. 'How dare you?' She stepped forwards, but Adam stopped her by moving in front of her.

'I'm afraid I have to ask you to leave the shop,' he said to Patrick, his voice neutral. 'You're upsetting my staff and the other customers.'

'Other customers?' Patrick looked round at the elderly shopper, who quickly retreated into Ancient History. 'Hardly.'

Adam sighed. He appeared completely relaxed despite Patrick's threatening demeanour and his refusal to rise to Patrick's insinuation defused the atmosphere. His voice was firm. 'Mrs Freeman has asked you to go; I'm now asking you to leave.'

'And if I don't?'

'Look,' Adam said, 'I'm running a business here. If I have to call the police to remove you I will. So why don't you just go.'

They stared at each other, Patrick more thick set than Adam, his body tense. Adam tall and lean, apparently unruffled, as comfortable as if he was dealing with a slightly perplexing book query.

'It's over, Patrick,' Isabel said.

He looked at her, his face red with anger. Then he turned and barged out, knocking over a pile of books and slamming the door behind him while the bell rang wildly.

Isabel realised she was trembling. 'I'm sorry, Adam,' she said. 'I had no idea he'd come here.'

Adam raised his eyebrows. 'Monday mornings are

certainly interesting when you're around,' he said. 'Sorry about that,' he called out to the elderly shopper who was scurrying to the door. 'Come again soon.' The door shut behind her. Adam started to pick up the books strewn over the floor in Patrick's wake.

'I suppose next time it'll be your husband,' he said lightly.

Isabel felt herself go scarlet. 'I'm sorry,' she said. 'My life's in a bit of a mess right now.'

'So you told me last Monday.'

'I'm sorry,' Isabel said again. Her legs were trembling with, she supposed, shock.

'Let's be grateful he didn't choose Saturday afternoon to come.' He rubbed the bridge of his bony nose. 'Think no more about it. Go downstairs and recover, if you want, and I'll hold the fort up here.' As he spoke the door opened. Both of them looked round quickly, as if worried that a rampaging Patrick might burst through, but it was nothing more sinister than a woman with a double pushchair. Adam went to help her negotiate the door and Isabel slipped downstairs, interested that Adam was not perhaps as cool as he looked.

She felt light-headed, as if by confronting Patrick she had released all her anxieties. She rubbed the top of her arm where he had gripped her. She had bitten him. It seemed impossible in retrospect. No wonder he had been so surprised. And she was surprised at herself, the primitive quality of her reaction. She had bitten him! She gave a little giggle, amazed at herself. She shouldn't have bitten him, but then, he shouldn't have held her, shouldn't have come back. She wondered why he was so persistent. Perhaps it was only because she had been the one to ditch him, when he was the one used to doing the ditching. And his refusal to take any blame was strange as no one else could have been responsible for sending the photographs.

'Isabel?' Adam's voice from upstairs. 'Could you please bring me up the figures on my desk?'

She took them to him, along with a mug of tea. There were now several people in the shop.

'Thanks. Okay?' His grey eyes were warm with concern.

She nodded. 'Yes. I'll take over if you want to carry on with these.'

'I don't need a computer for everything.' She watched him run a pencil down a column of numbers and add them up so quickly she could hardly follow.

'Wow. Are you really doing the maths that quickly?'

'Sure. Sign of a misspent youth.'

She watched, fascinated, as he did calculations as fast as he could write.

'Are you sure they're right?'

'Test them if you like. There should be a calculator about somewhere.' He looked around. 'Try that drawer.'

She searched and found the calculator.

'Okay, we'll do that column.'

'On your marks, get set, go!' Isabel punched in the numbers as fast as she could, but she was still slower than Adam.

'That's incredible. You ought to be able to do something with that.'

'Like what?'

'I don't know. Become an accountant?'

Adam laughed, his eyes creasing at the corners. 'No thanks.'

'Seriously, you ought to be able to do something more

than—' She stopped, embarrassed at what she had just said.

'More than running a provincial bookshop?'

She nodded. 'I didn't mean to be rude.'

'I know. Don't worry, most people make assumptions.' He doodled on his sheet of figures. 'I used to be a futures trader in the City, playing with numbers. I always said I'd stick it for five years then get out with my stash, but when the time came I thought I'd do just another year. And then another. You get hooked on it, the adrenaline, being faster than anyone else. Then it burns you out.'

Isabel tried to imagine Adam in the City, shouting 'Buy, buy, buy!' but couldn't. 'You're so good at maths, it's like magic,' she said. 'Couldn't you do something else with it?'

'Before I worked as a trader I was a Cambridge academic.' He shot her a look, as if to see how she was taking the information, and grinned at her surprise. 'Pure mathematics is even worse than the City for burn-out. Most people have done their best work by the age of twenty-four. Cambridge in the Eighties and Nineties was full of headhunters after people like me – maths PhDs at a loose end.'

'Why?'

'Speed. At the end of the day, trading is about speed, and the quicker you can do the calculations, the more money you make. When I was in the City, I was doing deals worth my entire year's turnover here every day, and it meant nothing. Pretend money.'

A customer bought a huge stack of books, obviously clearing his Christmas shopping list judging by the range, from a baby picturebook to the latest political memoir. Isabel rang up the money and carefully put the books into two carrier bags, all the while thinking about Adam and mathematics. His curly, dark head was now bent over the figures, pencil scribbling madly.

'Do you miss it?'

He looked up. 'Which? The City or the maths?'

'Either.'

'Both, sometimes. But most of the time, no. I play around a bit on the markets for fun, there's a poker game that meets once a month, and the shop keeps me sane.'

Poker. Shades of the Wild West. Another Adam that sat strangely with the diffident bookshop owner, in his faded moleskin jeans and soft suede shoes. But, thinking about it, she realised it made sense, the ability to calculate, the calm reserve. She looked at him shyly. 'Lots of people would find working in a shop would drive them mad.'

'But a bookshop like this is different. It's fascinating, like taking part in people's lives, you can tell what's happening to them by what they buy.' He glanced at her. 'I knew who you were, for instance.'

'Me? What did you know?'

'I knew you bought a lot of children's books, so I guessed you have children, and also fiction. There were some other books as well.' He looked sheepish.

Isabel mentally went back over what she had bought. *Rekindling the Passion,* then the divorce book.

'Mmm. I can see how books might be revealing.' She wondered what Adam read himself.

Adam fiddled with his pencil. 'It isn't the first time I've seen you and the man who came in today. A few Sundays ago, I was in the Italian café when you were there.'

Isabel thought back. Of course, the man with the newspaper on the next table who'd seemed familiar.

'Were you listening to us?'

Adam shrugged and smiled. 'Sorry. It was the most riveting conversation I've ever overheard. I take it you didn't go.'

'No.' Isabel was trying to adjust in her mind the idea that everybody seemed to know what she was doing almost before she did.

'Milbridge is a small town,' Adam said gently.

The kitchen still seemed too bright when she opened the door, but at least it was cheerful to come home to. The rest of the house seemed dull and dreary in comparison. Once the children were in bed and asleep she rang Neil's mobile. There was a lot of background noise, people talking, glasses chinking, and she wondered if he was at a party, but he sounded depressed and tired.

'Why don't you come back?' she said on impulse.

'Back?'

'I don't like to think of you in a B&B.' Music started playing in the background and she had to strain to catch his words.

'I miss the children,' he said.

'They miss you. I understand if you don't want to see me, but that doesn't mean you can't see the children.'

He said something she didn't catch.

'I can't hear you properly. Let's meet up and talk. Please?' Silence apart from the background noise. 'Neil?'

'I have to go,' he said, and cut her off.

She put the phone down and went into the sitting room to start making the curtains for the kitchen. As she cut and sewed, and sewed and cut, she thought about Neil. But whenever her thoughts started with Neil they ended up with Patrick. Then, when she thought about

Patrick her thoughts unerringly turned towards Neil. It was as if they were conjoined, as if each existed only as a reflection of the other. Patrick–Neil, Neil–Patrick. But whatever she'd felt for Patrick was dead now, burnt out like a violent storm. She didn't know how Neil felt, whether he could ever come back. It didn't really seem to be her decision, she just had to wait and see what Neil wanted. You can't make someone love you, just because you've decided it would be better for the children, she thought. And was there any point in staying married if love wasn't there? But then, what is love, in the context of a marriage? Liking someone an awful lot, feeling comfortable with them, knowing them. It didn't seem enough. Not an all-powerful, all-conquering emotion that moved mountains and shook the earth.

But I didn't love Patrick, she thought. There were times when she had thought she did, at the beginning. But never more than the children. Perhaps that was why he became so angry. Perhaps he thought she should have abandoned her children for her lover, as his mother had done. If it hadn't been for the photographs, she would have stayed with Neil, sighing wistfully at the memories of her mad affair when she was feeling bored. A little bit of spice, to add flavour to the everyday. She frowned. Patrick had said that she would never remain faithful, that if it wasn't him it would be someone else. If the marriage had been happy, he'd said, she would never have had an affair. Was that true? She dug around in her memory, trying to find an answer. Perhaps happy was the wrong word. She'd lacked contentment. She'd been restless. If it hadn't been for the photographs, perhaps she would have taken another lover, become a serial adulteress.

I love the children, she thought, but that didn't stop

me jeopardising their happiness. I love the children, yet I've wilfully disrupted their home.

The phone rang. It was Neil, this time with a silent background.

'I'd like to have the children this weekend,' he said abruptly.

'The whole weekend?'

'Why not?'

'No reason,' Isabel stammered, horrified at the thought of them going. 'What will you do?'

'Take them to my sister's. Heather would love to see them.'

'You know, I haven't said anything to them about—'

'I know.'

She wanted to ask him about his plans, what he intended. Every day of the past week she had been half expecting to see a letter from a solicitor drop through the door. Every day she had been relieved – and disappointed. Relieved because it meant that Neil was uncertain about what to do next, disappointed because it meant that she was left dangling.

They arranged that he would pick the children up on Friday evening and return late on Sunday afternoon.

Isabel put the phone down feeling as if someone had removed her insides and wrapped them round a rusty skewer. She had never been without the children for as long as a whole weekend. She decided she'd work in the shop on Saturday and on Sunday would paint the sitting room blue, a clear high-summer blue that you could imagine dissolving into infinity.

The weekend also seemed to stretch into infinity. Friday evening she spent clearing the sitting room and trying

not to feel as if her heart had been ripped out by the
children's joy at seeing their father and gleeful departure
with him. Neil had stayed in the car. Saturday was chaotic.
It felt as if the whole of Milbridge filled the shop, with
a stream of querulous customers demanding obscure
volumes. Even Adam became tetchy. Saturday evening
she had wanted to collapse with a bottle of wine, but she
started to paint the sitting room instead, finishing well
after midnight. On Sunday morning she did the second
coat although her arms were aching. Good thing I'm not
bothering with the woodwork, she thought. Afterwards
she sat in the kitchen to eat a ham sandwich for lunch,
exhausted, but admiring the curtains and the freshness
of the room. Impossible to feel sad when surrounded by
sunshine and sunflowers; impossible to feel sad when the
children were coming home. As she munched she thought
she'd do her room next, perhaps in a deep crimson.
Something dramatic and extraordinary.

Neil stayed in the car when he dropped the children
off. She ushered them into the house then ran out in the
rain to speak to him, her shoes slipping on the concrete.

'Come in,' she said, rain dripping down her neck. 'We
need to talk.'

'Not yet,' he said and drove off, spraying puddle water
in dirty arcs.

'When, then?' she yelled as the car was swallowed up
by the darkness. 'When?'

At work on Monday she surreptitiously read a book
about moving on after the end of a relationship. Accepting your loss, grieving, clinging on to the past. She'd
heard the words before, but had never applied them to
herself. At every opportunity she drifted back to the

book and read another chapter, hoping Adam wouldn't notice. Not that she thought he would have minded, but she felt he'd been exposed to quite enough of her emotional states.

They were setting out new stock when he said, 'What are you going to do with yourself?'

'What d'you mean?'

'Angela will be coming back after New Year, but I don't think Maria will. There'd be a job going here, if you wanted it.'

'I haven't thought about what happens next. Making it to Christmas seems hard enough.' She spoke without thinking, her voice bleak.

'Perhaps you should think about it,' he said gently.

'I've sort of been waiting for Neil to decide . . .'

'It's your life,' Adam said, straightening a pile of books Isabel had haphazardly stacked. 'But if it was me, I'd want to make some of my own decisions.'

'Like?'

'Like, it might be that bookselling is your ideal job. On the other hand something else might be.'

Isabel could have spat with irritation. 'I've been through that. I don't have any experience, I don't have any qualifications and I'm too old.'

'You can get experience, and you can get qualifications. It's a question of deciding what you want to do and then going out and doing it.'

'If it was so easy, everybody'd be doing it.'

Adam laughed. 'Wake up, Isabel. Everybody *is* doing it. Something like one in five students is a mature student. More or less everyone I knew in the City is doing something else now, like running a ski chalet or an organic farm, and the ones that aren't wish they were.'

'That's okay for them, they've got money behind them, or houses in London they can sell.'

'Sure. Look, all I'm saying is that people are changing careers and reinventing themselves all the time. There are loads of books for women returners. Do some research. Or don't: it's your life. If you want a job here, you can have it.'

'I'll think about it.'

'And the job?' He grinned at her and she couldn't help smiling back.

'Yes, and the job.'

'Good. Now, I want to clear part of Fiction away and make a larger cookery display.' And they moved books around for the rest of the morning until Adam was satisfied he'd maximised the space according to his calculations of profitability per square foot. Isabel loved the way he took his calculations so seriously, the way he'd stand weighing two books in his hands as if gauging their relative chances of success with the readers of Milbridge. Once he caught her looking at him.

'What's so funny?' he said, grinning at her.

'Nothing,' she said, giggling at being caught out.

'You think I'm mad, don't you?'

'Mmm. But in the nicest possible way.'

Isabel went to the library during her lunch hour and looked through their careers section. She discovered that the County Careers Office offered a free session on the computer, which threw up a selection of possible careers with as much variety as a bag of pick 'n' mix. She started to discuss career ideas with Adam, hesitantly at first and then with more confidence.

'Adam,' she'd start. 'What do you think of horticulture?'

'Depends what sort,' he'd answer. 'I can't see you in dungarees on a municipal lawnmower, but something like landscape design would be good.'

'Except I know nothing about plants. Well, not English ones anyway.'

'Exotic gardens are fashionable right now.'

'Why are you always so positive?'

'Natural optimism?'

'What about a lion tamer?'

'Working with animals. Plenty of travel opportunities. Snazzy outfit.'

'But if dogs have stinky breath, imagine a lion's breath.'

'Yeah, but you'd get a whip.' He raised his eyebrows and she giggled.

'Traffic warden?'

'Uniform, again. Outdoor lifestyle. A chance to be mean to people with shiny new cars and widen your vocabulary.'

'Seriously, what do you think I should do?'

'Seriously, I think you have to decide for yourself.'

'It's all right for you, you always knew what you wanted to do.'

'Not true.' He shook his head. 'I was always good at maths, so everyone assumed I would go and do maths. I didn't choose maths; it happened to be there.'

Isabel thought for a while. 'Still,' she said, 'you had a career, and are free to do what you like whereas I haven't, and I'm not.'

'Not what?'

'Free. I have children and a husband – I think.' She sighed. It would help if she knew what Neil was intending, if he was coming back. She didn't like to think of him in some horrible B&B or moving to a sordid bedsit.

Not that all bedsits necessarily were horrible or sordid, but that was how she saw them.

'It doesn't have to be all or nothing, you know. The choice isn't between working an eighty-hour week or drooping at home.' Adam straightened up, his tall frame unfolding like a laundry airer. 'Customers.'

Isabel went to help, thinking about what Adam had said. Perhaps she was concentrating on the difficulties, rather than looking for the possibilities. It struck her that she was managing to work full time, and although the children grumbled about going to the After-school Club, they seemed to be happy with it. But then there were the school holidays, and she couldn't see how she was going to manage those. She stopped herself. There she was again, looking at the difficulties rather than the possibilities. She had to think of possibilities.

'If I became a student,' she said to Adam later, 'I wouldn't have to worry about the school holidays. And when I graduated the children would be older, so it wouldn't be so much of a problem, and I'd be able to get a better job.'

'Sounds good. What subject?'

'Before I met Neil I wanted to read English.'

'So why not now?'

'It'd be a bit self-indulgent. I ought to do something more vocational.'

'Do something you enjoy. You can always specialise later.' He yawned and stretched, bony wrists emerging from his sleeves.

'I'm sorry, I'm being boring.'

'Not at all. Why don't you phone up for some prospectuses?'

'Now?'

'Use the phone in my office. You've got ten minutes.'

Isabel obediently went downstairs. The first call was nerve-racking, but nobody asked any awkward questions and she became blasé about making the calls, making three more in quick succession. She was just about to ring the fifth and last college when Adam stuck his head round the door.

'You've got a visitor.'

Isabel followed him up to the shop floor, wondering who it could be. Obviously not Patrick, judging by Adam's demeanour. As she reached the top of the stairs he retreated into the children's section, and she blessed his discretion in the face of what was likely to be another awkward encounter.

'Helen.' The last time she'd seen Helen was on the other side of the school playground. She was sure that Helen had seen her, but had avoided eye contact. And before that was the awful time on Helen's doorstep, when George had called her a bitch and told Helen to chuck Isabel out. Isabel clamped her lips together and crossed her arms.

'Hello, Isabel. Mary said you were working here.' Helen rubbed her hands together. She looked so nervous that Isabel softened.

'Are you well?'

'Yes,' Helen said, but she didn't look it. There were dark shadows under her eyes and her nails were raw. She took a deep breath. 'I came to invite you and Katie to tea. If you'll come.'

Isabel was astounded. 'What about George?'

Helen's face flushed. 'It's my house too,' she said, her air of defiance worthy of Joan of Arc about to go to the stake rather than a woman arranging for a little girl and her mother to come to tea. But Isabel knew how much the invitation meant.

'That's kind of you. Katie's missed Millie. But I don't want to get you into trouble. I thought George had banned me from the premises.'

'He has,' Helen said, 'but I don't see why I shouldn't invite who I want to my house.' She then spoilt the effect by adding, 'He doesn't get back until well after seven most nights.'

Isabel smiled. 'Katie would love to come for tea. And so would I.' She would, too. She felt so sorry for Helen. It must be awful being married to George, who Isabel knew to be a bully, and had wondered if he was something worse. She pressed her lips together, thinking about what she wanted to say. 'You know, these last few weeks, they've probably been the worst in my life, when I thought I'd lost the children—' She had to stop there. After a moment she continued, choosing her words carefully. 'But although it's been bad, here I am, and I think things are going to work out. I used to wish I could go back and change the past, but now, I'm not sure. Neil and me, we were stuck. And however painful it's been, I'm not stuck anymore. Do you understand what I'm saying?'

Helen flushed, and then quickly nodded. 'But I'm not brave, like you.'

'Oh, Helen, I've not been brave.' Isabel gently put one hand on her arm. 'Look, there are people, organisations, that can help. If you want.'

Helen blew her nose. 'It's not that easy,' she said.

'I know.' Isabel gave her a hug. 'But when you're ready, ask.'

* * *

On Friday evening Isabel opened a bottle of Rioja, to celebrate another week of work, spread the prospectuses out and read through them. And the more she read, the more the idea of going back to college to read English appealed. It seemed to bring a circularity to her life: she had given up her place at university in order to be with Neil and now she was no longer with Neil, she could go back to college.

Some of the prospectuses promoted the wonders of student life as if studying was some minor interruption to the serious business of sports, drinking and generally having fun. And the courses sounded fascinating, far more attractive than she remembered from twenty years back. There seemed such a huge range, not just English literature courses offering Anglo-Saxon or Victorian women novelists but modules in syntax, semantics, and sociolinguistics. Some of the combinations seemed wild: English and built studies conjured up visions of literate bricklayers discussing George Eliot as they trowelled mortar and built Flemish Bonds.

She looked at the grades required. Her own ancient A levels were nothing like as good as the As and Bs required for courses at the best-known universities, but most of the prospectuses said that entry requirements could be waived for mature students. Perhaps Adam would let her use the office phone again to ring up and ask. Then there was the money. She'd need enough to maintain herself and the children, and to pay tuition fees. She wondered how much her father's house was worth.

As she went upstairs to bed she thought about how peaceful her evening had been. She felt guilty, but it was pleasant just to be on her own, despite the difficulties. The weekend lay before her. She'd booked a visit to a local wildlife park that did Father Christmas specials – Michael was too old, but he wouldn't miss out on a 'free' present and Katie still believed. Then they'd go into Fordingbury and go Christmas shopping, with hot chocolate and cakes at a café for tea. She hoped the treats would make up for Neil's absence, or at least, make it less visible. On Sunday morning she was going to paint Katie's room lilac. It wasn't a very big room. Then in the afternoon she'd try to make a Christmas cake. Perhaps the children could make peppermint creams to give as presents. That was assuming they were still going to Neil's parents as arranged.

But I can arrange things to suit myself, she thought. I can do what I please. If I want to read English I can, and I can use my own money, I don't have to consult Neil. And once I get a degree, I can become a teacher and be with the children in the holidays. She started to drift off to sleep, mulling over her plans and smiling. She'd enjoyed teaching. This time next year I might have finished my first term at college. She stretched out and rolled herself snugly in the duvet. It made such a change to be looking forward to something rather than worrying about Patrick or Neil. On the edge of sleep she heard a noise. She listened, suddenly wide awake. There it was again, as if someone was cautiously opening the front door. And then a shuffle of footsteps. Somebody was definitely downstairs. Burglars. Or, and her mind shrank from this, Patrick. The big bed, which had seemed so cosy, suddenly seemed empty. She fervently wished Neil was there so she could wake him up and send him down to investigate.

She thought about lying still and hoping that whoever it was would go away. Burglars would take the television and video from the sitting room and hopefully leave it at that. The room was very dark, shadows menacing. She listened carefully. Silence. Then thump. And a creak. And another. Someone was climbing the stairs. She slid out of the bed as quietly as she could and slipped her dressing-gown on, all the while desperately thinking of what she could use as a weapon. The bedside light was the obvious choice. She scrabbled around in the darkness, trying to tug it loose, but the power point was somewhere under the bed, and she couldn't find the plug. Then she remembered the bookends, bought in Nairobi, carved wooden elephants on a soapstone base. Perfect: heavy enough, but not too heavy for her to hold.

She gripped an elephant tightly and crept towards the door. She always kept the door open in case the children called out for her, so it was easy to pull it wider and listen. The footsteps were coming closer. Her heart was thumping, blood was whooshing in her ears. She couldn't decide if she should wait, or scream, or lash out with the elephant and hope she connected with something. She could hear breathing. Taking a deep breath ready to yell she raised the elephant and switched the landing light on.

Neil stood in front of her, breathing heavily.

'I'm back,' he said.

20

'Blimey,' Neil said on entering the kitchen. 'It's a bit strong.'

'D'you like it?'

He looked around, his face as gloomy as the room was bright. 'It's only paint, I suppose. You could always go over it with something. Tone it down a little.'

'Have you seen the sitting room yet?'

'Oh no, what have you done there?'

'It's blue.'

'Blue.'

'It's nice. Come and see.' Isabel held out her hand to him but he didn't take it, although he stood up and followed her. 'Well?'

'Yup. It's blue.'

'Don't you like it?'

'No, not very much.'

Isabel watched him as he rocked back on his heels, hands on hips like a farmer surveying the damage to his crops after a rainstorm. It didn't seem the time to tell him that she meant to paint the bedroom – their bedroom – a Chinese lacquer red. The night before she'd offered to move into the spare bedroom but Neil had said he was too tired to talk. He'd clambered into their bed and lay, apparently insensible, while she'd hesitated at the edge of the bed. Moving into the spare room would give the impression that she didn't want him back, she thought, which wasn't what she wanted. Was it? In the end she slipped into bed and lay awake for the next three hours, wondering about where Neil had been and why he had come back that night, all the while listening to Neil's snoring and feeling frozen because he had snugly wrapped himself in three-quarters of the duvet so that her legs stuck out into the cold night air.

He'd come back, but seemed distinctly uncommunicative. She wondered what it meant. Perhaps he needed more abject apologies, more grovelling from her before he could magnanimously forgive her. She didn't think he was going to forget. The children were overjoyed, even Michael had jumped on the bed, whooping. Katie made her father burnt toast for breakfast, her little face wrinkled with anxiety in case he didn't like it. He managed to make a pretence of eating it, rather grudgingly, Isabel thought, although Katie was content. Isabel glanced at the clock. If they didn't get on they'd miss their slot at the wildlife park.

'Neil? I'd made a few plans for the day.'

'I've got things to sort out here.' He sounded distinctly huffy.

'No, you misunderstand me. I meant, do you want to come too? We're only going to the wildlife park to see Father Christmas, and then I thought we'd go shopping in Fordingbury.'

'You've got it all organised, you carry on.'

She wasn't sure if he wanted her to beg him to come with them or if he was genuine.

'I hope you haven't painted my study.'

'Of course not,' she said, although she thought she'd use a soft sage green should it ever become her study.

The wildlife park was bleak, the wind whipping in off the Downs. Family clusters stood huddled together for warmth, peering into enclosures to see red pandas and bandicoots. The butterfly house was popular, a steamy oasis of heat, but the contrast on coming out made the bitter wind feel like knives slicing across rosy faces.

She'd been right. Michael was too old, and so was Katie. Most of the other children were toddlers or nursery-school age. Katie sat on Father Christmas's knee, eyeing his white beard warily.

'So what do you want for Christmas' – he looked at his prompt sheet – 'Katie?'

'For my Daddy to stay at home and not go away any more,' she said in a clear voice. Isabel felt the words like a stabbing pain in her heart. She had tried so hard to pretend that everything was all right with Neil, that he was coming home. Now he was back, but there were no guarantees that he would stay there. At that moment she promised that if she had to eat humble pie for the rest of her life she would do it to give Katie her Christmas wish.

Father Christmas looked uncomfortable. 'Well, that's a hard thing to fit down a chimney. Is there anything else you'd like?'

'A puppy,' Katie said firmly. Isabel shook her head and Father Christmas moved on to Michael.

Michael looked terminally embarrassed although he was quick to supply a list of what he wanted for Christmas: a twenty-foot pole rod, a new keep net and a priest, which made Father Christmas blink in surprise.

'You use it for knocking fish out. Like a cosh,' Michael said, demonstrating with gusto. Father Christmas gave each of them a present – a tea set for Katie and a jigsaw of a steam engine for Michael – and beckoned the next family on with relief.

'Why didn't Dad come?' Michael asked, but Isabel hadn't got an answer for him.

Afterwards they traipsed round the Fordingbury shops. Although it was only mid-afternoon the Christmas lights were on, bright stars and angels blowing trumpets strung across the streets in looping swags. Shop windows glowed, piled high with goodies. There was a buzz of excitement in the air, and at the end of the market square a brass band was playing carols. Isabel bought a copy of *The Big Issue,* thankful that she wasn't homeless.

The children bought presents for teachers and Neil's family: Moira, Ian, Heather and her husband. Heather was expecting a baby in the New Year. Isabel knew that Heather wanted a boy. She was imbued with the Freeman attitude that boys were somehow better, even though it meant she'd been overlooked as a successor to Ian's business. Isabel's hand lingered over the diminutive toes of a blue sleepsuit. It seemed absurd to think of blue being only for boys and pink for girls and that it was tempting fate to choose either, especially when the alternatives were lemon yellow or mint green, both of which tended to emphasise the boiled goblin look of the newborn baby. In the end she bought a cheerfully bright mobile, and whisked the children off to the café for hot chocolate.

The children made a huge fuss of Neil when they got home, insisting that he read stories and put them to bed. Isabel worked quietly in the kitchen preparing supper, opening a bottle of Rioja to let it breathe. She laid the table carefully; she didn't want it to appear a celebratory meal, so no candles. On the other hand, she wanted it to look as if she'd made an effort. In the darkness of the garden she found some sprigs of evergreen – rosemary and a variegated euonymous – and a stem of winter jasmine. The yellow spikes reminded her of the nerines she had once picked in Patrick's garden, but that seemed long ago. The fragile beauty of the nerines would have shrivelled with the first frosts.

Neil didn't notice her flower arrangement, or if he did, he made no comment. They sat opposite each other, Isabel trying to get a conversation going while Neil gave monosyllabic answers. She wasn't sure what he wanted. Perhaps he was expecting her to beg his forgiveness, or perhaps they would fall back into being together without ever discussing what had happened. Perhaps he wanted to pretend that nothing had happened. But something had happened. It couldn't be swept under a bland carpet of politeness.

Finally she couldn't bear it any more. 'Neil, what's going on? Are you back, or what? I don't know if I'm about to be divorced or reconciled.'

'Do you want a divorce?'

'Do you?'

He didn't say anything to that, just stared at his hands. Isabel felt the word 'divorce' coil around the room like smoke. The big D word. She thought of other D words: depressed, despondent, disheartened. It was a struggle to think of any positive D words.

'I don't know what to say. Or what you want me to say,' Neil said at last. 'I want to be here, for the children. I want to keep the family together. But you—' he stopped and poured himself some more wine. 'Every time I look at you I see those photographs. The moment when I held them in my hands and realised what I was seeing . . .'

His hands shook when he raised the glass to his mouth.

'I'm so sorry,' Isabel whispered.

'Sometimes I wish you were dead.'

She hung her head, as if baring her neck for the executioner's axe. 'I know I deserve every horrid thing you can say about me.' She lifted her head. 'But if it hadn't been for the photographs, you wouldn't have known anything. I'm not saying that makes it better, but I had finished with him. It was over.'

'I don't know Isabel. I don't know if I could ever trust you again.' He got up and stood by the window, looking out into the darkness.

'But you have to. If we're going to live together again.'

He turned round. 'How do I know it won't happen again?'

She thought about making promises, but her promises would be worthless. 'You don't know. You can't. People don't come with guarantees. All I can say is that I won't risk the children's future again.'

'So for the children's sake, I'm to forgive and forget?'

'If you can.'

'I don't know if that's possible.' He sat down again and ran one hand over his hair. 'I can't talk about this now. I need to think.'

'Okay. Perhaps some other time.' She started to clear away the dirty plates in silence.

Neil drained his glass. 'I don't want to divorce,' he said abruptly. 'We don't do divorce in my family.'

'So your mother told me,' Isabel said. She wondered if this was going to be the deciding factor in her marriage continuing. Not because Neil forgave her, or loved her, but because the Freemans didn't 'do' divorce. It seemed a mean little reason, as if all ills could be solved by never referring to them and letting them dwindle into a miserable compromise.

Neil went upstairs to bed. Isabel tidied up in the kitchen, uncertain of what she was to do. In the end she, too, went upstairs. She undressed in the dark and slid into the cold bed, listening to Neil's steady breathing. She wondered what he was thinking. Perhaps he was lying there hating her. Or loving her and hating her at the same time. She didn't know if anyone other than a saint could forgive the sort of hurt she had given him. She curled up facing away from him and closed her eyes for sleep.

She was dreaming about being buried under flowers, rosemary tangling with nerines and winter jasmine. The weight on top of her was pressing down like stones, crushing the breath out of her. She woke, confused, but the weight was still there. Neil was on top of her, pushing into her. Still half asleep, she cried out.

'Shut up,' Neil muttered.

She was going to protest, push him off, then she remembered Katie wishing for her Daddy to stay forever, and she let her hands fall back.

There was a clip she had seen on television once, of two giant tortoises mating, the male perched precariously on top of the female, scrawny neck outstretched with effort, shells clashing. The female had offered no resistance, stood still with mouth clamped in a line of endurance. Isabel clamped her own lips together. She knew why he was doing this: this had nothing to do with pleasure. He was reclaiming her as his own after Patrick. Pushed up the bed, her head thumped against the headboard, she put her hand up to try to cushion the blows. Thump, thump, thump. Her fingers were hurting, rhythmically crushed between her skull and the hard surface of the headboard. Push, push, push. Her lower body burned with a dry, searing ache. But she made no effort to hurry him up, just lay passively accepting the pain, hoping it would be over soon. And it was. A sudden crescendo, then Neil rolled off and she was left to curl up again and try to go back to sleep.

The weekend ground on. The children frisked around a monosyllabic Neil who settled down amid the Sunday papers and the Grand Prix on the television as if he had never been away. Isabel piled Katie's things into the centre of her room and slowly painted it lilac. It'll match the shadows under my eyes, she thought, as her arms mechanically went up and down, up and down with the roller. Only Michael's room was left to paint, as Neil had refused to let her paint the bedroom in any colour, let alone crimson.

'I could try something less dramatic, like pale orange,' she tried.

Neil rolled his eyes. 'It's fine as it is,' he said, his voice as bland as the magnolia walls.

Monday morning was grey, as if the sun had decided it was pointless to emerge until Tuesday. Neil left for work, leaving behind the post, Isabel noticed. He obviously didn't want any more surprises on the commuter train. Also, most of it was for her. Two more prospectuses, Christmas cards from Saudi and Malaysia and a white envelope. She opened it and pulled out an invitation. Mrs Richard Wright. At Home. Isabel had to think for a second who it was from. It was ironic that someone so full of personality as Mary could be subsumed by her husband's name. She flipped it over. On the back Mary had written in neat, round writing: 'People have short memories. Do come, with or without.' Your husband, Isabel supposed. She flicked the card with her fingers, wondering what to do. Then she put it on the mantelpiece. It was kind of Mary to invite her.

By coincidence, she bumped into Mary at the school. She reiterated the invitation verbally, then lowered her voice.

'My dear, Patrick is devastated. He says—'

'Neil came back this weekend,' Isabel cut in quickly.

Mary paused, then said, 'I see.'

Isabel stared over the grey tarmac of the playground, not meeting Mary's eyes. 'It's going to be difficult,' she said carefully, 'but I think we're going to make a go of it.'

'Ah.' For a second Mary looked disappointed, then gave a little shake as if putting the mantle of PTA Chairman back on. 'Good for you. A very sensible decision.' She patted Isabel's arm.

I don't feel as if I've made any decisions, Isabel wanted to wail, sensible or otherwise. It's all happening to me and I don't get any choices. She rubbed her forehead with her hand, as if rubbing out the creases.

'You know you can call me and talk about it,' Mary said very gently. 'I would understand.' Isabel looked sharply at her. Did Mary mean that she'd had an affair?

Mary looked at the ground and Isabel could see the family resemblance between her and Patrick. 'All marriages have their rocky patches,' she said. 'It comes with the territory. So.' She sniffed, the usual brisk Mary reasserting herself. 'Ring me if you want to, or come round for coffee. And come to my party. It'll do you good.'

'I don't think—'

'Patrick won't be there, if that's what you're worried about. He's gone to Italy.'

She didn't want to ask, but had to. 'Alone?'

Mary shot her a look. 'Victoria's gone to London,' she said. 'I think she realised that Patrick was emotionally involved elsewhere. As much as Patrick can be emotionally involved.'

'I'm sorry,' Isabel said, but she wasn't sure if she was sorry for Victoria or Patrick. Or herself.

'Never mind, it wasn't your fault. Now, I must go. Look after yourself.' And she bustled off.

Isabel went to work.

Like most Monday mornings the shop was quiet. She trudged back and forth between the stock room and the shop floor, restocking the shelves, thinking about Patrick, about Neil, about choices and sensible decisions. Adam didn't say much either, as if he too was thinking. As she moved the books around she realised that some of the strength she had acquired from swimming was ebbing. The muscular tightness around her middle, the feeling of having a core of strength, was fading. She hadn't swum since the final break-up with Patrick.

At lunchtime she went down to the pool to pick up leaflets on the children's holiday programme. The air in the foyer was dense with steam and chlorine, hot after the chill outside. Through the glass she could see the swimmers, ploughing their way up and down the pool, sleek and mobile as seals. That was me, once, she thought. She leant her head against the hard glass, sick with unhappiness. But I've got what I wanted, she thought. A stable home for my children, complete with father. I've even got a job. It'll just take time to settle back to normal.

Business picked up in the shop over the afternoon.

In-between customers Adam asked if she had filled in the college application forms.

'Not yet.'

He frowned. 'Isn't the deadline soon?'

'After Christmas.'

'But it would be good to get the papers in before the deadline.'

'Neil's back,' she said suddenly. Adam didn't answer immediately.

'You must be pleased,' he said finally, sounding very formal and distant.

'Yes I am. Of course.' She felt close to tears.

'I'm pleased for you.'

'Thanks.'

They stood side by side behind the counter, not saying anything, watching the customers look through the books.

'Isabel? What's all this stuff doing, cluttering up the place?' Neil was back from work, scratchy with irritation. He was picking up the stack of prospectuses.

'They're mine,' Isabel said. She took a deep breath. 'I was thinking of going to college next year.'

'What for?'

'For me. Because I'm interested. Because I want to do something with my life.'

'I see. So who will look after the children while you're off being a student?'

'There are three universities within an hour's drive of here, plus the FE college at Fordingbury. It won't make any difference to the children. They're at school all day, and I'll have the same holidays as them.'

'What about money? You don't get grants any more, you know.'

'I know. I'm not eligible anyway, having been abroad.'
She gathered her thoughts. 'I'm going to sell my parents'
house.'

'But we use the rental money for the school fees.'

'I know, but the way property has been going, it's
worth a lot of money. There's enough to fund me going
to university as well as paying the children's school fees.'

'We agreed it would go on education.' Neil's face was
mulish.

No, Isabel thought of saying. You decided and I agreed.
But instead she said lightly, 'Why not my education?'

Neil rifled the prospectuses, the glossy pages making
a soft blur of sound. 'So, what will you do with your
education?'

'Teach.' She searched his face, trying to gauge his
response.

He leant back on his chair.

'I suppose there's no harm in trying.'

She waited to see if he was going to say anything more.

'What's for supper?' he said.

It was fortunate that Neil had stopped searching through
the mail before he left for work because a few days later
Isabel received a plump letter with a Roma postmark.
She tucked it into her bag without opening it, knowing
who it was from, wondering what he had to say to her.
The shop was busy so she had to wait until her morning break. She escaped into the stock room and closed
the door. Perched on boxes of books she took the letter
from her bag and opened it.

Inside was another envelope, containing three film
negative strips, a postcard of the Coliseum with an
address on the other side, and a small package wrapped

in kitchen paper. She sat with it in her hand, thinking of the beginning, the first kiss. She had felt so excited, expectant, electric with life and its possibilities. And now?

The door opened and Adam came in.

'Everything okay?'

In answer Isabel held out her hand. Patrick's signet ring glistened in the palm of her hand.

'I don't seem able to break free,' she said. It should have felt strange saying something so personal to her employer, but it felt natural to confide in him. Adam leant against the door, his face serious.

'Do you want to?'

'Yes. And no.' She fingered the ring. 'If I let go, I feel as if I'm closing the door on everything that's alive.'

'Do you love him?'

She shook her head.

'And Neil?'

'I don't know. I've been with him for ever, my whole adult life. Everything that I am, that I have, is bound up with him. I can't imagine life without him. Is that love? It's not violins and rockets, we just trundle along in our little world, every year settling deeper into the ruts.'

'It doesn't sound like love to me.' His face was sad, and she wondered about his past.

'The children love him.'

The shop doorbell rang and he moved as if to go.

'I must go back. Come up when you can.' At the door he turned back to her. 'Don't forget that there are always alternatives.' He looked as if he was going to say something else, but the bell rang again. He smiled at her and shrugged. 'I have to go.'

Isabel felt ashamed. It was Adam's shop, and she was the employee, yet he was the one who was going to deal

with the customers. She hurriedly shoved Patrick's letter
and ring back into her bag, and went up to join Adam.

She thought about what Adam had said about alternatives all day. Perhaps her choice was not, as she had
thought, between Patrick and Neil, but between staying
in a rut and moving on. Moving on didn't have to mean
moving to Patrick, or leaving Neil. She could move on
within her marriage, through developing herself. In that
way she could maintain the stable home for her children
that she so wanted for them. Talking about becoming a
student hadn't seemed real before, more an elaborate
party game, but now she realised that it was more
important than that.

When she got home she waited until Neil had gone
up to bed. The blue of the sitting-room walls was nearly
as blue as the sky behind the Coliseum. She wrote the
address on an envelope, then tore the postcard into pieces
and put them on the fire, along with the strips of film
negative. The cellophane curled and twisted as if in pain,
then dissolved into the flames. Finally she unwrapped the
ring. It was heavy in her palm, a beautiful gold circle.
Without trying it on she wrapped it up again, put it into
the envelope and sealed it. It was over.

21

Neil rang Mary's doorbell. As it sounded, Isabel felt panic rise inside her. She wanted to run, be anywhere else. Inside she could hear party noises, what sounded like hundreds of gossiping people. Neil must have sensed her panic because he put one arm around her waist so that when the door opened they were coupled together.

Mary had got staff in for her party. The door was opened by a young woman in a black dress and frilled white apron, with a bored expression on her face. They went in, Isabel wishing that she'd worn something smarter and more glittery. She could see by the way Neil was sticking his neck out as if his tie was too tight that he was feeling equally nervous. Glasses of champagne in hand, they made their way down the hall. Isabel was thankful that of the people she had seen so far she recognised no one, beyond Millie in her nightie, peeping through the banisters from the upstairs landing.

Mary's drawing room was crowded. Neil again put his arm around Isabel as if protecting her from the crush.

'Isabel, my dear, so pleased you could come.' Mary, pink face clashing with a gold sequined top, sailed majestically towards them. 'And Neil too, how nice. Now come and meet some people.' She briskly introduced them to a small group. 'Neil and Isabel Freeman, back in this country after years of ex-pat life.'

With Mary's introduction the conversation ran the usual path: which countries, what did you do out there, how long for? Neil did most of the talking, which was good as she felt wound up with the strain, too tense to make conversation. She looked up at him, watching his mouth, hidden under his moustache. It opened, red and fleshy as he talked. He kept talking about 'we' – we did this, we did that.

A waitress came round with canapés. Isabel ate one, although she couldn't tell what it was she'd just eaten. She hoped the children were all right: it had been the last day of school for them and they had come home carrying plastic bags bulging with exercise books and loo roll and cotton-wool constructions, paintings flapping, and stray bits of tinsel. It had been a wrench to leave them with the girl from next door but one. They were so clean and delicious after their baths, necks smelling of warm soap and innocence. They need security, she thought, suppressing a sharp pang of rebellion. They need Neil and me to stay together.

Isabel concentrated on the conversation, nodding and smiling. More canapés, more champagne. She began to relax. None of the people seemed to know of her, or if they did, they hid it under an impenetrable layer of sociability. One or two familiar faces went past, but Isabel acted as if nothing had happened, and they reciprocated. One of them, whom Isabel recognised from the sole PTA meeting she had attended, even went as far as to tease her about a meeting she had missed.

'Don't forget again, now,' she said gaily.

Mary had written that people had short memories, but to forget something as shocking as the photographs would imply the attention span of a flea. Isabel wondered what the reactions would have been like if Neil hadn't been there. After all, if Neil forgave her, then no one else had anything to say about it. She started to enjoy the party, although she stayed close to Neil's reassuring presence. Hesitantly at first, then with more confidence, she started to talk about her plans for university. It was heartening to realise how many people either knew someone who had gone to university as a mature student or had done so themselves. This is easy, she thought, relaxed on her third glass of champagne. Even if they know, no one is going to refer to Patrick. She turned to see where Neil had got to and bumped into a man standing behind her.

'Oops, sorry,' she said. The man turned and stared at her with bulbous eyes.

'Well, well, if it isn't Isabel,' George said.

Isabel stepped back, but she was hemmed in by the crush of other guests. George put his hands on her shoulders and kissed her, his palms moist with sweat, his breath hot on her cheek. One hand brushed – accidentally? – against her breast. He was standing close, too close, looming over her but she couldn't move away.

'I hardly recognised you with your clothes on,' he drawled, his eyes lingering on her body.

'Excuse me.' Isabel tried to push her way through the crowd, away from him, but George stopped her.

'Why so unfriendly?' he said, placing a fat hand on her bottom. 'We all know you're not exactly exclusive.'

He didn't bother to keep his voice down, and Isabel sensed a few heads turning. She caught the glint in his eye. He's enjoying this, she thought, he's enjoying my humiliation. But I don't have to be bullied by George, I've been through too much to let him get away with it.

'I think you need to cool off, George,' she murmured, and very deliberately poured her glass of champagne over the front of his trousers. He yelped and stepped back, but too late. Ignoring his splutters she tried again to escape through the crowd, and succeeded in reaching the door where Neil was talking to Mary.

Neil raised his eyebrows. 'You look flushed.'

Isabel nodded. 'It's awfully hot in there.' She heard a noise behind her and turned. 'Oh dear, it looks like George has had a little accident.' Her voice carried further than she meant to, so several heads also turned to see George pushing his way towards them, his trousers dripping wet. Someone laughed. George marched up to Neil and Isabel, scarlet in the face, his eyes bulging. He opened his mouth to speak, but was prevented by Mary cutting in.

'Never mind, George,' she said, putting a hand on his arm.

'But—'

'Now, come with me and we'll sort you out, there's a good chap,' she said, sweeping him away from Isabel and Neil, her manner that of a kind-but-firm matron.

Richard joined them. 'What was all that about?'

'George has got a little problem,' Isabel whispered in Richard's ear. 'You know.' She raised her eyes suggestively.

'Really? Goodness. Poor fellow,' Richard said.

'But don't tell anyone,' Isabel added, thinking that the Golf Club gossip machine might as well work to her benefit as her detriment.

'I wouldn't dream of it.' He stared after Mary and George. 'Who'd have thought it?' He gave himself a little shake. 'More champagne, Isabel? Neil? Your glasses seem empty.'

Richard topped up their glasses. 'I must circulate, but I'm so pleased you were able to come. Both of you.' He smiled at Isabel, and she blushed at his kindness.

'So what was that all about?' Neil said when Richard was out of earshot.

'I'll tell you later,' Isabel said, thinking back to George's face as he realised that she was actually going to pour champagne over him. She smiled. Not the world's wittiest riposte, but it'd do.

'What's so funny?' Neil asked. 'You really shouldn't laugh at poor old George.'

'Poor old George, my foot.'

'You looked at him as if he was something particularly nasty you'd just stepped in.'

Isabel glanced at Neil. Perhaps all this had started when Neil had told the story of the dissolving party dress to George. She remembered the way he'd leered at her then, the way his hands had felt on her shoulders tonight.

'I'm going to go to the loo,' she said. In the hall one of the waitresses directed her upstairs to what was obviously Mary and Richard's room, all frills, swags and flowery chintz contrasting with Mary's usual brusque manner. A couple of women were lolling on the bed, chatting.

'Are you waiting?' she asked.

They said no, and indicated the bathroom.

When she came out the women had gone, and another woman was standing examining the objects on top of a chest of drawers.

'Justine.'

As she turned round and saw Isabel, she looked so guilty, so dismayed that for a second Isabel wondered if she'd caught Justine helping herself to something of Mary's. But her dress was a skin-tight sheath, and tucking anything away would have been impossible. Justine's smooth, confident expression reasserted itself.

'I haven't seen you for ages,' Isabel said, trying to remember when she'd last seen Justine.

'I've been busy,' Justine said, moving away from the chest

of drawers and smoothing her dress down over her hips.

It occurred to Isabel that both of the women she had initially made friends with had been absent while she'd dealt with the fall-out from her affair. Only Mary had been supportive. Perhaps it was that thought that made her comment, 'Neil's back, you know.'

Justine tucked her hair behind her ears and sat on the bed. 'I know.' Her face was hard. 'So Neil has come home and forgiven you. Lucky you.'

'Yes, lucky me.' Isabel had a flashback to writing 'lucky clover' on the PTA agenda. It hadn't brought her much luck. She tried to read the expression on Justine's perfectly made-up face, but it was impossible to tell what she was thinking.

'Why didn't you go with Patrick?' Justine asked, tracing the pattern of the bedspread.

'How could I?' Isabel said.

'He seemed smitten.'

Isabel tried to keep her voice light. 'I expect it was the novelty factor of being refused.'

'Maybe.' Justine stood up. 'I'm sure Neil's told you his version of events, but I want to make it clear I didn't mean you any harm. We'll be meeting up at school, at social events like this, so it's best to be civilised. Or at least, civil.' She examined her nails. 'Mary's obviously decided to support you, and who am I to go against Mary? Especially as I don't have a loving husband to support me. And there was I thinking you were bored to tears with each other.'

'We're not,' Isabel said automatically, completely adrift.

'Obviously,' Justine said. 'Or boredom's better than risk. That's what Neil chose, but somehow I didn't expect you to. Still. Don't let's go there.'

Isabel started in recognition. She could remember Neil

using the expression, and thinking how strange it was. The world seemed to have changed angle, like a distorting mirror at a fairground. She touched the wall to steady herself. She could hear what Justine was implying, she just couldn't understand it. Then she thought of Patrick in the shop insisting that he hadn't sent the photographs, Patrick who avoided answers rather than lie. She had assumed he was lying because there wasn't anyone else with knowledge, opportunity and motive. Or so she had thought. Her body felt as wobbly as if she'd just got off a rollercoaster, her vision distorted, but as she focused on Justine the overlapping images settled themselves into sharp clear lines. Justine. And the photographs. She swallowed although her mouth was dry.

'How did you get them? From Patrick?'

'Patrick? No, why would he give them to me? It was your set, of course.'

There was a bitter taste in Isabel's mouth. She felt her whole body slump with the shock. 'When?'

'When I did your wardrobe. At first I was simply curious to see what they looked like, so I retrieved them from your bin. Then I thought they might be useful.'

'Why did you do it?'

'Well, obviously because—' Justine stopped herself, her eyes narrowing. She drummed her scarlet nails on Mary's dressing-table, as if buying time, deciding what to say. 'I should have guessed . . . He hasn't said anything, has he?'

'Who? Patrick?'

'No. Not Patrick.' Justine looked almost amused.

Isabel tried to think who else Justine could be referring to. It couldn't be . . .

The door opened and three women burst in, laughing and giggling. They caught the atmosphere in the room.

'Oops. Sorry,' one said and they started to back out.

'No, it's fine,' Justine said, smiling at them, her pretty face as smooth as an egg. She sauntered towards the bathroom, her bag swinging jauntily over one shoulder.

Isabel caught her arm, not caring who saw. She wanted to shake some answers out of Justine. 'Who are you talking about?'

Justine looked down at Isabel's hand on her arm, and Isabel dropped her hand. 'Thank you,' Justine said.

'Please, Justine,' Isabel said. 'Please.'

Justine looked at her with cold eyes, then smiled her pussycat smile. 'Why don't you ask Neil?' she said. 'Try asking your husband.'

Isabel waited until Neil had parked the car outside the house and turned the engine off.

'I spoke to Justine this evening,' she said, breaking the silence.

Neil shifted in his seat. 'Do we have to talk about this now? It's late and there's the babysitter to deal with.'

'I think it's important. Justine said she sent you the photographs.' She waited for his reaction, but he gave no sign of having heard her, half-hidden by shadow. 'When I asked why, she said I should ask you.'

Neil leant back in his seat, head on the headrest. His face in profile seemed relaxed. Unsurprised. The cold entered Isabel's marrow and she felt sick.

'You knew. You knew it was her. I don't understand what's going on.'

Neil turned to her, his face lit up by the street light. 'There's nothing going on,' he said, bland as a vat of magnolia paint. 'But there was.'

22

'I was flattered by the attention,' Neil said, leaning against the sink. 'What more can I say? I don't want to go into detail, any more than I expect you want to hear it.'

Isabel, elbows on the kitchen table, put her face in her hands and rested it there. Her head felt it might explode with information and questions and anguish and the blood thumping at her temples. She'd had to wait until the babysitter had gone home to ask, and now here she was. Neil and Justine. Neil and Justine. Only the comforting familiarity of her palms against her eyes seemed to keep her brain from spilling out over the yellow gingham tablecloth.

'When did it start?'

'Not long after you went to work for that man.'

'So at that dinner party . . .'

'Yes.'

Isabel reached back in her mind. She could remember thinking that Neil had been unfriendly to Justine, and being surprised because they had got on so well when they'd originally met.

'I feel I've been very stupid,' she murmured. 'So stupid.'

'You had other things on your mind.' She looked up at him. Neil rubbed the back of his neck. 'It's late. Let's call it quits. Both of us have had flings. Both of us have ended them. Going over and over who did what, and when, won't make any difference.'

'But why?' Isabel said.

'Coming here . . . I don't think you realise how difficult moving here's been for me. The move from being hands on, your own boss more or less, to working in an office, all the politics and manoeuvring. You weren't interested.'

'And she was?'

'Yes. Oh yes, Justine would be the perfect corporate wife, knowing who to suck up to, who mattered, playing the political game.' He sounded bitter.

Isabel felt guilty. She knew she'd taken little interest in Neil's work. She'd hardly considered what coming to work at head office would mean to him. But Justine had. Neil and Justine. She was stabbed with the pain of betrayal.

'How could you?' she cried out. 'I trusted you.'

'And I trusted you. I trusted you even though Justine had warned me about that man.' He shrugged. 'I'm not going to feel guilty about this. These things happen.'

'So we just forgive each other and say everything's okay.'

'What else is there?'

'You've made me feel like dirt these last weeks, made me crawl, made me . . .' A vision of the giant tortoises came into her head, and she hugged herself, rocking backwards. 'When all the time you were . . . It's so hypocritical.'

'And what about you? Did you think of the children? At least I left no evidence.'

'So it's okay so long as you don't get caught.'

'No. But my God, it makes it less painful.' He wiped

his hand across his face. 'Water under the bridge now. That's how it's got to be. Water under the bridge.'

She didn't, couldn't, answer him although she seethed inside with a jumbled mass of emotions. She felt like screaming and howling out her fury, but they were obviously going to be civilised and grown-up. At least, Neil was. Water under the bridge, brush it under the carpet, hide it under so many stones that it'll never see the light of day.

He yawned and pushed himself off the kitchen counter. 'I'm going to bed. Coming?'

'No. I'm going to stay here for a bit. I just can't take it in properly,' she said, putting her hand over her eyes.

Neil touched her hair. 'I'm sorry,' he said awkwardly. 'Perhaps I should have told you before. But there never seemed a good time. And I thought you were better off for not knowing.' He patted her shoulder.

'Not knowing,' she echoed. 'Not knowing. Being protected from the truth. If we all pretend nothing has happened, we can go on as before. Is that what you really think?'

But he had gone.

'It's funny,' she said to Adam on her last day at the shop. 'People are always trying to protect me from the truth, which makes it twice as painful when I find out.'

'Honesty is the best policy, or so they say,' Adam said, raising an eyebrow at her. 'What's brought this on?'

'Oh, Neil's been telling me some things.' And we're pretending they haven't happened, she thought, her head aching.

'Home truths?'

'Mmm.' She stretched her arms out. 'I feel I could sleep for a week.'

Adam looked sideways at her, but he didn't ask any more. It was one of the things that she liked about the shop, the conversations punctuated with dealing with customers, and working with Adam who never pried, never pushed her into saying things.

Instead he said, 'Have you decided if you're coming back? Maria's been in touch to let me know she's giving up work for the moment. We're closed until New Year, then Angela's coming back. I'll need someone else.'

'What are you doing for Christmas, Adam?' she said suddenly. She had a vision of him sitting alone in the flat above the shop. She'd never been in it, but she guessed it was modern and minimal, like his office. Very chic, but a cold place to spend Christmas.

'Big family gathering. My mother likes to go the whole hog so it's very traditional, extended family, lots of friends, lots of food, that sort of thing.'

'It sounds wonderful,' Isabel said, adjusting her mental picture from Adam, home alone with a small glass of sherry, to Adam at the centre of a maelstrom of affectionate family life. It certainly sounded better than Moira and Ian, Heather and her husband, and competitive mince-pie making, which was what her Christmas was going to be. 'I never had that sort of Christmas, being an only child.'

She served a desperate-looking man with a stack of books, obviously his last-minute Christmas shopping. When she'd finished she said, 'I always wanted to give my children a traditional family Christmas, in their own home with lots of friends as well as family. I thought that maybe we'd do it this year, but things haven't worked out like that.'

'I don't have children, so perhaps I shouldn't say this,'

Adam said slowly, 'but I think you have to be careful about giving children the things you wanted as a child, rather than what they actually want.'

He moved away to help a customer with a query. Isabel thought about what he'd said. Was she trying to give the children what she'd wanted rather than what they wanted? But surely all children wanted a stable home, with parents who loved them. The shop filled with customers rushing to buy books, whether as gifts or to keep them occupied over the holidays. They were busy until half an hour before closing when the crowds thinned, leaving only a few browsers.

'You still haven't answered my question,' Adam said. 'Are you coming back? And if so, when?'

'I'm sorry,' Isabel said. 'I should have told you before. Yes, I'd love to come back in the New Year, once term starts again.'

'Great,' Adam said. He looked delighted.

'I didn't realise it meant so much to you,' she said, embarrassed and pleased at the same time, trying to make a joke of it.

'I usually take several weeks off in February to go abroad. I couldn't if it was just Angela on her own.'

Which left Isabel feeling curiously deflated.

Adam finally ushered out the last customers, unlocking the door to let them go, and turned the shop sign to closed. Isabel put on her coat and scarf, and gathered up her bag.

'Here.' He handed her a brown envelope. 'Wages.'

'Thanks.' She'd thought about getting him a present, but had decided against it. He was her employer, after all, and she'd hardly known him very long. Only a few weeks. He unlocked the door for her, then bent and kissed her cheek.

'Happy Christmas,' he said.

'And to you.' She fiddled with the strap of her bag. 'And thank you. I'm glad it's not going to be goodbye.'

'Me too.' He frowned. 'You won't forget about applying to university, will you? It would be a shame to miss the deadline.'

'It's waited nearly twenty years; it'll wait another year.'

'That's what I used to say on the trading floor,' he said. 'I'll get out next year. I stayed too long and it broke me.' He touched a strand of her hair. 'Don't let it happen to you.' Isabel looked at him, his grey eyes clear and direct. She opened her mouth to speak, but he broke the contact.

'Go on, get on with you. I'm freezing to death here.'

She stood on tiptoe to kiss his cheek. 'Bye Adam. Happy Christmas.'

As far as Isabel could see, Michael and Katie had a good Christmas, although Isabel thought none of the adults enjoyed themselves. Isabel found Heather prickly at the best of times, but her new status as incipient mother had left her nerves raw. Anything and everything could be construed as criticism. A stolen mouthful of sherry trifle was seen as an accusation of abusing her unborn child, although all her mother had said was 'I'm surprised to see you eating that, Heather.' Moira grumbled about Ian's health, Ian grumbled about indigestion, which Moira then assumed to be the early stages of heart failure. Heather's husband spent a lot of time staring out of the window at the bleak granite landscape. Neil shut down completely, emerging from the latest paperback only at mealtimes or to watch an action adventure film on the television. Moira pursed her lips at his rudeness, but said nothing.

Isabel spent much of her time wrapped in layers of coats while she supervised Michael and Katie playing with Buster in the garden. She told herself they needed supervision because the garden ended in a river, which at this time of year was fast-flowing and swollen with rain, but she really wanted to be close to them, to make sure they were happy. And the sharp, clear air, however cold, was preferable to the acrimonious fug that swathed the interior of the house like ghostly Christmas swags. She found herself almost liking Buster, who was always keen for a game of football, never tired of being taken for walks and hardly ever nipped. In a rash moment she found herself promising to consider getting a puppy.

'A puppy would be fun for the children,' she said to Neil.

'And what happens to it if we go abroad?'

'But we're not going abroad again, are we?' she said.

Neil stroked his moustache. 'It might be for the best,' he said. 'A new start for us, where no one knows our history.' Isabel blushed, knowing he meant the photographs.

'And I'd rather be back in the field. This commuting . . .' He shook his head. 'It's bad now, and it's only going to get worse.'

'But we've settled back in the UK. We can't move again.' Isabel was surprised at how horrified she felt.

Neil shrugged. 'I don't think the children mind that much about moving from house to house, to be honest. Lots of families are in the same situation, ex-pats, service people. I don't think the children mind as much as you do.'

'What about my job? And going to college?'

'A poxy little job in a bookshop?' Neil laughed. 'I

hardly think that matters. And as for going to college, if you really want to, you can always get a degree through the Open University.'

Isabel clenched her fists in an effort to control her temper at his patronising attitude. 'Have you applied for a posting?'

'Keep your voice down, I don't want everybody in the house to hear.' But he wouldn't look at her.

'Neil, have you applied?'

'I've put out feelers,' was all he would say.

Isabel sat on the soggy bench in the garden, sightlessly watching the children play with Buster. Whatever Neil said or did, she couldn't, wouldn't, give up her dreams so easily a second time.

When they got back home, before she did anything else, even before putting a load of clothes in the washing machine, she dug out the university application forms and filled them in. She'd already discussed with Adam what her personal statement should consist of and now her pen sped along, black ink delineating her longing for change. She put down as references Mary Wright and Adam Rockcliffe.

She didn't tell Neil she'd sent the forms off.

On New Year's Eve Neil opened a bottle of champagne and Isabel cooked a special meal, but their hearts weren't in it and the bottle was left half-full. They went to bed well before midnight. Sex ensued, a furtive coupling in the dark, mercifully quick. Start the new year with a bang, thought Isabel, lying awake on her side of the bed.

The only bright spot was starting work again. Angela was back, a woman in her mid-fifties, Isabel guessed, with neatly permed hair and doleful eyes as if she expected the world to overlook her. Because Angela was there, Adam spent more of his time downstairs in the office, leaving Isabel to learn about Angela's husband's arthritis, her mother's senile dementia, her father's stroke, her sister's hysterectomy and the vast number of debilitating ailments suffered by her family. In the younger generation there were teenage mothers, multiple fathers, drug abuse, long-term unemployment, all recounted in tones of quiet acceptance. Isabel felt that just by knowing Angela she was statistically unlikely ever to suffer from disease, disability or anti-social behaviour, as Angela had cornered the market in personal disaster.

Adam went a few weeks later: first to Prague, then to stay with friends who'd left the City to run a ski chalet in Switzerland. He said he'd be gone for at least four weeks. It was strange being in the bookshop without him. Angela was nominally in charge as the more senior of the two women but as she fussed and fretted over the smallest of decisions, it was Isabel who suggested what they should do.

'I wish Adam was here,' Angela would complain. 'It's not the same when he goes away.'

Isabel made a non-committal answer, unwilling to admit to herself how different it was when Adam was away, how much she missed his reassuring presence. Angela loved talking about Adam, and was full of information about his past. Isabel tried to tell herself that she listened to gossip about Adam because it was preferable to the stream of diseased relatives, but it was curiously irresistible to learn that he'd been married briefly to someone in the City and had had a few relationships in Milbridge, although he'd steadfastly resisted the advances of Angela's niece, the one with forty-six piercings, including three 'down there' as Angela referred to it.

Isabel was turned down outright by two of the universities she'd applied to, but the third, the former FE college in Fordingbury, asked her to come for an interview, bringing essay samples.

'Essays!' Isabel wailed. 'I haven't done an essay for years.'

'If only Adam was here,' Angela said. 'He'd know what to do.'

'Well he's not,' Isabel said, more sharply then she'd intended. How on earth was she going to find some essay samples? She could hardly resurrect her old A level schoolbooks. She couldn't run to Adam for help and she wouldn't ask Neil. She thought for a few minutes, then laughed. 'I'm so stupid,' she said. 'Here I am standing in the middle of a bookshop. There must be at least one book on essay guidelines.'

She checked and, sure enough, there were several study guides.

That evening, after the children had been settled down, supper had been cooked and eaten, the dishwasher stacked, she started to have a go at writing an essay on Carol Ann Duffy at the kitchen table. It was ages since she had tried to do anything like that, and she wasn't convinced she had been any good at it when she was doing her A levels. But this time, she seemed to understand better.

Neil came in and sat down at the other side of the table.

'What are you doing?'

'Writing an essay,' she said, not looking up.

'What for?'

'I've got an interview.'

'What for?'

'I told you. A place at college.'

'I didn't think you were serious.'

She took a deep breath, about to explain why it mattered to her, then decided against it. 'Well, I am.'

'That's a pity.'

'Why?'

'I've been offered a posting to Ghana.'

She looked up at him then. 'Ghana?' Isabel said. 'We're not going to Ghana.'

'Why not?' Neil said. 'It's stable, reasonably safe, and there's a good-sized ex-pat community.'

'Because we've just moved here. What about schools?'

'There's an international school in Accra.' He scratched his ear.

'You know as well as I do that most of the boys will be sent to boarding school back home. If it's anything like Damascus or Muscat, there'd probably be only one or two boys in Michael's year, and I don't want that for him.'

'No reason why he shouldn't board.'

Isabel stared at him, open-mouthed. 'Board? Are you joking?'

'No. There's that school down the road, the one George and Helen send their boy to. It gets good results.'

'Absolutely not.' She shook her head, horrified at the idea. 'And what about my course? I might be starting a degree in September.'

'You can postpone it. Or do something else.' He spoke as if it was of no importance and the accumulated anger of the past few months swept over her.

'No,' she said. 'No. I'm not postponing it. I've postponed

enough. I'm not your property, trailing after you round the world. And nor are the children. It's unfair to expect them suddenly to up sticks and go to Ghana when for the first time they've got their own rooms in their own house.' She was breathless with defiance.

'And you expect me to sacrifice myself simply for the children to have their own bedrooms? I hate commuting, and I don't intend to carry on. I'm going to Ghana.'

Isabel looked at him. He was sticking his neck out in an aggressive manner, and she noticed how the skin round his neck had started to crease and wrinkle up like a tortoise. He resembled his father, laying down the rules, believing his loud voice would convince. She thought of Moira, freezing meals that no one wanted to eat, taking out frustration in petty vendettas. Then George and Helen, her personality drowned by the acceptance of his authority. She thought of the children, of Michael being sent away to board, of Katie being moved away from her friends yet again, brought up in a home of wintry politeness.

'Well? Are you coming with me or not?'

She was quite calm when she spoke. 'Not.'

23

Isabel and Neil maintained a pretence of togetherness. They were civilly distant with each other, never touching, careful not to impinge on each other's space. The distance between them made Isabel realise how far they had grown apart. Or how far she had grown away from him. They lay at night, each hunched under their bit of duvet, an unspannable abyss between them.

They didn't discuss divorce. It was not unusual among ex-pat couples for the wife and children to stay behind when the husband was posted to somewhere the wife considered unsuitable. But it was also known that marriages often didn't survive the separation.

The interview came closer. Isabel read as much as she could and got Angela to ask her test questions.

'Now Isabel,' she'd say, squinting at the book of sample questions. 'What is the value of studying a text in depth rather than just reading it for pleasure?'

And when Isabel answered, Angela would be very impressed.

'You'll have letters after your name in no time at all, just like Adam.'

'Thanks, but I think I'll settle for getting in first.' The trouble was, Isabel had no idea whether what she was doing or saying was right. She'd looked up sample essays on the net, and she thought hers seemed roughly comparable, but there was no way of knowing for certain. The interview was only a few days away.

Angela lowered her voice. 'It's funny about those letters. I mean, Adam's supposed to be a doctor, but he's ever so squeamish about blood. And he doesn't seem to like talking about illness at all.'

'It's not the same sort of doctor,' Isabel said, thinking about poor Adam listening politely to Angela's litany of illness.

'Speaking of which, did I tell you that my niece's daughter's gone down with rinderpest?'

'Rinderpest? That's something sheep get, isn't it? Or maybe it's cattle.'

'Well I'm sure that's what she said.' Angela looked put out.

'It sounds very serious, whatever it is,' Isabel said, and Angela brightened. She opened her mouth to start telling Isabel about the rinderpest, when the shop doorbell rang.

'Adam!'

He stood in the doorway, browner and leaner. 'I heard there was an emergency.'

Isabel frowned. 'Not as far as I know.'

'An interview?'

'What?' She turned to Angela who flapped her hands.

'I only sent a postcard saying you'd got an interview and had to write essays and everything for it, and how we didn't know what to do.'

'Oh, Angela,' Isabel said, torn between annoyance and being touched that Angela had cared enough to bother. 'You shouldn't have.'

Angela bustled off to make him a cup of tea while Adam took his things into the flat upstairs.

When he came back down Isabel said, her face scarlet

with embarrassment, 'I hope you haven't really come back because of a stupid interview.'

'I felt like coming back early.' Adam ran tanned fingers through his hair and shook his head. 'To be honest, I was bored. There were loads of old friends staying, but either they were married and treating it as a second honeymoon or they were chasing after chalet girls.'

'I can't imagine you chasing after chalet girls,' Isabel said.

'Oh, I've had my moments,' Adam said. 'But last night, we'd had a good day on the mountain, and had gone out to a club. And I looked around at all those people, everybody talking and drinking and having a good time, and I just wanted to be back here.' He looked at her sideways. 'Pathetic, or what?'

'Don't be silly. No one who knows you could ever think you're pathetic.' She traced a figure of eight on the counter with her fingertip. 'I'm glad you're here,' she said.

Angela spent the next few days clucking over Adam, bringing him cakes and doughnuts to fatten him up. Isabel kept her distance, feeling suddenly shy. She decided against letting him look at her essay attempts or coach her, although Adam had gently offered to help.

'You see, I want to know I can do it myself, without someone else helping me. Pulling the strings. It sounds stupid but—'

'It's not stupid. Don't worry, you'll be fine.' He paused. 'I expect your husband's been helping you.'

'No.' Isabel hadn't even mentioned the interview to Neil.

'Oh?'

'Neil's going to Ghana in the next few weeks,' she said. 'And you?'

'I'm not going.'

Adam played with a roll of sellotape, turning it over and over in his long thin fingers. 'That sounds a major decision.'

'Oh, no,' Isabel said. 'There's been no decision. It's just happened, and I suppose neither of us cares enough to stop it.'

'Would you like to?'

She shook her head. 'No. I think things have been over for us for a long time, we just didn't recognise it.'

'That's sad.'

'It is sad.' It should have felt strange talking to Adam about this, but it seemed quite natural. He's a good listener, she thought, even listening about Angela's niece's daughter and her rinderpest, which turned out to be ringworm.

'Do you know, I've felt so much sadness and unhappiness over the last few months that it's as if it's all been washed out of me. Now we are separating I feel, well, nothing. It's odd.'

Adam pushed up the sleeves of his sweater. Isabel could see that the cuffs of his shirt underneath were just starting to fray. 'Are you actually separating?' he said, not looking at her.

'Yes. We haven't said as much, but this is the end, and we both know it. Not that we've discussed divorce. Neil's family don't "do" divorce.' She pulled a face.

'Doesn't that leave you in limbo?'

'I don't mind. It's a halfway house, still safe, but I'm able to look outside and see what's going on.'

'You mean, all the constraints of marriage and none of the pluses? Like a bird that carries on hopping round the bottom of the cage even though the door has been opened.'

'You make it sound dreadful.'

'It wouldn't be my choice.'

'That's easy for you to say.'

'Maybe. It's like after a shipwreck. You can see the shore, but you're worried about striking out on your own so you're still clinging onto the wreckage. You know the wreckage isn't going to help you, in fact, you're doomed if you stay, but pushing off and leaving it is scary.' He sighed. 'I can only speak from my experience. When I was trading, I knew it was killing me, but I couldn't give up the lifestyle, the buzz, all that money. And each day I got more and more scared, and because I was scared I clung on all the tighter. And the shore got further and further away.'

'What happened?'

'I was pushed, in the end. No wonder, I was a wreck myself.'

'Did you sink?'

Adam looked away from her, his grey eyes unfocused as if seeing something other than the bookshelves. When he spoke his voice was low. 'Yes, for a little while. I did sink. And that was hard. But it was better than having it looming over me.' He turned to her and smiled.

'But you're stronger than I was then. You'll be fine.'

'What d'you mean?' Isabel didn't feel strong, she felt limp and confused.

'Look at what you've achieved. You've got a job, a home, plans for the future. And how long have you been back in this country? Six months? Seven?'

'I've also wrecked my marriage and become notorious in the process.'

Adam laughed. 'At least you've been doing things and not sitting at home weeping, waiting for something to happen.'

They stopped talking as a customer came into the

shop and started looking through the gardening books, eventually choosing one called *The New Gardener*.

New gardens, new beginnings. I suppose it is spring, after all, Isabel thought as she put the book in a bag. She could see that Adam was right, that she was clinging onto the wreckage, but it was hard to push away.

Her interview was late the next morning. Angela gave her a lucky rabbit's foot that had belonged to a great aunt before she'd been squashed by a collapsing wall on her way to bingo. Isabel's lips twitched as she met Adam's eyes.

'I can't guarantee this will be as lucky, but I hope you like it.' He held out a small tissue-wrapped package. Inside was a delicate silver bangle.

'It's beautiful.' She slipped it on her wrist. 'Thank you.'

He smiled. 'Good luck.'

The interview wasn't as terrifying as she'd thought it would be. One of the two interviewers, a young woman, seemed more nervous than she was, coughing and shifting on her seat. The other was a man of about her own age who spoke very slowly, his sentences trailing off into nothing. Isabel told them about what she'd read recently, her favourite authors, why she wanted to read English.

'I made the wrong choice when I was nineteen,' she said, twisting Adam's silver bangle round her wrist. 'This is what I want to do.'

Neil's taxi came late, so his departure was awkward. The children drifted off to watch Sunday-morning television leaving Isabel and Neil loitering in the hall, uncertain what to say. If they had anything to say at all, Isabel thought. All those years when she'd believed him to be her best friend, the one person she'd thought she could talk to about anything. And now there was nothing.

The taxi beeped outside.

'About time too,' Neil said, picking up his case.

The children rushed in, Michael leading, Katie at his shoulder, to hug and kiss their father goodbye.

'Bring me back a present!' Katie shouted.

'And what should I bring?'

'An elephant!'

'But it'll never fit in my case. There now, poppet,' he said, detaching Katie. 'Let Daddy go or I'll miss my plane.'

'Good,' Michael said, but he let go of his father.

They stood in the doorway and watched him carry his bags to the taxi. Neil opened the taxi door and paused for a moment, his head lifted as if he could already scent the warm Ghanaian air, and for a second she recognised the young man she'd married, the man in the photograph that Justine had admired all that time ago. Then he got in and closed the door.

On impulse Isabel ran out to the taxi, and banged on his window.

'Neil,' she said, not knowing what she was going to say until she said it, but when she'd said it the last piece of the jigsaw fell into place. He wound the window down. 'Neil, was Justine the first?'

Neil turned away from her, but not before she read the guilt in his eyes.

'Goodbye, Isabel.'

Isabel was unpacking books in the stock room. It was her least favourite job, wrestling with brown sticky tape and the foam squiggles used as protective packing. Not only did the squiggles escape the boxes at every opportunity, they would stick to her hair and clothes. She picked a broken one, shaped like a question mark, off her cardigan and studied it.

Why, why, why?

Why hadn't she known?

Because I'm stupid, because I trusted him, because he had the opportunity. Because, because, because.

I'm not very good at adultery, she thought. And as clearly as if he was beside her she heard Patrick saying 'Practice makes perfect'. She could picture him saying it too, patting the bed beside him. But I don't want sex without love, all the time fighting against caring, she said to him in her head. I don't want to have a bit on the side, I don't want to be a bit on the side. A bit on the side, where nothing mattered and no one got hurt and everyone behaved like adults.

Was that what Neil wanted? Too late to find out now, he was in a plane on his way to Ghana. She ripped open a box of travel books, remembering all the nights when Neil had lain on top of her, squashing the life out of her, and she had let him because it was easier to say yes than have an argument. Why had she let him? Why hadn't she realised? How could she have been so stupid? She snatched up a roll of packing tape and hurled it across the stock room, just missing Adam who was opening the door.

Luckily he had good reflexes and ducked in time. 'Are you all right?'

'No, I'm not all right,' she screamed at him. 'I'm fucking furious. You're all shits and bastards and I hate you,' and she spun round away from him, ashamed of her emotions.

Adam touched her shoulder. 'Isabel?' he said tentatively. 'Don't cry.'

His voice was so warm, so comforting that without

thinking Isabel turned to him and he held her while she cried.

'The worst thing is, I keep on thinking who else?' Isabel sobbed into his chest. 'Who else was there? Did it happen at every posting?' Oh please, not Frances, she thought. 'I can't trust anybody ever again.'

'Shh.' Adam stroked her hair. 'Of course you can.'

It didn't matter that he didn't know what she was crying over, it just felt good to be held by another human being, to be stroked and told not to worry, that everything would be all right. All she wanted was to stand there and be held by him. But as she calmed down reality asserted itself and Isabel remembered that she was standing in the stock room being held by the employer she'd just yelled abuse at like a fishwife. She wanted to stay there, but she couldn't. Reluctantly she pulled away from Adam's encircling arms.

'Sorry about that,' she said, gulping down the last lingering sobs. 'I'm a bit of a mess right now.'

He dug around in his pocket and fetched up a tissue. 'Here.'

Isabel took it and blew her nose. 'Sorry.'

'Would you like me to ask Angela to come down and be with you for a bit?'

'No, I don't feel up to any more information on gastroenteritis.' She grimaced. 'I must be the world's worst employee. Always in tears, abusing the boss—'

'Throwing things at him.' Adam stooped and picked up the roll of packing tape.

'I didn't mean to throw it at you, you just came in at the wrong moment. And I can't believe what I called you, when you've been nothing but nice to me.'

'Yeah, well, good staff are hard to find.' He turned the

roll over in his hands. 'If you want to take some time off, you only have to ask.'

Isabel felt guilty. 'I'm okay, really. Work's the best place for me. If you can put up with me.' She stood up and started to undo the nearest box, smiling to show she really was the good, hard-working employee he deserved. 'I've nearly finished these.'

Adam watched her, smiling slightly. 'I'm sure I can put up with you for a little longer.'

The envelope was laid out on the counter top, with Isabel, Angela and Adam watching it. Isabel smoothed it down, as if she could read the contents through her fingertips.

'Well? Aren't you going to open it?' Angela's eyes were round.

'Now it's come, I'm scared,' Isabel said.

'You silly girl. I don't know how you can bear to wait.' Angela reached out for the envelope. 'Would you like me to look first?'

'No,' Isabel snatched it away from her. 'I want to do it.' Now she had the envelope in her hands she felt she had to open it. But she didn't want to. 'Going to university was a stupid idea anyway,' she said. 'I'd be much better off doing something else.'

There was only a flimsy bit of paper inside. She read it, hand over her mouth.

'Go on, Isabel. What does it say?' Isabel shook her head at Angela, unable to speak.

Adam took the slip of paper from her trembling fingers. 'It's an unconditional offer.'

'What does that mean?'

'It means they want her very much.' He hesitated, then stooped and kissed Isabel on the cheek. 'Congratulations.'

I'm going to go to university, Isabel thought. I don't believe it. She took the piece of paper back from Adam and read it again. I'm going to university. This time I'm going to go.

She didn't stop smiling for the rest of the morning. She'd try to look serious, to look normal, and then this beam would take over, spread out over her face. She couldn't help it. It was just there. And every so often she'd simply have to make a little jump of excitement, or squeak with pleasure.

'I've just had some good news,' she told startled customers.

Angela went off for her lunch hour, leaving Isabel in charge upstairs, and Adam working downstairs. After a while he came up and joined her.

'I can't wait to tell the children,' she said. 'Even though I know they won't understand, I want to share it with them. What are you looking for?' Adam was rummaging through one of the drawers. He pushed it shut.

'Nothing.'

'I'm okay here on my own if you want to work downstairs. I'll shout if it gets busy.'

He hesitated. 'I wondered if you wanted to go out for a drink. To celebrate.'

'Oh, Adam, that'd be lovely. But we couldn't all go at once, not unless you shut the shop.'

Adam fidgeted with his cuffs. No wonder they were frayed, Isabel thought.

'I meant after work.'

'But I have to pick up the children and Angela has to get back.'

Adam pulled at a long thread. 'I meant after after work,' he mumbled to the till. 'And I didn't mean with Angela.'

'Oh,' Isabel said, her heart thumping. 'You mean a drink drink.'

'Or dinner,' Adam said, still apparently engrossed in the till. 'If you'd like.'

Isabel thought about it. Apart from Neil, she wasn't sure when she'd last gone out to dinner on a date. She'd only gone out with Patrick once, to the pub for lunch when he'd kissed her. And before Neil there were various meals consumed with various boys, but it would be stretching it to call them dinner. Dinner meant high-heels and babysitters and white linen napkins and bottles of wine in a wine cooler.

Would she like dinner? She looked at Adam.

'Dinner would be lovely. Thank you. Oh—'

'What's the matter?'

'I'm not sure I should. You see, I promised myself that I'd never go out with my employer again. And well,' she could feel herself going red. 'Dinner's going out, isn't it? So I ought to say no.'

'Mmm. I have to admit I did set a company rule when I started that I would never go out with an employee.'

'I wouldn't want you to break a company rule.'

'I had forgotten about it. To be honest, I haven't had any desire to break it. Until now.' He looked at her, and she felt herself flushing again. How strange this was, after all those years. But nice. She smiled as her heart started racing again. Oh yes, it was nice.

'But there's my promise to myself. And I don't want to break that. It's important to me.'

'I see. Well. It was just an idea.' He turned to go and Isabel suddenly felt if she didn't seize the moment it would never come again.

'No, Adam, wait.' Isabel found a bit of paper and quickly

scribbled on it. She handed it to Adam, who read it.

'What's this?'

'My notice. I'm going off to be a student.'

'Not for a while, surely?'

'October.' She looked at him sideways. 'But I'm sort of not your employee now, am I?'

'I suppose not,' Adam said, a grin spreading across his face. He turned and faced her. 'So, Isabel Freeman, would you like to come out to dinner with me?'

'I'd love to,' she said, beaming. 'I'd love to.'

The shop doorbell rang and Angela came in, arms stretched with heavy shopping bags. Adam went to help her, but she shook her head.

'No, I'm fine, Adam dear, I'm all balanced. That supermarket gets busier and busier. You'd think they'd put more people on the tills at lunchtime, wouldn't you? I'll just put these downstairs and then I'll be back up.' She bustled past them and as she went past, Adam stepped back and his hand touched Isabel's, warm and alive.

Angela came back up the stairs, patting her hair. 'That's better. Now, did anything exciting happen while I was out?'

Adam, busy tidying up the credit card slips into no particular order, looked sideways at Isabel. 'Maybe,' he said casually. 'What do you think, Isabel?'

Isabel pretended to be alphabetically sorting through the order forms, although the words were dancing in front of her eyes and making no sense at all.

'Definitely,' she said, smiling to herself. 'A definite maybe.'

Have a love affair with underwear at La SENZA™

FREE BRIEF OR THONG
WHEN YOU BUY ANY MATCHING BRA...

How to Claim:
To claim your free seductive undies, buy any bra and receive the
matching brief or thong free at any La Senza lingerie store.
Simply fill out the form and present it in store by 05.07.04.
For your nearest La Senza store call 020 8561 9784
or visit www.lasenza.co.uk.

Terms and Conditions
1) Offer excludes employees and their families of the promoter, Hodder & Stoughton, La Senza,
WH Smith or anyone promotionally connected. 2) Offer restricted to one purchase per person
3) Offer valid on the purchase of Adultery for Beginners between the 24th May and the 5th July 2004
at participating WH Smith outlets. 4) The offer must be redeemed in La Senza Lingerie stores by
5th July 2004, excluding Debenhams or Roches La Senza concessions and is not valid on internet
purchases. Present the completed voucher, to receive the free brief/thong 5) Leaflets or till receipts
which are altered, amended, defaced, damaged or copied, are invalid. The voucher has no cash
value. 6) The offer is a free brief or thong when you purchase the bra of any bra/brief or bra/thong
set. Offer open to different styles and sizes, subject to availability. 7) Only one voucher per
customer. As offer only applies to the purchase of one set, if more than one set is purchased within a
single transaction, the offer applies to the set of a lesser value. 8) Offer is not valid in conjunction
with any other discount or voucher. 9) The decision of the La Senza manager is final and binding.
10) Promoter: Hodder & Stoughton, 338 Euston Road, London NW1 3BH.

NAME

ADDRESS

POSTCODE

EMAIL

To be filled in by La Senza employee:

TRANSACTION VALUE

STORE NUMBER

Tick here if you do not wish to receive information
from La Senza or Hodder & Stoughton about future products and offers.

Offer closes 05.07.04